A Little IRRESISTIBLE

BREE FLEMING

LAST HARBOR PUBLISHING

www.breefleming.com

ISBN: 979-8-9908707-0-3

ISBN: 979-8-9908707-1-0 (Ebook)

Cover art by Qamber Designs

For Elliot
for reminding me to believe in myself
(and be strong!)

ONE

Nell McLean didn't believe in fate.

Kismet, karma, destiny—whatever you wanted to call it, Nell didn't subscribe to it. Not since she was twelve years old and her entire life had gone off course like a go-kart with a loose front wheel. Fairy tales were fine for children, but in the real world, there were no happy endings and there was no such thing as meant-to-be. She didn't believe in ever-afters or wishing on stars. She didn't even read her horoscope.

Which was, she reflected later, actually kind of a problem. Because if she had believed in fate, she would have turned on her heel and dashed right back out the door the second she'd spotted Whit O'Rourke seated at the bar.

But since Nell didn't believe there was any sort of arcane cosmic presence guiding her future, she didn't flee screaming into the night like the terror-crazed victim in a horror movie. Instead, she did what any totally sane and one-hundred-percent rational woman would do: she ran into the bathroom to hide.

What the hell is he doing here? was her first thought.

Followed quickly by: *Crap.*

She stopped herself there, because even she knew better than to start wondering—silently or otherwise—what else could possibly go wrong. Nell might not believe in fate, but she did believe in bad luck, and tonight she was having the worst of it. The three hours since she'd landed in Minneapolis had been one mishap after another.

Plane stuck on tarmac for over an hour? Check.

Flat tire on her rental car? Check.

Dead phone? Check.

Torrential rainstorm turning the streets and gutters outside into some kind of Biblical flood? Aaaaaaaaaaand check.

Add in the fact that she was broke, unemployed, and about to need a new place to live, and Nell was basically a misfortune magnet. At this point, she wasn't going to rule out the possibility that she'd angered a vengeful god or that a witch somewhere had cursed her.

And all of that was before she'd seen Whit.

She poked her head out of the bathroom, just to make sure she hadn't hallucinated him. Yep, there he was. She recognized him instantly, and not only from his artfully rumpled hair or his perfectly sculpted jawline. His presence filled the room. It always had. She could feel him there, physically, like that electric sizzle in the air that comes right before a lightning strike. If she hadn't been soaked through and dripping rain, all the hairs on the back of her neck would be standing on end.

Smothering a groan, Nell ducked back into the bathroom. Not that she thought he'd noticed her. Even if she hadn't hurtled her way into the bar looking like the proverbial drowned rat, Whit had other matters to occupy his attention—such as the curvy bleach-blonde who had sidled her way up to him and, at last check, appeared to be whispering in his ear. Or possibly licking it.

And wasn't that just completely unhygienic?

How—and with who—Whit O'Rourke spent his time wasn't something Nell wanted to think about. She generally preferred not to think about him at all. She had, in fact, spent the past four years trying to forget his very existence, which was why it had taken her sister calling upon their sacred oath to get Nell to agree to this ridiculous scheme in the first place. And while Nell could confidently say this wasn't the stupidest idea her sister had ever come up with, that was only because

Paige had once tried to sell her on eBay when they were kids. Even then, Paige had been a budding entrepreneur. And also kind of an idiot.

But dwelling on what got her here wasn't going to solve her predicament, so Nell tried to put Whit out of her mind and focus on the more immediate crisis. Like the fact that she was now hiding in a bathroom in a bar that was decorated wall-to-wall with fish trophies and smelled like the unholy trinity of fried food, draft beer, and vomit.

She grabbed a handful of paper towels to dry her hair and gave herself a quick glance in the mirror. Then she grimaced. Her every emotion tended to show on her face, and right now she was somewhere between fire engine and fuchsia. Not to mention her makeup was smeared, there was mud on her jeans, and since the paper-thin jacket she'd chosen to wear wasn't waterproof, both it and her ancient University of Chicago T-shirt were plastered to her chest. She was the walking, talking definition of bedraggled.

All right, Nellie, she told herself. *First things first.*

She had to figure out where her hotel was and then get herself out of the bathroom, out of the bar, and out of Whit O'Rourke's general vicinity before another calamity happened, like someone spilled beer down her shirt, or a ceiling tile fell on her head.

What she really needed was a new phone, one with a battery life that lasted longer than she could hold her breath. She tried smacking it with the heel of her palm—which didn't work, but sort of made her feel better—and then worked up the courage to ask the woman washing her hands next to her for directions to the Marriott.

She was about to take another check of the restaurant and then sneak her way back out of the bathroom when a couple of college girls in Minnesota Blizzards shirts entered. And she could tell from the first few words they spoke—if not simply from their flushed faces and excited laughter, or the fact that one of them was actually wearing an O'Rourke 27 jersey—just who the subject of their discussion was.

"Better?" one of the women asked, adjusting her shirt to lower her neckline before checking her makeup in the mirror.

"Oh, please," her friend in the jersey answered. "He is not going to go home with you, no matter how you arrange your boobs. Isn't he dating some model?"

"Not anymore! They broke up last month."

Nell had known that already. Whit's breakup with social media darling Lilah Hart was the precise reason Paige had sensed an opportunity. He was newly single and just as in need of a fresh start—or rather, a flashy relationship to give the internet something else to gossip about.

According to Paige, it would be purely a PR relationship. She and Whit would pretend to rekindle their brief-but-popular romance, shifting the focus from past embarrassment to future conjecture... and deflecting the hurricane of scandal that was currently headed straight for her.

Nell had expected Whit would laugh himself silly at Paige's expense, but apparently his deranged sense of humor had prevailed, since he'd told her he'd consider it. With one condition.

And there it was. The one teeny, tiny, insignificant problem with Paige's plan.

Whit wanted an apology. From Nell. In person.

Nell could remember Paige's exact words. The conversation was permanently seared in her memory, like marking the date of a catastrophe. Fifty years from now, long after she'd forgotten being left at Lincoln Park Zoo as a kid or the name of her first grade crush, she'd be able to say exactly where she was and what she was doing when her sister had officially lost her mind.

The *where* had been Nell's apartment and the *what* had been cooking up comfort food. She'd been busy wallowing in her own misery when Paige had come hurtling in like a whirlwind, throwing the door open dramatically and collapsing into the sofa with her face buried in her hands. Nell had barely gotten a word in before Paige began detailing their grandmother's soon-to-be-public transgressions.

Nell had tried to be reassuring. "You are not the company, Paige. Weren't you wanting to distance yourself from the Forrester name anyway? Build your own brand?"

"My brand is based on the Forrester brand. I'm Paige *Forrester*. If they can't trust the Forrester name, they can't trust me."

That's what happened when your super secret skin cream formula touted as all natural, a hundred percent organic, gluten free, and vegan turned out to just be gluten free. Forrester Cosmetics would be lucky if they got off with a scandal and not a class-action lawsuit. As soon as the news broke, their stock was going to plummet—literally and figuratively.

Nell, who had cut herself loose from their grandmother's company the second she turned eighteen, would have laughed for a week straight if it hadn't been for Paige. "You could use your middle name," she'd suggested. She didn't know a lot about branding, but she figured removing all associations with the Forrester label could only be a good thing.

"Can you please take this seriously?" Paige had responded. "This is my entire life. I've built a career out of being the public face of the company. The second the story hits, I'm going to be ruined."

"You do remember you're speaking to a member of the recently unemployed, right?"

"It's not the same thing. You can just get another job. Being Paige Forrester *is* my job."

Nell bit back a sarcastic retort. She'd loved her job. Losing her position at Bellwater Academy might not be akin to actual ruin, but it had felt an awful lot like it. And it wasn't as though she would be swimming in job offers after she'd gotten into a heated confrontation with the father of a student. Nell hadn't thought the incident would be worth firing her over—even if she *had* used language she normally reserved for only the most extreme provocations—but the school's largest donor, who just happened to be the man's uncle, had disagreed. Given the choice between keeping Nell and keeping funding that helped pay tuition for children whose parents couldn't afford it themselves, and... well, Nell would have fired her, too. She wasn't going to be the reason underprivileged kids were denied opportunities. But that didn't make it hurt any less. And since Bellwater wasn't the only school Frank Grantham, entrepreneur and philanthropist, donated to, her job prospects were looking decidedly grim.

Still, Paige had a point. For someone who traded on the public's good will, image was everything. "Is there some way you can get out in front of it?" Nell asked. "Soften the blow?"

"And do what? Admit the company has been lying to consumers for decades?"

"Well, what does the PR team say?"

"They won't talk to me. Grandmother has them on lockdown."

"Can't you hire another firm, just for yourself?"

Paige sliced a hand through the air. "Stop, Nellie. I don't need you in fix-it mode, I need you to listen. I've already got a plan."

Nell hesitated. Paige's last plan had involved a photo shoot that led to a five-star restaurant catching fire. And Nell hadn't forgotten the eBay incident. "Do I want to know?"

"Probably not, but I'm telling you anyway. I have an idea on how to shift the narrative," Paige said. Her eyes glinted dangerously. "I'm going to give people something else to talk about. And you're going to help me."

A prickle of foreboding crept its way up Nell's spine. "Help how?"

"I need you to talk to Whit."

The plastic bowl Nell had been pulling from an overhead cupboard clattered to the floor. "Whit? As in *Whit O'Rourke?*"

"Do I know someone else named Whit?"

"I'm just confused as to how he entered the conversation," said Nell. Confused *and* horrified. Even after four years, just the sound of his name was enough to make heat climb up her cheeks, something she hoped Paige was too distracted to notice. "What does Whit have to do with any of this?"

"He's a solution."

"So is hydrochloric acid. That doesn't mean you should mess with it."

"You know what I meant. He's going to solve my problem."

"*How?*"

"By dating me." Nell opened her mouth to respond, but Paige was quicker. "Before you freak out, don't worry, it won't be legit. This is strictly a PR move. Whit is way too intense for me, anyway."

"Which is why the two of you never made any sense in the first place," Nell retorted. "Have you run this by Gabi? You can't tell me she signed off on it."

Paige looked away quickly. "We broke up."

That surprised Nell even more than the mention of Whit had. "When did this happen? Gabi didn't say anything to me." Which was likely because Nell had insisted they stop putting her in the middle of their disputes. Having your sister date one of your closest friends was great—until they broke up. Repeatedly.

This would be the fourth time they'd called it quits in the past two years, and Nell knew without asking what had caused the latest hiccup. Gabi and Paige were perfect for each other in every way... except that Paige was terrified of commitment and refused to go public with their relationship.

Paige had never kept her sexuality a secret, but being bisexual in theory was one thing, more of a quirky trait than an accepted reality. Their grandmother—who had chosen to add bigot to her list of charming qualities—would never allow the face of her company to openly date another woman, even if that other woman was every bit as beautiful and glamorous as Paige was. According to their grandmother, it was bad for the brand. And as long as she was in charge of that brand, her word was law.

"It doesn't matter when it happened," Paige said, waving a hand. "What matters is we're done. For good this time."

Nell would have been a lot more upset if she'd actually believed that. "You're thirty years old. You really need to stop letting Grandmother control your life."

"She doesn't control my life. She controls my bank account. Which is exactly what I'm trying to fix, and is exactly why I need Whit."

"I still don't see how he can possibly help."

"Because you spend all your time hanging out with eight-year-olds. In the world of adults, there are two things that sell: sex and scandal.

If I want to erase the scandal, I need sex, or at least the illusion of it. Do you know how much attention I got when Whit and I were dating? My social media engagement skyrocketed."

"And do you remember how it ended?"

Nell remembered.

Media shitstorm was the *polite* way of putting it.

"That's sort of the problem," said Paige. "Here's the thing. I already talked to him. And he said he'd think about it, if..."

"If...?"

"If you apologize."

It had taken Nell a full minute to come up with a response that didn't include either of the phrases *when I'm buying ice skates in hell* or *right after we colonize Mars*.

"Seriously, that's it?" she'd finally asked. "He wants an apology? Give me his number, I'll text him right now. Dear Whit, I am so sorry I accidentally announced to the world what a tool you are. I should have waited a few weeks, since you would have undoubtedly revealed it all by yourself. That sound good?"

"*Nell.*"

She gritted her teeth. "Fine. What do you need me to do? You want me to call him?"

"Well... he gave me his address and said if you fell on your knees and begged his forgiveness, he might agree to my plan."

"I want to erase from the cosmos that time I walked in on Grandmother and her personal trainer, but that doesn't mean I'm getting it."

"Oh my god. You promised never to mention that to me again."

"If I have to suffer, you have to suffer."

"I'm already suffering!" Paige complained. "Come on, you *owe* me. You asked me to talk to that real estate guy for you. And if that's not enough to convince you, then I'm calling in the pact."

Nell bit her lip. Asking Paige to intercede with Frank Grantham had been a desperate move on her part, and she wasn't proud of it. She'd spent her entire adult life trying to dissociate herself from the Forrester name, and at the first sign of trouble, she'd gone running for help. But after all her own attempts to reach out had been rebuffed, her family's influence had seemed like her only chance. In the end, it hadn't mattered.

Still... she did owe Paige. And even if she didn't, Paige had used the one argument she knew Nell wouldn't reject. In the fifteen years since its inception, Nell had never once gone against the Forrester-McLean Sisters Pact. The pact had been sealed with their pinkies and bound with a promise, and it didn't matter that they were technically only half-sisters. Breaking it was absolutely unthinkable. An offense against nature. Straight up sacrilege.

"If I do this," Nell told her, "you're putting me up in a nice hotel, you're paying my airfare, *and* you're telling Gabi the truth. I'm not letting you break her heart over something so stupid."

Paige just curled a sly little smile. "Already booked. Pack a bag, Nellie. You leave on Thursday."

So now here she was: hiding out in a bathroom, stuck listening to the college girls debate which part of Whit's anatomy was most worthy of admiration.

"He's a pitcher. It has to be his arms," said the woman who had been adjusting her boobs in the mirror.

The jersey girl wasn't convinced. "Counterpoint: his ass."

"His ass is usually hidden by the pants. He needs tighter pants."

"Um, have you somehow not seen that nude photo shoot he did?"

Nell was about three seconds away from committing a misdemeanor, like pulling the fire alarm and running shrieking from the bar—but thankfully, they decided to take their discussion on the road and exited the room before Nell was forced to take matters into her own hands.

She waited a couple of minutes, just to be safe, then gave herself another quick check in the mirror and eased toward the door to head back into the restaurant. Drawing in a slow, calming breath, she squared her shoulders and stepped out of the bathroom.

And right smack into Whit.

Literally. As in, that was the precise sound her forehead made as it impacted him in a sudden, dizzying collision. Her head connected with his chest so that she got a face full of soft cotton shirt and hard muscle and the scent of warm skin. Nell was too dazed to react, or she would have yelped out a quick apology and hurried on her way. Instead she just stood there flailing while Whit regained his balance.

"Whoa, careful there," he said, catching her shoulders with his hands to steady her.

She knew the second the realization hit him.

He glanced down at her, a soft half-smile curving his lips. The next instant, his grip tightened. His eyebrows slammed together. His teeth clenched. Then he released her, pulling his hands back light-ning-fast—and freeing her so abruptly that she nearly lost her balance again.

"Motherfucker," he said. Only he laughed it. Like it was the most hilarious thing in the world that Nell, in all her drowned-rat glory, had pitched headfirst into his impossibly-broad, thickly-muscled, annoy-ingly-solid chest. "*Nell?*"

"That's me," she said, then winced. *Brilliant response there, McLean.*

She had to resist the urge to retreat. Up close, Whit O'Rourke was the stuff of fantasies—or nightmares, depending on your perspective.

Paige wasn't wrong when she'd called Whit intense. It was those eyes of his. They were a rich, deep brown, fringed with thick lashes, but heavy-lidded, like he'd just rolled out of someone else's bed. He had a way of looking at her that always made Nell feel as though he could see through her clothing, right to bare skin. His gaze could drop panties. His voice was straight up sex. With his dark tousled hair, perpetual stubble, and those wide lips that were always half a second from sliding into a smirk, he was the living embodiment of smolder.

Though he definitely wasn't smoldering at her right now.

"What *exactly* are you doing here?" he demanded.

"Leaving," she said through her teeth, and made to brush past him.

"Oh, no, you're not." His arm shot out in front of her, barring her exit.

"I carry pepper spray," she warned.

She would have spun on her heel and marched back into the bathroom, except that she had the sneaking suspicion he would've followed her. Shoving him aside definitely wouldn't work, seeing as he was six-foot-three and two hundred pounds of prime-of-his-life athlete, and she was a five-foot-six lapsed vegetarian who struggled to carry thirty pounds of groceries up the stairs. And trying to duck under his arm would only lead to disaster. Instead she retreated down the corridor, out of sight of the main part of the bar, so at least they wouldn't have an audience.

He loped ahead, moving in front of her to cut off any attempt at escape.

"I'm actually a hallucination," she told him. "You're passed out drunk. In a couple of minutes, you're going to wake up in a puddle of drool with a coaster stuck to your chin."

His eyes narrowed. "If I were passed out drunk, I'd be dreaming up someone a lot more naked and a lot less you. Let's try this again. Why are you here?"

Nell scowled. "Because someone has a voodoo doll of me somewhere and they're busy casting a hex."

"Right. Because *I'm* the pain in *your* ass."

She folded her arms across her chest. "Why do you think I'm here? You're the one who demanded I apologize. *In person.*"

For a second he just stared at her, like she'd suddenly started speaking another language. Then he started to laugh. Not a small, amused chuckle, either. Oh no. Full on belly laugh.

She was surprised he didn't actually clutch his sides and double over.

"Paige seriously sent you out here?" he asked when he'd finally paused to draw breath. "Damn. She must really be desperate."

Nell's sentiments exactly, though she wasn't about to share that with him. She went right on glaring.

"So let's have it," he said, lifting a hand to wipe at his eyes, which were looking suspiciously moist.

"Have what?"

"Your apology."

Nell bit her tongue to keep herself from making a snotty remark. "I'm sorry."

Whit stuck a hand behind his ear, cupping it. He tilted his head. "What was that?"

"I said"—*deep breaths, Nellie, deep breaths*—"I'm sorry."

"Sorry for what, exactly?"

She had rehearsed this. She'd written it down and memorized it, every sentence, every syllable, so that she wouldn't be tempted to go off-script. "I'm sorry I revealed sensitive information about you to the public. It was wrong of me. It was never my intention to harm you or your career, and I sincerely apologize."

"Then why did you do it?"

Seriously? "I didn't mean to."

"Bullshit. You knew exactly what you were doing."

She hadn't, actually—but she knew he'd never believe that.

It had been a heat of the moment thing.

After his breakup with Paige had gone public, Whit had said a few unflattering things in the media. Paige had taken the high road and wouldn't retaliate—so Nell had done it for her. She'd stepped in front of the camera when a would-be influencer with an unfortunately large social media following happened to spot them and asked why Paige and Whit had broken up. Nell could still remember, word for word, exactly what she'd said.

Because all those performance-enhancing drugs he takes don't help him perform in bed.

Once the words had left her throat, Nell had known she'd messed up. But it wasn't as though she could just call them back. They were out there, in the air, and *on* the air. The clip had gone viral. It had been played on evening news segments and Good Morning America.

That would have been the end of it, if there hadn't been some truth to her statement. Whit really had taken PEDs. Nell knew it because Paige had told it to her—in confidence. Whit had been dealing with a forearm injury and wanted to speed up his recovery. It was nothing illegal. It was just against the rules of Major League Baseball.

Whit had never actually tested positive. He'd come to a compromise with the league, earning himself a sixty-game suspension instead of an eighty-game one. But his reputation had been in shreds.

Still, she failed to see how any of that was actually her fault. She hadn't caused his injury. She hadn't persuaded him to cheat or forced him to break the rules. She'd just *unintentionally* let it slip that he had.

"I said I was sorry," she bit out. "What more do you want here?"

"See, that's the thing about apologies. Just because you say it doesn't mean I have to accept it."

He was clearly enjoying this *way* too much. And he was entirely too close to her. She could feel the warmth of his body radiating out of him, like he was his own personal space heater. She fought down an anxious, fluttery sensation in her chest.

Enough was enough, Nell thought.

Paige had said he'd wanted her to get down on her knees and beg.

Well, if that was what he wanted? That was precisely what he was going to get.

Her pulse hammering, Nell let her bag drop to the floor, and then slowly, deliberately, sank to her knees.

Whit stared at her. "What are you doing?"

"What does it look like?"

"Um..."

"I'm doing exactly what you demanded. Groveling. This was what you wanted, right? For me to humiliate myself the way you imagine I humiliated you? Fine. I'm sorry I *accidentally* revealed to the world that you *purposely* took banned substances. I'm sorry you were forced to face the consequences of your own actions. I'm sorry you were exposed to the world as the cheater you are. I'm sorry your fans learned you were a fraud unworthy of their worship. Should I keep going, or are you satisfied yet?"

Whit didn't answer. He was stone-faced, his jaw rigid and his mouth a thin line. His hands were clenched into fists. For a long moment, he simply stood there, his eyes locked on hers.

Neither of them spoke. Nell wasn't even certain if they breathed. She felt frozen. The space around them had grown quiet, all the noise and the music and the chatter fading into silence so that the only sound she heard was the frantic pounding of her own heart. An expression she couldn't name flickered across Whit's face. He lowered his gaze. His lips parted.

Then, without a word, he turned on his heel and left.

TWO

He'd been in a foul mood when he left the bar, the kind of foul that had him stalking out into the night heedless of the rain, his teeth gritted and his hands clenched, a sour taste in his mouth. He'd had to bite back a sharp retort when his Uber driver made a snide comment about a bad start last season and then promptly asked for an autograph. Old Whit might have signed with a false name or a quickly scrawled *fuck off*—but he was New Whit, and New Whit didn't let anything rattle him. Not reporters, not hecklers, not self-appointed sports analysts who couldn't tell a slider from a four-seam—and not Nell Forrester.

At least, not until she'd gone to her knees before him and flung all his sins in his face.

He'd fallen asleep with her voice ringing in his ears and woken with her taunts still echoing. He was a cheater. Unworthy. An impostor. A fraud. He deserved everything he got.

And the worst part of it was, she wasn't even wrong.

At this point, a hangover would've been a hell of a lot more enjoyable. He was seriously considering having beer for breakfast.

Whit rolled over in bed and stared up at the ceiling. He had about fifty things to get done before he had to hit the road, not to mention a three-hour drive north into the great Minnesota backwoods followed by a slew of awkward reunions he was already dreading, but all he could think was—*Nell Forrester.*

He should've known Paige was crazy enough to actually send her.

Well—scratch that, he had known. He just hadn't thought Nell would ever agree to it. Whit had figured she'd rather douse herself in gasoline than offer up an apology to him. She'd never been shy about her disdain for him, so when Whit had jokingly told Paige his condition for going along with her deranged plan, he'd assumed Nell would laugh Paige right out the door.

But then, this wouldn't be the first time he'd underestimated Nell's devotion to her sister.

Nell fucking Forrester.

His entire body had gone into deep-freeze the moment he'd recognized her, like he'd stepped barefoot into a polar vortex. Instant frostbite, brutal and numbing. As a result, he'd gone on the offensive when he should've just walked away. He couldn't even remember the last time he'd seen her in person, but the video of her revealing to the world that he'd taken PEDs was a permanent fixture in his mind. Those big innocent eyes and cutesy girl-next-door looks of hers might fool some people, but not Whit. Not anymore.

The ironic thing was, he used to like her. A lot more than he should have, all things considered. Sure, she was prickly, but she'd been entertaining as hell, even if he couldn't quite figure out what it was he'd done to offend her. She'd been sharing an apartment with her sister back when he'd been dating Paige, and right from the start, she'd made it clear she disapproved of him.

The smart move would have been to ignore her, but Whit was a born competitor; he hadn't been able to resist provoking her, especially once he'd discovered just how easy it was to get under her skin—and how quickly her temper flared once he did. Her eyes turned stormy when she was angry, he still remembered that. And when she wasn't, she had a warm, frothy laugh. Maybe he'd gone out of his way to argue with her, but none of the teasing had been malicious, not on his end. He'd enjoyed their sparring matches and assumed she had also. His mistake.

Why she'd been so protective of her sister was still a mystery to him. It wasn't as though he'd shared some deep emotional connection with Paige. They'd only dated for what, two months? Three? That was just shy of his usual relationship cut-off point. Whit had strict rules about relationships to avoid exactly these sorts of messy complications. He preferred to date high-profile women who preferred to date high-profile men, women who already had their eye out for an upgrade by the time they were done with him. Paige had fit the bill perfectly, even though there had never been much chemistry between them. Their relationship probably would've fizzled out on its own, if not for his injury.

And everything that followed after.

It had been a dark time for him, made darker by his own poor decisions and a narrative that had swiftly spun out of control.

He'd been on a high that whole season, coming off a Cy Young win the year before and cruising toward a second, until the wear on his arm had caught up to him. Officially, it had been a forearm strain. But everyone knew what that meant: he was going to need Tommy John surgery—also known as ulnar collateral ligament reconstruction, a procedure to replace a tendon in his arm. That would require a year of recovery, followed by several more months ramping back up. After that, it was a roll of the dice if he'd ever be as good as he had been. Whit had already undergone the surgery once, his first year of college, and had battled his way back to dominance through sheer stubbornness and force of will. The prospect of another surgery... that had felt less like a dice roll and more like a death sentence.

Whit hadn't been willing to leave it up to the fates a second time. Instead, he'd listened to a trainer who had advised him on a way to speed up his recovery that was safe, effective—and against the rules of Major League Baseball. It was meant to be secret, a one-time transgression that would afterward go unspoken, and if the guilt gnawed at him, that was something he would deal with in private. He would never have told Paige if she hadn't overheard him discussing it with his trainer. And while it hadn't surprised him that she'd blabbed to her sister, seeing his shame broadcast on national television was something no amount of media training could have prepared him for.

Maybe if he'd shown even a hint of remorse, things would have gone differently—the disaster might have been averted, or at least quickly forgotten. But instead of owning up to his mistakes, Whit had self-destructed. Over the next few months, he'd done everything in his power to prove his critics right. He'd punched a reporter, gotten into brawls both on the field and off, had a messy and highly publicized affair with a reality TV star, and wrecked a motorcycle going twenty miles over the speed limit.

The crash had been his wake-up call. It had been pure luck that he'd survived at all, let alone that he'd escaped from it virtually un-scathed—a fact that still woke him in a cold sweat some nights. Since then, he'd kept his image squeaky clean. He'd submitted to intrusive, humiliating interviews that dissected every part of his life, and filled his calendar with charity events and photo ops. The Whit O'Rourke Apology Tour had spanned both coasts and most of the Midwest. But in the end, none of it had helped. The damage had already been done. Almost overnight, he'd gone from rising star to the Bad Boy of Baseball. From generational talent to just another PEDs user. With no one to blame but himself.

But after four years—after suspension, after surgery, after a pro-longed recovery built entirely on his own hard work and refusal to quit, he'd once again fought his way back to the top. General managers didn't care about his past. They cared that his fastball still hit nine-ty-nine and he had a career ERA under 3.00. When he'd reached free agency a year ago, he'd been courted by most of the competitive clubs before deciding to go home and play for the Blizz. He'd dealt with the shame and moved on.

Dealing with Nell Forrester was another matter. Even before she'd started talking, he'd seen the accusation in her huge brown eyes. *You haven't changed,* those eyes had said. *You're the same selfish prick you've always been.* And once again, he'd been hell-bent on proving her right.

Determined to put her out of his thoughts, Whit rolled himself out of bed, tugged on a pair of jeans and an old Blizzards warm-up T-shirt, and trotted down the stairs toward the kitchen.

The woman snoring on the couch in his living room made him stop in his tracks.

For one horrified second, he wondered if he'd been more drunk than he remembered. He'd been alone when he'd walked into his house last night. Hadn't he? Whit furrowed his brow, the specter of his first few months in the majors hanging over him, when he'd downed enough alcohol to fuel a semi and woken up with a different woman every morning—sometimes more than one.

Then the woman rolled over, and he saw the faint blue streak in her long, butter-blonde hair.

Right. Allie. He'd been so focused on Nell, he'd forgotten he'd told his sister she could have the couch for the night after her flight to Minneapolis had been delayed. She must have let herself in sometime after midnight and decided not to wake him.

He made his way to the sofa and nudged her lightly. "You're not dead, are you?"

She probably wouldn't have rolled over if she were dead. But still, he figured he might as well check.

His sister grabbed her pillow and used it to cover her face. "Go away."

"I said you could crash here. I didn't say you could drool all over my couch."

She lifted her head to blink blearily up at him. "I'm not drooling."

"Yeah, and before you start, up and at 'em." He snatched the pillow out of her hands before she could protest. "We need to be out of here by nine if we want to hit Fallen Oaks by lunch."

"What kind of monster wakes up before eight?"

"The kind of monster that's on a schedule."

"Well, I *don't* plan on being there by lunch."

"Then I hope you've found yourself another ride," Whit tossed over his shoulder as he headed for the kitchen.

With a grumble, Allie hauled herself off the couch and padded after him. "As a matter of fact, I do have another ride. Freddie's picking me up."

"Say what?" Whit swung toward the counter to start his pot of coffee. "You wanna run that one by me again?"

"Sure thing," Allie replied. "Freddie. Is. Picking. Me. Up."

"You're bringing Freddie? Freaky Freddie?"

Her first year of college, Allie had chosen to diverge from her sports-obsessed family by dating the geekiest, least athletic guy she could find. That had been Frederick Arroyo, a skinny Puerto Rican engineering student with a passion for science fiction and tabletop gaming, who had disappointed her severely by proving to be an avid fan of both sports in general and baseball in particular. On the other hand, he'd also annoyed the shit out of their father thanks to his relentlessly upbeat attitude and encyclopedic knowledge of obscure baseball trivia, so Allie had stayed with him until she'd transferred to an out of state school her sophomore year.

Freddie hadn't taken their break up well. He'd gotten drunk and peed on one of the statues of the school's founders, earning him the nickname Freaky Freddie from Whit's other sister, Rory.

Personally, Whit had always liked Freddie. He'd even given him a signed bat at a Blizzards game last season. But as far as he'd known, Allie hadn't been in contact with the guy for the past couple of years.

Allie stuck her hands on her hips. "First, you had better not call him that. And second... yes. Yes, I am." She turned away—but not quite fast enough to hide the slow, sneaky smile that curved across her face.

A little light bulb went off in Whit's head. "This is about that stupid contest you're having with Rory."

She lifted a shoulder. "I confirm nothing."

Whit sighed. His younger sisters had already tried—and failed—to rope him into their Piss Off Dad Contest. Besides being the height of immaturity, their timing could not have been worse. If they managed to screw up the groundbreaking ceremony, they'd be lucky not to find themselves cut off. "And *Freddie* is your brilliant plan? Dad is gonna toss you out on your ass the second he spots him."

"Really? Do you think he'll be mad?"

"Think Pompeii."

"Then I am definitely walking away with the trophy."

Whit's brow wrinkled. "Hold up. You guys can't use the trophy for your idiotic contest."

The O'Rourke Family Trophy had sat in their father's office for the better part of twenty years. An old, bent chunk of metal that had served as the reward for some local Little League tournament back in the fifties, the trophy was the pinnacle achievement of the O'Rourke household. Every year, Whit and his sisters had competed for the glory of winning it all: temporary custody of the trophy itself, a small raise in their allowance (permanent), no chores for three blissful weeks, and—of course—gloating rights.

Whit had been the final winner of the trophy, claiming victory over his sisters when he'd been accepted into Vanderbilt his senior year of high school, and he'd been lording it over them for more than a decade. As far as Whit was concerned, that trophy was his.

Allie apparently didn't agree. "Sure we can. We just have to steal it from Dad's office."

Not if Whit had anything to say about it. He didn't particularly want to get embroiled in his sisters' childish schemes, but there were some lines you just didn't cross.

"Don't you think it's time the two of you considered something really outrageous?" he asked. "Like, say, pretending to be adults?" He expected this sort of behavior from Allie, who was the baby of the family and somehow still clinging to teenage rebellion at the advanced age of twenty-four, but Rory going along with the scheme had surprised him.

Allie made a *pffft* noise. "You're not going to win the Piss Off Dad Contest with an attitude like that."

"Good thing I'm not particpating."

"Of course you're participating. Dad is pissed off at you by default. That's like starting the game three runs ahead."

Whit leaned back against the kitchen counter. "You didn't have to drag Freddie into it, you know. If you really want to annoy Dad, you could just ask what he sent Mom for a wedding present."

"Mom is off-limits," Allie said, in a tone that told him the *off-limits* rule would be starting immediately. She flopped into one of the kitchen chairs and busied herself on her phone.

Which he supposed was her way of signaling that any discussion of the Piss Off Dad Contest was at an end. But that didn't mean Whit wasn't going to do his best to spike his sisters' wheels. His father wasn't the only one who wanted—hell, needed—this week to go smoothly. Whit's reputation was finally on the mend, but it was a slow process, and displaying a united front with his father, who would never have let any such scandal taint *his* legacy, would go a long way toward repairing it.

The problem was, Allie was right. Even before Whit had proved himself the family disappointment, he and his father had never had the easiest relationship. *Strained* was one way of putting it. *Combative* was another. Whit preferred to think of it more as a balancing act. In the center of a teeter-totter. Over a volcano.

His whole life, he'd been one misstep from plunging into an inferno.

That misstep had come when the PEDs scandal broke. Publicly, his father had stood by him—said all the right words, released the right statements, the benevolent, supportive father ready to guide his errant son back onto the path of righteousness. Privately, whatever tenuous peace Whit and his father had forged in the years since his parents' divorce had been exploded. Their single phone call on the subject had quickly devolved into a shouting match. Since then it had been a lot of terse conversations and petty arguments. He doubted his father would even have invited him this week, except that he wanted the entire family present for the groundbreaking ceremony.

The Fallen Oaks Fishers being named the Double-A affiliate of the Blizzards and having their own minor league stadium constructed in the center of town was an achievement Whit's father had been working toward for the better part of a decade, long before Whit's own fall from grace had tarnished the O'Rourke name. For the city, it meant commerce: media attention, an influx of tourism, the creation of new jobs—not to mention, the entire week leading up to the groundbreaking was filled with O'Rourke Family Foundation charity events. For Whit's father, it meant cementing himself in the annals of baseball history, proving he could still be a part of the game fourteen years after he'd stopped playing.

For Whit, it was a chance to show he was no longer the Bad Boy of Baseball the media had painted him as. His dad had convinced the legendary sportswriter Jerry Garwood to come out of retirement to cover the groundbreaking, and there was no way Whit was going to pass up that particular stroke of luck. Garwood was respected around the league, and not just by journalists. His in-depth profiles of players had won him a devoted audience; he was smart, he was fair, and though he'd retired before Whit's scandal had broken, he'd always gotten along well with the O'Rourke family. Even without a one-on-one interview, Whit could rely on his coverage to be positive.

"Um. Hey. Whit?" Allie asked, interrupting his thoughts. "What did you do last night?"

Whit grimaced, Nell's face hovering before him. He didn't think *acted like a raging dickwad and then had my character eviscerated* was the sort of answer Allie was looking for, so he just asked, "Why?"

Allie's grimace matched his own. "Because—and we can file this under things I never thought I would say to my brother—*Meltdown* has a picture of you getting a blowjob from a groupie."

Whit snorted. *Meltdown* was an internet tabloid, a knockoff *TMZ* with few scruples and less legitimacy that had surged into prominence over the past decade. Whit had been featured on it more than once during the height of his scandal, but since most of what they published was pure bullshit, he'd done his best to ignore it. Which was exactly what he planned to do now. "That definitely didn't happen."

Allie shoved her phone at him.

"Holy shit." Whit gaped at the screen. That was his face, all right. That was the Clash T-shirt he'd been wearing yesterday. The giant bass mounted on the wall to his right and the backdrop of beer signs clearly marked the location as Gills. The bar was dimly lit, the rest of the decor fading into anonymity in the darkness of the hall behind him—though, of course, the problem wasn't what was behind him. It was what was in front of him. Or rather, *who* was in front of him.

Nell Forrester, on her knees, the back of her head lit like a halo by the glare of the neon sign above her.

The photographer had taken the shot at the perfect angle. Whit knew that Nell hadn't actually been all that close to him. And that his jeans had absolutely not been unzipped. But the image staring back at him from his sister's phone made it seem as though, well...

"Don't you think I'd be looking a little happier?" he asked, unable to tear his eyes away from the innocent-but-incriminating image before him.

"*That's* gonna be your defense?"

"No, my defense is that it's bullshit. It's one blurry picture from a bad angle."

"Actually, it's three. And now, if you'll excuse me, I need to go bleach my eyeballs."

He snorted again. "There was nothing sexual going on, believe me."

"And she was what, just down there looking for her keys?"

"If this were legit, there would be video. And if there were video, you'd be able to hear that the only thing she was doing with her mouth was insulting me."

"You sure about that?" Allie snatched her phone back out of his hands. She hesitated a moment, shuddered, and then turned the screen toward him. "I am going to need so much therapy after this."

A second later, Nell's voice floated toward him. "*Should I keep going?*"

"Holy shit!"

Obviously, the video had been edited. Nell's tone had been slowed and softened so that she sounded almost crooning, and the rest of her sentence had been cut off. The only other noise was the low din of chatter in the background and the faint hum of machinery. Someone had very carefully spliced the audio to create the most damning soundbite they could.

"Look," Whit gritted out, his fingers tightening. "What's happening in that video is not a blowjob. It's a *hit* job."

His blood went icy, cold fury washing over him.

Nell had set him up.

He didn't know how. He didn't know why.

But he did know she wasn't going to get away with it.

"Didn't your publicist call you yet?" Allie asked. "Or your agent? Or, I don't know, *anyone?*"

"I've had my phone turned off." He saw the look of genuine concern on Allie's face and forced himself to stop glowering. "Relax, Allie. No one is going to believe this shit."

As soon as he said it, he knew he was wrong.

Of course they would.

The world was ready to think the worst of him. They *wanted* to think the worst of him. They were just waiting for him to falter again before they pounced.

"On the bright side," Allie said, "I'm pretty sure you just won the Piss Off Dad Contest."

Whit felt his jaw clench. If the circumstances had been different, he might have just shrugged it off. Hell, a few years ago, he might even have laughed. He wouldn't be the first professional athlete to be caught with his pants down—never mind that his actually hadn't been. Most either ignored it or released an embarrassed mea culpa proclaiming how sorry they were for the pain they had caused their wife or girlfriend or family or whoever. The story died down. A fresh scandal broke. The transgression was forgotten. And the world moved on.

This time it wasn't going to be so simple.

Like it or not, he was going to have to deal with the situation. That meant calling Rebecca, his publicist—who probably wouldn't believe him, either. Thankfully, her job wasn't to believe him; it was damage control. He'd connected with her during the fallout of his PEDs scandal, and after his downward spiral had finally reached rock bottom, she'd taken the tattered shreds of his reputation and begun the painstaking process of stitching them back together. She was the best in the business, clever, careful, and absolutely unflappable. If she could turn an All-Pro quarterback's two month rehab stint into a secret charity function, she could make a fabricated story and a three-second video disappear.

As for Nell—

He'd deal with Nell himself.

She was damn well going to regret screwing with him.

The sound of an engine sputtering outside caught his attention. Whit turned to peer out the blinds, then flicked a glance at Allie. "Looks like your knight is here on his shining steed."

She blinked at him. "What?"

"Sir Frederick, outside, on a motorcycle."

"Please tell me you're joking."

Whit shrugged. "You can still come with me," he tossed behind him as he exited the kitchen and made his way to the front door.

Outside, Freddie stood grinning on the doorstep, clad in torn jeans and an old leather riding jacket, a helmet tucked under one arm. He'd exchanged his glasses for contacts, Whit noted, but aside from that—and a rather sorry attempt at a goatee—he looked as though he hadn't changed much from his college days: a little short, a lot scrawny, and entirely too eager.

"Hey, Freddie," said Whit. He hooked a thumb over his shoulder. "If you want to use the bathroom before you guys head out, it's down the hall."

"Oh, come on—*still?*" said Freddie. He chuckled good-naturedly. "One incident of public urination and you're branded for life."

"You should ask Whit what he's been doing in public lately," Allie said. She'd wrapped herself in her coat, moving toward the door and peeking out from behind Whit to gaze at Freddie in dismay. "Freddie, I said I wanted to leave at noon."

Freddie tilted his head slightly, squinting toward her. "You said eight."

"I was drunk. Or delusional. I *meant* noon. And what on earth is that thing? Are you having a mid-life crisis?"

"I'm younger than you are."

"Then you have no excuse. Do you even know how to ride that?"

"I rode it here, didn't I? What are you doing?"

"I'm hiding. I am filthy and unshowered. Please go away and come back at noon, in an actual vehicle."

"Aw, babe, you always look gorgeous."

"I don't know, she does kind of smell," said Whit.

His sister smacked him on the shoulder.

Whit sidestepped her, then moved back and nudged her forward, through the door, toward Freddie. "You kids have fun."

"How am I supposed to bring my luggage on that?"

"I'll throw your bags in my car," said Whit. "No worries. See you at Dad's!"

"Yeah, yeah, laugh it up. *While you can*," Allie muttered darkly. She turned and followed Freddie to his motorcycle—but not before sticking her middle finger up at Whit. A minute later, they were on the road.

Leaving Whit alone to manage his latest disaster.

THREE

THE GOOD PART ABOUT having a publicist who wouldn't have been fazed by anything shy of cannibalism—and maybe not even that—was that she didn't immediately fly into crisis-management mode or harangue him for his piss-poor decision making and phenomenally terrible timing.

The bad part was that it took her a good five minutes to stop laughing.

"Let me get this straight," she said. "You want me to release a statement saying you *weren't* receiving sexual favors in a public space, but instead—and please, stop me if I have this wrong—instead, you demanded that your ex-girlfriend's sister get down on her knees and grovel before you in order to beg your forgiveness for revealing your use of unauthorized substances to the media."

A muscle in Whit's jaw twitched. "Well, when you put it like that, it does sound kind of bad."

"Try convoluted. Or better yet, *insane*."

"It was a joke. I didn't think she'd actually do it!"

A miscalculation he had no intention of repeating. Ever.

"You're not really helping your case here," Rebecca replied. "At this point, we'd be better off going with the blowjob story." And then she started laughing again.

"So, what, you want me to apologize?"

"Of course not. Though that would certainly be the easiest way to take care of it."

"I'm not going to apologize for something I didn't even do. The whole thing was a fucking setup."

"First, you have no proof. Second... honestly, Whit, no one cares about your sex life. This isn't the calamity you think it is. Compared to what we've already been through? Please. The best thing to do now is not draw attention to it. We'll say the whole thing was taken out of context, you'll be the butt of a few jokes on social media and take some heat in the clubhouse. That's it. Just go to your dad's little shindig, try not to ruffle any feathers, and wait for the whole thing to blow over. No pun intended."

Except that the very mention of his *dad's little shindig* was already enough to make him break into a cold sweat. His sex life—or what the media had decided was his sex life—might not concern Rebecca or the greater sports community, but the hometown that had reviled him even before his PEDs scandal had validated their disdain? That was another story. The same people who had gloated over his failures were no doubt already whipping the small town gossip machine into a frenzy about his sordid extracurricular activities. The Bad Boy of Baseball had done it again. And he hadn't even done anything!

He wasn't about to breathe a word of that to Rebecca. That would really give her something to laugh about: All-Star ballplayer afraid to face a bunch of aging former jocks and armchair analysts who had peaked in high school. "Fine, if that's how you want to handle it."

"Trust me. You've already been to the World Series of scandals. This one isn't even college ball. But... bit of friendly advice? The next time you've got a woman on her knees—I don't care where, I don't care *why*—try to make sure you don't have an audience, okay?"

On that cheerful note, she promised to keep him apprised of any updates and ended the call. Whit stared at his phone, wondering how in the hell he'd gone to bed in a completely normal, rational universe and woken up in bizarro world.

Rebecca was right about one thing. A couple of his friends were already sending him lewd texts and idiotic memes, and another kept trying to offer advice on hiding affairs. His most recent girlfriend, Lilah, sent him half a dozen messages ranging from sympathetic to reproachful. Even his manager on the Blizzards had messaged him.

The early hour had granted Whit a reprieve from everyone he knew on the west coast, but his mother, who was out of the country and several time zones ahead, sent a quick message of support. *Honey, I'm not going to judge, but please remember to be safe. Love you!*

His dad was less understanding about the situation.

I think it's best you sit this week out.

That was the single text Whit received from his father on the subject. No demands—or opportunities—for explanation. Nothing but the word of Ryan "Skip" O'Rourke, meant to be obeyed without question by all sycophants and underlings, offspring included. Woe be to he who didn't heed it. Coming from Whit's father, the text was tantamount to a command. One that, despite the knots currently twisting in his stomach, Whit had absolutely no intention of following.

Part of him wanted to take the excuse and run. He could spend the next week relaxing, far away from the media, his father, and the vultures in Fallen Oaks who were waiting to swoop in and feed on his corpse. But that was the coward's way out, and Whit wasn't about to be a coward. Not this time.

There was going to be hell to pay, all right. And he was just going to have to pay it.

***

The slamming of the car door behind her sounded like a death knell.

Her death knell, to be specific.

You did this to yourself, Nell thought, taking a deep breath and squaring her shoulders as she gazed at the charming two-story stone house fringed with ivy that sat at the end of the block. A weathered cobblestone walkway wended its way through the frost-tipped grass to a sunny yellow door where a leftover jack-o-lantern was beginning to droop on the front step. In the side yard, a couple of overgrown lilac bushes were creeping their way toward the house, several thin, twisting birches were hung with bird feeders, and a wind chime dangling from an overhead window stirred in the breeze, sending a faint, clanging melody toward her. Not the sort of home she'd pictured belonging to Whit, but maybe he hadn't gotten around to upgrading to soulless suburban mansion yet.

Or maybe she had the wrong address. She could always hope, right?

Though that would only delay the inevitable. She had promised Paige that she'd apologize to Whit. She had come to Minnesota with the express purpose of doing precisely that.

Worse, she had the uncomfortable feeling that after last night, she might actually owe him one.

A thought that didn't make the prospect any more appealing.

Don't panic, she told herself. *Don't think. Just get it over with and go home, and then you can forget this entire nightmare ever happened.*

Nell's surge of triumph after leaving the bar had lasted just long enough for her to get checked into her hotel. Then reality had landed on her like a bucket of ice water. She had let Whit get under her skin, and instead of taking the high road, she'd gone nuclear. She might think Paige's PR-romance scheme was pointless, ridiculous, and doomed to failure, but she couldn't have done a better job of blowing it up if she'd used an actual torpedo. It didn't matter that Whit apparently hadn't informed Paige of the debacle. The look on his face as he'd turned away could have frozen every one of Minnesota's ten thousand lakes. He'd rather be tied to a rocket and shot into the sun than do anything to help her.

And the stupid thing was, it hadn't even been about him. Not completely. Nell had seen the hard, smirking twist to his lips, heard the disdain dripping from his every syllable, and something inside her had snapped. The carefully restrained part of her that had been cruising toward a meltdown ever since she'd lost her job at Bellwater had finally reached its boiling point. All the turmoil of the past two weeks had come rushing in at her, all the anger and frustration and helplessness, and for that one instant, he hadn't just been Whit.

He'd been Braden Gaskell, the swaggering, sneering, over-grown-fratboy who had gotten in her face and then gotten her fired when she wouldn't let him bully her the way his son bullied the sweetest, most sensitive kid in her classroom.

He'd been Frank Grantham, who had decided without ever meeting her that she was unfit to educate children, and robbed her of the only truly meaningful part of her life.

She might not believe in fairy tales, but she spent her share of time reading them, and in that moment, Whit had been her villain, the dragon she needed to slay, the giant she needed to topple. By some miracle, she had found the exact words she wanted to say exactly when she wanted to say them. And god, it had felt good.

Until she'd realized she'd screwed up. Colossally.

So here she was. Apology, Take Two. Less sarcasm, more penitence. She could manage that.

At least she was prepared this time. Sure, her stomach was currently doing enough somersaults to land her a job at a circus, but the flat tire on her rental had been replaced, her phone was fully charged, the weather had cleared into brisk blue November skies, and her hair was under control in a safe, if boring, ponytail. Thanks to a quick stop at Starbucks, she was coffee-fueled and clearheaded. All she had to do was somehow get through the next five minutes.

Steeling herself, she marched up the little stone walkway, forced her jaw to stop clenching and her fingers to unfurl, counted silently to ten, and rang the doorbell. Somewhere inside, the high tone chirped merrily and then fluttered into silence.

Nell waited. A few agonizingly slow seconds ticked past. Then a few more. She rolled back on her heels, hugging her arms against her, and closed her eyes, biting down on her lip as she ran through the script in her mind. She'd rehearsed it over and over again in her head during the drive from the hotel. As long as he didn't slam the door in her face—a probability she wasn't willing to discount—she could do this.

I know I'm probably the last person you want to see right now, but I wanted to tell you that I really am sorry. Whatever my own personal views of you might be...

No, wait. Scratch that last line.

You didn't deserve what I said last night. It was ungenerous and unkind. I'm sorry.

She opened her eyes again, her brow furrowing as she gazed at the cheerful yellow door. There hadn't been so much as a peep from inside the house. No slap of footsteps or creaking of floorboards, no muffled words. He probably had cameras, she realized. He probably wasn't even going to bother answering. He was just going to leave her out there, standing on his doorstep like an idiot. Or maybe he hadn't heard the doorbell. Maybe he wasn't home. Maybe he was still sleeping. Or on the toilet. Or on a call. Or—

Oh god, what if he wasn't alone?

Since that last possibility was fairly high on her list of nightmare scenarios, Nell was about to turn right back around and walk—okay, run—to her car, when she heard the click of the lock and the soft whine of hinges as the door was yanked open, bringing her face to face with a surly, scowling, and honestly kind of menacing Whit O'Rourke.

For half a second, they simply stared at each other, Nell in her thin blue windbreaker, the breeze tugging at her ponytail, her lips slightly parted, Whit barefoot and broody. He must have just gotten out of the shower. His dark brown hair was wet, sticking up in chaotic little spikes that curled at the tips, and his T-shirt was actually damp enough to cling to his chest. His eyes were narrowed on her, and the look of fury in them was so intense, Nell took a quick step back.

Nell gulped. She'd anticipated his irritation. She was more than half expecting him to just throw the door shut with a resounding crash. But she hadn't expected this cold-eyed, nostril-flaring, teeth-grinding rage. He looked ready to combust. Instinctively, she edged back another half step.

But Nell hadn't come here to retreat. Drawing in a quick breath, she lifted her gaze to meet his. Straightened her posture. Exhaled.

"I know I'm prob—"

That was as far as she got into her speech before he caught her by the arm and hauled her unceremoniously into the house, slamming the door behind them.

"Are you recording this?" he hissed, eyes flashing.

Then, to her utter outrage, he snaked his arm toward her purse, yanked the little clover-green bag off her shoulder, and started digging through it.

"What are you *doing*?" she demanded, trying to wrench her purse out of his grasp. Since she was bound to come out the loser in any game of tug-of-war with this deranged jock, she slapped frantically at his hands—but that only jostled the bag, causing her wallet to go bouncing out of it toward some indeterminate spot down the hall. Next, her keys dropped directly onto her foot. Nell yelped. "Recording *what?*"

Whit tightened his grip on her purse, jerking it out of her reach. "Your next hit job."

Her what now?

Was he on something? Had he progressed from performance enhancing drugs to actual illegal ones?

"If you're trying to mug me, I don't carry cash," she said. "Or drugs. Or whatever it is you think you're going to find in there. Now—give—it—back!" She lunged forward, clutching at the side of her bag. As soon as her fingers found purchase, she stuck the heel of her free hand directly in the center of Whit's chest and shoved. As hard as she could.

Whit was caught off guard. His arms wheeled as he took a quick, stumbling step backward. Half of her purse went with him.

The other half didn't.

Nell could only watch in horror as lip gloss, hair ties, tampons, a bottle of Tylenol, and a couple of old gum wrappers went spilling onto the floor at their feet.

Her phone went the way of her wallet. It sailed into the air—up, up, up, in a high, heroic arc, followed by a rapid descent as it cracked to the ground with a sound like a gun going off.

Speechless, Nell stared. The brief flicker of hope that her phone had miraculously survived its flight was quickly extinguished. The back had popped off and the screen was shattered.

Righteous fury took over. She swung toward Whit who had retreated from the entryway and stood a short distance from her, his arms folded, glaring.

"Nice going," he said, raising a sardonic eyebrow.

It took every last bit of self-control she possessed not to snatch up her broken phone and hurl it directly at him.

"You are so paying for that," she snarled.

Whit's lips twisted. "Just take it out of your cut from *Meltdown*. But hey, as a heads-up, you might want to do it soon, before I sue your ass."

Nell heard something that sounded suspiciously like a growl leave her throat. She could actually feel herself twitching. And since she didn't want to find out firsthand if blood boiling was really just a metaphor, she tried desperately to think of something calm and soothing. Like the color blue. Or a sailboat on placid waters.

Or Whit O'Rourke, skewered on a spike.

His eyes narrowed again. "You aren't mic'd, are you?"

"Why on earth would I be mic'd?" she retorted. "I swear to god, if you try to frisk me, I'm calling the cops." At least, she would if she still had a phone. Since she didn't, she dropped into a crouch and began gathering her scattered belongings and the remains of her purse. Her *favorite* purse, which, okay, was five years old and had definitely seen better days—but that didn't give him the right to rip it in two.

At least now she could return to Chicago with a clear conscience and tell Paige she had dodged a bullet, because there was no amount of public-relations goodwill that could make up for being saddled with a man who had blown right past *asshole* and settled firmly on *sociopath*.

Paranoid sociopath, if his rambling about *Meltdown* were any indication.

"What are you doing here, anyway?" the sociopath asked, rubbing his jaw as he looked her over. "Did you just come to gloat?"

"I was planning to apologize." She scooped up the hair ties and tampons and tucked them into her jacket pockets. "Against my better judgment. Now? Now I am going to drive to the airport, get on a plane, go home, and be eternally grateful for every single one of the four hundred miles between us. I'll send you a bill for the phone."

"Yeah, I think I've had enough of your apologies." There was an edge to his tone she didn't understand—but then, she didn't understand half of what he'd been saying. He was leaning back against the wall, his arms still crossed, his brow more creased than an accordion.

Then, abruptly, the corners of his mouth tipped upward. Nell wouldn't have called it a smile. At least not a friendly one.

More like a cat getting ready to pounce.

"As long as you're here," he said, "you're going to set the record straight about last night."

Nell stuck her lip gloss in her pocket and paused to look at him as an uneasy feeling began to creep its way up the back of her neck. "Set the record straight about what exactly? What a tool you are?"

"Like you don't know."

"I hate to break it to you, but I don't exactly have you on my Google Alerts."

"So it's just a coincidence that *Meltdown* has a video of you down on your knees in front of me?"

It took a moment for his words to connect. Mainly because they didn't make any sense. "*Meltdown* has what?" She climbed back to her feet and mirrored his stance, arms folded, chin up. Then she frowned. "Why would *Meltdown* want a video of us?"

"Think about it."

Nell bit down on her lip, rolling his words over in her head. While she would have been perfectly happy to erase the past twenty-four hours from the whole of space-time, their encounter at the bar hadn't exactly been newsworthy. Unfortunate? Yes. Uncomfortable? Absolutely. But of national interest? Hardly. Except...

Meltdown has a video... of you down on your knees in front of me.

"No way," she said, eyes widening.

His eyebrow lifted again.

Heat scorched its way up her cheeks. "But I wasn't doing anything!"

"Believe me, I am well aware."

"But..." Nell stared at him, floundering. She was going to have to change her name, flee the country, and join some Buddhist monastery deep in the Himalayas. Or maybe hitch a ride with the next NASA rover on its way to Mars, because if she stayed anywhere in the vicinity of Earth, Paige was going to murder her. Nell was supposed to convince Whit to help handle one scandal, not stir up an entirely new one. Not to mention—

Sudden dread pooled in her belly. Her entire body went cold. She could actually feel the blood draining from her face. If Frank Grantham didn't turn out to be the end of her career, this definitely would. She'd just gone from unemployed to unemployable.

"Please, please, please tell me you're making this up," she breathed.

"Yeah, I wish."

Mars wasn't far enough. She was going to have to book a ticket straight to the sun.

She closed her eyes, trying to quell the panic that threatened to overwhelm her. She just needed to think for a moment. Maybe it wasn't as bad as Whit was making it out to be. Maybe...

Her eyes snapped back open. Nell might not have Whit's name on her news alerts, but Paige definitely did. And if Paige had been able to recognize Nell in the video, there was zero chance she would have been silent about it. Nell's phone would have been blowing up from the second she rolled out of bed.

"Hold on," Nell said, a sudden, dizzying hope rising. "My face is in this video?"

Whit hesitated. "Your head is."

That meant *no*.

"So what you're saying is that they have a video of you with a woman. Not specifically with me."

"It *is* you."

"But we're the only ones who know that."

Whit's jaw tightened. If his scowl got any deeper, she thought, his face would actually be concave.

Nell couldn't help it. The high-speed rollercoaster her emotions had been on for the past two weeks finally derailed. Giddy relief washed through her, making her legs feel a bit like jelly. She backed toward the wall and sagged against it. A gurgle of laughter worked its way through her chest and out her throat. She clapped a hand over her mouth, trying to squelch her giggle.

It was definitely not funny.

Except that it kind of was.

Whit stared daggers at her. "You're seriously telling me you had nothing to do with it? Who else would it have been?"

Nell fought back another laugh. "Anyone in the bar looking to make a quick buck?"

"Why would they bother?"

"Why would I?" she countered. "You're not my favorite person on the planet, but if you think I've been nurturing some deep-seated grudge against you for the past four years, just waiting for my chance at vengeance, you really need to examine that ego of yours."

"Fine." He cocked his head to the side as he looked at her. The corners of his mouth curled back into their cat-smile. "Then you won't have any problem helping me clear up this little misunderstanding. What time is your flight?"

She eyed him warily. "Why do you care?"

"Because we need to change it. You're not leaving tonight. You're coming with me."

Four

Whit wasn't certain exactly when the idea had struck him.

When he'd opened the door to find Nell standing there—the architect of his downfall, all big-brown-eyed soulfulness and rosy, wind-kissed cheeks—his first instinct had been to shut the door in her face. He didn't want to be anywhere within a ten-mile radius of her, much less close enough that he could smell the faint floral scent of whatever shampoo she used. Instead, some circuit in his brain had misfired. The second she started speaking, a sudden, blind panic had gripped him. It hadn't occurred to him to simply turn and walk away. His only thought had been that he'd be *damned* if he let her get more footage of him.

Then, somewhere between her giggling like a maniac and protesting her innocence, the realization had hit. The solution was standing right here in front of him, five-feet-six of pain-in-the-ass answer-to-his-problems. *If* she were telling the truth and she had nothing to do with the video, then she was exactly what he needed to set the record straight.

Not entirely, of course. The national media was out of the question; his publicist was right about that. The last thing he needed was someone connecting the dots between the woman in the video from yesterday and the woman from the video four years ago. Whether he liked it or not, Nell was intimately tied to the scandal that had destroyed his reputation. That meant she had to stay as far as possible from this one. She couldn't say anything to the press, not without stirring up a whole lot of ghosts he'd thought he'd finally laid to rest.

But there was one audience she *could* explain it to: his father. She was a foolproof guarantee that his dad wouldn't try to send him packing. Skip O'Rourke might rail at his son in private, but he would never do anything to make himself look bad in front of an attractive woman.

Plus, Nell's presence might convince the more critical residents of his hometown to shut the hell up. He doubted anyone in Fallen Oaks would believe *his* excuses for the video, but they might well be swayed by the sweetly sincere image that Nell presented. She had good girl written all over her. She just looked so damn wholesome: cute, casual style; minimal makeup; chestnut hair pulled into a wavy ponytail that swung against her shoulders when she moved; that whole *smile that could light up a room* thing she had going on—not that she'd ever directed it at him. She even had freakin' freckles. There was just the slightest dusting of them across the bridge of her nose, like some artist had sprinkled them there as an afterthought to add the finishing touch. She was picture perfect. If Whit showed up with Nell at his side and she explained that they were both victims of a malicious bit of libel, that would bring the subject to a definitive close.

As much as it might nettle him, Whit was going to have to set his personal feelings aside. Whatever had happened in the past didn't matter. The history between them was exactly that—history. He was no longer a twenty-five-year-old hotshot terrified of losing his edge. He was a little older and a lot wiser, and he wasn't going to let anything, especially not Nell Forrester, derail his career again. Right now, she was his get-out-of-jail-free card. And he intended to cash in.

"Excuse me, *what?*" she asked, blinking those huge brown eyes at him and clutching the remains of her purse to her chest. "Coming with you where?"

Whit hitched a shoulder. He should have started this out a bit differently, but thinking wasn't one of his strong suits when it came to Nell. "A town a couple of hours north of here."

"No way. The only place I'm going with you is an Apple store."

"We can hit one on the way."

"Okay, I'll bite. *Why* would I go anywhere with you?"

That was the sticking point, Whit thought. She had absolutely no reason to help him. And if her little giggle fit were any indication, she was deriving entirely too much enjoyment from his current predicament.

He was going to have to make it worth her while. And he had an unhappy suspicion there was only one offer she would be willing to accept.

Still, he might as well try.

He made an effort to seem casual, tucking his hands into his jeans pockets and letting out a low, whistling breath. "So you can explain to my family that the video was taken out of context."

It took a moment for his words to register. At first she just looked at him, her head tilted and her lips slightly parted. She paused. Processed. Stared. Her lips quivered.

Then her giggles returned in full force.

"Oh, no," she said. "No, no, no, no, no. This is your problem, not mine. I can't be seen in public with a known degenerate."

"I'm glad I can provide you with so much entertainment, but I'm being serious."

"So am I," she replied. A statement that might have been more convincing if she hadn't laughed while she said it. "Can't you just explain it to them yourself?"

"Do you think I'd tell them the truth if the video actually *had* been real?" he asked. "Yeah. Neither will they."

"I still don't see how this is a me issue. It seems like it would be in both our interests for me to remain anonymous."

In general, she was right. But while he had no doubt that obsessive internet sleuths could easily connect Nell to her previous video, he didn't credit the general populace of Fallen Oaks, whose main recreational activities included beer pong and ice fishing, with that much savvy. Irritating as it was, she was his best option.

"Hey, I'm not in that video by myself," he told her. "Maybe you didn't send the footage to *Meltdown*, but you're still responsible for this mess."

The pink tinge to her cheeks made another appearance. "Really? That's the tactic you're gonna go with? That this is somehow *my* fault?"

At least she'd stopped laughing.

"I suppose you want me to apologize again," she added.

Whit smothered a sigh. "Fine. You hate my guts. I get it. I don't need you to like me, I just need you to give up a few hours of your time to help me deal with a situation that, like it or not, you're involved in."

"I'll give you five minutes. Get your family on FaceTime and I'll tell them all about how you were framed. Sort of."

"No go. It has to be in person."

"This whole thing wouldn't have even happened if you weren't so big on things being in person."

"But since it did happen, I need you there, face to face, in order to make it unhappen."

Nell shook her head. "I have to return my rental by four."

"I'll have someone drop it off. We can take my car."

"Uh-huh. And we're supposed to make it to this town without murdering each other *how?*"

"We're both adults. I think we can handle a car ride."

"We couldn't handle ten minutes in a bar."

"At least this time there won't be any witnesses," he pointed out.

"That's not much of an argument." But for one fleeting instant, he thought he saw the corners of her lips twitch upward.

He almost had her.

"It's *one* day," he wheedled.

And then he smiled at her.

Not just any smile, either. The same slightly flirty, slightly bashful, eye-crinkling, aw-shucksing smile he'd been using to get himself out of trouble ever since he was old enough to get into it. The same smile he'd used in college to win over punctuality-obsessed professors and to charm sorority girls out of their panties. The same smile an ex-girlfriend of his had once described as *devastating*.

Whit didn't necessarily think he was devastating, but he'd received enough attention from the opposite gender over the years to know that women, in general, found him attractive.

Unfortunately, woman, in specific, appeared to be immune. "A day I would rather spend doing anything other than being trapped in a car with you for two hours."

Three and a half hours, each way, but he'd let her find that part out later. "I'll replace your phone."

"You'd better be doing that anyway." She lifted a hand in a brief, helpless gesture. "I do actually sympathize with you, and whether or not you believe it, I'm sorry this happened. I would help if I could. But I absolutely cannot be linked to that video. Nightmarish levels of embarrassment aside, it would kill whatever is left of my career."

"I thought you worked for your grandmother."

"*Paige* works for our grandmother. *I* work for a school. I mean, I used to. And if you think they'll let me teach a bunch of second-graders after committing a public sex act, you are much further removed from reality than I thought."

A schoolteacher. He should've known. "My family isn't about to go running to the media."

"You don't think they'll recognize me?"

She had a point. There wasn't a single member of his immediate family that hadn't watched the clip of her spilling the secret of his PEDs use to the press, probably more than once.

On the other hand, four years had passed. The sports world had long since moved on. And Nell looked different now. Back when he'd been dating Paige, Nell's hair had been honey-blonde in color and styled in a chin-length bob.

"You were blonde. And your hair was shorter. Just smile a lot, try not to look like you're about two seconds from banishing me to the principal's office, and it'll be fine."

"I didn't agree to do this!" She set her hands on her hips. "And since you seem to be a bit confused on the subject, let me be very clear: I am *not* agreeing to do this."

Whit drew in a breath. Here it was. The moment he'd been dreading. Nell had nothing to gain and everything to lose from helping him. Which meant...

"All right, here's the deal. You do this for me, I'll help with Paige's PR problem."

Nell's mouth dropped open. "Seriously?"

"Scout's honor."

"You're actually going to go along with her stupid plan?"

Whit had no intention of dating Paige, not even as a publicity stunt. Even if he had the inclination to, the Vikings had about as much chance of winning the Superbowl as Paige's plan had of not backfiring in some spectacular—and highly public—manner. Not to mention, Paige was just as connected to his PEDs scandal as Nell was. What he *would* do is get Rebecca to come up with an alternate method of rescuing Paige from whatever disaster she had brewing. Rebecca might deal primarily with the world of sports, but she'd started out in media relations for a high-powered law firm, and she thrived on crisis management; he had no doubt she'd take it on if he asked her. Paige must have her own PR people, but clearly they weren't up to the task, if this was the idea they'd run with.

"We can discuss terms on the road," he said. "I'll work out the details with Paige."

Nell didn't answer. She glanced away from him, her gaze lowered, her fingers drumming against her hip. A tiny divot appeared in her brow. He could almost see the gears in her head spinning.

"If I do this," she said finally, "we're not telling Paige. She'd never let me hear the end of it."

"Absolutely."

"As far as she's concerned, I came here, apologized, it was totally amicable, and then I left."

Triumph was so close he could taste it. "One hundred percent amicable."

"And you're taking care of my rental."

"I did say I would."

"Okay," she said—a little shakily, he noted. "You can have one day, provided we can get my flight changed. But I have a condition."

Of course she did. "And that would be...?"

"*I* want an apology from *you*," she said.

If she thought that would faze him, she had a lot to learn. He wasn't going to back down this close to a victory. Instead, he decided to throw her a curve.

"How do you want it? On my knees, or standing upright?"

Her face went from seashell pink to bright, blaring red.

He wasn't going to dwell on just how satisfying that was.

"Um, upright is fine," she squeaked out.

Whit took a step toward her, and then another, making a sweeping gesture with his arm. "You have my sincerest apologies for breaking your phone, tearing your purse, and in general acting like a dick." He quirked an eyebrow at her, waiting.

Nell cleared her throat. "Thank you."

"Great. Go grab your stuff and let's hit the road." He wasn't about to give her the opportunity to change her mind.

"Why do I feel like I just sold my soul to the devil?"

"You *rented* your soul to the devil. And the sooner we get going, the sooner you get it back. After that, you never have to see me again."

"Promise?"

"Promise."

It was one day.

They could survive each other for one day.

Famous last words, he thought, and headed up the stairs to collect his bags.

***

Nell had definitely lost her mind.

That was all she could think as Whit put his shiny chrome-blue Audi on cruise control and the Minneapolis skyline receded behind them, the land on either side of the highway opening into the gentle roll of cornfields and sudden, small bursts of forest: she had lost her mind.

She wasn't supposed to be here. She was *supposed* to be in Chicago, working on her resume. But now, instead of catching the first flight back home, she had boarded the plane straight to crazytown. There was no other explanation for why she had agreed to travel to some small town in the great up north and inform complete strangers that she had not, had never, and *would* never be in any situation with Whit O'Rourke that could be remotely described as sexual—all so that Paige could parade him around as arm candy in a futile attempt to make the world forget their grandmother's vegan beauty products were actually made out of Bambi.

You owe me one, Paige, she thought, with another quick glance in the rearview. Yes, she had asked Paige to speak to Frank Grantham for her—but she hadn't made her go on a freaking road trip with him!

This went way above and beyond the call of duty, as far as Nell was concerned. The Forrester-McLean Sisters Pact—signed by Nell and Paige at the ages of twelve and fifteen respectively, two days after they'd landed in their grandmother's strict and sterile estate—might cover hell, high water, and any number of zany plots and schemes, but it did not cover two-hour-long car rides with demented ex-boyfriends. If Nell actually managed to get through this (and that was a very big *if*), she was going to hold this over her sister for a decade.

In the meantime, she intended to devote the next two hours to browsing the internet on her newly upgraded iPhone. True to his word, Whit had bought her a replacement. They'd stopped at an Apple store before leaving Minneapolis, and while Nell had been transferring her data, he'd been sorting out her travel arrangements and dealing with her rental car. Easy as that, she was booked for a return flight to Chicago tomorrow evening. But having the logistics of it settled hadn't done much to calm her frayed nerves, especially not after she'd discovered that Paige had sent her a flurry of panicky texts.

You haven't gone to see Whit yet, have you? Wait until you hear from me, okay?

Please tell me you're not there right now.

PLEASE tell me you did NOT go off script.

Has Gabi texted you? Don't mention where you are. I didn't tell her about the apology part.

Um, hello?

HELLOOOOOOOOOOO NELLIE.

Nell had shot back a rapid reply saying she was holed up in her hotel room and that she'd wait for Paige to give her the go ahead.

So here she was. Lying to her sister. And she planned to keep right on lying to her for as long as she was on this miserable misadventure.

She never lied to Paige. She didn't like lying to anyone, not even their grandmother—and lying to their grandmother was a basic defense mechanism. Now she was on her way to tell Whit O'Rourke's family the video that had somehow found its way to *Meltdown* was all part of a hilarious accident that had turned an innocent joke into a salacious headline.

She had very definitely lost her mind.

To make matters worse, ignoring Whit wasn't nearly as easy as she'd hoped. Nell was wholly and uncomfortably aware of his presence beside her. Even when he wasn't talking to her, she could feel him there. Breathing. Being. She could smell the faint scents of soap and aftershave wafting off him—something cool and woody that made her think of deep winter forests and log cabins and cozy fireplaces and several other entirely inappropriate images. And there was not nearly enough space between their seats. Despite the chill autumn air, Whit hadn't bothered to put on a coat, and with his bare arms still sun-kissed from summer and his thin gray T-shirt taut across the well-muscled line of his shoulders, Nell could swear she could feel his body heat. Sitting so close to him was bad for her equilibrium. She should've demanded he act chauffeur and give her the entire backseat.

Keep your hormones in check, Nellie, she told herself. *He's still Whit O'Rourke, remember?*

What she needed to do was focus on his shortcomings. Her libido might not know what was good for her, but her common sense did. Whit was a professional athlete, a player in every sense of the word, hardwired to score both on and off the field. To him, women were plentiful, interchangeable, and ultimately disposable.

Yes, he was a little irresistible. Yes, he radiated testosterone and had a smile that could make a grown woman forget her own name. And yes, he smelled good—okay, *really* good. But that was no reason for Nell to ignore that his fiendish desire to humiliate her was the reason they were in this situation in the first place.

Paige's words floated back to her. *He said if you fell on your knees and begged his forgiveness, he might agree to my plan.*

There. That was the helpful reminder she needed to keep her heartbeat nice and regulated.

"What did I do now?" Whit asked.

Nell's gaze jerked toward him. "What?"

"You look like I just kicked a puppy."

"Oh. It's nothing. I was just thinking."

"About me kicking puppies."

Why in the world was he talking about puppies? "About what exactly I'm going to say to your family." *Liar, liar.* "And how I'm going to manage to keep a straight face while doing it."

"Please don't imagine them in their underwear," he quipped, tossing her a grin.

A grin that made her pulse kick up a notch and her clothing feel significantly tighter than it had just a moment ago.

Not to mention, she was now imagining *him* in his underwear. Boxers, she thought, the image swimming before her—boxers resting an inch or two below his navel and hugging his narrow hips, all warm, bare skin and broad chest and hard muscle glistening faintly with sweat.

Stop it, Nell!

"I'm not sure that would keep me from laughing," she said with a shaky little exhale.

"You haven't met my grandfather. Believe me, the thought of whatever might be lurking under his overalls is the stuff of horror films." He gave an exaggerated shudder.

Nell gaped at him. "Grandfather?" she echoed. "I have to explain I wasn't performing oral sex in some skeevy bar to your *grandfather?*"

"I wouldn't worry about it. He only hears about half of what you say, anyway," Whit answered, like that was supposed to make her feel better. Then, after flicking a quick glance in her direction, he reached behind his seat to grab one of the bags of junk food he'd picked up at the convenience store where they'd stopped for gas, rummaged through it to remove an energy bar, and shoved the bag toward her. "Here, in case you get hungry. I'd rather not stop for lunch."

Lunch? Nell glanced at the clock, an uneasy suspicion beginning to form. It was only quarter past ten. "I thought you said this town was two hours away."

"I said it was a *couple* of hours away."

"Couple means two."

"I was being figurative."

"All right, then how many literal hours away is it?"

"Three," he said. And then, in slightly lower pitch, he added: "And a half."

Something gurgled out of her throat. Half laugh, half scream, all exasperation. "Were you planning on sharing this bit of information with me? Or were you just hoping I'd be too oblivious to notice the time?"

"You're supposed to read a contract before you sign it. That's one of the main rules of negotiation. You really should have asked for specifics."

"I didn't *sign* anything."

"And there's the other half of your problem."

"You're not actually kidnapping me, are you? Because Paige knows I'm here. If I'm never heard from again, you are gonna be suspect *numero uno*, pal."

"Hey, you were the one who brought up murder."

"If that was meant to be comforting, let me tell you, it isn't."

Three and a half hours. Nell groaned. Paige had better be amply prepared with gift baskets and baked goods by the time she got home. At this point, they had left debt-of-gratitude behind and were fast approaching firstborn-child territory. But since there wasn't much she could do about it at the moment, Nell settled for shooting Whit a dirty look, then reached into the grocery bag and dug out a candy bar.

She leaned back in her seat, propping her feet up on the dashboard before shifting her gaze toward him. "So who exactly *am* I going to be meeting? Besides Grandpa of the unmentionable unmentionables."

Whit glanced at her feet, but refrained from commenting. "My dad. And maybe my sisters."

Nell tried to remember what information Paige had provided about Whit's family. Not much. Paige's interest in him had been mainly aesthetic. "Your father played baseball, too?"

"You could say that," Whit said with a wry little quirk to his lips.

"Let me guess. He's famous."

"Mostly for being an asshole."

"Like father, like—"

"Don't even say it."

Nell flushed. "Sorry."

Beside her, Whit shifted his arm to glance at his watch. "Twenty-three minutes."

"Until when?"

"That's how long it took for you to insult me."

"Did you seriously set a timer?" She wasn't certain whether to be amused or offended.

"Oh, I set a timer all right."

"It's been over an hour since we left your house."

"Twenty-three minutes since we got on the highway," he corrected. "And if we're keeping score here, we're at O'Rourke 1, Forrester 0."

"Wait a second," she said, drawing her legs back down and pulling herself upright in her seat. "Why do you get a point if *I* insulted *you*?"

"It would be too easy otherwise."

Great. They were having a jackass competition, and she was losing. Nell crossed her arms. "You can't just make up a game. I didn't agree to play."

"You can always opt out. Of course, that means you forfeit."

"Fine. If we're keeping score—"

"I always keep score."

That didn't surprise her in the least. "*If* we're keeping score," she continued, "then technically, I didn't actually insult you. I never finished my sentence."

A muscle in his cheek twitched. "Point for intent."

"And my name isn't Forrester. It's McLean."

"You're married?"

The surprise in his tone tempted her to say yes, but since she didn't want to add *invented a husband* to her list of recent transgressions, she opted for the truth. "It's always been McLean. Paige got our mother's last name. I got my dad's. We're half-sisters."

"The video identified you as Eleanor Forrester. I've got a pretty clear memory of that."

She bit her lip. That damn video. "I guess they didn't fact check."

"Well, whoever the hell you are, you're still losing."

"I want my point back. I didn't know we were competing."

"Rule number one of the O'Rourke household. You're *always* competing."

"Well, rule number one of the Forrester-McLean household is"—she floundered a second, trying to think of something a little more appropriate than *whatever you do, don't tell Grandmother*—"um, always play fair."

Instantly, Whit's shoulders tensed.

It took her a second to make the connection. *Play fair*. Of course that was going to be a sore spot with him. He probably thought she was calling him a cheater. Again.

She could have kicked herself. She'd managed to insult him without even trying. She was definitely going to lose this competition.

"Okay. O'Rourke 1, McLean 0," she said grudgingly. "But I want to know what I get if I win."

"You're not going to win."

"Maybe I just need the right incentive. What do I get?"

"Besides the satisfaction of being a better person?"

Nell opened her mouth to retort—and then clamped it shut again. He lifted an eyebrow at her.

"Nice try," she said.

"Good take. But you're still not gonna win."

"You really think you can go the next three hours without insulting me?"

"Absolutely." He withdrew something from the car's center console and held it in front of her.

Earbuds.

Since she couldn't think of a response that wouldn't have lost her another three points, Nell slumped in her seat, stuck her feet back on the dashboard, and settled in to nap.

FIVE

THREE HOURS LATER, NELL was discovering there was something worse than being stuck in a car with Whit O'Rourke—and that was being stuck on the side of the road with Whit O'Rourke, next to a car with a popped tire and a bent mirror that had narrowly escaped adding a deer as a hood ornament.

Although it might have been an elk. Or even a moose. Nell wasn't totally certain, since she'd squeezed her eyes shut the second Whit's sudden expletive had alerted her. One moment she'd been sipping coffee, texting Gabi—who she was *also* lying to—and trying not to dwell on the fact that she'd lost another point in the jackass competition thanks to an ill-timed phone call from Paige; the next, a furry, antlered creature roughly the size of Godzilla had pranced out onto the road. Whit had cursed, Nell had shrieked, then there had been a whole slamming-of-brakes, screeching-of-tires, flailing-of-arms (hers) bit that played out like a slow-motion dream sequence. The car had come to an abrupt and noisy halt. Nell's shiny new iPhone had flown out of her hand and straight into the windshield. Her cup of lukewarm gas station coffee had done a sudden flip, dumping its contents directly down her chest and soaking straight through her jacket and blouse. The deer—or whatever it actually was—had blinked once in their direction and then pranced off the road, unscathed.

All of which had brought her to her current situation: standing slumped against the hood of Whit's Audi, dressed in a sweatshirt that was way too big, chewing her fingernails down to the quick while Whit paced back and forth in front of her. She was going to have to revisit that whole *under the sway of a deep and malevolent hex* idea. If this most recent calamity were any indication, she was living out the Forrester family karma in real time. Curse of the cosmetics, Bambi's Revenge.

She hugged her arms against her, watching Whit as he moved. Pacing aside, he'd maintained his calm a lot better than she had. As soon as the car had stopped, he'd checked to make sure she wasn't injured, then steered them gently off to the shoulder to assess the damage. And since all of her packed clothing was dirty, he'd sifted through his own luggage and pulled out a fresh T-shirt and hoodie so that she didn't have to walk around wearing half a cup of coffee. Now he was on hold with his roadside assistance company, drumming his fingers on the side of his leg as he turned toward the stretch of pines and underbrush that nestled up against the highway.

She had to give him marks for chivalry, she supposed, plucking at the hem of the blue-and-gray Blizzards hoodie that came down past her knees. And aside from his stunt with the earbuds, he'd been on his best behavior during the drive, entertaining her with stories from when he played for Chicago and asking her about teaching. But it was still his fault they were there in the first place.

Nell sighed softly, her breath fogging in the cool air. According to Whit, they were only a few miles out of Fallen Oaks, but they might as well be on the moon for all she could make of their surroundings. The vast swathes of farmland and hay fields had gradually given way to forest as they'd made their way north, and now all she could see were clusters of towering trees, none of which actually appeared to be oaks. The wind had picked up, tugging at her clothes and hair. The air smelled like pine needles and burnt rubber. It might only be a ten minute drive into town, but it certainly *felt* like the middle of nowhere.

She wondered if there were bears.

Whit swung back toward her, apparently finished with his call. "You might want to wait in the car. We could be here a while."

"Define *a while*," Nell said uneasily. "Because if it's another three and a half hours, I'm calling an Uber and heading straight for the airport."

If they even had Uber in the middle of nowhere.

Which, come to think of it, they probably didn't.

Maybe she could rent a dog-sled.

Whit shrugged. "They said up to forty-five minutes. Unless you feel like walking."

"Don't tempt me. If I sit too long in a stuffy car, I'll throw up."

"In that case, you definitely shouldn't wait in the car," he said as he loped around to the back of the Audi and started rearranging the trunk to access his spare tire, thrusting aside a couple of fleece blankets, a first aid kit, a set of jumper cables, about a dozen baseballs, and two large bubblegum-pink suitcases dotted with travel stickers he'd said belonged to his sister.

Nell followed him, frowning. "Forty-five minutes for the Blizzards' star pitcher? Shouldn't you get some sort of special celebrity treatment?"

"I'm not that much of a celebrity."

"We passed three billboards with your face on them."

"Around here, that usually just means I'm trying to sell you a house."

"There was a woman at the bar last night wearing your jersey," she added.

He paused in his game of suitcase Tetris to glance at her. "Just one?"

"One that I saw," she answered quickly. "I was a little distracted." Not to mention, she'd spent the majority of her time in the seedy little sports bar trying to avoid being spotted by Whit. She hadn't exactly been making a close inspection of its patrons.

Though she did have a pretty clear memory of the generously-endowed spray-tanned blonde who'd been all but sitting in Whit's lap.

Whit turned, leaning back against the car with his hands tucked into his jeans pockets and his long legs stretched out in front of him. The wind ruffled his hair, coaxing it into thick, unruly waves. With the afternoon light gleaming against his sinewy, sun-bronzed arms, she could just see the faintly puckered flesh of the crescent-shaped surgery scar that ran along his right elbow. "How did you know to find me at Gills, anyway?" he asked, tilting his head as he gazed at her.

"I didn't. I was *trying* to find my hotel."

"So it was just a coincidence?"

"You still think I somehow set you up?" she asked.

"I'm not ready to rule out the possibility that someone did."

"Unless that someone caused my flat tire and controls the weather, I think you're gonna have to put this one down as plain old bad luck."

"Hold up a sec," Whit said, straightening, his eyes suddenly locked on her face. "This is your second flat tire in two days?"

"This flat tire is yours, not mine."

She decided not to mention the hex.

She wasn't actually *really* hexed anyway.

Probably.

"But we are talking less than forty-eight hours here," Whit said. "Just to be clear."

"Why?" She peered at him suspiciously. "You're not actually going to make me walk, are you?"

"Two flat tires," he repeated, "one of which dropped you directly into my path. And then you broke your phone."

"*You* broke my phone. And my purse!"

Whit ignored that. He pushed himself up from the Audi and took a couple of slow strides toward her. "What you need," he said, a tiny wrinkle appearing in his brow as he looked her over with the same meticulous intensity he'd used to assess his car, "is a good luck charm."

"I was thinking more along the lines of an exorcist."

"What do you normally use?"

"For exorcisms?"

"For luck. Say you had a job interview. Or a date. I mean, you do date, right?"

She opened her mouth to respond, but before she could lose herself yet another point in the jackass competition, Whit rubbed his chin with one hand and continued. "Don't you have some ritual you follow? A favorite shirt? Lucky underwear?"

"I don't have lucky underwear, and if I did, I definitely wouldn't tell you."

"Maybe if you did, we wouldn't be in this mess."

"*I* am not in any mess. *I* am just helping *you* out of yours. Which I'm seriously beginning to reconsider."

Instead of answering, he took another step toward her, and then another, until he stood only a foot or so away. With his gaze still focused on her face, he raised a hand to tug at the edge of the silver chain he wore around his neck, lifting it free from his T-shirt. The slender metal strand glinted in the chilly sunlight.

Nell had noticed the chain before but hadn't thought much of it. Paige had told her most baseball players wore a necklace or chain of some sort. It was like one of the unwritten rules of the game. Play ball? Wear chain. Many were plain, but some held crosses or other ornaments. Whit's necklace, she saw, had a small, scuffed baseball suspended from it, no larger than a nickel, complete with white cowhide exterior and tiny red stitching.

"Here," he said, holding the chain slightly—but only *very* slightly—away from his body. "Kiss this."

"Excuse me?" Nell asked. Partly because she wasn't certain she'd heard him right. Mostly because she was afraid she had.

"It's my good luck charm. I don't have an exorcist handy."

"You have got to be kidding me."

"Nope. I kiss it before every start."

"And do you win every start?"

"A hell of a lot more than I lose. You can check my ERA."

"I'm not checking your anything. And I am not kissing your ball."

Whit's eyebrows shot straight upward.

"Your *baseball*," Nell said. "I am not kissing your *baseball*."

"Why not?"

"Because it's ridiculous. And completely unhygienic."

"Afraid you'll get cooties?" he asked, like he was one of her second-graders.

"Yes," said Nell, in her most patient teacher voice. "I am afraid I'll get cooties. So put your ball back where it belongs."

"Hey, it's your bad luck."

"Tell that to *Meltdown*."

"You're the *source* of the bad luck," he amended.

Nell crossed her arms. "If I kiss that thing, I want a point back."

"You can't negotiate points."

"Take it or leave it."

"Fine. You get a point back. Pucker up."

The fact that her pulse accelerated when he said *pucker up* was really just too pathetic for words, Nell thought. Especially since she had little doubt the attraction she was fighting was entirely one-sided. He'd certainly never spared her more than half a glance before this whole debacle. Whit had dated models and actresses and, well, Paige, who had definitely held the winning ticket in the Forrester-McLean genetic lottery. Even without the lingering animosity Whit must feel toward her, Nell wasn't exactly his type. Whereas tall, dark, and athletic was pretty much everyone's type. It wasn't her fault her hormones went into overdrive whenever she was in close proximity to him. It was basic biology.

And since that proximity was about to get a whole lot closer, she was just going to have to ignore the way her heart was slamming and her stomach was doing flips. Because really, the only thing more mortifying than harboring an irrational and unwelcome attraction to Whit O'Rourke would be him knowing about it.

With that thought in mind, Nell straightened her shoulders and stepped toward him. He was so tall that she was going to have to stand on her tiptoes to reach the baseball, but she had a feeling that demanding he remove the chain might fall under the category of protesting too much, so she edged slowly forward until she was close enough that she could feel the heat of his body and smell the faint tang of his skin beneath his aftershave. Telling herself not to think about how low his jeans were riding on his lean hips, or the way the wind pulling at his thin shirt perfectly outlined his chest, she lifted herself onto her toes, shut her eyes, and gave the baseball a quick, decisive peck.

"There. Happy?" she asked.

Then she made a mistake. Instead of immediately retreating, she opened her eyes and peered up at him.

And felt like she'd been hit by a truck.

Or if not a truck, at least a mid-sized sedan. Whatever it was knocked the breath right out of her lungs and set her senses reeling. A jolt of pure sexual awareness raced through her.

Whit hadn't retreated, either. He was looking right back down at her, a faint, ironic lift to one eyebrow, the corners of his mouth curved in an expression that was half smile, half smirk. Up close, she could see his eyes were starred with tiny flecks of gold. She could see the fine glisten of sweat on his collarbone, and the strong, steady tick of his pulse. He was near enough that if she angled herself forward just slightly, she'd be able to feel the soft cotton of his T-shirt beneath her fingers. Another inch or so and her thighs would brush his.

Back up. Back up, now!

Nell swallowed, every nerve in her body humming with tension. If she had any sense of self-preservation, she would turn and run. Flip whatever switch had set her instincts to fight instead of flight and dash straight off into the woods without a backward glance. Better he think she'd gone crazy than realize how desperately she was battling the awful, traitorous impulse to raise herself onto her tiptoes, curl her arm around the back of his neck, and drag his head down to hers.

Except—

Except that he hadn't moved. Not so much as a step. He was still holding the chain gently away from his chest, letting it dangle between them. His eyes were still fixed on her face. Was she only imagining it that his gaze had dipped ever-so-briefly to her lips?

Her mind flashed out a warning. Her body ignored it. He was an open flame with his bedroom eyes and sultry stare—and right now, all of that high-octane heat was aimed directly at her. She couldn't have looked away if she'd wanted to. Meeting that heavy-lidded gaze sizzled with danger and felt like a dare.

Somehow he'd gotten even closer. His free hand was touching her arm, the tips of his fingers coming to rest just below the curve of her shoulder. She closed her eyes again.

Only to open them a second later when the sudden rumble of an approaching vehicle broke whatever hazy, lust-induced trance Whit had lulled her into.

Nell took a hasty step backward and folded her arms across her chest. Good lord. The man needed to come with some kind of warning label.

"See?" said Whit, clearing his throat as he reached to tuck the chain back inside his shirt. "Good luck charm working already."

For one panicked instant, she wondered if Whit could somehow peer into her thoughts—until she turned and realized that the vehicle making its loud and lumbering way toward them wasn't a car but a battered old Chevy tow truck, its faded red paint beginning to flake, a dent in its hood the size of a bowling ball. It slowed as it passed them, pulling off onto the shoulder in front of Whit's Audi. The engine gave one final rumble as it came to a stop.

Whit's expression hardened when the driver's door opened and a man in blue coveralls stepped out. "Or maybe not." He muttered something under his breath.

Nell didn't answer. She was too busy trying not to hyperventilate. She exhaled slowly, making an attempt to get her rocketing pulse under control, and sent a little prayer to the heavens that her face didn't look as flushed as it felt. Nothing had actually happened, she told herself. That faint crackle she'd felt in the air around them had been an illusion, the product of an overactive imagination and an underactive sex life. Whit had not been about to kiss her. And she had definitely not been about to let him.

But still, if she had to be stuck on the side of the road with one of Paige's exes, why couldn't it have been Gabi?

She should have demanded hazard pay.

The thought of Paige was enough to send her crashing back down to earth. Her stomach plummeted. Guilt gnawed at her. Even if something *had* almost happened—*and it absolutely hadn't!*—she had no business letting it almost happen with Whit O'Rourke.

He was still gazing down the road at the tow truck, his hands shoved into his pockets and his jaw tightly clenched. The driver had turned, shutting the door behind him with an abrupt, decisive thud, and was now making his leisurely way toward them.

Grateful for the distraction, Nell took in a long breath of the crisp autumn air and studied the driver as he approached. He looked about thirty, give or take, with a handsome, boyish face, dark eyes and light brown skin, his crop of black hair tousled by the wind. A jagged scar ran the length of his forehead, starting just below his hairline, bisecting his left eyebrow before it curved toward his temple. It lent him a sort of piratical look, Nell thought—although the effect was ruined by the blue coveralls. Not to mention the thick wire-framed glasses perched on his nose. According to the plastic tag pinned to his chest, his name was James.

It was clear from the way Whit had tensed that he knew the man. And that whatever history lay between them, it was anything but pleasant.

"Whit," the man said, in a tone that made the temperature drop a good ten degrees.

Beside her, Whit inclined his head slightly. "James."

"I didn't know you were in town."

"I'm not in town." Whit gestured toward the car. "Which is the problem. You're still working for your aunt?"

James's face was carefully impassive. "I work for the city. Kate was understaffed, so I'm helping her out."

"I'm guessing she didn't bother to mention who you'd be meeting."

James didn't reply. His gaze flicked to Nell, then back to Whit. "Are you planning to introduce us?"

Nell drew in a quick breath. Right. They had prepared for this. They had a plan. A story. A completely unbelievable story, in her opinion, but Whit was the one who had to sell it to his family. She was Eleanor Lacey, aspiring sportswriter. She'd been interviewing Whit for an upcoming article when she'd dropped her recording equipment and bent to retrieve it. Simple enough to remember. And one hundred percent fiction, aside from the name.

Whit had chosen the narrative. All she had to do was repeat it.

James's attention shifted back to her. Ignoring the anxious, fluttery feeling in her stomach, Nell lifted a hand to smooth a few loose strands of hair away from her face, straightened up in her best effort to appear professional, and met his gaze with a bright smile. She wasn't going to screw it up this time. No going off-script, no sarcastic comments or biting retorts. Whatever the cause of this man's hostility, it wasn't her concern. She'd made a deal with Whit, and if she didn't hold up her end of the bargain, he had no reason to hold up his. And while Nell might not enjoy lying, the six years she'd lived in her grandmother's house had taught her a lot about playing pretend.

She stuck a hand toward James. "I'm—"

Before she could get another syllable out, Whit slipped his arm around her shoulders and tugged her against him. "This is Eleanor. My girlfriend."

Six

Nell froze.

Girlfriend?

The word seemed to explode in the air like a firecracker: loud, echoing, and (at least to her ears) startling enough to send small animals scurrying into the thickets. Which was exactly what Nell wanted to do. If she'd been thinking clearly, she'd have tried to laugh it off, then come up with a quick rejoinder or witty comment to put Whit in his place—which was at least twenty feet away from her and not molded to her side like a drowning man clinging to a life preserver.

Nell was not thinking clearly. In fact, she wasn't thinking at all. She was too stunned to react. It was a good thing Whit was holding her up, or she'd have toppled face first into the road.

GIRLFRIEND??

"I'm bringing her to meet my dad," Whit added. His hand had settled at her elbow, the tips of his fingers grazing the fabric of her sleeve, the arm he'd curved around her back the only thing keeping her upright—and effectively keeping her trapped. She was pinned to his body with her shoulder tucked against his chest and her hip snug against his thigh. And while he may have *sounded* cool and collected, he was humming with tension and he felt like a furnace.

A nervous laugh worked its way out of her. She was a little appalled she was even capable of making such a noise—it was practically a *titter!*—but decided it was forgivable, given the circumstances. Short of calling Whit a liar, there didn't seem to be much she could do, so she gave James her best attempt at a smile. "I go by Nell."

Then she brought her foot down on Whit's. Hard.

Something that might have been a yelp squeaked out of him, but he covered it with a cough and adjusted his grip on her, nearly lifting her off the ground as he steadied them both. "Or Nellie."

"Nellie is reserved for small children," she said through her teeth. "Maturity level aside, no one here qualifies, *Whitney*."

"Your sister calls you Nellie," Whit pointed out.

"She named me. She can call me whatever she wants."

He tilted his head to glance down at her. "Your sister named you?"

Now why had she told him that? "I'm lucky she named me after a neighbor and not her stuffed bunny." She turned back to James. "It's nice to meet you. You're a friend of Whit's?"

James frowned, making his pirate scar bend inward. "Yeah. We go way back," he said gruffly, hitching a shoulder before turning to Whit. "I didn't think we'd be seeing you this week."

Whit just went right on smiling. "You thought wrong."

The rest of their conversation—which was an exercise in passive aggression that would've impressed even her grandmother—involved the details of getting the tire changed, so Nell spent it trying to come up with ways to punish Whit that wouldn't end with her being tossed in jail. Like sticking all of his baseballs together with Gorilla Glue. Or programming his car to play nothing but talk radio.

The second James returned to his truck to get his gear, she rounded on Whit. "What the hell do you think you're doing?"

Whit had the grace to look abashed. That was something. Not much, but something.

"I said I'd explain the video to your family," Nell continued. "I did not sign up to be your freaking *girlfriend*. You're supposed to be fake dating my sister, not me!"

And boy, if that didn't win some sort of prize for bizarre statement of the year.

"Hey, you went along with it."

"Under duress!"

"Relax. It's not going to mess up Paige's little media show. No one in Fallen Oaks cares who I'm dating."

"Then why did you just introduce me as your girlfriend?"

"You'd rather he assume you're my weekend hookup?"

"Oh my god," Nell said. He was right. Who else would Whit be taking to his hometown, wearing what was clearly one of his own hoodies? James would have taken one look at her and decided they were sleeping together. "I hate this. I hate *you.*"

"Yeah, I'm pretty clear on that one."

"And before you even *think* of adding another point, that wasn't an insult, it was a statement of fact."

He sobered. "Do you want me to tell him you're just here helping me out?"

"No. I'd better be your girlfriend," she grumbled. "But we are avoiding everyone else in this town, and we are telling your family the truth, okay? No ridiculous story about how it was all just a hilarious accident." The truth didn't make either of them look particularly good, but at least she could tell it with a clear conscience.

Whit brushed a hand through his hair. "All right."

He'd agreed to that easier than she'd expected. It sort of deflated her righteous fury. "Well... good." She nibbled on her lower lip, glancing past him to where James was crouching down to fiddle with something on his truck. It was none of her business, but—

"So, what'd you do?" she asked. "Wait, let me guess. You slept with his girlfriend."

Whit, who had been gazing down the highway at some object in the distance, turned back toward her and frowned. "Why do you assume it's my fault?"

"Are you saying it's not?"

"I didn't sleep with his girlfriend."

"His mother?"

"Yes. I slept with his mother."

"*You slept with his mother?*"

Whit rolled his eyes. "I didn't sleep with anyone, so get your mind out of the gutter. We grew apart, Nosy Nellie, that's all."

"Haha, very original."

"I thought so," he answered. She shot him a glare and he cracked a grin. "Are we done with Twenty Questions? Because you might want to wait in the car after all."

She blinked. "While he's changing the tire?"

"Unless you feel like making more friends," Whit said. He hooked a thumb over his shoulder at the truck making its way down the road. "No one in this town can mind their own business, so if they're a local, there's a good chance they stop."

Nell didn't wait to find out. She swung about and darted back to the car, diving into the passenger seat with Whit's soft, chuckling laughter floating behind her.

***

After three and a half hours in a car with Nell—plus another forty minutes on the side of the road—Whit had come to one inescapable conclusion: he seriously needed to get laid.

That was all there was to it. His body was sex-deprived and starving and desperately in need of the kind of workout that only a bout of vigorous, enthusiastic sheet-tangling could provide, or he would never have let whatever latent attraction he felt for her override his common sense. And override it it had. There was no denying the subtle physical tug he'd been feeling ever since Nell had bent over at the gas station just outside of Minneapolis, her tightly-fitted jeans providing him with a generous view of that gently-rounded bottom and those long, slender legs. Since then, he'd tried and failed to steer his thoughts in a less disastrous direction. Ignoring her had proved impossible. Reminding himself that she was off-limits even if she weren't an enormous pain in the ass had only tempted the perverse part of himself that couldn't resist a challenge. Whatever rational thought he'd had left had gone out the window the moment he'd seen her gazing up at him, flushed and flustered, all wide eyes and softly parted lips. He'd damn near kissed her before James's untimely—or rather, extremely *timely*—intervention.

So, okay, maybe the attraction wasn't all that latent. It definitely hadn't been latent four years ago, which had been more of a problem than he'd cared to admit. And he wasn't going to pretend she wasn't good-looking. Pretty, even. The silky wisps of hair that had come free from her ponytail had framed her face with loose curls, accentuating her caramel-colored eyes and the delicately sculpted line of her jaw. Her mouth was sensuous and prone to smiling (when she wasn't using it to argue with him, anyway), and she might look the very image of the girl-next-door, but the crooked little scar curving along her upper lip was a potent reminder that every nice girl had a naughty side.

But she was also the last woman on earth he should ever think about kissing. A few hours ago, he'd been happily imagining the expression on her face when he found the most cutthroat lawyer money could buy and slapped her with a couple of lawsuits. Now he'd just introduced her as his girlfriend.

Definitely not his best idea—though it had been less an idea than a reaction.

He'd been living with the antipathy of his former classmates for so long, he hadn't thought he'd let the icy disdain and naked hostility get to him. He'd been wrong. The confrontation with James had sent him hurtling straight back to high school, all the anger and hurt as fresh as it had been a decade ago, all the history he'd thought well-buried surfacing with roughly the force of a four-seam. He'd gotten the same tight, panicked feeling in his chest that he'd had four years ago when three separate doctors had told him he needed surgery. The same surge of adrenaline that had propelled him toward self-destruction after. The same quiet dread. And beneath it, the old, familiar bite of guilt.

He'd wanted to run. Just the sight of that scar slicing down James's face had made his stomach churn. For an instant, he could have sworn he'd caught the smell of burnt rubber. Then, instead of running, he'd used Nell as a buffer. It had been a stupid, desperate move—and an ironic one, considering she'd made no secret of her own dislike for him. Still, however low her opinion of him might be, it didn't compare with the utter contempt James held for him.

But then, she didn't know the worst of his sins.

Introducing her as his girlfriend hadn't been entirely for his own benefit, of course. He'd had to protect her reputation. What hopeful sportswriter would torpedo her career by getting involved with an athlete? That had to cross some serious professional and ethical boundaries. Eleanor Lacey, aspiring journalist, would've had a lot of explaining to do.

With that amused thought, he darted a quick glance toward Nell, who was sitting beside him with her arms folded. She'd been quiet since they got back in the car, her head turned toward the window, her body scooted as close to the door—and away from him—as she could manage. So he'd probably said something to piss her off again.

At least the ordeal was nearly over. He wasn't looking forward to the upcoming conversation with his father, but once it was done, he could send Nell and whatever ill-advised attraction he felt for her safely back out of his life.

"This is it," he said, easing his car into the long curve of driveway that led up to his father's house. Ahead, the sprawling two-story building with its white stucco exterior and wide picture windows came into view.

"Just so we're on the same page this time, we're going with the truth," Nell said as Whit pulled his Audi around the side of the house and put it in park. "Agreed?"

"You mean the truth where you were only apologizing to me so I would pretend to date your sister?" he asked, stepping out of the car and waiting for her to emerge on the passenger side before clicking the lock on his key fob. "That truth?"

"Maybe we should skip that part."

"There's some word... I can't quite think of it—goes along with *omission...*"

"It's not lying," she huffed. "It's cutting down on unnecessary details."

"Uh-huh. Just remember you're supposed to be on my side here, so try to keep the insults to a minimum. And be nice."

"I'm always nice."

He raised his eyebrows.

"Okay, I'm usually nice. Can we please just get this stupid thing over with?"

Smirking, Whit jogged the last few steps to the front entrance, Nell grumbling as she followed along behind him. The door had been left open a crack, which was unusual. He'd half expected to find his father had locked him out—and then changed the locks. But maybe whatever antics his sisters had gotten up to had provided a distraction. Clearly *something* was amiss. From inside, he could hear the sound of raised voices, and a couple of sharp yelps that sounded a lot like—

"Is that a dog?" Nell asked.

"My dad doesn't have a dog."

"Well, someone does," Nell said as Whit tugged the door open and ushered her inside.

Chaos greeted them. Whit hadn't taken more than three steps into the hall before a small terrier wearing a gray and red argyle sweater came streaking across the floor. The dog swerved as soon as it saw him, stopping to aim a few sharp yips in his direction, and then resumed course. It had left a small puddle of urine on the hardwood floor, Whit noticed—though no one else seemed to be paying the slightest attention to the dog. Or to him, for that matter.

He blinked, taking in the tableau. Gerda, his father's seventy-year-old housekeeper, was sitting on one of the blue upholstered dining room chairs, drinking scotch straight from the bottle and muttering in German. A frazzled-looking young woman carrying an iPad was pacing back and forth in front of the main staircase while a second terrier barked at her heels. Allie and Freddie stood near a side window, Freddie making soothing noises while Allie gestured wildly with her hands. Somewhere deeper in the house, Whit's dad was yelling into a phone—presumably—his voice reverberating down through the halls.

"Who are you?" the woman with the iPad asked, pausing to stare at them with wide, panicked eyes the color of cornflowers.

"Whit O'Rourke. Who are you?"

Her forehead wrinkled, but the panic vanished. "Oh. I thought you weren't coming. I'm Maggie, Skip's assistant. He's busy." She went back to pacing.

A thump sounded from above, followed by the telltale noise of a fist slamming into a wall. But since no one else seemed in any hurry to investigate, Whit stayed where he was. His first thought was that something had gone wrong with the stadium. Contracts falling through, an investor backing out—maybe the city was dragging its heels on a couple of details, or someone had gotten an injunction. That didn't bode well for Whit's chances of reputation rehabilitation. There couldn't be much of a groundbreaking celebration without a groundbreaking.

Allie had spotted him. She lifted a quick hand to shush Freddie and came flying toward Whit, barreling at him so fast she had to skid to a halt to avoid a collision.

"Where have you been?" she demanded. "Rory just won the Piss Off Dad Contest!"

"I don't care about the stupid—"

He broke off mid-sentence. If Rory had managed to top *bogus footage of public fellatio in a national media outlet,* she must have done something truly egregious. "What'd she do? Get herself arrested?"

"She married Satan!"

Something that sounded suspiciously like a laugh wheezed out of Nell.

"She joined a cult?" Whit asked. "We aren't talking the literal Prince of Darkness here, I assume."

"Trust me, this is way worse."

Whit frowned. "Don't tell me she got back together with Scott." If Rory had somehow married her scumbag of an ex, their dad wasn't going to be the only one pissed off.

"Come on, Whit. *Satan.*"

It took him a second to put the pieces together. "Rory married C.J. Saint?"

Fourteen years ago, Saint had been a twenty-year-old hotshot rookie freshly called up to the bigs—cocky, careless, and determined to keep himself in the show. Whit's dad had been a thirty-six-year-old veteran, fighting the relentless pull of time on a body that had already been stretched to its limits. Their clashes in the clubhouse had led to Saint being traded. Their collision at home plate a few months later had torn Skip's ACL and ended not only his season, but his career.

The bad blood hadn't stopped there. Whit didn't know the precise details, but comments his father had dropped now and then led him to believe the feud was ongoing. His own interactions with Saint had been brief and few. From what Whit had heard, in the years since Saint had waltzed away with Rookie of the Year, he'd gone from reckless arrogance to being a bit of a loner: quiet, broody, focused, and unforgiving.

There was no way that Rory, who as far as Whit knew had never even met the guy, would just up and marry him. She might have inherited every ounce of their father's competitiveness, but unlike Allie, she wasn't entirely lacking in common sense. And Rory of all people knew better than to marry a ballplayer—especially since she was two months out of a three-year relationship with a man who had publicly cheated on her.

"Relax," he told Allie. "She's pranking you. Both of you. Not even Rory would marry someone just to win a stupid contest."

His father's screaming into the phone aside.

"Oh, no, she married him," said Allie. "When I got here, Dad was talking about hiring a hitman!"

This time Nell definitely laughed.

"And we weren't invited to the wedding?" Whit asked. "I'm hurt."

"She's not lying. She sent us the video of the ceremony. From Vegas!"

Admittedly, that was rather elaborate for a prank. And it occurred to Whit that Rory was one of the very few people who hadn't contacted him about *Meltdown* article. Still, if he'd wanted to add gambling to his list of vices, he'd have wagered a good chunk of his contract that Rory had simply upped the ante in his sisters' silly competition. Even if he could believe her choosing to take over the dubious honor of Least Favorite O'Rourke Child by eloping with their father's arch-nemesis—which he couldn't—she definitely wouldn't have done it without telling him. He hoped Rory was prepared for the fallout, because as far as jokes went, this one was rather sadistic.

Although it was also pretty damn funny.

"Stop laughing!" Allie hissed. "Dad's gone ballistic. He's going to disinherit her, and when I refuse to shun her for the rest of eternity, he's going to disinherit *me*."

"Lucky for you, you have a rich older brother," Whit said. Not that he planned to fund Allie's aimless lifestyle of traipsing across Europe or South America or whatever continent she'd chosen this year, but he also didn't think she was in any real danger of being cut off. Rory, on the other hand...

He cocked his head toward the staircase, where Skip's roars had gone up a few decibels. "So which one of them is he yelling at? And where did the dogs come from?"

Allie waved a hand. "The depths of hell, according to Gerda. Dad's dog-sitting for one of the guys." A slight furrow appeared in her brow as her gaze darted toward Nell, then back at Whit. "If you don't care about the contest, why did you bring a groupie here?"

"Don't be rude, Al," Freddie murmured, coming up beside Allie and slipping his arm around her shoulders. He grinned at Whit.

"Sorry." Allie shrugged, directing a thin smile at Nell. "I have no tact. Nice to meet you, whoever you are." Then she wriggled away from Freddie, stalked across the hall to the dining area, snatched the bottle of scotch from Gerda's suspiciously unsteady hand, and took three long swallows.

"She's taking it hard," Freddie said before turning to follow her.

Whit was debating whether to give Nell a tour of the house or forage in the kitchen for something to eat when the shouting from upstairs abruptly ceased.

"Either she hung up on him or he's having a heart attack," Whit said, flicking a glance at Nell. "Come on."

She looked horrified. "You think *now* is a good time to talk to your dad?"

"We'll still be here next spring if you want to wait around for a better one." Taking her pained expression and faint shudder as assent, he started forward, carefully sidestepped the puddle of dog urine on the floor, and headed for the stairs.

Seven

His father's office sat on the upper floor of the house, down the hall from what had once been Whit's bedroom and was now a converted workout room. A memory flickered as he picked his way up the staircase, trailing his hand along the banister: the groaning fifth step, betrayer of midnight excursions and teenage rendezvous, silent now, since his father had long since had it fixed. In the years since first Whit and then his sisters had left for college, renovation had become something of a passion for Skip. The office, with its oak panel door and wide back windows that overlooked the lake, was one of the only rooms that hadn't changed in the last decade. The rest, Whit's father had slowly but surely transformed from a rambling family abode into a sort of living museum, filled with old game photos and baseball memorabilia: plaques, jerseys, merchandise, magazine covers, awards; anything that bore Skip O'Rourke's name or the number that had become the most important part of his identity—good ol' Number 15, which his club had retired right along with him. Wall by wall and room by room, he'd made it a shrine to the career he'd felt had ended too early. And eradicated any trace of the woman who had once put her soul into making it a home.

As a child, that home had been idyllic: spacious but cozy, comfortable rather than pristine, the walls cluttered with family pictures and haphazard art projects. Skip had bought the place after signing the deal that cemented his status as not only a rising talent but a superstar in the making. He'd plucked his young family from their Baltimore suburb and dropped them in his beloved Fallen Oaks because he wanted them to have a sense of *stability*—a true place to call home, he said, instead of picking up stakes with every new contract or sudden trade.

The reality had been much more chaotic. Instead of moving with contracts, they'd moved with the seasons. Each summer, Whit's mother had packed her children up to be with Skip during home games, first in Baltimore, then a year in St. Louis, another two in Los Angeles, and finally Baltimore again for the remainder of his career. When the school year started, it was back to Minnesota's great up north, the sleepy town of quiet forests and long winters. Spring was a toss-up: some years saw them spending a week or two in Florida or Arizona while Skip's team prepared for the upcoming season; more often, Whit went months at a time without seeing his father.

He hadn't minded at first. He'd missed his dad, of course; he'd missed watching the players at batting practice, and hanging out in the clubhouse, and the thrill that ran up his spine each time Skip stepped up to the plate. He'd spent every day at the ballpark willing himself into the future, when he would be the one standing in the flood of the stadium lights with the cheers roaring around him and the crowd chanting his name. But he'd understood that his mother needed him. He was her rock, the man of the house while his dad couldn't be.

It wasn't until he was older that Whit realized his father preferred to keep his family safely out of sight. Skip O'Rourke had wanted to enjoy a particular kind of lifestyle, and having a wife and kids got in the way. Stability had just been an excuse. What he'd wanted was freedom.

His mother's voice drifted to him. *You have to let it go, Whit. He's your father. He's the only one you get.* She'd told him that a couple of weeks ago, shortly before he'd walked her down the aisle of the little Scottish chapel where she'd held her recent wedding. Rather than ruin her day, Whit had kept his thoughts to himself—but it galled him that she still defended Skip. For eighteen years, she'd had forgiving him down to a science. And every time she forgave him, she'd lost a little bit more of herself. It had taken a near-tragedy to convince her to leave the marriage while there was still some part of her left, and the fact that she was thriving now didn't just erase that.

He paused a few feet from the office door and shot a quick glance at Nell. She was keeping slightly behind him, her body stiff. She looked about two seconds from spinning on her heel and bolting for the nearest exit. He couldn't blame her for being nervous, even if she *was* at least somewhat to blame for the mess they were in. But strange as it was—and he'd give up baseball before he'd ever admit to it—he liked having her there.

Not that he was afraid of facing his dad. It was just that Nell's presence made him feel... less alone. And he never felt more alone than when he was with his father.

Still, given the mood his dad was in...

"I'd better go in first," Whit said, signaling for her to wait before easing the office door open and moving quietly inside.

The old, familiar scents of whiskey and leather greeted him. He breathed them in a moment, forcing himself to relax. Even as a kid, this had been Whit's favorite room in the house; entering it now was like stepping through a portal into the past. While his father might have rededicated the rest of the place to the legend of Skip O'Rourke, this room was still a tribute to the greats: Ruth, Mantle, Williams, Aaron, Mays; there was a signed Jackie Robinson card framed in loving display above the big cherry wood desk and a Roger Maris home run ball on one of the built-in bookcases. An entire wall had been given over to Skip's personal hero, Tony Oliva, and in the far corner, next to a couple of antique figurines, sat the coveted O'Rourke Family Trophy with its little gold baseball player caught in permanent swing. Nearby, a few photo frames hung slightly askew—presumably from the sudden impact of a fist connecting with the wall beneath.

Whit's father stood behind the desk, leaning forward on the heels of his palms. He was staring down at his phone, but even from across the room, Whit could see the grimace on his face and the tension running through his shoulders. He was sort of twitching, like he was about to either bellow his fury at the heavens or dramatically sweep everything off of his desk. There was nothing Skip hated more than having his will thwarted… except, of course, for having his legacy tarnished. The last time Whit had seen his father this angry, he'd been the one on the receiving end.

Whit studied him, sizing him up like they were staring at each other across the plate—though in this case, his father was the umpire, short-fused and ready to toss him out of the game. A man of rigid rules and stubborn pride, utterly convinced of his own infallibility. It had been almost a year since they'd stood in the same room together, but aside from the faint growth of beard and the fact that he now dressed like a businessman instead of a ballplayer, Whit didn't see that anything had altered. It never did.

Unlike a lot of aging sports heroes, Skip hadn't let his body go after retirement. He was as fit at fifty as men ten years younger, and all that hot sun and hard-drinking hadn't done much but put a little gray in his hair and deepen the lines on his face—a face that was enough like Whit's own that he had a pretty good idea of how he'd look in a couple of decades. But that was where their similarities ended. Whit may have followed his father's footsteps into baseball, but he didn't intend to follow them out of it. He wasn't going to spend the rest of his life mourning his youth. When he could no longer cut it, he'd make a clean break. None of this living in the past, reminiscing about the good old days. Instead of making a museum of his memories, he'd donate whatever he couldn't bear to throw away.

Until that time came, however, he had a reputation to clean up and an image to maintain. One ordeal at a time.

Whit strolled casually forward, the low slap of his footsteps loud on the hardwood floor.

His dad glanced up. No hint of surprise or outrage registered on his face. He just pushed himself upward from the desk and gave Whit a grim, narrow-eyed stare. "I told you to stay home."

And I haven't followed your orders since I was thirteen years old and one of your girlfriends showed up at our hotel in a towel.

But you didn't win with Skip O'Rourke by getting defensive. The only way you won with Skip O'Rourke was if you didn't play.

Whit plucked the signed Maris ball from its stand and flipped it toward his dad. "Catch."

Skip grunted, snagging the ball one-handed. "You break anything in this room, you're replacing it." He tossed the ball back.

Whit caught it, shuffling the baseball back and forth between his hands before throwing it to Skip again. "How's your fist?"

His father's frown deepened to a glower. "I suppose Allie filled you in." He flipped the ball to Whit.

"I don't know why you guys are taking Rory seriously." If there was one person in the family with a temper to rival their father's, it was Rory. Which meant she hadn't pulled this prank merely to win some contest. "You planning to share what it is you did to piss her off?"

"Rory will do whatever the hell she wants," Skip said bleakly. "She always has."

"I take it she's also been uninvited from the week's events," said Whit. *Flip.*

"At least she's smart enough to keep her private life private." *Flip.*

"So you've got one kid out of three. Really putting the *family* in O'Rourke Family Foundation, there." *Flip.*

His father set the baseball on the desk. A vein in his neck throbbed. "Should I have asked your mother? I hear she's in Scotland with the latest addition to her husband collection."

"You could try being happy for her, you know."

"I give it six months."

Considering his new stepdad was thirty-two years old and dumb as a brick, Whit thought that was a little generous—but Skip was the last person who should ever judge her choices. "Are you sure you want to be casting stones?"

The vein throbbed again. "I'm not the one dragging our name through the mud here, kid."

"I guess that means you don't plan to hear my side of the story before booting me out on my ass."

"Is there a side of the story that isn't a headline on *Meltdown?*"

"Then what about a little fatherly loyalty? You can't be completely unfamiliar with the concept."

"You've been in the game long enough to know you only get so many strikes."

"And you took one look at a sleazy tabloid and decided my guilt."

"Let's cut to it," Skip said, folding his arms and adopting that same, familiar stance from Whit's childhood, Zeus booming out from Mount Olympus to lay down the law on the mere mortals below. "You're not here because you give a damn about the stadium or the foundation. You're here because you want the publicity that comes with it. And that was fine—yesterday. But I have too much on my plate to deal with cleaning up another one of your messes. You want to stay in the press's good graces? Learn to keep your pants zipped."

As though Skip O'Rourke had ever once in his life met a temptation he'd wanted to resist. Whit felt all that old anger surface. "Just following your shining example, Dad."

"I didn't flaunt my affairs to the public."

Only because he'd retired before the rise of social media and smartphones. Skip had managed to come out of the steroid era unblemished, but both of them knew the league had covered up plenty of other sins. Some of whom charged by the hour. Whit curled a lip. "Just to your wife and kids."

Something flickered in Skip's eyes. His nostrils flared. "You're not staying, end of story. You want fatherly loyalty? Fine. As your father, it's time for some tough love. You fucked up. Now you get to face the consequences. Maybe next time you'll think before risking your reputation for a cheap thrill."

The quiet voice from behind him made Whit jerk in surprise.

"It wasn't Whit's fault."

Neither of them had heard Nell enter the room, but as the door closed behind her with a gentle thud, Whit swiveled and Skip slammed his palm against the desk.

"Who the hell are you?" Skip barked.

Nell's chin came up. "The cheap thrill. And before you ask, yes, it was me in the video, no, it wasn't what it looked like, and yes, we are suing. Any more questions?"

His father took one glance at her before shooting Whit a look of sheer disgust. "You brought a *groupie* here?"

So much for his plan of introducing Nell as a wholesome girl-next-door type, the sort of woman who rescued kittens and organized bake sales and had never so much as said a swear word in her life. *This* wholesome girl-next-door looked ready to murder someone. Even with the golden afternoon light haloing her, showcasing the smattering of freckles that dappled her nose, she seemed less like an innocent, fresh-faced cherub and more like the archangel of doom.

"Nell's not a groupie, Dad," he said, hurrying toward her with long, purposeful strides. "Give us a minute, would you?" He wrapped an arm around Nell's shoulders to aim her back toward the door and away from his father. Far, far away. She must have realized he'd simply lift her off her feet and haul her off like a sack of potatoes if she tried to resist, because she didn't utter a word of protest.

As soon as he'd maneuvered Nell safely back out of the office, he released his grip and dropped his voice to a whisper. "What are you doing?"

"Exactly what you dragged me out here to do." Her words came out on a huff of air, but her inability to meet his eyes said it all.

"I told you to wait in the hallway."

"Nosy Nellie, remember?"

He glared at her.

"I thought you could use some help," she added, sounding guilty.

"And a fantastic job you're doing of that."

She grimaced, glancing down at her borrowed Blizzards sweatshirt. "The next time I spill coffee on myself, I'm just going to walk around naked."

"Because no one would mistake you for a groupie then."

"This wouldn't be a problem if you didn't have groupies in the first place."

"I *don't* have groupies," he retorted. When she gave him a pitying look, Whit scowled. "What, you think I encourage them?"

"I don't remember you complaining about that spray-tanned blonde crawling into your lap."

"That sounds like jealousy to me."

She planted a hand on her hip. "Are we going to do this thing or not?"

Or not seemed like a good idea to Whit, but since he didn't want to give Skip the satisfaction of chasing him off with his tail tucked between his legs, he supposed he'd better do what he could to salvage the situation. "Fine. Just... try not to antagonize him."

"What do you call what you were doing?"

"He's my dad. I was born to antagonize him." He shoved a hand through his hair. It grated to have to explain himself to a man who had once smuggled a stripper disguised as a bat boy into Camden Yards, but Whit's stay in town would go a hell of a lot smoother if he and his father could reach some sort of agreement. "Look. My dad isn't stupid. We're going to need to lay it out to him flat, no bullshit. If he doesn't accept it, that's his problem."

And mine. But he'd cross that bridge when he came to it.

"I still think a phone call would've been better."

"He can hang up a phone call." Which was undoubtedly what Rory had done once Skip started yelling. "Or ignore it. He can't ignore us face to face."

"If you say so."

Shifting, Whit pushed the heavy door open with the heel of his hand and stepped back into the office.

Within, Skip had seated himself behind his desk, tapping his fingers rhythmically against the smoothly polished surface as he frowned at something on his laptop screen. The Maris home run ball had been returned to the shelf, Whit noted, a relic of a bygone era back in its proper exalted place. At the far end of the office, one of the windows had been tugged open to let the cool air roll in off the lake, the scents of autumn mingling with the whiskey-and-leather aroma that clung to the walls. Old leaves and mildew, the hint of wood smoke; heralds of the coming winter. Somehow that felt like an omen. And not a good one.

Whit cleared his throat. "Dad."

The look on Skip's face when he glanced up was more weary than enraged. His shoulders, normally as rigid as the rest of him, had worked their way into a subtle slump. "I've said my piece, Whitney."

"Then let me say mine."

Skip waited a beat, then gave a quick, curt nod.

Whit's chest felt suddenly tight. He opened his mouth to speak but no words came out.

You remember Nell, Dad. She told the whole world I had cheated at the one thing that ever meant anything to you.

He swallowed.

Funny story. She was on her knees because I told her she had to beg forgiveness for destroying my reputation. Ironic, right?

Somehow, he didn't think his dad would appreciate the irony.

He didn't need to conjure up the disappointment he would see in his dad's eyes. It was already there, had been there from the moment Whit first admitted he'd broken the league's most sacred rule.

He hated that it still mattered to him. Hated that even if he couldn't live up to his father's lofty ideals, he still craved his respect.

"Never mind," he bit out. "Think whatever the hell you want."

He swung around and headed for the door.

It took him half a second to realize Nell hadn't followed him. And another half second to process that she was moving in the wrong direction. Instead of taking the offered escape and beating a swift retreat, she was making a beeline for his father. Whit hurried after her, but before he could reach her—catch her, stop her, *anything* her—she'd halted in front of the wide cherry wood desk and thrust out a hand.

"We weren't introduced properly," she told his dad.

Whit's breath came out in a whoosh. "Nell, you don't have to—"

"I'm Nell. Whit's girlfriend."

He stopped in his tracks.

Skip's eyebrows slammed together. He turned his stony gaze on Whit. "Girlfriend?"

Since he didn't think telling his father that Nell was a crazy woman he'd picked up on the side of the road would do much to help his case, he lifted his shoulders in a weak shrug. "Surprise."

"I'm sorry to barge in on you like this, Mr. O'Rourke," Nell continued.

Whit tried again. "Nell—"

But Nell was gaining confidence. Head lifted, spine straight, she met the icy gaze of Skip O'Rourke—who had made a career out of intimidating everyone from rookie call-ups to tough-as-nails veterans—without flinching. "I want to set the record straight. Whit isn't to blame for what happened last night. I was on my knees because I was asking his forgiveness. The circumstances of that are private, so I hope you won't ask me to share them. I'll just say that seeing that video was definitely the most mortifying moment of my existence. Followed closely by this one."

She didn't look mortified, Whit thought. She looked determined. And entirely earnest.

A truly terrible idea started to take root in his head.

His dad shot him another glance, but this time his expression was mostly baffled.

Whit leaned a shoulder against one of the bookcases, folding his arms as he cocked an eyebrow at his dad. "I told you she wasn't a groupie."

Skip cleared his throat. He rose from the desk, realized that he'd been ignoring Nell's outstretched hand, and instead of shaking it, enfolded it briefly in both of his. "I apologize for the misunderstanding, Miss..."

"Lacey," said Nell.

"McLean," said Whit.

"Lacey-McLean," Nell corrected quickly. "It's easier for my students if I go by Miss Lacey. But you can call me Nell."

Whit had to admire her quick thinking. For someone who had been so insistent on telling the truth, she sure was good at acting.

That terrible idea of his grew a little.

"Students?" Skip echoed.

"I teach second grade."

His dad seemed more flummoxed than ever. Whit decided to take advantage of it. "See, Dad? Totally blameless."

"I wouldn't say *totally* blameless." Nell gave him a sidelong glance that told him he'd better not push his luck. "But the article isn't true. The pictures were taken out of context and the video was edited."

"We're letting my publicist handle the media," Whit added. "So no comment, if anyone asks."

Skip had stopped paying attention to him. It must have finally occurred to him that he'd made an ass of himself in front of a young, attractive woman, and he was busy trying to gain her good graces by flipping the charm switch. He stepped out from behind the desk and, to Whit's considerable annoyance, gave Nell that same lopsided aw-shucks smile Whit had tried on her only a few short hours ago. "Glad to meet you, Nell."

"Likewise. Though I wish it were under *slightly* less embarrassing circumstances." Her laugh came out somewhat shaky, and Whit wasn't certain if that was her playing it up or genuine nerves. She dropped her hands to the hem of her sweatshirt, plucking at the fabric. "Normally, I'd wait a couple of months before doing the whole meet the parents thing, but I guess *Meltdown* had other plans."

Skip was quick to reassure her. "I wouldn't worry too much about it. The news cycle tends to move fast. Give it a couple of weeks and no one will even remember it."

Whit thought he should win another Cy Young for the sheer level of control it took to bite back a snarky comment. He divided a glance between Nell and his dad. Nell was looking cute and frazzled, all but drowning in his sweatshirt as she nibbled on her bottom lip. His father was clearly trying to put her at ease, transformed now from angry ump barking out orders to genial host.

That terrible idea buzzed in Whit's head.

It would never work. It was crazy. Demented. Absolutely, one hundred percent bonkers.

And yet...

"Teacher, huh?" Skip continued, aiming another one of those lazy smiles at Nell. "How'd you get tangled up with him?" He tipped his head toward Whit.

"Bad luck," said his loving girlfriend.

Skip chuckled.

Since Whit wouldn't put it past his dad to straight up start flirting with his girlfriend—never mind that she wasn't actually his girlfriend—he slipped away from his spot by the bookcase and moved to Nell's side, looping an arm around her waist. She tensed as he drew her against him, but she didn't try to break free, and after a moment she relaxed, exhaling softly.

She smelled good. Like warm vanilla and some sort of floral shampoo.

"Worked out well enough for me," Whit said, sliding his hand to her shoulder and giving her a quick squeeze.

It was dawning on him that perhaps Paige's PR romance scheme wasn't all that ludicrous... at least on a much smaller scale and in the much shorter term. And with a very different woman. If he'd been smart, he would never have planned on coming to Fallen Oaks alone in the first place. He'd have waited to break up with his latest girlfriend until after the groundbreaking ceremony. Lilah had been sweet, easygoing, and gorgeous. Sure, she'd gotten a bit clingy at the end and had taken the breakup harder than expected, but he could've dealt with that for another few weeks if it meant having a plus-one to provide a diversion. Lilah would have been the ideal candidate to keep malicious busybodies at bay and make all his former friends writhe with envy. But Nell...

Sure, she'd professed to hate him not half an hour ago, but if he could set aside the minor issue of her having spilled his darkest secret to the world, she could be convinced to tolerate him for a week or so—given the right incentive.

Maybe that flicker of an idea wasn't so terrible after all. Maybe it was actually just a little bit perfect.

"We really need to get checked into our hotel," Whit said, reaching a decision. "I assume we're invited for dinner."

Nell stiffened and his dad looked pained.

"If you're not still planning to send us both packing, that is," Whit added.

The lines in Skip's forehead deepened. "You really should've given me some warning, Whit. I already canceled your hotel."

Whit fought back another retort. "No problem. We'll stay here."

"That's really not necessary," Nell answered quickly. She lowered her voice, giving him a dark look from under her lashes. "Remember that urgent business I have? How I need to get back to Minneapolis tonight?"

"Don't worry about it, babe. Didn't I tell you I'd take care of it?" He moved his foot before Nell could bring hers down on it.

"I don't need you to take care of things for me, *babe*."

On second thought, the less time Nell spent with his dad, the better. Keeping his arm firmly around her, he steered her toward the door. "You know what, Dad?" he called over his shoulder. "Don't even sweat it. We'll stay with Grandpa. I'll text you once we're settled in."

EIGHT

As WHIT EASED HIS Audi out of his father's driveway and onto a winding back road lined with oak trees and evergreens, Nell tried to imagine she was in the midst of some strange, alcohol-induced fever dream. Any moment now, the world would rewind itself, and she'd wake up in her own bed, in her own apartment, where she would fumble toward her phone to text Paige all about the wild and wacky ways of her subconscious. They'd have a good laugh, Paige would tell her to lay off the rosé, and time would spin forward once more, with Nell safe and sound and four hundred miles distant from any member of the O'Rourke family.

Except, of course, that didn't happen. The sun didn't reverse its course overhead. The potholes scattered across the road didn't jolt her awake. She tried squeezing her eyes shut, but when she opened them again, she was still deep in the backwoods of Minnesota, still trapped in a car with the man she'd falsely announced was her boyfriend, and the sudden chiming from her phone wasn't an amused response to her zany nightmare, but a reminder she'd set for herself to start working on cover letters.

That was one bright side to her current catastrophe, she supposed. It made her last catastrophe seem a bit less... well, catastrophic.

Nell blew at a strand of hair that had come loose from her ponytail, aiming a sidelong glance at Whit. She hadn't spoken a word to him since he'd whisked her out of the house and into the car, hustling her along like she was a bomb about to go off. She hardly trusted herself *to* speak. A single thought kept repeating itself over and over in her mind, like a particularly irritating song stuck on loop: *Eleanor Lacey McLean, what have you done?*

It was definitely bad when she was using the full-name-scolding tactic on *herself.*

She didn't know what had come over her. She'd told herself not to get involved. Whatever messy family drama Whit had going on was his business. But one moment she'd been standing in the hall outside his father's office, trying desperately not to eavesdrop on what was clearly a private and deeply personal conversation... the next, she'd found herself striding across the threshold and putting on the performance of her life.

She should've just told the truth. She could hardly have made the situation any worse if she'd laid the facts out plainly. But she didn't know that she'd have made it any better, either. And somehow, for reasons that escaped even herself, she'd needed to make it better. She'd heard the pain in Whit's voice and something inside her had shifted. The same instinct that had cast Whit as the villain in her storybook had now reframed him as the victim. His father was the big bad wolf, all sharp claws and bared teeth, and Whit was the innocent in need of saving; of course she'd had to step in. It had been an act of kindness, of generosity, and if some small part of her—some *very, very small* part—had felt a guilty thrill at announcing herself as his girlfriend, well, she was only human.

Not that that would matter to her sister. Paige would murder her if she ever found out about this. Unless that whole fever dream thing panned out.

Nell thought it might be a trifle cliché to pinch herself—especially since she knew full well she wasn't actually dreaming—so instead she leaned over and smacked Whit on the arm. Not hard enough to hurt, but hard enough that he scooted farther over in his seat before turning his head to glance at her.

"What was that for?"

Like he didn't know *exactly* what that was for. Nell's eyes narrowed. "Where are we going? And if you say anything other than the airport, I'm opening this door, rolling to the side of the road, and staying there until some kind soul shows up to rescue me."

Or until she got run over by a tractor. And given her luck, the tractor seemed a lot more likely.

"You don't think that might be a bit of an overreaction?" Whit asked. In response to her glare, he added, "You weren't going to spend the night at the airport anyway."

She crossed her arms. "So you're taking me to my hotel, then."

"It's more of a farmhouse than a hotel. You're not allergic to cats, are you?"

"You have lost your mind if you think I'm staying with you at your grandfather's."

"I'm sorry, who was it who just told my dad we were dating?"

"That was—"

"*I'm Nell*," he said in falsetto. "*Whit's girlfriend.*" Then he giggled.

"I didn't giggle!" She could feel heat creeping up her face and bit down on her lip. "Anyway, I was doing you a favor."

"Oh, I'm not complaining," he said, tossing her his patented sideways grin. The same grin that had never failed to make her heart do a funny little flip. Which was exactly what it did now. "You were perfect. Except, you know, for that one teensy complication where now my dad thinks we're dating."

"There's no complication. Just tell him I had an emergency or something. In a couple of weeks, you can say we broke up, and then rebound with Paige." Nell winced. That sounded convoluted even to her.

"I think you might need to work on your definition of complicated."

"And your solution is what?"

"It's not a solution so much as a proposition."

Given what he'd said to his father about being invited to dinner—plus the fact that he was currently kidnapping her—Nell had a pretty good idea of just what that proposition was. "You cannot be serious."

"You don't even know what I was going to say."

"Were you *not* about to suggest I spend the next week telling everyone in this town I'm your girlfriend? Because that was a stupid idea when Paige came up with it, and it's an even stupider idea now."

For many reasons, not the least of which was the way her pulse accelerated whenever their eyes met. Or how she could still feel the pressure of his fingertips on her hip from when he'd slipped his arm around her, a physical echo playing itself against her skin.

Or how badly she'd wanted to kiss him earlier.

"I don't think the two of us dating was precisely Paige's idea," said Whit.

"*Pretending* to date," Nell amended quickly. "And you know what I meant."

"I'm just trying to be specific."

"Well, it was a specifically stupid idea. Both times."

"Yet you still hopped on a plane to convince me to go along with it."

"I have never regretted anything more in my life, believe me."

He chuckled. "Come on, I'm not all *that* bad, am I?"

Nell wasn't about to take that bait. "I don't see why you need me. We already cleared things up with your dad. Sort of."

"It's not really my dad I'm worried about. General sentiment in Fallen Oaks wasn't exactly favorable toward me even before this morning's developments."

"And I'm supposed to help that how?"

"Same way you did before," he said. "Just act all cute and nervous, and if anyone starts asking questions, flash your dimples at them."

Cute. Like she was some big-eyed baby animal, or a little kid with a missing front tooth. It was depressing how much that bothered her. "I don't have dimples."

"Whatever you did, it was effective."

"You do realize how crazy you sound, right?"

Whit lifted a shoulder. "Hey, it worked on my dad."

Nell floundered, struggling for a response, any response. Between Whit and Paige, Nell would have put money on him being the more sensible of the two. He might be arrogant and argumentative, strolling through life with that air of utter certainty that came from getting everything you want—but he'd always seemed soundly rational. Now he appeared perfectly content to follow Paige's descent into lunacy. Only worse, because he'd somehow decided *Nell* was his get-out-of-scandal-free card. It was absurd.

Even if it *was* just the tiniest bit gratifying.

No! It wasn't gratifying, it was ludicrous. And absolutely out of the question.

Finally she sputtered out: "I can't stay here pretending to be your girlfriend!"

"Why not?"

"For one thing, Paige would kill me. I agreed to this to help *her.* Not you."

"You are helping her. And Paige never even has to know."

"You're suggesting I lie to my sister for a week?"

"Aren't you lying to her now?"

He had a point. Her last text to Paige had been a promise that she would shortly be on her way to Whit's house in Minneapolis to render her apology. Brief and reassuring—and total fiction, something Nell felt guilty enough about already.

"How are we supposed to convince an entire town we're dating?" she asked. "We can't go five minutes without arguing, and in case you've forgotten, you hate me."

"I don't hate you. You're the one losing the insults competition."

A reminder she definitely did not need. "The fact that we *have* an insults competition doesn't seem like it might be cause for concern?"

"I'm willing to forfeit."

"Wow. How can I say no with that incentive?"

He grinned again.

Nell tried to ignore the way her heart was knocking against her ribs. "My point is, mutual loathing isn't much of a basis for a relationship, fake or otherwise."

"Then why did you try to kiss me?"

"That's it. Stop the car!"

Immediately, Whit slowed the Audi, coasting onto the shoulder before putting the car in park. He shut off the engine and twisted around to face her. "I'm sorry. That was out of line."

"*Way* out of line. And, for the record? Completely untrue."

It was mostly untrue, at any rate. She hadn't actually tried to kiss him. She'd just *thought* about kissing him. And then imagined, for the briefest of moments, that he'd meant to kiss her.

But she also wasn't going to admit that to him.

"This may come as a shock to you," she continued, "but not every woman in the world is falling all over herself to be slobbered on by the great Whitney O'Rourke."

His grin widened. "Sweetheart, if there's one thing I don't do, it's slobber."

She eyed him balefully.

"Sorry." He shifted in his seat, rubbing at the back of his neck with one hand, leaving the other draped over the steering wheel. "Not much of a mystery why I can't stay in anyone's good graces, is it?"

He looked—and sounded—entirely repentant, but Nell wasn't in the mood to be charitable. "You weren't exactly in mine to begin with."

"No kidding." When Nell didn't answer, a soft sigh whistled out from between his teeth. "All right, so what's your starting position?"

It was a sign that her mind was permanently located in the gutter that the word *position* conjured up images of bare limbs and bed sheets. "My what?"

"For negotiations. What do you want? Hit me."

She made an effort not to gape. "Are you trying to hire me to date you?"

"*Pretend* to date," he said, lifting a hand to wag his finger back and forth. "And I wouldn't have put it in quite those terms."

"You'd better not be backing out on helping Paige."

"I'm not backing out. You'll note I asked what *you* want. You're gonna have to give me some suggestions here, since I'm guessing season tickets to the Blizz won't be enough to seal the deal."

Nell opened her mouth, shut it, then opened it again. "If you really need someone to parade around town, I'm sure you can find some other woman to suffer your presence for the week."

"Suffer, huh? Cute. Too bad my dad already thinks you're my girl-friend."

"Well, since I'm not in the market for a signed Whit O'Rourke *any-thing*, unless you can somehow get me my job back, our relationship is going to be very short-term and very long distance."

Whit straightened upright, fully alert and alarmingly focused. He leaned toward her, eyes glittering. "How'd you lose it?"

Nell blinked. "I wasn't being serious. You can't actually get me my job back."

"Now I want to know, so 'fess up."

She fidgeted, playing with the hem of her borrowed hoodie. "I got into an argument with a student's father."

"That's it?"

"The argument was rather heated."

"Mm-hmm. *Raised your voice* heated or *dropped to your knees and told him what a scumbag he is* heated?"

"I might have used a worse word than *scumbag*."

"And here was I, thinking you didn't swear."

That nettled her. "I teach little kids. Most of the time, I try to keep my language age appropriate."

"I take it this guy said something *in*appropriate?"

"His son was bullying another student in my class. I asked for a meeting to address the behavior, and it was pretty clear where his kid got it from. It sort of devolved from there."

"Champion of the underdog, huh?"

"No one deserves to be bullied," she answered fiercely.

"Spoken like a woman with no younger siblings." When she shot him a glare, he just smirked. "So what did you say?"

Nell hunched her shoulders, slinking down low in her seat. "I told him to go fuck himself."

Whit, predictably, started laughing.

She hit him again. Harder this time. "It's not funny!"

His laughter stopped, but the amusement in his eyes lingered. The corners of his mouth tipped upward. "I bet it felt good though, didn't it?"

Nell struggled to keep an answering smile from forming on her own lips. It *wasn't* funny! She should never have lost her temper in a professional setting, no matter the provocation. She was supposed to be a role model, not a cautionary tale. But Whit wasn't wrong. It had felt good—at first. "Right up until I found out his uncle is the school's largest donor. After that it was lose me or lose funding, and the school made the smart choice."

"You don't have a union or something?"

"Bellwater Academy is a private school. They can pretty much do what they want." Her throat tightened, but the wave of panic that normally hit whenever she thought about being fired was notably absent. Which was probably why she went right on talking instead of keeping her mouth shut. "That means I have no job and no money, and unless I figure something out soon, I'll also have no apartment. I'm not really looking forward to spending the next couple of months in Paige's guest room while I job hunt."

"What about your grandmother? Isn't she rich?"

"I wouldn't ask her for money even if I thought she'd give it. You don't get anything from Grandmother unless you're willing to follow her rules."

"Which you're not."

"I don't want to be another prepackaged Forrester product for her to put on display." Realizing what she'd just said, she hastily added, "It's different for Paige. She doesn't mind being in the spotlight, and she's better at manipulating Grandmother than I am. About most things, anyway." It was ridiculous that she felt the need to justify her choices to him, but she couldn't seem to stop to herself. "I never lived up to expectations, and whenever I failed, it was made clear to me that I'd need to find a way to measure up or I wouldn't be"—she made air quotes—"afforded the benefits of the Forrester name."

"Harsh."

An understatement, but the trouble her grandmother's cosmetics empire would shortly be facing *did* take a bit of the sting out of it. "I decided I didn't want Grandmother controlling my life, so I cut financial ties after I graduated high school. I had money in a trust fund that paid for college, but that's it."

A calculating look crossed Whit's face. "So you're broke and unemployed. I can work with that." He tapped his long fingers against the steering wheel. "What's this donor's name?"

Nell hesitated. Losing her job had been her mistake; it was her problem, and she didn't need anyone to swoop in and rescue her—least of all Whit. Asking her sister to intervene had been one thing, but using a flimsy connection to a man who couldn't care less about her felt like a line she shouldn't cross. If she did cross it, what then? She couldn't stay in Minnesota for a week. She had responsibilities, and those responsibilities did not include taking care of a grown man who should be more than capable of taking care of himself. Not that it mattered, since she doubted he could actually help her.

But a small voice in her head whispered, *What if he can?*

Her heart thudded. "Paige already tried talking to him."

"No offense to Paige, but I think I might have a bit more clout."

"I thought you said you weren't much of a celebrity. And what about the video?"

"I'm owed a few favors."

The thin sliver of hope she'd been holding twisted painfully. She fought against it. Making any sort of deal with Whit was out of the question. Absolutely outside the realm of possibility.

Unless it wasn't.

"He's not going to be very receptive," she told Whit. "I called his office so many times his secretary blocked my number."

"I enjoy a challenge."

"They said if I didn't stop showing up at the building, they'd file a restraining order."

"*That* you're making up."

"Okay, yes," she admitted, "but the one time I *did* go there, the receptionist told me Mr. Grantham was unavailable without an appointment and booked until the end of the year."

"Frank Grantham? The sleazy real estate guy?"

She decided to ignore his use of the word *sleazy.* "You've heard of him?"

"I did live in Chicago for six years," said Whit. "He's the one you need persuaded?"

For a second, Nell could see her classroom with its careful array of desks and brightly colored chairs, the posters and art projects taped to the walls, the reading nook in the corner with its overflowing shelves. She could see her students' eager little faces and the cubbies where they kept their backpacks. She could smell glue sticks and crayons.

You can just get another job, Paige had told her. Nell didn't want another job. She wanted *her* job. She wanted it back. But she also wanted it back the right way.

"I don't want him pressured into having me reinstated," she said. "I just want a chance to plead my case." That wouldn't be crossing any line. It would just be tiptoeing right up to it. A compromise that she could live with—*if* it worked.

Whit's sideways smile made another appearance. "Done. But are you sure you can do that without getting, um, 'heated'? I've met Frank Grantham, and I hate to be the one to tell you this, but dickhead runs in the family."

"I'll do what I have to," Nell answered, trying to sound more self-assured than she felt. "Do you really think you can get me a meeting?"

"How's this: I'll make you a bet. Give me three hours, and I'll get it done. If I'm right, you stay the week. Well, eight days, to be specific, since the groundbreaking is next Saturday."

"And if you're wrong?"

"I won't be. But if I'm wrong, you can name your reward."

"What if I ask for your Audi?"

"I'll buy another."

"What if I ask for a kidney?"

His eyebrows lifted. "Why would you want one of my kidneys?"

"Hypothetically. You said I could name my reward."

"Then I guess it's a good thing I'm not gonna lose."

"You're pretty confident." *Or desperate*, she thought. The problem was, she was desperate, too. "I don't have any clean clothes."

"I'll take you shopping."

"What am I supposed to tell Paige?"

"Do you need to tell her anything? I thought she was going to Cabo for some resort endorsement. You really think she's going to find time to worry if you're actually back in Chicago? Tell her the apology went off without a hitch and she can happily spend her time networking and recording videos."

Nell frowned. He was right, but... "You're making her sound shallow."

"Not shallow. Just busy. It's her career, I get that. I've done my share of swimsuit modeling."

And nude modeling, she thought, recalling the infamous photo shoot he'd done for the successor of *ESPN*'s Body Issue. Another reminder she definitely did not need.

But it was true that Paige was going to be distracted for the next week and a half. And if she *did* happen to find out... Paige might not understand what had prompted Nell to jump to Whit's defense in the first place, but she knew how devastated Nell had been to be fired from Bellwater; she would understand why Nell had stayed.

"All right. You have a deal." Strangely, her whole body felt lighter. Like something that had been dragging against her had subtly loosened its grip. "But I want the meeting right when I get home, not next month and *definitely* not next year. And you'd better hope you can manage it, because I'm going to spend the next three hours thinking up what to demand if you lose."

"Just as long as you don't go back on your word once I win."

"I never go back on my word, O'Rourke."

"Uh-huh. I guess we'll see about that."

She leaned back in her seat and put her feet on the dashboard again. "I guess we will."

Nine

WHIT PARKED HIS CAR in the rugged patch of dirt that served as the driveway leading up to his grandfather's garage. Nearby, a sleepy-looking tabby was stretched out on the hood of an old powder blue Ford pickup, the same rickety road hazard his grandpa had been driving for the past thirty years, since no amount of bargaining or bribery could convince him to retire it. A few years back, Whit had offered to replace it with a brand new, top of the line F-150, and his grandpa had told him in no uncertain terms that he didn't need charity. He'd rather drive around in a rust bucket held together with chewing gum and prayer than accept money earned from—as he put it—grown men playing a child's game. At this point, Whit fully expected he'd demand to be buried in the damn thing.

But at least the presence of the junkyard atrocity meant that his grandpa was at home, which solved his most immediate problem. Breaking and entering seemed like a needless waste of time when he was already on a tight schedule. He had to get this Grantham thing taken care of before Nell started regretting her decision, and a quick glance at her face told him she'd already left second thoughts behind and was well on her way to third, fourth, and fifth.

"Welcome to Hotel O'Rourke," he told her as he shut off the engine of his Audi. "Amenities include a fantastic view of cornfields and a rooster that crows at all hours."

"You're really planning to stay on a farm?" Nell unbuckled her seat belt and twisted around to look through the back windshield, peering out at the land with open interest. He followed her gaze. His grandfather's farm was the quintessential homestead: single-story house with a brick chimney and a neatly fenced wraparound porch; weathered livestock barn with adjacent silo; a windmill for the well. There was even an antique milk can tucked up against the side of the garage, a few dried cornstalks poking out from the top. The only thing the place lacked was a clothesline with a couple of flannel shirts whipping about in the wind.

"*We* are staying at a farm," he corrected. Then, because he couldn't resist, he added: "I hope you like fresh milk."

She wrinkled her nose. "If you're trying to get me to change my mind, you're on the right track."

"You want your job back, don't you?"

"Depends. If getting my job back means drinking milk five minutes out of the udder, I think I'd rather just find a new one."

"Didn't you just tell me you never go back on your word?"

"You haven't won yet. And as far as your grandpa's concerned, I'm lactose intolerant."

"Isn't that commonly known as a fib? What would your students say?"

"I'll be sure to give myself detention."

Whit grinned and hopped out of the car, giving the landscape a quick survey. He hadn't been out to visit since signing with the Blizzards, and his grandpa had fallen a bit behind on chores. The porch needed painting, the lawn needed to be raked and mowed, and a shutter on one of the windows was hanging askew. The whole roof should probably have been redone years ago, but he supposed Skip had been too busy trying to work out the details of the stadium to worry about whether his father's house was threatening to fall down on his head. Not that Whit's grandpa would have welcomed the interference. The elder Whitney O'Rourke—*Bucky* to everyone but his late wife—was on the wrong side of eighty and declining in health, but steadfast in his insistence that he could manage just fine on his own. The same way he'd been managing for the past thirty odd years, ever since his only child had left to play ball instead of staying to work the family farm.

These days, there wasn't much of a farm left. Over the past few decades, the sprawling acres that had once been Bucky O'Rourke's livelihood had dwindled until it was barely even a hobby operation. Most of the land had been rented out or sold to neighboring establishments, along with the bulk of the machinery. Bucky still hired seasonal workers from among the local high school students, but the only properties he regularly worked were a couple of cornfields and a small vegetable plot, and the barn housed three times as many cats as cows. Cows that, despite his teasing of Nell, were mostly ornamental, since they no longer produced milk.

Skip wanted Bucky to sell whatever remained and retire. Bucky had stated it would be over his dead body, and since his family knew him well enough to believe he meant it literally, that had been the end of the discussion. For now.

In the meantime, the porch needed painting. That much Whit could do, provided he could trick his grandpa into letting him.

He breathed in the cool afternoon air as he stepped around the car, nudging a few of the leaves that had collected in the driveway with the edge of his shoe. The chickadees that had been flitting about near the eaves of the garage chirped at him. A brisk wind nipped at his shirt. He'd missed this, he realized—the comforting stillness of open country and the scent of cut hay, the fallen leaves and damp earth. They'd arrived too late for the peak of the fall colors, but a couple of birches were still holding onto their ochres and golds, and the old maple that overlooked the porch flamed starkly red. That same maple had stood there as long as Whit could remember, stubbornly keeping its leaves long after the rest of trees were bare. In a few hours, the setting sun would slant through the branches, dappling the porch with shadows. He could picture his grandpa sitting on the swing with a book and a beer, watching the twilight roll in.

"I haven't spent a lot of time on farms," Nell said as she climbed out of the car behind him. She stood for a moment with her hands planted on her hips, her head tipped skyward. The loose wisps of hair that had worked free from her ponytail tangled in her face. "It's pretty here."

"When it's not buried in forty feet of snow." Whit loped the rest of the way to the porch, then paused with his hand on the door to toss a quick glance over his shoulder. "By the way, my grandpa hates baseball, so try not to mention it."

"I thought all American men over the age of fifty liked baseball."

"Grandpa enjoys being contrary."

"This is your paternal grandfather?"

"Whitney O'Rourke the elder," he replied. "Third generation farmer."

"So I'm guessing he wasn't too thrilled when the fourth and fifth generations didn't follow in his footsteps."

"And now you know why he hates baseball."

The inner door was already open, so Whit yanked at the screen door and stepped inside without knocking. The lights were off but the drapes were pulled, and the afternoon sun filtering in gave the entryway a soft buttery glow. Within, the house looked exactly as it had all throughout Whit's childhood: the same cream-colored floral wallpaper beginning to peel at the edges; the same scuffed wooden furniture that was too old to be modern, too new to be considered antique. The bookshelves built into the walls of the small living room were still jammed with Louis L'Amour paperbacks, and the picture frames that hung over them still displayed jigsaw puzzles instead of paintings. The clock over the fireplace chimed out the hour. The air smelled of coffee and cigarettes.

Frowning, Whit followed the scent into the kitchen, where he found his grandfather at the dining table, assembling his latest puzzle with one hand and holding a cigarette in the other. An empty Mason jar sat nearby, repurposed as an ashtray, the bundle of fake daisies that had formerly occupied it shoved toward the edge of the table. Without a word, Whit stalked across the room and leaned over the sink to tug the window open, nudging aside the cat that had been sunning itself on the sill. Then he turned to his grandfather, plucked the cigarette from his hand, and stubbed it out on the side of the jar before dropping it inside.

"I thought you said you were quitting," he said.

"And hello to you, too," Bucky replied, reaching to pull a new cigarette from his shirt pocket. He sighed when he saw Whit's expression and let his hand fall. "For your information, mister, I am quitting." A rueful smile spread across his face. "Tomorrow."

"Does Dad know you're still smoking?"

"Your dad can mind his own business," Bucky answered cheerfully, "and so can you."

"I'll be sure to write that on your tombstone."

"You can write what you want. I'll be dead." But he withdrew the rest of the pack from his pocket and handed it to Whit. "Happy now?"

"Happier, anyway." Whit took a short step back and studied his grandfather. Bucky had never been a large man, but nothing—not even his own son and grandson towering over him—could convince him of that fact. He'd lost a couple of inches over the past few years and somewhere along the way his frame had gone from stocky to stout, but though his movements had slowed and his shoulders had begun to stoop, he still carried himself with the air of a man on a mission. Today he'd chosen to forgo his traditional overalls, opting instead for a pair of jeans and a shirt of faded blue and green flannel that had seen better decades. He looked tired, Whit thought, noting the shadows beneath his eyes. Tired and old. "Are you getting enough sleep?"

Bucky took a sip from his coffee mug and regarded Whit with a mixture of irritation and affection. "I sleep when I'm tired, I eat all my veggies, and I only have one beer before bedtime. You want to know about my prostate, too?" He lifted his bushy white eyebrows, then hooked a thumb toward the doorway of the kitchen, where Nell stood fidgeting. "You didn't come here to prod me about my health. Who's your friend?"

Whit hesitated. Lying to his dad was one thing. Lying to his grandpa was basically the eighth deadly sin. And since he didn't think Nell would agree to sleeping arrangements that involved the two of them sharing a bedroom, let alone sharing a bed, he was going to have to come clean. "This is Nell. She's a friend of mine. Dad thinks we're dating, so don't tell him otherwise."

Bucky reached into his shirt pocket for his missing cigarettes, then tried to play off the motion by withdrawing the small pair of glasses he used for reading. He slid the glasses onto his nose and peered at Whit, blinking as his vision adjusted. With his bald head, drooping mustache, and disgruntled expression, he put Whit in mind of a grumpy walrus. "Why does he think you're dating?"

A quick glance at Nell told him he was on his own this time, so Whit just shrugged. "It's complicated."

"Meaning you lied to him."

"More or less."

"Mm-hmm. Well, he won't hear about it from me," Bucky promised. He tipped his head toward Nell. "She the one who was polishing your knob for you?"

It was impressive how quickly Nell's complexion went from nervously pale to bright flaming red.

"Jesus, Grandpa," said Whit.

"No need to get huffy." Bucky poked at his glasses. "I'm not judging. I'm just asking."

"Since when do you read *Meltdown?*"

"It's a small town. Just about the only person who didn't text me is my pastor."

Whit sighed. Not that he'd expected any different. At this very moment, someone was probably collecting funds to put up a billboard. *Whit O'Rourke, Professional Pervert.* "Sorry to scandalize the neighborhood, but since you asked, that's not what was going on."

Nell apparently remembered she was meant to be contributing, because she made a kind of fluttery, flailing motion with her hands and then blurted out, "We're suing!"

"Thanks. Very helpful," Whit drawled.

"I told you I wasn't going to be any good at this," she complained. "You are suing, though, right?"

"Since you keep announcing to the world that I'm going to, I suppose I probably have to."

Bucky divided a look between them. "If she's not your *girlfriend*, why is she wearing your clothes?"

"Coffee mishap," Whit answered. "Can we crash here for a few days?"

"Not if you're going to make a habit of coffee mishaps. If I don't get my morning caffeine, I get crabby. Skip didn't have room for you?"

"He's pissed about my bad press."

"I hope you told him to pull his head out of his behind. He cares too much what people think about him. So do you, kiddo."

Easy for him to say, Whit thought; his grandpa had never had his face in a tabloid or been a headline on CNN. He also knew that was an argument he wouldn't win. "So can we stay?"

The bushy eyebrows raised again. "You know the rule about sleep-overs."

"Did you miss the part where I said we're not dating?" Whit wasn't sure if he should be flattered or offended. Bucky had instituted the rule when Whit was seventeen years old and had spent most of his senior year of high school living at the farm. Appropriate, he supposed, for a horny teenager angry at the universe and bent on self-destruc-tion—not that it had done any good. But Whit was nearly thirty and long past carving notches.

He noted that his grandfather had neglected to state the rest of the rule. Whit could recall it verbatim. *No sleepovers, remember that no means no, the lord gave you two hands to keep you from getting lonely, and if you're gonna do it anyway, keep it wrapped up.* The gospel according to Bucky O'Rourke.

"You didn't do much 'dating' in high school, either, as I recall," Bucky said dryly.

Whit didn't know what was more alarming—that his grandpa seemed intent on embarrassing him, or that it was actually working. He avoided looking at Nell. "I'm thirty years old."

"You're twenty-nine, and my roof, my rules."

"What do you want me to do, swear on a stack of bibles? *I solemnly swear I will never have sex.*"

"Seeing as I don't want my only grandson struck by lightning, I guess we'll have to forgo that," Bucky replied, chuckling. "I'm just messing with you." He aimed a smile at Nell. "You can have Whitney's old room." He jerked his chin at Whit. "*You* can have the couch."

Whit leaned back against the kitchen counter, folding his arms and crossing one foot in front of the other. "Here I was thinking I'd be banished all the way out to the barn."

"You keep fussing over me and you will be." A devious glimmer came into Bucky's eyes. "And since you're going to be living off my hospitality, I figure you won't mind being put to work."

Whit considered bringing up the flaking paint on the porch, but doubted it would be that easy. Bucky was nobody's fool. The second he suspected Whit was trying to look after him, his back would go up and his foot would come down. "If you're looking for someone to strangle your rooster, I'm your man."

Bucky squinted at him from behind his glasses. "I'd call your bluff, but you might pull a muscle backpedaling. You can go muck out the barn."

Whit looked at him in amusement. "What, now?"

"You got something better to do?"

Catching his eye, Nell—clearly horrified at the prospect of being abandoned with his grandfather—shook her head frantically and mouthed the word *no.* She tapped a finger against an imaginary watch.

Whit ignored her. "I have a couple of calls to make," he told Bucky. "But I can multitask. You want to get Nell settled in?"

"She can help finish my puzzle."

"Great." He took a few long strides toward the side door that opened out into the backyard, then turned to toss his car keys toward Nell. She was still staring daggers at him, but clapped her hands together and caught them. "If he gets too obnoxious, feel free to run him over."

"Just for that, you get barn duty tomorrow, too," Bucky called after him.

"And don't let him pick up a cigarette!"

***

By the time Whit had cleaned out the stalls in the old pole barn and replaced all the soiled hay with fresh bedding, he'd contacted three of his former teammates in Chicago—plus one of the coaches—and called in a favor from an assistant manager. Then, since he'd decided that might qualify as overkill and invite scrutiny, he called two of them back. In the end, he left the details up to his friend Charlie, whose All-Star name power and status as a recent MVP pretty much guaranteed *someone* in Frank Grantham's immediate circle would take his call. All Charlie had asked in return was that Whit participate in his charity bowling tournament in January, which Whit would have agreed to do anyway. Simple, easy, and entirely painless—provided it worked. He wasn't certain what he'd do if it didn't. Negotiate new terms, probably. It wouldn't be the end of the world if he had to pack Nell back up and wave her off on a flight to Chicago, but now that he'd set his mind on a plan, he didn't want to deviate from it. That and he hated to lose.

His worries wound up being needless, as Charlie worked his magic in record time. Whit had just finished putting out feed for the barn cats and was heading back into the house when Charlie messaged him that the meeting was set.

Simple, easy, and entirely painless.

For him, anyway. Nell clearly didn't know much about Frank Grantham if she believed a brief interview would convince him to save her job. Grantham was a self-serving narcissist with an overinflated ego and an underused moral compass. His charitable contributions weren't causes but carefully selected tax breaks, and if Nell thought he would give a damn about her school or the students in it, she was deluding herself. Grantham might agree to have her rehired, provided she were willing to grovel, flatter, flirt, and otherwise humiliate herself enough to soothe his vanity, but that failing—and from what he'd seen of Nell's temper, it *would* fail—she was in for a massive disappointment.

He still had half an hour until the agreed upon deadline hit, and since he'd sweated through his T-shirt and smelled like the more fragrant parts of a cow, he dug a change of clothing out of his suitcase and hopped in the shower before going in search of Nell. He'd heard the blue Ford sputtering its way down the road while he was in the barn, so he assumed his grandfather had gone into town. He also assumed Bucky had been wise enough to overcome his compulsion to entertain guests and had left Nell to her own devices—an assumption that proved correct when Whit peeked into the guest room and found her curled up in the window seat with her legs drawn up and her knees serving as a book rest.

Since she was totally absorbed in whatever she was reading, he stood in the doorway and watched her. She'd taken off her shoes—sensible flat-heeled slip-ons with a cream-and-blue butterfly pattern, set very neatly against the wall—and with the cuffs of her jeans turned up, he could see the faint ink of a tattoo on her left ankle. Her toenails, he noted, were painted the color of cherries. Not the shade he'd expected from her, since she seemed to prefer softer, more neutral tones, but then, he hadn't expected the tattoo, either. It made him think of the little scar on her lip; an innocent detail that whispered of something wicked. The curtains were open and the late afternoon light spilling in caught in her hair, giving it a rich, coppery luster. Sitting there with her lashes half-lowered and the sun on her skin, she looked picturesque. And startlingly pretty. Pretty in a way that made him think of lazy mornings spent rumpling bed sheets and made him wonder what else she wore in red.

That was a dangerous direction for his thoughts to head down, so he shoved the image aside. Jamming his hands in the pockets of his jeans, he took a short step forward and cleared his throat. "Good book?"

She started at the sound of his voice and turned toward him, looking sheepish. "I bought it for my flight."

That would have been the perfect opening to let her know her flight needed changing... but he'd instructed Charlie to have Grantham's office call her at the last possible moment. And he was enjoying watching her squirm. "I see Grandpa didn't send you running for the hills," he said instead.

She shut her book and set it aside, giving him a reproachful look. "You mean after you ditched me with a total stranger five minutes after I'd met him?"

"Given your sentiments toward me, I figured a total stranger might be a step up. Did he grill you?"

"He wanted to know where I'm from, what I do, and how we met."

"Yeah, he definitely thinks we're sleeping together."

Nell groaned. "Fantastic. The one person we actually told the truth doesn't believe us."

"You've gotta appreciate the irony, though."

She glared at him.

Whit shrugged. "So what did you tell him?"

"I said my sister introduced us."

"Smart."

"We didn't talk long. After we finished his puzzle, he made me a sandwich, showed me the guest room, and told me to get out of his hair."

"Funny, considering he doesn't have any." Reflexively, he reached up and brushed a hand through his own hair, still damp from the shower.

Nell caught the gesture. "Worried?"

"My mom's dad died with a full head of hair, so I'm probably okay. Of course, he also had a heart attack at forty, so I guess I should watch my cholesterol."

She swung her legs down from the window seat but didn't stand, leaning back on her palms as she looked at him. Tilting her head, she motioned toward the far shelf where a couple of old tournament trophies were gathering dust. "Your grandpa said this room used to be yours."

"Only for a few months. I lived with him a while during my senior year of high school." He gave the room a quick, impassive study. The furnishings were sparse—a dresser topped with a couple of old knickknacks; a bookshelf; a bed flanked by twin nightstands; a lamp shaped like a flower vase—but everything had been kept tidy and neatly arranged. The trophies had been his sole contribution to the decor. Not much had changed in the past decade, but despite his grandfather's best efforts, the room had never felt like his. Whit had spent more time sneaking out of it than staying in.

"Because of your father?" Nell asked.

"It's a long story." One he had no interest in sharing.

She must have realized it wasn't his favorite topic, because instead of prying more, she pivoted. "You don't mention your mom much."

"She and my dad divorced when I was a teenager. She's currently honeymooning in Scotland."

"Scotland?" Nell gave him a pained look. "You'd better be planning on a phone call, because I am not taking this explanation tour international."

Whit chuckled. "Mom's pretty laid back." He still wasn't quite ready to end the suspense, so he leaned into the doorjamb and cocked his head slightly. "What about you? I think I remember Paige saying your mom passed away."

A brief shadow moved across her eyes. "When I was twelve. Pancreatic cancer."

"I'm sorry."

"It was a long time ago."

He doubted that made it hurt less. "That's why your grandmother raised you?" Considering what she'd told him of her grandmother, that had to have been difficult.

"We went to stay with her after Mom died. I wouldn't say she raised us."

"What about your dad?" He knew Paige was an orphan, but Nell had mentioned a father.

"I never saw much of him. He and my mom were only married a year. After she died, he wanted custody... but that would've meant leaving Paige. He didn't have a lot of interest in being a father, anyway. What he really wanted was a payout. The judge let me decide who I wanted to live with."

"And you chose your grandmother."

"I chose my sister. Paige needed me more than I needed a deadbeat dad."

So her habit of rushing to her sister's defense had started young. She had a thing for playing hero, he'd noticed. And rarely to her own benefit. "What about now? Do you keep in touch?"

"He calls me once or twice a year, usually because he needs money."

Which meant she was an orphan, too, or near enough to it. "Be careful not to tell my grandpa that. He'll try to adopt you. He collects strays."

Nell aimed a pointed look at the foot of the bed, where a suspiciously feline-shaped lump was snoring beneath the faded patchwork quilt. "That explains all the cats."

"These are just the indoor cats." There were four of them, at his last count. But he wouldn't have been surprised if his grandpa had added one or two since his last visit. "You should check out the barn. They've pretty much taken over the place."

She stood, stretching her arms over her head, and then bent to put on her shoes. Those cherry red toenails vanished. "Tempting as that is, we should probably get going."

Whit played innocent. "Going?"

"To my hotel," she said, giving each word a slow emphasis. She tapped her imaginary watch again. "It's been three hours. Time's up, O'Rourke."

"Two hours and fifty-seven minutes, by my clock."

"So I have three minutes left to decide how big I want my private jet?"

"Just how rich do you think I am?" he asked in amusement.

"A lot richer than you're about to be, if you didn't get me my meeting."

"Do I seem nervous?"

Her gaze sharpened. "Are you saying you got it?"

"I'm not saying I didn't."

"I hope you're not expecting me to just take your word for it."

Right on cue, her phone rang.

"You might want to answer that," he said.

Her mouth made a perfect O. Pure shock showed on her face as she fumbled for her phone, but when she answered the call, her voice was calm and professional. Teacher voice, he thought: patient, personable, attentive. She nodded along as she spoke, absently twirling the ends of her ponytail with her free hand. Whit watched her dazed expression with satisfaction, ready to gloat the second she hung up the call.

What he wasn't ready for was her reaction.

It took a moment. The dazed look remained as she slipped her phone into the front pocket of the Blizzards hoodie and wiped her palms on the sides of her jeans. A soft breath whistled out of her. She turned toward him. Whit opened his mouth to make an obnoxious remark.

And then didn't speak.

Her whole face was lit up. She looked like a little kid who'd been given a puppy for Christmas. Like a rookie call-up who'd just hit a walk-off home run. Her smile was wide and radiant. The sheer joy she exuded made him feel like all the air had been sucked out of his chest.

A situation that was in no way improved when she proceeded to throw her arms around him and squeal.

Whit was too stunned to do anything but stand there. He didn't know if the noises she was making contained any actual words, but if they did, he couldn't decipher them. She was nearly vibrating with excitement. She was also bouncing up and down. Literally bouncing up and down, which meant her breasts, currently brushing against him, were bouncing up and down right along with her. She might not have a lot going on in that area, but it was more than enough to redirect his blood flow straight to his groin.

Something that was quickly going to get embarrassing for both of them if he didn't put a stop to it.

He carefully disentangled himself and caught her by the sides of the arms, holding her still. "Something tells me you loathe me just a little bit less right now."

Her squeals ended in a shaky laugh. "Sorry." She took a couple of steps in retreat, wiping at her eyes. "And thank you. I should've said that first. Thank you. Do I want to ask how you did it?"

He cleared his throat. "I told you I was owed a few favors."

"The perks of celebrity."

"The perks of having celebrity friends, in this case."

It was hard to gloat over someone so grateful. He felt another stab of guilt—especially since it wasn't as though he'd done it out of the kindness of his heart. And he knew, even if she didn't, that she'd been bargaining for a poisoned prize. When she broke into a fresh volley of thank yous, the guilt kicked up a notch.

He tried to ignore it. He wanted to ignore it. He tried to remind himself that she was still *Nell*, no matter how adorable or delighted she looked. Still the same woman who had taken it upon herself to announce his PEDs usage to the world. Not to mention made that ridiculous dig about his sexual prowess.

But it wasn't easy to remember any of that when she was standing there lit up like a Christmas tree. He'd have to be exactly the asshole she thought he was to see the hope shining in her eyes and not feel a pang of misgiving.

Whit sighed and dragged a hand through his hair. "I need to say something. I'm probably going to regret it, but I need to say it. I'm not sure this meeting is going to work out the way you imagine it."

"I'm not going to mess up my chance, believe me."

"I just think you should manage your expectations. Grantham isn't exactly going to be open to what you have to say."

That brought her down to earth a little. "Meaning I shouldn't tell him to go... you know."

"That would be a good starting point."

A faint wrinkle appeared on her brow. "If you don't think I know how to play nice, why did you just coerce me into spending a week as your arm prop?"

"Bribed you into spending a week as my arm prop," he corrected. "And you're more like cannon fodder. If someone gets too irritating, I'm planning on hurling you at them and running away."

"Brave of you."

He shrugged.

"I can behave myself if I have to," she said. "I spent six years getting good manners drilled into me by the high queen of cosmetics, remember?"

"Good manners will get you in the door. They're not gonna get you your job back."

"I've done my research on Grantham."

"Yeah, and like I said, I've met him. He's a dick."

"So you don't think I can handle him?" When a snicker escaped him, she stuck her hands on her hips. "Why are you laughing?"

"I'm trying to decide if you'll get angrier at me for saying you can handle a dick or saying you can't."

Just like that, her sunbeam smile turned into a glare.

"Hey, you said it, not me." He moved forward and swiped his car keys from where she'd left them on the window seat. "I just thought I should warn you. Anyway, I hope you made a list."

"A list?"

He dangled the keys in front of her face. "I won the bet, Miss McLean. It's time to go shopping."

TEN

By eleven o'clock that evening, Nell wanted nothing more than to stumble her way to the bed in the guest room, flop onto the mattress, yank the quilt up over her head, close her eyes, and sleep for about seventeen hours. There was no part of her that wasn't exhausted. She was so tired, she didn't even care—much—that Whit's idea of sleeping attire amounted to nothing more than a pair of plaid boxers and a tissue-thin T-shirt. She couldn't even muster up a snotty remark when he pointed out she'd managed to get toothpaste on her brand new pajama top. All she could think about was finding the nearest pillow and flinging herself into the sweet bliss of unconsciousness. She was going to sleep the sleep of the dead, and if any rooster dared to rouse her before she was good and ready, she'd be eating chicken soup for dinner.

Her brain had other ideas.

The second her eyes shut, her thoughts started churning. The day replayed itself again and again in her head like she was stuck watching some disaster film marathon, starring herself—except that instead of being eaten by dinosaurs or getting disintegrated in a nuclear explosion, at the end of it, she still had to explain herself to Paige. Worse, every single frame of it featured Whit's face. That crooked grin, so quick to appear, had become imprinted in her consciousness. Those dark, heavy-lidded, gold-flecked eyes taunted her. During the day, she'd been able to push her worries aside and ignore the warning signs. Now, alone with her thoughts, she was coming to the uneasy, unavoidable realization that she was in trouble. Big time.

Not that the past few hours had been the nightmare she'd anticipated. Whit had been on his best behavior when he'd taken her shopping in the nearby town of Dower Hill, refraining from commenting on any of her fashion choices, and offering to pay for everything—an offer she'd declined, since the last thing she wanted was to feel even more indebted to him than she already did. Replacing her phone was one thing; replacing her wardrobe felt decidedly too intimate. And intimacy with Whit of any sort was to be avoided at all costs. When they'd gone out to dinner with his family that evening, he'd been charming and attentive, just like she was his actual girlfriend, and every time he'd smiled her way or his arm had brushed hers, she'd had to remind herself it was only an act. Something she was having less and less success at. Twice she'd caught herself watching him and forced herself to look away. Whenever their gazes had met, she'd felt like she'd been kicked in the stomach.

That was when she'd known, in the awful, inevitable way you know you're about to witness a car crash, that it was back. The unpardonable sin she had thought she'd left behind her forever. The one secret she'd kept even from her closest friends.

She had a crush on Whit O'Rourke.

Again.

Shit. Shit shit shit. Shit!

There were some circumstances that required stronger language than the watered down expletives she tried to limit her vocabulary to. This was definitely one of them.

At least she'd admitted it to herself now. It wasn't just a simple attraction. It wasn't her hormones going crazy at the sight of a sexy, vital, *virile* man. She had a stupid, irrational, unreasonable, and completely unhealthy crush on Whit O'Rourke. The same crush she'd had on him four years ago when he'd been dating her sister.

Nell groaned. She was the worst person on the planet. She'd had a crush on her sister's boyfriend. It didn't matter that she had never acted on her feelings; even having them in the first place had been a betrayal.

She had fought the infatuation desperately, concentrating on all the reasons he was bad news: his overblown ego and cocky attitude, his carelessness, the revolving-door of models and C-list actresses that made up his love life. Not to mention the fact that he'd never shown the slightest hint of romantic interest in her. And why should he have? He was dating her sister. If he'd so much as aimed a flirty comment in her direction, her opinion of him would have sunk from *oversexed playboy* straight down to *scum of the earth.* The only consolation she'd had was that Paige had never picked up on her distress. Nell had been careful to keep her thoughts to herself and not do anything that would sabotage her sister's relationship. Outwardly, she'd been supportive. Privately, she'd been in turmoil.

The fallout from his breakup with Paige had brought an abrupt and decisive end to Nell's infatuation—at least she'd thought it had. Ever since then, she'd been crushless and guilt-free, happily dismissing Whit as another asshole jock with more arrogance than empathy, not worth her or her sister's time.

Now she was right back where she'd been four years ago, her stomach in knots and her traitorous heart full of yearning. She would be furious with herself if she still had the energy. All it had taken was a few hours and a couple of lazy grins and her crush was back with a vengeance. And there wasn't a damn thing she could do about it, since she'd given Whit her word she'd stay the week.

Her best option was to remain professional. This was a business arrangement, nothing more. The important thing was that she'd gotten Paige her media distraction—and gotten herself a chance to keep her job. When she and Whit were in public, she would play the part of the devoted girlfriend; when they were alone, she would maintain a polite and careful distance. And when the week was over, her ill-advised crush would fade back into the past where it belonged: brief, unknown, and entirely unmourned. Permanently. In the meantime, all she could do was try to keep her heart from overruling her head and hope to avoid calamity.

She drifted to sleep cataloging Whit's various faults and woke to the sound of the rooster. After several attempts to drown out the noise by clutching a pillow to her head, she dragged herself out of bed and made her way to the kitchen.

Whit, leaning back against the counter with his legs stretched out before him and his ankles crossed, greeted her with the deeply unflattering, "You look like hell."

"I'm not human until I've had caffeine," she moaned, rubbing at her face. "Please tell me there's coffee."

"Grandpa likes his a little strong," Whit warned, but he reached into one of the kitchen cupboards and handed her a mug with a cutesy snowflake design and a small chip along the rim.

"I don't care if I have to chew it. Give it to me."

Strong was an understatement, but Nell barely tasted it. She downed the bitter liquid fast enough that it left a pleasant, tingling burn in her throat, and by the time she reached the bottom of the mug, she felt almost alive again. Unfortunately, with alertness came the awareness that she was standing barefoot in Whit's grandfather's kitchen, her eyes bleary and her hair bedraggled, her pajama top still flecked with a smudge of toothpaste near the collar. Whit, naturally, looked like he'd stepped out of a GQ ad. She gave him a grumpy frown before heading off to the shower.

Nell's cannon fodder duties weren't scheduled to begin until later that evening. The official groundbreaking festivities wouldn't kick off until Sunday afternoon—with some sort of exhibition baseball game made up of former players—but Skip had set an introductory reception for Saturday, which Whit informed her they'd be attending. She expected he'd simply ignore her until then, but he must have grown restless waiting around the house, because he dragged her on a tour of his grandfather's farm. So much for her plan to keep her distance.

She watched him out of the corner of her eye as they walked, trying to ignore the way her stupid heart skipped a beat every time his arm brushed hers. He'd changed in the years since she'd last seen him. Physically, he seemed stronger, leaner, the effortless athleticism of youth hardening into something less casual and more durable—and exponentially more intoxicating. But it wasn't only his body. There was an edge to him now that hadn't existed before, and a hesitance, that smooth arrogance undercut with uncertainty... and vulnerability. All of which only made him more dangerous. He'd been easier to dismiss when she could think of him as nothing more than a cocky, self-absorbed jock with the approximate depth of a puddle. Now she had the uncomfortable feeling that she might have judged him unfairly.

What she couldn't figure out was why he'd insisted upon her staying. She wasn't deluded enough to imagine he'd spontaneously developed feelings for her. He blamed her for damaging his reputation; it was pure desperation that had led him to hijack her in the first place. So what was it about his hometown that had him convinced he needed a girlfriend to hide behind?

The reception that evening only added to her confusion. Whit was buzzing with nerves even before they entered the banquet hall, and by the time they'd reached the refreshments table, he was so tense she thought she'd need a vise grip to pry him loose from her arm. She couldn't understand it. Most of the guests had some connection to the stadium or the groundbreaking—investors and city officials, along with several of the "old-timers" who would be participating in Sunday's game and a handful of sports journalists—and they didn't treat Whit any differently than they treated his father. James was a notable exception, but since he was attending as an employee of the mayor's office, he maintained an aloof politeness and carefully avoided Whit. No one mentioned the video. That may have been due to Nell's presence, but she doubted Whit cared about a bit of innuendo or a few suggestive comments.

The only actual hostility came from another former schoolmate of Whit's, a combative, red-faced loudmouth who went by the name of Petey and probably spent the bulk of his time trying to relive his high school glory days. Nell would have dismissed the entire thing as jealousy... except that it was clear Whit didn't. Since she didn't think telling Petey to go fuck himself would help matters, she told him to get a life instead, and then steered Whit in the other direction.

The rest of the night passed without incident, save for a minor flub when someone asked how long they'd been dating. Whit said a few weeks; Nell said a month. They smoothed it over easily enough, but Nell's anxiety kicked into high gear. Lying was bad enough. Being *caught* lying was nightmare territory. She agonized over it while falling asleep, was still worried the following morning, and after stewing about it throughout breakfast, she walked to the barn to talk to Whit.

He was mucking out stalls in a pair of old jeans he'd dug out from the guest room closet and a loose-fitting flannel shirt. He had his sleeves rolled up to the elbow, where the soft discoloration of his surgery scar was visible in the slanting morning light. A few errant bits of straw had made their way into his hair, and with the thin sheen of sweat on his skin and the taut, rhythmic motion of his muscles as he bent and lifted, he looked rustic and earthy and disturbingly masculine. She was close enough to him that she could see the dusting of hair on his forearms and smell the faint tang of exertion. The way her pulse quickened told her she should turn back around and hide in the house until it was time to leave for the old-timers' game.

Instead she pulled herself up onto the stack of hay bales that took up one side of the barn and watched him.

He turned toward her, setting the pitchfork aside as he leaned back against the doorway of a stall, his arms folded. The top few buttons of his shirt were undone, revealing the dark fuzz of hair that curled along the hard planes of his chest. The little baseball charm sat on its silver chain, dangling just below his collarbone. One of his eyebrows lifted questioningly.

Nell straightened, forcing herself to look away from that tantalizing V of exposed skin. "I've been thinking."

"That can't be good."

"It occurred to me that if we're going to pull this off, we need to work out a few details."

"Such as?"

"Personal information, to begin with," she said. She'd spent half her morning shower coming up with horrific scenarios where she committed some terrible blunder in front of his family. And the other half imagining lathering Whit's bare chest with soap. "I don't even know when your birthday is."

"It's not like we're trying to get you a green card. You really think people are going to quiz us on birthdays?"

"You really want to look like an asshole if they do?" She bit her lip. If she managed to get her job back, she was going to have to sit herself down and binge-watch a bunch of kids' movies before her potty mouth turned permanent.

Whit only laughed. "May third."

"August eleventh."

He made a soft whistling noise through his teeth. "Leo and Taurus. That's a bad combination."

"If astrology were a real thing. And if we were actually dating. You just knew that off the top of your head?"

"An ex of mine was really into horoscopes," he said on a slightly defensive note. "What else do you want to know?"

"I'll get to that." She leaned backward on her hands, the coarse threads of hay beneath her tickling at her palms. "First, we need a story."

"Our track record with stories hasn't been great so far."

"Exactly my point. We screwed up last night, and I don't want it to happen again. Here"—she sat upright, digging a hand in her jeans pocket to withdraw the piece of notepaper she'd tucked there earlier that morning—"this is the list of things you should know about me. You can study it before we leave for the game."

A flicker of amusement crossed his face. "Are you giving me homework, Miss McLean?"

"It's a short assignment."

He took the paper from her and flipped it over. "You wrote on both sides."

"I was being thorough."

"I see *thorough* doesn't include your coffee addiction," he said, giving the list a quick skim.

"It's not an addiction. It's a medical necessity."

"Uh-huh. So… wait. We're supposed to have been together a month. Isn't this kind of overkill?" He leaned back against the stall and ran a hand through his hair, dislodging the bits of straw that had tangled there. "I couldn't tell you half of this about the women I've dated, and I guarantee you they knew even less about me."

Nell opened her mouth to tell him that some people actually *liked* getting to know their partners—then she stopped herself. This was exactly the dose of reality she needed. Whit might have more depth than she'd wanted to believe, but when it came to romantic affairs, he was all surface. He liked his relationships casual, uncomplicated, and with their own predetermined expiration date. The only intimacy he was interested in was the physical variety, which was why her attraction to him was so misguided. He never kept a girlfriend for more than a few months. If she and Whit had truly been dating, he'd already be planning his exit strategy.

She pushed herself up from the hay bales and hopped to the ground, giving him a shrug that she hoped was nonchalant. "You're right. I wasn't thinking." She held out her hand for the paper.

"I didn't say I wouldn't read it."

"There's no need."

"I wasn't trying to hurt your feelings."

She didn't want him thinking she actually cared, so she stuck her free hand on her hip and gave him her most winning smile. "No hurt feelings, I promise. My teacher instincts got the best of me. I haven't graded anyone in over a week."

That flicker of amusement returned. "You were planning to grade me?"

"Pass/fail only. You can give that back now."

"But I'm not finished with it."

"I told you there's no need."

"I didn't even get past allergies. What if someone asks me about your family?"

"You already know the basics. Dead mom, deadbeat dad, grandmother who is single-handedly keeping the polar ice caps from melting. Can I have my list back, please?"

"How much is it worth to you?" he asked, dangling it above her head.

There was no way she was getting drawn into a game of keep-away with this overgrown eight-year-old, so she folded her arms and switched tactics. "You know, your dad tried to bribe me at dinner the other night."

That got his attention. His hand, which had been waving back and forth as he fluttered the list in front of her, went still. "Excuse me?"

"He said he'd give me two hundred dollars if I convinced you to let someone else manage the old-timers' game today."

"Only two hundred? I'm a little offended."

Nell took a casual step toward him and let her arms fall to her sides. "He bumped it up to five when I turned him down."

"He's just afraid I'll show him up."

"You're not playing, are you?" She inched forward. "I thought it was for retirees."

"He's afraid my team will show him up," Whit amended. "Which we will. And you're still not getting your list back." To prove his point, he tucked the paper into one of his jeans pockets and smirked.

Defeated, Nell slumped back against the hay bales.

"Where was I during all of this?" Whit asked.

"You'd stepped outside to make a phone call."

His eyes narrowed. "I'd say I'm surprised he'd flirt with you in front of his girlfriend, but that's Dad for you."

"He wasn't flirting with me. And what girlfriend?"

"Maggie."

Nell frowned. Skip had introduced Maggie to them as his assistant, and nothing in his manner toward the young woman had hinted that their relationship went beyond the professional. If anything, he'd seemed less comfortable in his conversations with her than with Nell herself. For her part, Maggie had seemed somewhat timid, with the aura of a nervous cat, ready to bolt at the first sign of trouble. During the reception, she'd kept to the sidelines as much as possible. "I thought she was his assistant."

"Like I said—that's Dad for you."

Nell didn't answer. It was clear that whatever tension lay between Whit and his father ran deeper than a bit of bad press, and she was already too emotionally invested in a connection that would be as fleeting as it was fake. Her curiosity would just have to go unsatisfied. A week from now she had to pass Whit off to Paige with her conscience clear and her heart intact. He was right; the less she knew about him the better. And since the best way to resist temptation was to avoid it altogether, she made up an excuse about having to catch up on some messages and fled back to the house.

ELEVEN

"THIS PLACE IS PRETTY busy," Nell said as Whit pulled his Audi into the parking lot of Fallen Oaks High. "I thought the game didn't start until four."

Whit grimaced, easing the car into one of the reserved parking spaces near the front of the main school building—one of the few spaces that was actually still available. Around him, the low hum of chattering crowds filled the air as he cut the engine. Nell was right. It wasn't quite two o'clock and most of the lot was already packed like it was a giveaway night at the ballpark. But then, his dad had wanted to go all out to kick off the week of festivities, and he'd managed to bribe, badger, cajole, or otherwise enlist some two dozen retired ballplayers into coming to his exhibition game. The majority of them had been out of the show for a decade or longer, but even if the younger kids didn't remember them, plenty of teens had grown up idolizing them. There were a lot of heroes here.

He found his fingers clenching on the steering wheel and forced himself to relax. Given how much money his dad had thrown at advertising the thing, the bulk of the spectators were likely to be tourists gathered from around the state—and probably Wisconsin and the Dakotas—rather than Fallen Oaks locals. The odds of running into anyone he knew were a lot lower than they'd been for the reception last night. And if they did happen across someone he'd rather avoid... well, that was what he had Nell for.

It was bound to happen sooner or later. He accepted that. He'd already had encounters with James and Petey, and he doubted his bad luck would stop there. Fallen Oaks was a small town with a long memory, and most of his former schoolmates hadn't strayed far from home. But if he were going to run face first into the ghosts of his past, he'd rather it not happen here, the site of the haunting.

Whit did a quick survey of the landscape, his gaze skimming along the chrome shine of parked cars and the old gray brick building that hadn't seen a renovation in at least twenty years. More than a decade had passed since the last time he'd stood on this stretch of ground, but the unexpected familiarity of it made all the hairs on his arms stand on end. Back then, a towering oak had grown in the center of the parking lot, jutting skyward out of a raised flowerbed bordered with smooth white stones. It had since been cut down and replaced by a couple of bushes and a wooden sign carved with the words *Welcome to Fallen Oaks High School.* The entire lot had been repaved at some point, and all the lines marking the spaces appeared freshly painted. Everything else was the same, right down to the flaking metal on the flagpole and the giant bronze statue of a muskrat—the school's longtime mascot—locked in its eternal pose near the building's front doors.

"Let's get this over with," he murmured. He stepped out of the car and put on his aviators, shoving his hands into his pockets as he turned in the direction of the baseball field. The weather was crisp and cool, the sky that deep, clear blue that belonged only to the first two weeks of November. The sun beat down against the pavement and skidded along the grass, making everything gleam. It was a beautiful day for baseball.

Out of nowhere a memory surfaced: the last home game of the season, sophomore year of high school. Whit had been sidelined with a sprained ankle, but he'd been in the dugout to cheer on his friends. Bottom of the ninth, down by one, James had been perched on first base when Sawyer Brewster came up to the plate. Sawyer, struggling with his swing for the past several games, had been given the order to bunt. Instead he'd hit a moonshot straight over the head of the center fielder. Whit had forgotten all about his ankle as he went screaming out onto the diamond with the rest of the team while Sawyer did his victory trot around the bases.

"I thought you wanted to come," Nell said, climbing out after him. She walked around the back of the car to stand beside him, using her hand to shield her eyes from the glare of the sun. "I could've made an easy five hundred bucks."

"Nothing's easy with my dad," Whit retorted, shaking off the memory. He rolled his shoulders to loosen some of the tightness he felt building in the muscles of his neck and back, then turned his attention to Nell. He doubted his dad had been serious in his bribery attempts, but it was clear he'd been trying to charm her. "And I hope you reminded him you're taken."

"It wasn't like that."

"Next time he flirts with you, tell him you're not into geriatrics. That'll shut him up."

"He wasn't flirting with me!"

Whit smiled. "I'd better stake a claim, just to be safe." He opened the trunk and fished around until he found one of his Blizz caps, which he set on Nell's head, positioning it over her ponytail. The hat was too big on her, so he tugged the edges down behind her ears, tucking back a few stray wisps of silky chestnut hair. She glared at him from under the rim.

"Gotta rep the team," he said. He took her hand and laced his fingers through hers, just to piss her off. "You're my girlfriend, remember?"

"Let's get this over with," she echoed sulkily.

She was quiet as they made the slow trek across the grass toward the baseball field, though she didn't try to wriggle her hand free. Whit watched her out of the corner of his eye. Concentrating on Nell was a hell of a lot more fun than dwelling on the fact that he was back on what had once been his home turf, so he studied her as they walked, noting the obstinate set to her jaw and the creasing of her brow. She'd dressed for the weather, pairing a long-sleeved blouse with a burgundy cardigan that fell to mid-thigh—though she wasn't wearing socks, and he could just see the edge of her tattoo peeping out from below the rolled cuff of her jeans. The sun had left a warm rosy glow on her skin, emphasizing her freckles. She looked cute. More than cute. She looked... something that was completely inappropriate for him to be thinking, much less put into words.

Whit had given up pretending he wasn't attracted to her. He was a young, healthy, active, heterosexual male; of course he was attracted to her. It was pure mathematics. Whit thought about sex forty times a day, give or take—and since he'd spent nearly every waking moment of the past *two* days with Nell, it was only natural he'd fit the two together. She was a young, healthy, active, heterosexual female. Add in the fact she was strikingly pretty, had a softly curved ass that he just knew would fit perfectly in his hands, and those long, slender legs that he could so easily imagine wrapping around him... well, there wasn't any mystery why his hormones had gone haywire. He remembered her bouncing up and down in his arms, the tantalizing friction of her body against his, and thought about how much more tantalizing it would have been without all those layers of clothing.

Proof that his body didn't always agree with his brain, since Whit knew damn well that acting on his impulses would lead to disaster. And he hadn't forgotten her revealing his PEDs usage to the world. Even though he'd long ago accepted that the blame lay squarely on his own shoulders, there had been too much turmoil, too much fallout for it to fade easily.

Gazing at her now, he wondered how different the trajectory of his career would have been if they'd never crossed paths. What would he have done if she hadn't stepped in front of that camera? Would he have had the courage to come clean on his own? Or would he have kept his mouth shut and let the years slip by in silence, the guilt slowly eating away at him?

It was a question he didn't want to ponder. He had the uneasy feeling he wouldn't like the answer.

Crowds were already gathering near the stands, so he steered Nell around the far side of the field to where his father was holding court with the collection of sports journalists he'd flown in to cover the game. Whit recognized a few of them, including a writer for *ESPN* who had done an in-depth profile on him after he recovered from his surgery. Jerry Garwood was notably absent, but Skip had explained he wouldn't be arriving until later in the week. Whit doubted any of the reporters would recognize Nell, but since he wanted to keep her out of the national spotlight, he left her to chat with Allie—who was under strict instructions to go along with the girlfriend charade—before joining his dad.

He spent the next twenty minutes answering questions while doing his best to remain charming, affable, and evasive as hell. Thankfully, when it came to the piece in *Meltdown*, Rebecca's press release had done most of the work for him. He laughed off a couple of suggestive comments, and whenever a reporter brought up the video, he deflected by telling them he was there to support his father and that he'd be happy to speak about the O'Rourke Family Foundation and its causes. After disentangling himself from a sports analyst who wanted to book him for an interview on an upcoming podcast, he rescued Nell from his sister and took her on a tour of the facilities.

Despite himself, Whit was impressed. His dad had gone all out. The area had been transformed from a small-time field into a bustling venue with security, concessions, ushers, and a dedicated area for signing autographs and holding photo ops. The bleachers at Fallen Oaks High weren't built to accommodate the numbers Skip had wanted, so additional seating had been constructed for the occasion. The smell of hot dogs and popcorn wafted on the breeze, and the air was filled with that same giddy, restless vibe that could be felt in ballparks across the country. Whit breathed it all in as he led Nell to the visitors' dugout to mingle with the players of the team he'd be managing.

He knew most of those men from his childhood, men with big personalities and the talent to match. Age had softened their edges—along with their bellies—but they were still fierce competitors, and none of them did anything by half. The game was in their blood, and a decade or so off the field didn't change that. When they played, they played to win. Watching them take practice swings as they traded trash talk back and forth made him wonder if maybe his father had arranged this whole thing just for an excuse to play ball with his friends again. He could only hope none of them played themselves into a heart attack.

It wasn't until he saw Bellamy Swan that he realized his dad had set him up.

Swan was only a couple of years older than Whit, but he'd left baseball after a mere four seasons in the majors when he'd run head-long into every athlete's worst nightmare: that mysterious ailment known as the yips. The yips defied logic and understanding and were all but impossible to overcome; when they got you, unless you were stubborn enough and lucky enough, you were done. Swan might have been stubborn, but he hadn't been lucky. For three years he'd thrown straight filth; then, out of nowhere, he'd fallen apart. He had no command, he had no velocity, and when he wasn't walking batters he was belting them.

And Skip had set him as Whit's starting pitcher.

Whit swallowed a curse. Since it was an exhibition game, his team only had two pitchers, and Dusty Gaines had spent most of his career as a closer. Add in the fact that Swan didn't exactly qualify as an old-timer—he was there representing his father, a former teammate of Skip's who had passed away in the spring—and it would be a colossally bad PR move to switch him out. Not to mention cruel. Whit would just have to hope that a few years away from the pressure of the big leagues would help Swan find the strike zone. Otherwise, they were in for a massacre.

"This is for charity, right?" Nell asked, peering at the clipboard he was using to adjust the lineup card. Behind her, some of the guys were going through warm-ups, and Francisco Sánchez was doing his favorite trick of standing a bat on the top of his head. "Your dad said it was only supposed to go six innings."

Six innings followed by a meet and greet where the players would sign autographs and take photos with fans. That was the real draw for most of the crowd, not a shortened game with a bunch of aging ballplayers huffing and puffing their way around the bases. But that didn't mean Whit didn't intend to do whatever he could to win it. "Remember the number one rule of the O'Rourke household," he said, tapping his pen against the clipboard.

Nell rolled her eyes.

He spotted his dad across the diamond in the home dugout barking out instructions to Maggie, who looked completely out of her depth. Technically, Skip had named Maggie as manager of the home team; realistically, it was obvious that Skip was planning to manage it by himself. Whit hadn't exchanged more than a few sentences with his dad's girlfriend—or *assistant,* as Skip would have it—but from their limited interactions, he'd gotten the impression Maggie didn't know much about baseball. His dad claimed to have hired her a couple of weeks ago to help out with the stadium details, which was as transparent as it was laughable, since Skip had a legion of agents and lawyers making sure nothing slipped through the cracks. What Whit didn't understand was why Skip was bothering to lie about their relationship. Sure, Maggie was young (twenty-seven, according to Allie), but she wouldn't be the first younger woman Skip had tangled the sheets with. Maybe it was sheer force of habit; he'd spent so much time hiding his various mistresses, by now he just did it as a reflex.

Whatever the reason, Whit didn't hold it against Maggie, and he had no intention of embarrassing her if she was the one who wanted their connection kept secret—though he was sorely tempted when his dad jogged over to the visitors' dugout and tried to kick out Nell.

"No girlfriends in the dugout," Skip said, giving Nell an apologetic tilt of the head.

Whit had been planning to seat Nell behind home plate with Allie and Freddie, but there was no way he was letting his dad get away with that little bit of hypocrisy, especially not after Skip had stuck him with Bellamy Swan. He shot a pointed look in the direction of the home dugout. His dad pretended not to notice.

Whit folded his arms, keeping his clipboard tucked under an elbow. "What do you think she's gonna do, go out there and steal signs?" When his dad didn't budge, Whit shoved the clipboard toward Nell, who scrambled to catch it. "She's bench coach. If you'd like to lodge a complaint, send your manager over and I'll discuss it with her."

Skip only grunted.

After they had finished ironing out the last few remaining details and the guys completed their warm-ups, Skip did one final media roundup, the captain of the Fallen Oaks softball team threw out the ceremonial first pitch, and the game was on.

"Aren't you afraid I'll jinx you?" Nell asked, standing beside him while Sánchez stepped up to the plate to face Dee Romero, a first ballot Hall of Famer with two Cy Youngs and a Pitching Triple Crown under his belt.

"I think my dad already took care of that." Romero sent a sinker to the outside corner and Sánchez's bat met air. A low whistle escaped Whit's lips. Romero might not be able to compete with the younger generation of pitchers who threw harder and faster—but damn, that was a sweet pitch. But since admiring the opposition seemed a tad counterproductive, he shifted and sent a sidelong glance toward Nell. "If you want to kiss my ball again, all you have to do is ask."

"I didn't see you kissing it."

"Only before a start."

"You can't really believe that works."

"I believe in hedging my bets." He let his gaze drift down her. The thin breeze billowed her cardigan and tugged at her blouse, providing a brief glimpse of bare skin at her hips as she stretched on her tiptoes to gaze at the action on the field. Her jeans, he noted, were the perfect level of snug, though the cardigan kept all the best parts of her back end out of view. Only the very edge of her tattoo was visible at the moment, a splash of dark ink above the knob of her ankle. "I noticed you didn't mention your tattoo on your list."

She turned toward him, her cheeks tinged pink. "Can we please just forget about that stupid list?"

"Not a chance. What's your tattoo?"

After a quick glance around, she lifted her knee and propped her foot on the lower rail of the dugout, sliding the cuff of her jeans upward. "It's my mother's handwriting. I got it right after I turned eighteen." She let her leg fall. "Paige was supposed to get a matching one, but Grandmother wouldn't allow it, of course."

"Seriously? That thing is tiny. It's not like you're rocking full sleeves."

"Aesthetic is everything to Grandmother," Nell replied. "Forget about tattoos—when I was sixteen, she wouldn't let me go out with a boy because she didn't like his *haircut*. After she found out I was seeing him anyway, she threatened to make me switch schools. And she definitely didn't approve of you, by the way."

Whit had never even met the notorious Josephine Forrester, so this was news to him. "Why? What's wrong with my aesthetic? I have great hair."

"Something about grown men going to work in pajamas."

"Then it's a good thing she never saw *my* tattoo."

He was one of the only guys in the major leagues who didn't actually have a tattoo, but that flummoxed look on Nell's face was exactly what he'd been aiming for, and his lips curved upward as he turned his attention back to the game. His smile didn't last long. At the plate, Sánchez had struck out swinging, and Dee Romero made short work of the next two batters. Just like that, the top of the inning was over and it was time for Bellamy Swan.

The crowd got on their feet when he was introduced—son of the late, legendary Patrick Swan, making his first appearance on a mound in over six years. Swan didn't even seem to notice the applause. He was locked in, pure focus, standing in that lonely realm where nothing mattered but the ball in his hand and the guy at the plate. Unfortunately for him, the guy at the plate was Skip. And it wasn't in Skip's nature to give anyone a pass.

"Try not to pull anything, old man!" Whit hollered as his father stepped into the batter's box.

"Your day will come, kid," Skip shot back.

Swan's first pitch was high and inside. The second was a called strike that was enough of a gift it should've come with a bow attached. On the third pitch, Skip ripped a home run into left field.

The crowd roared. The air buzzed. Skip pumped a fist as he made his victory lap. Then, instead of following tradition and pointing skyward as he crossed home plate, he pointed at Whit and winked.

"Remind me again that this is for charity," Whit gritted out as his dad returned to the dugout, greeted by a hail of cheers.

"What about the number one rule of the O'Rourke household?"

"We're moving to the second rule."

"You can't win 'em all?"

"If you can't get a win, get *vengeance*."

"You just made that up."

He pulled his phone out of his back pocket and shot a quick text to Allie. *What's the second rule of the O'Rourkes?*

Her response took less than a minute.

Payback. Why? Is this about Dad hitting that homer?? If you're plotting something, I want in.

Smirking, Whit handed his phone to Nell.

"I am officially afraid of your family," she drawled.

Whit flashed a grin. "Buckle up, baby. We're just getting started."

TWELVE

BY THE BOTTOM OF the third inning, Nell had learned three things about baseball players: they did a lot of sweating, they did a lot of swearing, and they did a lot of spitting. Even with all the bottles of water they chugged, she was surprised they didn't shrivel into raisins from dehydration.

Nell didn't think of herself as squeamish. She'd been vomited on by sick students and peed on by hamsters. She'd dealt with bloody noses and lice infestations. She'd been given bug collections as birthday presents. But really, this was excessive. There was no inch of the dugout that wasn't covered in sunflower seed shells or saliva—or both—and Nell had long since abandoned any attempts to watch where she stepped. When she got back to the farm, she was going to have to hose down her shoes with Lysol.

Some of the players, she'd discovered, also held grudges. Decade-long grudges, from what she could tell. There was a running dispute about whether a ninth-inning bunt (particularly egregious, apparently) that had ruined a perfect game was "bush league" or fair play, and a couple of the guys were tossing such creative insults back and forth in both English and Spanish, she could only hope all the little kids in the audience would cover their ears.

And if that weren't enough of a culture shock for Nell—who spent her days doling out reminders about inside voices and respecting boundaries—there was also the ass slapping. The players did a *lot* of ass slapping. Not her ass, thankfully; at least not yet. But whenever one of the guys made a nice play, he got a quick, congratulatory smack, and if he scored a run, his triumphant return to the dugout was met with cheers, hoots, high-fives, and a barrage of swats on his rear end. Then usually he'd spit. Saliva and ritualized spanking: definitely not the way she'd imagined spending her day. At this point, she wasn't really certain how her life could get any weirder.

She flicked a glance at Whit, who stood leaning against the dugout rail, his arms resting on the high metal bar and his gaze pinned on the field. No one had yet slapped *his* ass. And there it was, tucked snugly into the close-fitting jeans he hadn't bothered to trade for baseball pants. She remembered the women at Gills discussing which part of his body was most worthy of admiration. One of them had definitely mentioned his ass. She wondered what he'd do if she gave it a tap.

Hands off, Nellie. Boundaries, remember?

Sighing, she pushed herself away from the railing to find a spot on the bench. Next to her, the small metal figurine of a wizard holding up a sword sat staring woefully at her. She could not for the life of her say where the statue had come from, but the players had taken to calling it their "rally wizard" ever since Eddie Ames had hit a bases-clearing double after waving it over his head. She wondered if she should give it a try. She could use a bit of luck just now.

Those unsavory thoughts of hers were becoming a problem, especially since it was getting harder and harder to pretend that there was nothing more to Whit than a sexy smile and an ego the size of Alaska. Seeing him in his natural habitat, a jock among jocks, the patron saint of swagger, able to trash talk and launch sunflower shells with the best of them—when he wasn't shoveling bright pink bubblegum into his mouth, anyway—should have been a turn off. Instead she'd found herself fascinated. It was clear he was in his element, a fierce competitor humming with restless energy and driven by the need to give it his all. And it wasn't just the game itself he thrived in. He was good with people. She was used to his smooth, easy charm, so she wasn't surprised by how effortlessly he'd handled the reporters before the game, or by the quick camaraderie he'd formed with his team. But when he'd stopped to give autographs to a group of kids and made sure to include a timid little girl hiding shyly behind the others, Nell had felt herself melting.

What she needed, she decided, was a boyfriend. A real one. Or at the very least a date. Some other, non-disastrous outlet for her romantic yearnings. As soon as she got back to Chicago, she was going to call up Evan Greyland and invite him for coffee. Evan's daughter had been a student of Nell's last year, and when he'd asked her out during a field trip to Adler Planetarium, she'd turned him down—but they'd become friends on social media, and he'd recently indicated he was still interested. That would help turn her thoughts in a less destructive direction. The only reason her crush had returned was because her love life was virtually nonexistent.

And even before it was nonexistent, it had been pretty dismal, if she were being completely honest. Her only serious boyfriend had been in college, when she'd wanted to revel in all her newfound freedom and had thrown herself headfirst into a relationship with the teaching assistant in her freshman English class. They'd been on a camping trip in the Upper Peninsula when she'd found out he was married. She'd packed up her car and her shattered heart and ditched him at a campground, leaving him to explain to his wife why he needed a ride home from Michigan in his underwear. Since then, she'd had a series of lukewarm relationships, few of them lasting long enough for her to meet the parents or keep a toothbrush or a spare drawer. Which was not the same as Whit's flavor-of-the-month approach to dating. She *wanted* to fall in love. It was just that all her lovers left her feeling vaguely... unsatisfied.

Paige told her it was because the men she dated were boring. She'd had her heart broken by a bad boy, so now she refused to take risks and purposely chose men who couldn't keep her interest. None of them were right for her, because boring men needed boring women so they could buy little houses and raise boring children: psychology according to Paige Forrester—the woman who broke up with the love of her life every five months like clockwork.

Evan wasn't boring. If anything, he was intimidating. He spoke three languages, he'd climbed to the summit of Everest—*and* K2—and he'd spent a year in the Peace Corps. What Nell couldn't figure out was what he saw in *her*, which was half the reason she'd turned him down in the first place. But if he wanted to go out with a woman whose most strenuous climbs involved staircases and whose only other language was Pig Latin, she figured that was his business.

The decision to call Evan made her feel a bit better, so she managed to relax, leaning back on her hands and tipping her head skyward to breathe in the clean autumn air. She closed her eyes, listening to the hum of chatter from the stands. To her surprise, she liked being here. Maybe the excitement was contagious. She'd never had much interest in professional sports, figuring she had better things to do than watch a bunch of grown men with too much testosterone grunt their way up and down a field or try to pummel each other with sticks—but the energy of the crowd and the sheer joy the players exuded made her own pulse quicken. The atmosphere was kinetic and heady. The air was electric.

"Catching a nap?"

Her eyes flew open. Whit had turned to face her, resting against the dugout rail with one arm still propped along the bar, his legs stretched out before him and his head tilted just slightly as he looked her over. The brim of his baseball cap shadowed his face, but she thought she detected a note of disappointment in his tone—or disapproval.

"Just enjoying the nice weather," she said, fighting a faint sense of embarrassment.

"You're missing the game."

"I'm listening to it."

"Then listen over here. I'll help you follow along."

"I don't need help," she huffed, getting to her feet. The rally wizard fell over, and she hastily set it back upright, giving a quick glance around the dugout to make sure none of the players had noticed. Most of them were on the field, so it looked like she was safe. She folded her arms as she gazed at Whit. "I'm not totally ignorant of the rules of baseball."

"Uh-huh." Whit snapped the piece of bubblegum he'd been chewing. "Indulge me."

The *I'm-so-charming* look on his face told her he'd been indulged way too often in his life, especially by women, but since she'd be calling Evan as soon as she got home, what could it hurt? She shrugged and moved alongside him, ignoring the sudden tingle that ran up her skin when her arm touched his. Copying his stance, she leaned against the railing and peered out toward home plate, where the pitcher for Whit's team—who couldn't be much past thirty and had the lanky build of a swimmer—was facing a guy who looked like he'd just wandered onto the field after auditioning for a role as a part-time mall Santa. It didn't seem to her to be a fair match-up, but no one else appeared to think it was strange, and she turned her attention back to Whit. "Shouldn't you be busy plotting your revenge?"

Whit and his dad had been trading insults back and forth between the dugouts for the duration of the game, but their words lacked any viciousness, so she figured it was their own bizarre form of father-son bonding. So far, however, Whit hadn't been able to make good on his payback plans, even after his sister had sneaked into the dugout and offered to sabotage Skip by doing something that involved pine tar and athletic tape—or, that failing, by bribing the umpires. Whit had kicked her back to the stands when she started screaming the word "balk" every time one of his players stepped up to the plate.

Now the corners of his eyes crinkled as a slow smile spread across his face. "Just wait."

She didn't have to wait long. After Whit's pitcher struck out Santa, the lineup flipped over and Skip stepped back up to the plate.

"I considered just walking him," Whit said. He exchanged a quick, conspiratorial look with his pitcher. "But this is better."

This, according to Whit, was a plan to "pitch around" his father. Skip wouldn't be satisfied with simply taking a free base, Whit said—he wanted to hit. That meant they could get him to chase bad pitches. And from the groans of the audience, they were *very* bad pitches. Skip didn't take the bait when the first two throws were so low they nearly touched the dirt, but on the third and fourth pitches, he tapped the ball foul. The fifth pitch was something else entirely. The ball moved much more slowly than it had in the previous throws, and just as it crossed the plate it seemed to dip downward. Skip's bat met air.

Just like that, he'd struck out swinging.

Skip slammed his bat to the ground in disgust, then sent a searing look toward his son as he realized he'd been played. "That only works once," he warned.

"Once is enough," Whit said, winking. He shoved another piece of bubblegum into his mouth.

"Isn't he going to be plotting *his* revenge now?" Nell asked.

"Who cares? That was so worth it." The grin he gave her made her knees feel a little wobbly. It was really a good thing she'd be dating someone else by this time next week.

Until then, however, she had a role to play, so she rested her arms against the railing and settled in to watch the game. To her surprise, Whit was a good teacher, answering her questions without making her feel like an idiot for asking them and pointing out details she'd have otherwise missed. In the top of the fourth inning, when he ordered what he called a *squeeze play*, he told her what to watch for. By the bottom of the fifth, Nell knew that a fielder's choice counted against a player's batting average, but a sacrifice fly didn't. Most of his talk of pitches went over her head—and him demonstrating various grips didn't help the way he seemed to think it should—but his enthusiasm was infectious. When Francisco Sánchez hit a game-tying home run in the top of the sixth, she found herself cheering right along with the rest of the team.

Whit also related the saga of the infamous ninth inning bunt, a twelve-year-old feud between Ray Wakefield, the shortstop for Whit's team, and Dee Romero, the opposing team's pitcher. According to Whit, Dee hadn't allowed any base runners for an entire game—until Ray came up to bat in the bottom of the ninth and ruined Dee's bid to make history by bunting for a meaningless hit in a game his team was losing by eight runs.

"And your dad thought it was a good idea to invite them both here?" Nell might not have a full grasp of the situation, but the anger simmering between the two had become abundantly clear when Dee had celebrated after striking Ray out. Twice.

Whit shrugged. "They'll behave themselves."

Which they did. Right up until Ray stepped up to the plate to face Dee a third time.

Nell didn't hear what was said, but she didn't need to. The gestures they made at each other were more than enough to get the point across, besides being wholly inappropriate for an audience that included small children—not to mention Nell, who could have gladly gone her entire life without being subjected to the amount of pelvic thrusting and testicle grabbing that made up their angry pantomime. For heaven's sake, these men were old enough to be grandfathers! A fact they'd apparently forgotten the second they set foot on the field, since neither of them paid the slightest attention to the players attempting to calm them down. Tensions rose, tempers flared, and before anyone knew what was happening, Ray had tossed his bat into the dirt and was charging toward the pitcher's mound.

Whit swore and shot a quick look at Nell. "Stay here." In one fluid motion, he vaulted over the dugout railing and went racing toward the infield. She stared after him as around her the volume from the crowd reached a fever pitch, a torrent of cheers and heckling that quickly drowned out the voices on the field.

After that it was chaos.

Nell was so busy watching Whit, it took her a moment to realize that he wasn't alone. He hadn't gone more than a couple of steps before the entire dugout emptied behind him, every last player scrambling to follow in his wake. Eddie Ames, who had once again been waving the wizard figurine in the air, pressed the little statue into Nell's hands as he hustled to join his teammates.

Meanwhile, the players already on the field had converged upon Ray and Dee, and all Nell could see was a tangled mass of grizzled, heavily perspiring middle-aged men in various states of disheveled. At least two of them had already lost their hats, and somehow, someone's shoe had flipped into the air, narrowly missing one of the umpires who was trying to separate the players. Whit had been swallowed up within the sweaty human amoeba, and she couldn't see Skip, but Maggie stood on the outskirts of the fray, wringing her hands and looking helpless.

Nell felt a rush of sympathy for Skip's assistant-slash-girlfriend, who appeared completely overwhelmed by all the shouting, shoving, and general mayhem unfolding before her. The sheer panic she exuded made her seem less like a nervous cat now and more like one that had been thrown to the wolves. She was the lone woman in a sea of testosterone and posturing, and since Skip had apparently abandoned her, Nell figured Maggie could use a little support. Tucking the rally wizard into one of her front jeans pockets, she headed for the steps.

There she hesitated.

She knew she should stay in the dugout. Whit had *told* her to stay in the dugout. Not that she felt the need to follow his orders, but she was definitely out of her depth when it came to a bunch of angry, adrenaline-fueled jocks who had no idea they were supposed to get wiser—or at least more mellow—with age. Hair-pulling and arm-pinching she could handle. Headlocks and right hooks? Not so much.

But how could she just stand there while poor Maggie was looking so desperate? Maggie had that little-kid-left-at-the-zoo expression on her face, and boy did Nell remember *that* feeling. And Whit had technically named Nell bench coach. That meant she was part of the team. She had an obligation to help.

With that thought in mind, she adjusted the Blizzards cap on her head, straightened her shoulders, and rushed toward the tumult.

What happened next was in no way her fault.

She never made it to Maggie. Before she could reach her, the brawl shifted sideways and Whit emerged, dragging Ray backward with an arm locked around his upper body. Or rather, *not* locked around his upper body, since Ray managed to wriggle his way free, kicking his legs outward as he hurled himself back into the melee with the guttural war cry of a man who felt he had suffered a grave injustice. Whit, caught off-guard and off-balance, lost his footing and went down.

With a gasp, Nell swerved toward Whit, intending to help him back to his feet. The throng swerved with her. Someone lurched. Someone else swayed. She ducked aside to avoid a collision with a man whose bushy white beard identified him as Santa. Then, feeling herself stumble, she took a couple of long, staggering steps to right herself... and caught an elbow in the back.

Nell flailed. Directly into Whit.

Whit, halfway to his feet, went crashing right back down again and landed face-first in the grass. Nell went with him. Her hat flew off her head and did a sharp pirouette through the air, vanishing somewhere between the third baseline and the dugout. She had a brief, dizzying sense of weightlessness. Then her forehead slammed against the solid plane of a shoulder blade, she got a mouthful of cotton shirt and a breath of sun-dampened skin, and her hips collided with Whit's.

Whit howled.

"Sorry! Sorry!" Nell squeaked, struggling to lift herself off him. She lay sprawled in an undignified heap, her chin grazing his shoulder and her chest flattened against his back. Any second now, the adrenaline would subside and the embarrassment would kick in, but at the moment she hurt too much. As it turned out, that ass she'd spent *way* too much time admiring was a lot harder than it looked.

Whit pushed himself—and her, by extension—upward with his arms and growled, "Get off me!"

"I'm not *that* heavy," she muttered, flopping into the grass beside him. She could feel her cheeks starting to burn. At least the brawl had moved on without them. She thought it had, anyway. Her head was throbbing and her vision was sort of swimming, so it was difficult to be sure.

"You stabbed me!"

"What? No, I didn't."

Her eyes widened as she realized the wizard figurine was no longer in her pocket. It had remained behind with Whit, its tiny metal sword embedded in...

Oh no.

She had very definitely stabbed him in the ass. The sword had gone straight through the denim of his left jeans pocket and lodged itself in the flesh beneath. It wasn't very *deeply* embedded, but she doubted that mattered much to Whit, who currently had a wizard poking up from his rear end.

Without thinking, she grabbed the figurine and pulled.

Whit howled again.

Nell winced. "It's out now."

He uttered a string of syllables she couldn't make sense of, then heaved himself to his feet, gripping her arm and pulling her bodily up with him. "I told you to stay in the dugout."

"I thought Maggie could use some help," she said weakly.

"What were you going to do? Announce yourself as her girlfriend?"

That was a little unfair, she thought, but he was the one bleeding from a sword wound to his posterior, so she supposed he had the right to be irritable. She rubbed at her aching forehead with the palm of her hand. "Sometimes I act without thinking."

"Yeah, I've noticed. The champion of the underdog strikes again. You ever consider therapy for that superhero complex of yours?"

"I don't have a superhero complex, and if I did, why would I want to get rid of it?" It was on the tip of her tongue to mention that *he* had been her most recent underdog, and the only reason she was even there was because he'd decided he needed a girlfriend as a bodyguard, but the stormy look in his eyes made her think better of it.

Whit snorted. "Maybe so you don't get yourself fired again?"

"That wasn't me trying to be a hero. That was me losing my temper." Something she would in no way do during her meeting with Frank Grantham, since, no matter what Whit believed, she *was* capable of playing nice.

"Because you were trying to be a hero. Give me your sweater."

She blinked at him. "Why?"

"There are about a thousand people with smartphones watching us and I'd rather the world not know I have a puncture wound in my ass."

Biting down on her lip, she shrugged out of her cardigan—her *new* cardigan that she'd just spent thirty bucks on—and handed it to Whit, who didn't even bother to thank her. He just grabbed the sweater and tied its sleeves around his waist, as though that would somehow draw less attention to him than a minuscule bloodstain on the back of his jeans. Then, instead of doing what any normal, reasonable human being would do and hurrying off the field to find himself a first aid kit, he turned and headed back toward the melee.

"Shouldn't we apply pressure or something?" Nell asked, trotting after him.

"Be my guest," he tossed over his shoulder.

Since any further close encounters with Whit's backside were to be avoided at all costs, Nell changed her mind about following him and went to check on Maggie.

THIRTEEN

"I DON'T NEED TO go to the emergency room," Nell gritted out—for the third time, since no one had paid any attention to her first two protests.

No one being Whit, his father, the on-site medic, two EMTs, Allie, Freddie, and a small congregation of players who were apparently feeling guilty for their role in knocking her face-first into two hundred pounds of solid muscle. None of *them* appeared to be suffering any ill-effects from the brawl, she thought sourly. Somehow, all the pushing and punching had resulted in nothing more than a handful of scrapes and bruises and one swollen lip—if you didn't count her and Whit.

She still didn't get a response, so she tried raising her voice a little. "I don't need to—"

"That knot on your head says otherwise," Whit finally replied, turning to face her. He'd gotten over his irritation with her and now looked entirely too cheerful for a man she knew had a strip of gauze bonded to his ass with medical tape, but the go-ahead home run Ames had hit as soon as the game resumed had apparently improved his mood. He'd even given her back her sweater. Like she wanted it now.

"You're the one bleeding," she huffed.

"What do you call this?" His thumb grazed her forehead just below the hairline, where a thin trickle of blood was already drying.

She batted his hand away.

They were gathered near one of the first-aid stations Skip had set up on the grounds, which was sheltered from view of the stands by a large canopy—though she doubted many people had missed the ambulance driving across the field. After the skirmish had been broken up and tempers had been soothed, the teams had done a quick appraisal of injuries before finishing out the top of the inning. During the break, they'd decided to delay play in order to reassess.

Unfortunately for Nell, general assessment of her was that she might have a concussion. A bump on the forehead, a pounding headache, and, okay, a *slight* bit of nausea that she was desperately wishing she'd kept to herself, and suddenly they were carting her off to be poked, prodded, scanned, and scrutinized. The only justice was that Whit was in need of a tetanus shot.

She knew she was putting up more of a fuss than was strictly rational, but the months she'd spent in hospital waiting rooms while her mother went through treatment after treatment and test after test had given her an aversion to everything from urgent care to MinuteClinics. She never went to the doctor if she could avoid it. This instance, in her opinion, was one hundred percent avoidable. But she didn't want to admit the reason for her reluctance to Whit—who would probably just tell her she needed therapy again—so instead she gave him a smile and said, "I'm fine. Really."

"Nice try, but Dad doesn't take chances when it comes to head wounds or insurance liability."

"Right. Insurance. You know, that thing I lost when I lost my job?"

"We have it covered," he said, with the sort of easy assurance that just made her want to grind her teeth harder.

"This is revenge, isn't it?"

"Yes. This is revenge. I'm getting back at you for stabbing me in the ass by making sure you don't have a concussion." He shook his head slowly. "Jesus, is there anything you *aren't* difficult about? I tell you what—if we see a stray dog on the way to the ER, I'll make them pull over so you can rescue it."

"You weren't worried about concussions before."

"Sorry if I was a little distracted by being stabbed."

"Put her in the damn ambulance, Whitney!" his dad growled.

Whit's eyebrow raised. "You heard the man."

He made a move toward her like he was going to scoop her right off the ground and deposit her in the ambulance if she didn't follow orders, so she quickly complied—but not before aiming a dark look in his direction. "I hope you get gangrene."

The emergency room turned out to be an urgent care facility rather than a hospital, which was a small relief, but Nell still wasn't happy about being bullied into going there in the first place. The waiting room with its over-bright fluorescent lighting was like every other waiting room she'd been to, neutral, sterile, with carefully selected art prints framed on the walls—wildflower studies, in this case—and stacks of magazines piled on short, square tables. A couple of potted plants added a touch of green, and there was a play area in one corner to entertain little kids, but the sounds were the same, the smells were the same, and her hands felt clammy as Whit ushered her into one of the upholstered chairs that had been arranged near the front desk.

She was too restless to sit. The refreshments area set up along the back counters proved to have run out of coffee, so while Whit spoke with the receptionist, she walked over to the empty play area and skimmed through their selection of children's books.

"Good choices," she murmured when Whit joined her. He was holding a pair of clipboards with what she assumed were medical forms. Great. "Someone here has excellent taste."

He cocked his head, squinting at the picture book she held. "Aren't they a little below your age group?"

"And right about at your reading level," she retorted before she could stop herself.

"Still pissed I made you get on that ambulance, huh?"

"It's more the three hours we'll be stuck waiting here just to be sent home with an ice pack and a bottle of Tylenol."

"Sucks to be you, McLean. You're on concussion protocol."

It only ended up being fifteen minutes before Whit was called back to have his puncture wound seen to, but another twenty had passed by the time Nell was summoned to an exam room. Not much of a change in scenery, she thought. Another sterile room, painted beige, with a couple of counters holding glass canisters and a computer monitor displaying its psychedelic screensaver. She busied herself on her phone, checking texts and catching up on correspondence. She was in the middle of composing a message to Gabi (conveniently leaving out any mention of her location) when the door clicked open and a slim blonde figure in a dark green sweater slipped in.

Nell didn't even bother asking how Whit's sister had managed to locate her, much less sneak her way into an exam room. Allie was an O'Rourke, and Nell had already learned they had a knack for getting their way.

"So," Allie said, trailing her fingers along the metal shelf that sat near the door. "You're *not* dating my brother."

Impressive how she managed to make it sound like an accusation.

Nell watched her warily. At dinner the other night, Allie had been polite but aloof, dividing most of her remarks between her boyfriend and Whit, and since Nell wasn't certain how much Whit had revealed to his sister, she decided to tread carefully. "Is that a problem?"

"But you *were* with him in the bar on Thursday."

"What did Whit tell you?"

"First he said the whole thing was a setup. Then he said it was an accident." Allie shifted, turning her back to the door as she tapped an impatient foot against the tile. "So which is it?"

"I wasn't trying to set him up."

"It seems to have worked out well for you."

"Yeah. Ambulance rides and urgent care centers are every girl's idea of a dream date."

"Maybe not, but I'm guessing the date part is what counts."

"Did your brother happen to mention he basically kidnapped me to get me here?" When Allie just favored her with a perfect imitation of Whit's eyebrow raise, Nell sighed. "I'm not a crazy stalker or an undercover reporter for *Meltdown*, so if you're planning to interrogate me, can it at least wait until they give me some drugs?"

"Really milking that head injury, I see."

Since losing her temper was dangerously close to becoming a habit, Nell changed the subject. "What is Whit's deal, anyway?" she asked, retreating to the other side of the room and mimicking Allie's stance. She figured two could interrogate. "Why does he think everyone in town hates him?"

Allie blew a puff of air out from the side of her mouth. "Because he's an idiot." A thin frown flickered across her face and vanished. "He told you everyone hates him?"

Nell thought of James's icy looks and Petey's open hostility. "More or less."

Allie's suspicious expression turned faintly curious. "Who exactly are you? Whit never bothered to explain."

"According to him, I'm cannon fodder."

"Interesting."

Nell didn't have a chance to ask just what was interesting about that. A soft knock sounded at the door, and she chirped out a quick, grateful, "Come in!" She might not be looking forward to having a total stranger poke at her, but at least the O'Rourke Inquisition would be put on hold.

Except that when the handle turned and the door inched open, it wasn't a doctor who appeared. It was Whit, a cup of fresh waiting-room coffee in one hand and an orange and black Halloween-themed Band-Aid plastered to his left arm. Ridiculously, her pulse kicked up a notch at the sight of him. To cover it, she shot him the exact same death glare she'd used when she'd caught one of her students trying to finger-paint the class hamster.

"Peace offering," he said, holding up the cup of coffee. He took another step into the room, noted her irritable expression and crossed-arms, then stopped and stared at Allie. "What are you doing here?"

Precisely what Nell wanted to know. Didn't anyone actually work at this stupid clinic?

Allie shrugged. "You left your car at the school. I figured you'd need a ride, so I took Dad's. Your team won, by the way."

"You mean you wanted to ambush Nell."

"I'm just making sure she's not up to anything nefarious."

"Nefarious isn't Nell's style. Leave her alone."

"You're no fun."

"Too bad. You'll have to find someone else to harass." He passed the cup of coffee to Nell, then turned back toward his sister. "And speaking of nefarious... have you heard from Rory?"

Instantly, Allie scowled. "She said she knows what she's doing, she's sorry she didn't talk to me sooner, and she'll tell me all about it when she gets back from her honeymoon."

"Damn. She's really trying to sell this thing."

"She's in Cancún!"

"Well, there you go. Rory always said she wanted to honeymoon in Italy."

"Why aren't you taking this seriously?"

"Because there is no way she married someone just to piss off Dad," he retorted.

"Then why wouldn't she tell me the truth?"

"You're staying with Dad. If you weren't flipping out, it would spoil her game. Sorry, sis, but you're just a pawn on the Grandmaster's chess board."

"Maybe she wanted to marry him," Nell offered. The matching looks of disgust the O'Rourke siblings shot her made her quickly put up her free hand. "Or not."

She was spared any further commentary when the doctor finally arrived and shooed Allie and Whit back to the reception area—but the diagnosis of a mild concussion did nothing to improve her mood.

"Well?" Whit asked when she found him in the waiting room. As she hesitated, he gave her that smirking eyebrow arch that told her he had an *I-told-you-so* ready and waiting if she so much as mentioned the word concussion.

"Don't worry, the baby's fine," she said, loud enough that a couple of older women seated nearby turned to stare.

"Hilarious," said Whit.

Allie had defrosted enough to crack a grin.

Nell set a hand on her hip. "What did I tell you? Tylenol and an ice pack, and one giant waste of everyone's time and money." And a follow-up exam in a few days she had absolutely no intention of keeping.

"Your time, our money," Whit replied.

"How's your ass?"

"I'd let you see for yourself, but I'd probably get arrested."

"Or wind up on *Meltdown*," said Allie. "Again."

Whit's injury apparently no longer hurt—or he was too macho to admit it—because he didn't utter a word of complaint on the drive back to the high school. Nell sat in the backseat and watched the town slide by through the window of Skip's sleek silver Bentley, trying not to breathe on the glass. Being in such an expensive vehicle after so many years of the run-down used cars she'd driven ever since she'd cut herself off from Grandmother's money made her feel itchy. It didn't help that Allie seemed to think speed limits were simply suggestions, and Nell's nausea made an unwelcome return as the car took a sharp right that sent a small cascade of fallen leaves spinning through the air.

A quick check of her phone told her it was closing in on eight o'clock. Dark had long since fallen, transforming the curving roads and long boulevards into dusky landscapes of twisting oaks and bare branches. Downtown blurred by and gave way to residential areas where leftover Halloween decorations and harvest-themed lawn ornaments mingled with strings of early Christmas lights. Allie was forced to slow as they drew nearer to the high school, since traffic was still slightly congested from the remnants of crowds exiting the baseball game. Most of the clean-up crew had finished up for the night, though lights could be seen twinkling in the direction of the field and a few cars remained in the lot. An after party for the players who were staying in town was being held at one of the local hotels, but since Whit didn't like the idea of leaving his car at the school late into the evening, he'd asked Allie to drop them at the edge of the parking lot so he could drive to the party himself.

Allie pulled up near the lot's entrance and brought the Bentley to an abrupt and noisy halt, earning her a sarcastic remark from her brother.

Nell was just glad it was over. After fumbling a moment with her seat belt, she slipped gratefully into the cool evening air and stood with her hands on her hips, tipping her face up to the breeze as the Bentley roared away again. A sliver of moon hung overhead, the stars dizzily bright in the deepening darkness.

Whit's hand in the small of her back made her start.

"You all right?"

She assumed from the note of concern in his voice that he was worried about her supposed concussion and not his sister's NASCAR aspirations, so she waved him away and headed for his car.

Looking across the lot, she could just see the back of Whit's Audi poking out from behind a minivan that had been parked in one of the neighboring spaces. Otherwise the area was nearly empty. There was an SUV with its parking lights on a short distance from the field, and an older model pickup truck had been left diagonal across a couple of spaces next to what she assumed was a maintenance shed, but the rest of the lot had been cleared.

She let her gaze wander along the property as they walked, taking in the tiny grove of pines that flanked the lot and the tall wooden sign rising starkly from the center of the parking rows. To her right, she could make out the high school, a single-story building of cement pillars and faded red brick, dark now except for the dim glow of security lights. She glanced at Whit. "This is where you went to high school?"

He'd been keeping pace with her, a leisurely stroll for those ridiculously long legs of his, but now he paused to kick at a clump of leaves the wind had blown in from the street. "Part of the time. I finished out my senior year in Dower Hill."

"When you lived with your grandfather."

His shoulders lifted. "They changed the town boundaries a couple of decades ago. Poor Grandpa ended up with a different address in a different city without ever changing houses. Pissed him the hell off. It worked out for me, though."

"That was why you moved in with him?"

"That was one reason." He raked a hand through his hair. In the moonlight, his eyes were almost black. For the briefest of instants, she thought she saw something there—a flicker, a glimpse of something a little lonely, a little sad. Then it was gone. The ghost of a smile crossed his face. "Feeling homesick?" he asked, tipping his head toward the building.

She felt a surge of disappointment and told herself she had no right to it. Whit didn't share his private life with his real girlfriends, never mind a pretend one. And that was his business, not hers. A fact she was going to have to accept, or she'd be in for a lot more than disappointment.

"Maybe a little," she said.

He started to move again, and because he had set the pace this time, she had to hurry to keep up. The breeze tickled at her face and sent a chill along her arms. She tugged her sweater tighter.

"What made you go into teaching?" he asked when she reached him, a switch in conversation that told her the subject of his high school days was well and firmly closed.

"The obvious answer. I love kids."

"Yeah, I know, you wrote that on your list. A lot of people love kids. But why choose teaching?"

It was on her lips to remind him he preferred not to know much about the women he was dating. Then it occurred to her that was precisely why he was asking. They weren't dating and never would be. They were...

God, were they becoming *friends*?

He stopped walking to peer at her. "What?"

"Nothing!" she squeaked out, hoping the horror she felt didn't show on her face. She pulled the sleeves of her sweater down over her palms, fidgeting with the cuffs as she took another couple of steps forward. The wind was stirring again, and she breathed in the faint, lingering scents of cut grass and fried food. She could sense Whit watching her and quickly curved a smile. "I suppose I just knew I wanted to be a teacher. I always enjoyed school."

"What a nerd."

A nervous laugh fluttered out of her. "Guilty. I used to play school at home every chance I got. I had a magnet board with the alphabet and I would set up all my stuffed animals for story time."

"Still nerdy, but cute."

"Plus, I got to send Paige to detention. I'd make her go sit in the closet whenever she forgot to raise her hand."

"Strict disciplinarian, huh?"

"I've mellowed out since then."

Whit's snort told her he didn't believe her.

"Really, though, it was probably because of my mom," she said.

"She was a teacher too?"

"Kindergarten. I'd say it runs in the family, but I think for her it was more of an accident. She was rebelling from Grandmother and found out she liked it."

"Teaching kindergarten was a rebellion?"

"Grandmother expected her to get her MBA," Nell explained. "And what Grandmother expects, she usually gets."

"Still... most kids would opt for piercings and tattoos."

"Well, Mom did get knocked up by two different men. That has to count for something."

"Absolutely. A true revolutionary." It was too dark to see his expression, but she could hear the smile in his tone. "Is your mom the reason you feel the need to rescue everyone?"

Nell opened her mouth to respond that she did *not* have some kind of weird hero compulsion, but realized she'd just be wasting her breath. "You tell me, Dr. O'Rourke, since you seem to have me all figured out."

They were only a few yards from his car now, nearly at the minivan that had been parked a few spaces before it, but Whit stopped, cocking his head to the side as he gazed at Nell. "Not completely. I still can't figure why you thought Paige needed rescuing. Maggie, I get. I think it was stupid, but I get it. Taking up for your students is justified—though you clearly need to work on your methods. Standing up to my dad even makes a twisted sort of sense. But what the hell did you think you were protecting Paige from?"

"When?"

"When you *revealed sensitive information to the public,* as you put it. And then said I was bad in bed."

"Oh." Instant heat shot up her cheeks. "Maybe I just didn't like you."

Except that she had liked him. Way too much.

And still did.

"Now you're trying to hurt my feelings."

Nell hurried forward again. Her chest knotted. She didn't want to talk about that awful moment when she'd stepped in front of the camera and exposed his secret. Had she thought he deserved it then? Possibly. More likely she hadn't been thinking of the consequences at all. He was right that she'd wanted to protect Paige. It was that instinct that had thrust her forward to face down the so-called reporter, ignoring her sister's startled protests. But had it been more than that? Had some bitter, twisted part of herself wanted to punish him for her own sake?

She didn't want to think that—but she did know that she wasn't about to have that conversation here and now. With a quick glance behind her, she jogged the last few feet to the minivan, stepping around it.

Then stopped short. Her breath came out in a gasp. "Whit."

Fourteen

The thing was, Whit reflected as he stared at the broken taillights and slashed tires of his Audi, he wasn't even all that surprised.

Shocked, yes—initially. He'd seen all the blood drain from Nell's face and had taken those last few steps at a run, his breath coming hard and his adrenaline spiking. He'd rounded the minivan in less than a second, expecting... he didn't know what he'd been expecting, but some asshole using his car as a piñata had definitely not been at the top of the list. For a moment he'd been speechless. And not just speechless, but frozen in place, completely empty of thought and sense. He'd felt a vague awareness that Nell was speaking to him, but the words hadn't registered. It wasn't until she'd reached out and touched his arm that he'd reacted, uttering the only response that had seemed appropriate at the time: "*Motherfucker.*"

But he wasn't surprised, at least not by the vandalism. The extent of the damage—that was something else. Not only were the tires sliced and all the lights smashed, but the entire driver's side had been keyed, the rear windshield shattered, the bumper dented, and the word *CHEATER* had been scratched across the trunk in huge jagged letters. A cheap department store baseball bat had been left lying just above the damning word, surrounded by tiny shards of glass.

"Whit," Nell said again, her fingers grazing his shoulder.

The pity in her voice was unbearable. He jerked away.

Shifting to the side, he did a quick scan of the lot. The damage had to be recent or someone would have reported it. But no unusual shapes caught his eye, no flicker of movement or sinister shadows lurking in the distance. Except for the minivan parked nearby and the pickup truck that had been left next to the tool shed, the area was empty. The only sounds were the low hum of highway traffic and the quiet rustle of his own breath. Whoever had chosen to make this little statement hadn't had the balls to stick around to see it received.

Which was probably a good thing, Whit thought. He really wanted to punch something, and the last thing he needed was a hand injury.

The glow of Nell's phone caught his attention. He turned, watching as she picked her way through the wreckage and began snapping pictures. When she reached the driver's side door, she stopped, sliding her fingers beneath the handle. Whit peered at her. "What are you doing?"

"Wondering why the alarm didn't go off." She gave the handle a sharp tug. The door swung wide with a soft mechanical groan, and Nell took a step backward, using her phone as a flashlight to search the car's interior. "Do you normally leave your car unlocked?"

"Never in my life." He slapped a hand to his right front jeans pocket. The denim lay flat beneath his palm—flat and empty. "The brawl," he said, frowning.

"You lost your keys?"

"Or someone on the field was one hell of a pickpocket."

"I hope you've got a spare," she murmured, gripping the top of the frame with one hand while she bent forward and ducked her head into the Audi. Since Whit couldn't muster up the energy to inspect the car himself—and figured he may as well appreciate the view of her behind she was presenting—he stood back and watched. "It doesn't look like there's any damage to the interior."

"Fantastic." He'd lost his spare key over a month ago and hadn't gotten around to getting a replacement. Not that it mattered, since he doubted he'd be driving his car again at any point in the near future.

He'd probably just get a new one.

He shoved his hands into his pockets. "I guess we'll need a ride."

Nell straightened back up again, closing the door with a heavy thud as she turned to stare at him. The wind had been playing in her hair, whipping loose strands in front of her eyes, but even in the pale gleam from the school's security lights he could see the indignant look that spread across her face. "Someone turns your car into a Carrie Underwood song and all you can say is *we'll need a ride?*"

"What do you want me to say?" He nudged one of the deflated tires with the tip of his shoe. A hard, humorless laugh worked its way out of his throat. "I told you this place had it in for me."

"That doesn't make any sense. Someone just happened to notice you lost your keys during the game and also happened to know exactly where your car was parked? I don't buy it. And why not just steal it?"

"You have a better explanation?"

"I don't know. Maybe you have a stalker. *Someone* edited that video and sent it to *Meltdown.*"

"The only people with this much animosity toward me were born right here in this town, and I can guarantee you none of them were at Gills on Thursday." He couldn't, exactly—not with absolute certainty, anyway—but the idea that some bitter Fallen Oaks local had tracked him down at the bar, then waited around just in case he managed to make an ass of himself on camera, seemed a lot more outlandish to him than a simple crime of opportunity.

Nell hugged her arms. "Whit, you really need to call the police."

He doubted the city would even bother to send someone, but it must have been a slow night, because not only did the dispatcher assure him an officer would shortly be on the way, barely five minutes had passed before a patrol car pulled up and a man in the bright blue uniform of the Fallen Oaks Police Department stepped out. By then, Whit had texted Allie to inform her that he and Nell wouldn't be making it to the after party and had let his grandfather know they'd need a ride back to the farm as soon as they finished their report.

Whit realized his mistake when he saw the officer's face. It wouldn't have mattered if there had been a rash of burglaries down Main Street, a hostage situation at the rec center, or a triple homicide. This particular cop would have found the time regardless. Slow night or not, Sawyer Brewster had come here to gloat.

Hey, Flash, sweet play on that grounder, man.

You and me in the big leagues, buddy. All the way to the Show.

Whit tensed, feeling all the air leave his lungs. His stomach twisted. If the vandalism had been a shock to his system, Officer Brewster was like a nuclear bomb. His mind went blank and his blood went cold. None of his family had bothered to warn him. Had they known? His father had to have. His grandfather, too. Bucky and Sawyer had always been close. But not a word—not the two words that would have kept Whit from returning. *Sawyer's home.*

He wondered how long he'd been back. Last Whit had heard, Sawyer had been applying to law schools somewhere out east; he wasn't even supposed to be in Fallen Oaks, let alone walking around in a uniform he'd always claimed to despise. But here he was, the fourth generation of Brewster to wear the badge, looking as hard-edged and irritable as the father he'd worked so hard to escape.

Karma, Whit thought. He'd known even before he'd pulled out onto the highway and turned his car north that a reckoning was coming. More than a decade overdue, but better late than never.

He glanced at Nell. She'd moved to his side without a word, sliding her hand into his as she aimed a tentative smile at Sawyer. Playing her role as the sweet, supportive girlfriend—the exact reason Whit had convinced her to stay in Fallen Oaks in the first place. Now he wanted her a hundred miles away. A thousand. Somewhere she wouldn't be able to see just how close he was to crumpling.

Heard your daddy got you off with probation.

Even after all this time, the words stung in his ears.

I hope you burn in hell, O'Rourke.

A million years ago, give or take, Sawyer Brewster had been his best friend. They'd met the same day Whit's father had moved the family to Fallen Oaks, almost the same hour. Five years old, and right from the start, they'd been inseparable, kindred spirits and polar opposites: Whit quick to temper and quicker to laugh; Sawyer quiet, reserved, serious. The brother he'd never had. Along with James, they had been the undisputed kings of the Fallen Oaks High athletics department. The triple threat, their baseball coach had called them. Whit had the arm, James had the power—and Sawyer, he had the speed. Even as a freshman, no one had been faster around the bases. He'd set the school record for steals his first year and broken it each year that followed.

Except the last.

"What are you doing here, Sawyer?" Whit asked finally. Somehow he managed to keep his voice steady.

Sawyer tapped the badge on his chest. "My job." The hard edge was in his voice, too, beneath the derisive tone and the sneer that curled his lips. He made a slow circuit around the Audi, beaming his flashlight along the shattered glass and the slashed tires, letting it hang a long moment over the word carved into the trunk. The letters gleamed up, bright as a neon sign against the chrome. Sawyer let a slow whistle out through his teeth. "Looks like someone's got a grudge. Can't really fault their accuracy though, can you?"

"No."

"I'd ask who you've fucked over lately, but I imagine the list is pretty long. So why don't we start with what happened?"

Whit didn't answer. He was trying to remember the last time he'd seen Sawyer. A few days before leaving for Vanderbilt, probably—some late summer evening only a week or two shy of September. Right after Sawyer had finally been released from the hospital. Over a decade had passed since then, and the face that had once been as familiar to Whit as his own was alien now, a grown man where the boy had been, the wry humor that had lurked in his light blue eyes replaced with a cool cynicism. Instead of awkward and gangly, he was tall, lanky, tough. Under his cap, his wild tawny hair had been clipped short.

He looked good for a dead man, Whit thought. Healthy. Fit. There was no trace left of the gaunt stranger that had screamed at Whit to get the fuck out of his house.

Not that Sawyer had been dead for very long. Two minutes, maybe less, between the time Sawyer's heart had stopped and the time the ambulance had arrived on scene, Whit doing desperate chest compressions all the while, counting beats, distantly aware that he'd cracked Sawyer's ribs in the process. It hadn't mattered. It hadn't been Whit's frantic efforts that pulled his friend back from the darkness, but a paramedic with an AED.

A strained whisper came from beside him. "Whit, could you, um, let go a little?"

He looked down and realized he was nearly crushing Nell's hand with his grip. "Shit. Sorry." He let her hand drop, wiping his sweaty palm against the front of his jeans. *Let it roll off,* he thought, trying to imagine himself back at the ballpark, all bright lights and roaring crowds, turning his focus inward as he stepped onto the mound. When he was on the field, he'd always been able to locate that concentration, that calm. Whit O'Rourke didn't collapse under pressure; he let it all roll off.

He left his arms loose at his sides, forcing himself to relax. If he couldn't actually find that inner calm now, he could at least give the appearance of it. And he'd better do it fast, he thought, before Nell got it into her head that he needed defending. God only knew what would come out of her mouth this time.

Curling his lips into his cockiest smirk—the one he used right before striking out everyone from MVPs to daredevil rookies who thought they could challenge him—he turned back to Sawyer and did his best to sound bored. "Do you really want a statement, or are you just here to enjoy the spectacle?"

Sawyer rocked back on his heels and matched him smirk for smirk. "I can do both."

For the next few minutes, they kept up a pretense of civility. Sawyer took their statements—including Nell's theory of a stalker—and examined the car, the points of damage, the placement of the other vehicles in the lot and their distance from the school, scouting the view from various angles in case there might be surveillance footage. Robbery was quickly ruled out as a motive, since Whit had already done a search of the interior and the only things missing were an extra pair of sunglasses he'd left in the glove compartment and a tacky hood ornament that belonged to his ex. After Sawyer had finished up his notes and taken the baseball bat into evidence, he advised Whit not to hold his breath; unless that footage turned up anything, these sorts of crimes usually went unsolved. Easy enough to decipher that code. The report would be going to the very bottom of the endless pile of petty incidents and department cold cases, if they didn't simply close it with suspect unknown.

It wasn't until Sawyer had finished his report and turned to leave that the simmering undercurrent of hostility rose to the surface.

Half a step from his patrol car, Sawyer twisted around, leaning back against his vehicle with his arms folded and his ankles crossed. The smirk on his lips was almost a snarl now. Under the brim of his hat, his eyes had taken on that hard, brittle gleam. "Don't you just love the irony? Whitney O'Rourke. Vandalized. *Here*. Not really karma, though. You still ended up with everything you wanted, didn't you? Doesn't much matter how you got there."

Let it roll off. "Nope." He could feel Nell bristling and draped his arm over her shoulder, drawing her tightly against him to keep her still. He couldn't take her jumping to his defense again. Not now, not here.

Not when he damn well didn't deserve it.

Sawyer's lips curled. "Whatever it takes, right?"

"That's right."

"I suppose some things don't change... but then, all that money never could buy character." Straightening, Sawyer turned to yank open the door of his patrol car, then paused again. He rubbed his jaw with one hand. "I've gotta admit, I was surprised to see you here. Weren't you banned from the premises?"

"For a year."

"Really? That wasn't a lifelong thing?" Sawyer shook his head slowly from side to side. "Huh. I guess someone didn't want to piss off Daddy. Though it looks like not everyone's quite so forgiving."

"Any time you want to take a swing at me, Sawyer, you go right ahead. First one's free."

"Tempting, but then I'd have to book myself for assault, and who needs all that paperwork? Still, you might want to rethink sticking around town. It would be a real shame if anything worse happened." He touched the brim of his hat and nodded at Nell. "You have a good night now." With a soft whistle that Whit recognized as the tune to the Fallen Oaks High School song, Sawyer ducked into his patrol car and shut the door. A moment later he was gone. Whit stared after him, watching the glare of his taillights disappear down the road. Their passage seemed to leave an imprint on the air. Two angry red eyes, harsh and accusing. Only after they faded did he remember to exhale.

He let his arm go slack and glanced down at Nell, wondering what the hell he was going to say to her. He knew he should say *something*. Explain, or at least try to. Offer up some flimsy excuse for what had just happened. Or he should just tell her that she was off the hook. That he'd changed his mind about staying, about all of it, and come morning, he was going to rent a car—steal one, if he had to—that he was going to turn out onto the highway and floor it, putting this godforsaken town behind them. Fallen Oaks would vanish in a puff of exhaust fumes and Nell could be back on a plane a few hours later, and Whit... well, who had he been fooling, anyway? What had he hoped to accomplish, *here* of all places? His reputation had already been firmly cemented, and at the end of the day, none of it mattered. No one cared what the media called him as long as he could still throw a ball.

In the end he didn't have to say anything, because Nell gave him his third shock of the evening. Without words, without warning, she turned, wrapped her arms tightly around him, and pulled him into a hard, fierce hug.

Whit didn't move. He recognized the hug immediately for what it was—nothing sexual or suggestive, not any sort of invitation, but an act of such simple kindness that he wanted to lay his head on her shoulder and weep. His throat felt thick, his every nerve raw and exposed. Rather than give in to an instinct that would undoubtedly embarrass them both, he kept himself perfectly still, his spine ramrod straight and his arms plastered to his sides. He didn't try to speak. He just stood there and let himself be hugged, breathing in the summer-sweet fragrance of her shampoo and that intoxicating, indefinable scent of warm skin, the heat of her body melting into his as he listened to the solid, steady rhythm of her heart.

It ended too soon. Only a few seconds had passed before her arms unlocked and she released her hold, taking a step backward and tugging at the wrinkled fabric of her sweater that had become bunched between them. She set a hand on her hip and tilted her head in the direction Sawyer had gone. One corner of her mouth tipped slowly upward. "Okay. You definitely slept with *his* girlfriend, right?"

A startled laugh choked out of him. "What if I told you I did?"

"I wouldn't believe you." She made her way to the back of his Audi, brushed away the glass that had been scattered over the trunk, then lifted herself up and perched there with her legs dangling against the dented bumper and her gaze fixed on Whit. Her eyes were dark pools in the moonlight. "You think he did it?"

"This? No. This would be too underhanded for him. And too crude. I did sort of expect him to arrest me just for the hell of it, though."

"Would you really have let him hit you?"

"I knew he wouldn't."

"But you *would* have let him." She shifted, propping herself up with her elbows on her knees, and peered at him curiously. "Why? I mean... I know the answer is none of my business, but *why?* You weren't even trying to defend yourself."

The words were out before he could stop them. "I'd think you of all people would know I'm not worth defending."

Nell's lips parted. Her eyebrows dipped together. There was that pitying look again, the one that was so much harder to take than simple disdain. He turned away.

"You don't have to tell me," she said softly.

The strange thing was, he wanted to.

He didn't know why. Didn't even want to examine that why. It defied all sense and logic, but there it was, this compulsion to lay it all bare, to erase that pity from her eyes and let her see just how bad he really was.

Without thinking, he found himself moving up beside her. She said his name and he barely heard it. His blood was pounding in his ears. She was the last person he should ever want to confide in, but Whit was no longer operating on reason. He knew he should change the subject, or come up with some half-assed lie, or even tell her, rightly, that it was none of her business. He *knew* he should. But he didn't.

Instead he leaned back against the trunk of the car, drew in a ragged breath, and prepared to tell her how he'd betrayed the best friend he'd ever had.

Fifteen

"We used to be friends," Whit began. Funny how his voice sounded so calm, so steady. He let his hands rest against the bumper, laying his palms flat against the cool metal. "Sawyer was actually the first friend I made when my family moved here. His aunt worked as a nanny for the people next door, and she babysat him during the week, so most of the time we got tossed together to entertain each other. Worked out well for me, because I'd have been bored out of my mind otherwise. I had two little sisters, and when you're five years old, that seems like the worst possible fate, believe me." Being an only child, Sawyer hadn't understood the curse of baby sisters, but he'd been more than happy to help Whit escape whenever Allie came toddling after them. And eventually running after them. "So we became friends, and it stuck. Sawyer was kind of the fourth O'Rourke kid growing up—his home life was shitty, so he basically lived at my house when we were in town. Back then, he was as good at baseball as I was. Better, when it came to speed. Get him on first base, and he'd be on third before you could blink. He couldn't pitch worth a damn, but man, he was an incredible hitter. We had this plan to go to college together, get drafted. The whole thing."

"You must have been really close."

"Yeah, well, things change." He flicked a glance toward Nell. She sat huddled in her sweater, hugging her elbows, her feet propped on the edge of the bumper and her hands tucked under her armpits, shoulders hunched. The wind had picked up and the temperature had dropped quickly—something he should have realized earlier, instead of just sitting there and letting her shiver. He straightened. "You're cold. We should wait in the car until my grandpa gets here." Which reminded him he still needed to text Bucky to come pick them up, if he didn't want to end up walking several miles of country roads in the dark.

Nell shook her head. "I'm fine. It's fine."

"Give me a sec." He slipped around the side of the car and opened the rear driver's door, crawling halfway inside to yank down the back-seat and access the trunk. After a bit of blind fishing, his fingers caught one of the fleece blankets he kept for emergencies. Snagging it, he returned to Nell and draped it loosely over her shoulders. "Better?"

She wriggled around a bit, drawing the edges of the blanket together to make a snug cloth cocoon around herself. "Thanks," she said, eyeing his thin T-shirt. "How are you not freezing?"

Whit shrugged. "You get used to it."

"I hope that's not your way of calling me a wuss."

"Nah. Minnesotans pride ourselves on being immune to the cold. Except Allie. It drops below forty degrees and she bundles up like she's taking a trip to the North Pole."

Nell reached to tuck away the stray locks of hair the wind had tangled in front of her face. The Blizzards cap she'd been wearing during the game hadn't made it with them to the emergency room, and he could see the faint bruise near her hairline where she'd knocked her head against him. While that debacle had been entirely her own fault—and he definitely wasn't going to let her forget it, at least not as long as he had a bandage stuck to his ass—he couldn't help feeling a little guilty. "How's the head?"

"Nothing a little Tylenol and a lot of coffee won't fix." She tugged the blanket tighter as she looked at him. "Do you want to tell me the rest?"

Did he?

He jammed his hands into his pockets. "Yeah."

Odd as it was, it felt good to talk about it. He *hadn't* talked about it, not in years. He couldn't talk about it with his family. Too much baggage there. Definitely not with any of his current or former teammates, either. He was close with some of the guys he played with—he'd even been in a few of their weddings—but not *bare your soul and dig up past trauma* close. One of his girlfriends? Forget it. His chosen romantic partners didn't have any particular interest in him as a person; that was the whole reason he chose them. The ironic thing was, the one person he *could* have talked about it with was Sawyer. A lifetime ago, when they'd still been friends.

Whit closed his eyes and leaned back against the car, drawing a deep breath into his chest, savoring the sting of the frosty air as it met his lungs. This was the hard part, what came next. "You know that feeling you have when you're seventeen? Of being invincible?"

"Not really."

"Well, I had it," he said grimly. He felt all the old bitterness rise up, the specter of his former self: cocky, arrogant, angry, reckless. The boy he'd tried so hard to put behind him. "I thought I was invincible. My whole life revolved around sports, and by the time I was in high school, I knew I had a destiny. Having a famous dad helped, but I was good—I was *really* good—and not just at baseball. All of us were, Sawyer and James and me. Multi-sport athletes, gods of the field and the rink. James was more practical about it; he wanted to go to college, and sports were his ticket out of here. But Sawyer and I had big league dreams. Until..."

Until.

There it was. The one word that changed everything.

He tipped his head back, gazing up at the maze of constellations that mapped the sky overhead. He'd forgotten just how bright the stars were out here, away from the constant, crowded blur of city lights. "I told you how I transferred schools."

"I figured you didn't want to talk about it."

"Yeah, well, this is why," he said. "It was right at the start of my senior year—barely two weeks into September. Something happened, and... well, it doesn't matter, but the result was that I got kicked off the football team. That pissed me off, but I would've accepted it. Understood it, even. I didn't really care about football, and I knew they were going to punish me somehow. Then, a week later, they decided to extend it to every team. Baseball, basketball, hockey... you name it. I was completely banned from sports. They probably wouldn't have let me play ping-pong. It didn't matter much for college—I'd been in touch with coaches and had already decided on Vanderbilt. But I wanted to play. Since they wouldn't let me play here, I changed schools. Just showed up at my grandpa's house and told him I was moving in."

And Bucky, being Bucky, had let him.

His grandpa had been his rock back then, and he'd needed one desperately. He'd been unmoored, untethered, lashing out at everyone. Moving to the farm had been his best choice—almost his only choice—and even now he couldn't view that part as a mistake.

"My friends saw it as a betrayal. It probably was, but I didn't care. I was angry at the world, in full-on teenage rebel mode, convinced that the injustices I'd suffered meant I could do whatever I wanted. I was never what you'd call a model student, but after I got kicked out of sports, I started skipping classes, ignoring homework, getting detention, skipping that. That didn't change much when I switched to Dower Hill. Absolutely killed it on the field, though. They let me get away with it because the athletic department needed me. Your basic asshole jock." He slanted a look toward her. "And let me spare you a bit of commentary by saying—whatever you think of me now, I was a thousand times worse."

"I wasn't going to say anything." She sounded miffed.

A smile hovered at the corners of his lips, then vanished. "Maybe things would've settled down eventually. Sawyer and I weren't speaking by that time, but we'd had arguments before and they never lasted. The bigger problem was James. He took over as quarterback of the football team after I left, and he'd convinced the cheerleaders to chant my name and spell out the word *traitor* the night we played each other. The schools were huge rivals at the time, and that didn't help matters. Especially after we curb-stomped them." He drew in another of those slow, steadying breaths. "I found out later it could've been a lot worse. Our cheerleaders had been planning to retaliate by outing James as gay."

"God, that's…"

"Shitty?"

"I was thinking more along the lines of *unspeakably cruel.*" A wry note crept into her voice. "I guess you really didn't sleep with his girlfriend."

"For the record, I've never slept with anyone's girlfriend but my own." As far as he knew. There had been a couple of questionable college hookups, but he wasn't about to admit that when he was already in the middle of telling her the worst thing he'd ever done. "James is open about his sexuality now, but he wasn't back then. Only a few of us knew, and we kept it quiet. Small towns aren't known for being welcoming to gay high school quarterbacks."

"Poor kid."

"Yeah. Thankfully, one of the cheerleaders told the coach what the rest of the squad was up to, and they put a stop to it. But it still sparked some rumors, and James and Sawyer blamed me for it."

"You didn't try to explain things to them?"

"I was an angry seventeen-year-old. I figured they should know me better than that." He felt his fingernails biting into his palms and forced his hands to loosen. "And then, well… then I really did betray them."

"Them? Or James?"

"I didn't out him, if that's what you're asking. I wasn't *that* much of a douchebag," Whit retorted. "A couple of weeks after I transferred, some of the guys at Dower Hill decided I needed to prove my loyalty. I'd messed up during a game and I guess they thought I blew it on purpose. So one night, we drove out here, drew a giant dick on the football field with diesel fuel, and then broke into the school to trash the locker rooms. Typical rival stuff."

Nell held up a hand, letting the blanket slip off her shoulders. "Sorry, I'm still at *drew a giant dick on the football field.*"

He grinned. "Well, we weren't gonna draw a small one."

"I'm so, so glad I don't teach high school."

It was probably a good thing she didn't, Whit mused, letting his eyes graze her body as she adjusted the blanket. He doubted they'd let her walk around in those tight jeans, but he could just picture her flitting about the classroom in a pencil skirt with a short-sleeved button-down open at the collar, like a naughty librarian. She'd have all the horny teenage boys salivating over her.

Not to mention horny formerly-teenage boys, if he wasn't careful.

Whit cleared his throat. "Things got out of hand when a couple of the guys suggested we make a bonfire of the athletic equipment." He hunched his shoulders, letting his body sink lower against the car. "We hauled everything out into the parking lot and piled it up. That's when I found out just what their *test* was. They wanted me to do it. They all got back in their cars and said they'd see me at practice the next day. Then they left me there with the pile of equipment, the rest of the diesel, and a match."

"Did you do it?"

He closed his eyes. "Yep."

"Oh, Whit."

"That wasn't even the worst part. Sawyer and James had somehow gotten wind of what we were up to. My best guess is one of the guys at Dower Hill tipped them off. Maybe it was some sort of hazing for me, I don't know—however it happened, they showed up in the parking lot barely thirty seconds after I'd lit the bonfire. God knows why I hadn't just left, but there I was, watching everything go up in flames, guilty as hell." Sometimes he thought he could still *smell* it—that faint, acrid scent, burning away the past. Deep down, some part of him had even enjoyed it. The melting plastic... the flecks of ash. The heat. He'd felt like he was purging something.

Instead he'd been destroying it.

"I was too much of a coward to face them," he continued, voice thick. "The second I saw them, I took off—just dove into my car, turned the ignition, and floored it. Didn't even look back. I was half a mile from the school before I realized they were following me. There had been freezing rain earlier that evening and the roads were slick, but I didn't care. I just kept pushing the car faster and faster, trying to outrun them. It was the stupidest thing I could have possibly done, but I got lucky. Sawyer and James didn't. They took a curve too fast and hit a patch of ice. The car flipped, went skidding across the road, and hit a tree. James was wearing his seat belt and ended up with a broken arm and that slice across his face. Sawyer went through the windshield."

"Oh, god," Nell breathed.

"I stopped when I heard the crash, ran back as fast as I could. James was still in the car. He was unconscious, but he was breathing. But Sawyer..." It was an image Whit would never forget as long as he lived: his friend lying motionless in a cushion of dried grass and old leaves. The only time in his life that Whit had ever prayed. "I called an ambulance and tried to perform CPR, but it didn't do much good. The fire at the school had already been called in, and we weren't far from the fire station, or Sawyer probably would've died. As it was, he spent a month in a coma and the better part of a year in the hospital. The doctors thought he'd be paralyzed. Sawyer proved them wrong. He eventually made a full recovery. But he never played baseball again."

Or any other sport, for that matter. And the boy who had once been greased lightning on the basepaths had become a harsh, embittered man and ended up right back where he started, while Whit had achieved every goal he'd ever set out to.

Yeah, he had some karma coming to him, all right.

"So, there you have it," Whit said with a small, helpless shrug. "I didn't sleep with his girlfriend. I just ruined his life."

Nell's voice was soft. "It sounds to me like you saved it."

"The paramedics did that."

"You can't blame yourself for an accident, Whit."

He pushed himself up from the car, kicking at the red plastic splinters that lay scattered below the bumper. "I didn't tell you this so you could absolve me. I know exactly what I did, and so does everyone else in this town." Being the son of a living legend went a long way, but when Whit had tossed that match, he'd gone from being the pride of the city to its greatest disappointment, and he'd taken James and Sawyer down with him. Three rising stars extinguished in a single act. James had only suffered minor injuries in the crash, but he'd quit playing sports altogether; instead of heading out east to some big name university, he'd gone to a community college in Bemidji. Whit had put Fallen Oaks in his rearview and hadn't looked back.

"Why were you kicked off the team in the first place?" Nell asked.

"Drunk driving," he bit off.

"Really? I'm surprised they didn't just sweep it under the rug. I thought even high school athletes pretty much got away with murder."

"The principal had it in for me."

She was quiet a moment. "Were you actually driving drunk?"

"I was booked for it, until my dad got them to throw out the charge."

"You took the fall for someone else."

He couldn't look at her. The last thing he wanted was more of her pity, and if he told her the rest of it, that was exactly what he would get. "I'm afraid that's all the confession I've got in me for tonight. You wanted to know why the town hates me, that's the story. Vandalism, drunk driving, betrayal... take your pick. All those guys I went to school with were just waiting for me to fail. Which, of course, I did." He shrugged again. "But I guess that's why they say karma's a bitch."

A thin laugh skidded out of her. "I think you mean I am."

Whit shot her a sharp glance. "I never said that."

"I *am* sorry," she murmured, and now she was the one who wouldn't look at him. She sat fidgeting with the edges of the blanket. "Really. I never meant to sabotage your career. I hope you can believe that."

Whit's sigh was bone-weary. "You didn't sabotage my career. I did."

But Nell wasn't finished. "You were right before," she told him. "When you said I was trying to rescue Paige. You were right. I was pissed off by something you'd said about her, and I let anger cloud my judgment. That's why I did it. And I truly am sorry."

His eyebrows drew together. "What did I say about Paige?"

"You implied she was cheating on you."

"No, I didn't."

"You said the two of you had a difference of opinion on what the word *exclusive* meant."

Shit. "That could've been either one of us," he hedged.

"That's not how the press took it."

Whit hesitated. He remembered the comment now. Most sports reporters didn't care about athletes' personal lives—even when those personal lives involved swimsuit models and high-profile cosmetic company heiresses. It had been his bad luck to make a thoughtless remark in front of one who did.

The incident with Paige hadn't even been a big deal, just a bit of flirting with a visiting team's athletic trainer that had gotten out of hand. Yeah, she'd made out with the guy, but her relationship with Whit had already run its course anyway. If he hadn't been in such a dark place at the time, it probably wouldn't have mattered to him.

But there was no way Whit was going to say anything remotely negative about Nell's beloved big sis. He'd learned that lesson already. "I think this is a discussion you need to have with your sister," he said. Then he frowned. "I didn't make that comment until after Paige and I had broken up. You hated me before then."

A guarded look came into her eyes. "I didn't hate you."

"Every time you saw me, you looked like you wanted to set me on fire."

"You went out of your way to argue with me!"

"Okay, but in my defense, that was purely for entertainment value. And I didn't start that until *after* you'd made it clear you thought Paige was slumming it."

She suddenly became very interested in studying the blanket's stitching. "You don't have the best track record with women. I was just being overprotective. I can't help it."

"I don't have a bad track record with women."

"What was your longest relationship?"

"What was yours?" he countered.

"We're not talking about me."

"Which means short. That's a little hypocritical of you, Miss McLean."

"You asked why I didn't like you; that's what I'm telling you. I was worried—"

"So you admit you didn't like me."

He swore he could hear her teeth grinding. "—I was worried that you would break Paige's heart."

"We dated for like two months!" A good chunk of which he'd spent on the road, since it had been during the season.

Though he'd also had a bit of unexpected free time after being slapped with an eight-game suspension when his elbow had accidentally caught an ump during a bench clearing.

Still. His relationship with Paige had been brief and, truth be told, kind of boring—if you didn't count how it ended. No hearts involved. That was the entire point.

"It wasn't two months, it was two and a half," Nell said.

"It was—"

"The end of April to the middle of July. That's two and a half."

Whit's gaze narrowed. "You have an awfully good memory about a relationship you weren't even in."

Nell opened her mouth. Shut it again.

He was going to just let it slide. He'd gotten what he wanted from her—a reason for her bristling animosity and snotty behavior, even if it was (in his opinion) a ridiculous reason. Four years had passed, and they were both a bit older, hopefully a bit wiser, and definitely on much better terms. There was no point in needling her about something that ultimately wasn't important. He *should* just let it slide.

Except that she wouldn't meet his eyes.

Except that she was blushing.

It could have been the wind. All that crisp air brushing against her, leaving a bright, rosy flush on her skin. But he didn't think so. That wasn't the chilly November temperature putting a bloom in her cheeks. Oh, no.

That was guilt.

The light bulb went off. The lightning bolt struck. And Whit knew *exactly* why Nell had dedicated so much time to convincing herself—and him—that she disliked him.

"Holy shit," he breathed. "I've figured it out."

"Figured what out?" She looked nervous. Her tongue poked out, wetting her lips. Was that intentional? His gaze zeroed in on that little dip in her mouth. Intentional or not, it was definitely enticing.

"*Damn,*" he said softly, a rumble of laughter forming deep in his chest. He couldn't believe he hadn't seen it before. All that barely concealed hostility... all those irritable looks. The prickly attitude, the insults—the favored defense mechanism of love-struck boys and girls in playgrounds the world over. What better way to hide interest? "You had a crush on me."

She bolted upright, her hands slapping down against the trunk and the blanket sliding off her shoulders. That flush crept even higher up her cheeks. "You're delusional."

There was no way he was going to let her wiggle out of this. He put a little smoke in his voice and gave her his silkiest grin. "You know, I didn't mention this before because I figured you'd just go ballistic, but you're kinda sexy when you're mad."

Her nostrils flared. "I did *not* have a crush on you."

"What would you prefer to call it? An overwhelming desire to bump pelvises?"

"Your ego is absolutely out of control."

"Just like your attraction to me."

The look she gave him could have frozen a supernova. "All right, this deal is off. I don't care if it's breaking my word, I am out of here as soon as I can figure out how to hotwire a car."

Time to switch tactics, he decided. Teasing her might be fun—okay, *incredibly* fun—but there were so many more satisfying ways to torment someone. Several of them popped into his head as he let his gaze roam over her in a long, lazy perusal. "I never said the attraction was one-sided. I'm not trying to upset you. I just think it's time we admit that there's something going on between us, and it's only gonna be worked out in one way."

"I have no idea what you're talking about."

The smart move would be to back off. He knew that. If he hadn't still felt so raw, so totally off-balance, maybe he would have. But his nerves had been stretched taut, his emotions had gone through a blender, and his self-control was barely hanging on. He didn't even care if he was rushing headlong into another mistake. He had a lifetime of bad decisions behind him, and he wasn't about to stop now, not when she was close enough that he could smell that warm, heady fragrance that clung to her hair and skin. His mind shut off and instinct took over. Instinct wanted to taste the forbidden fruit. He inched even closer. "Like it or not, we've got chemistry."

He saw her gulp. "We've also got history. You know, the history where you dated my sister, and also you don't like me?"

She was grasping at straws. Whit crooked an eyebrow. "I like you just fine. And this isn't about feelings. This is about lust. Pure, old-fashioned lust."

"Lust is a feeling. One that, for the record? I am *not* feeling."

"You're a terrible liar, Nellie."

"Sorry to disappoint you, but you're not nearly as irresistible as you think you are."

"Do you need a demonstration?" he asked.

"I think you need your head examined."

"There's one way to find out."

Without waiting for an answer, he dropped his hands to her hips and tugged her forward, pulling her straight off the car, holding her hard against him.

He felt her breath hitch. Her eyes went huge.

But she didn't attempt to break free.

He lifted a hand, trailing his fingertips along her jaw, his thumb coming to rest on her chin. With gentle pressure he drew his thumb downward, parting her lips. "You really gonna say I can't kiss you?" he asked huskily.

She didn't answer.

"Yeah. That's what I thought," he said, and covered her mouth with his.

SIXTEEN

Nell knew it was a mistake.

No, worse than that—so much worse. It was the most calamitous, catastrophic, self-destructive mistake she could possibly make. This was crazy. *She* was crazy. She couldn't let Whit O'Rourke kiss her!

But oh, god, she wanted him to. Wanted it so badly she could scarcely think.

Quickly, she tried to rationalize it. Maybe it would be a bad kiss. Or even just mediocre. She'd spent so much time building it up in her head—what it would be like to kiss him, what it would *feel* like—that reality couldn't possibly compare. All that smolder of his would fizzle out the second their lips touched. And what infatuation could survive such a massive disappointment? One kiss, and she'd be cured.

Anyway, she had a head injury. She wasn't accountable for her actions. He was taking advantage of her vulnerable state with all that talk of pelvises and chemistry. Completely unethical of him.

Even she couldn't quite believe that one.

The truth was, she had no one to blame but herself. She *knew* it was a mistake.

And she did it anyway.

When Whit bent to kiss her, she didn't even try to resist. She was right there, meeting him, her mouth just as hungry as his, her traitorous hips pushing against him while her hands crept up his shoulders to curl around his neck, keeping him pinned. Cool fingertips met hot skin. The very air between them sizzled. And she knew instantly that she had been wrong, so wrong. There was nothing mediocre about this kiss.

It was the sort of kiss that wasn't just mouths or lips. The moment they made contact, Nell felt it everywhere. Every inch of her skin tingled with it, every nerve ending a live wire, fully charged, ready to spark. How something that started so soft could be so seductive, she didn't know, but from the first brush of his lips against hers, she felt herself melting. She clutched at him desperately, the only solid object in a world that had suddenly tilted.

Embarrassing, really, how easy she was.

Somehow, she had the presence of mind to pull back. She forced her arms to loosen, her hands to stop molding themselves against him. "You win, O'Rourke." She tried to sound casual. It came out raspy. "You were right. We just needed to get that out of our systems."

His thumb was tracing a path along her jaw, feather-light, making her shiver. "I win, huh? What do I win?"

"Gratification."

He grinned. Wide. Wicked.

"That's not how I meant it," she said quickly.

"Gratification is good," he whispered. His gaze was on her lips again. "But I want your confession."

He hadn't stepped away, and his nearness was making her dizzy. She tried to inch backward, but she had nowhere to go. The cool metal of the bumper was pressing against her legs. "I already said you were right," she told him.

"Right about what, exactly?"

She felt a flash of temper and clung to it like a lifeline. Of course he had to gloat. "Chemistry."

"You mean lust."

There was no way she was going to make that admission, even though it had to be obvious, given that she was still sort of panting. But he probably couldn't tell how much she was sweating under her shirt. Or that her pulse seemed to be located entirely in the upper portion of her lower extremities. "Let's call it curiosity. *Mild* curiosity. Now thankfully appeased."

God, she was a liar.

A dangerous glint came into his eyes. "I don't know," he said, in that husky tone she felt all the way to her bones. "I don't think all that lust is out of my system yet."

His mouth came down on hers again. And this time, he took no prisoners.

If the first kiss had been seductive, this one was demanding. He shoved a hand into her hair, pulling it loose from the ponytail so that it came tumbling down onto her shoulders while he cupped the back of her head, tilting her face up to meet his. She had a brief, foolish impulse to resist, to prove to him that she *could* resist, and clamped her lips shut, keeping her body entirely motionless. But Whit only laughed, a low, sensual sound that she felt rather than heard, and then his tongue was there, grazing against the seam of her mouth, coaxing, massaging. Nell gasped. Her hands somehow found their way to his hips and worked their way upward. All thought of resistance vanished. All thought vanished, period.

She gave in. Completely.

Mistake number two, but who was counting?

The terrible thing was, it didn't feel like a mistake. It felt like an epiphany.

And like agony.

Whit was thorough in his torment. His mouth urged hers open, gentle, insistent, taking his time with her, tugging, tempting. He tasted like salt and bubblegum, sharp and sweet, and he explored her with infinite patience, using his lips, his tongue, his teeth. Nell, less patient, deepened the kiss, plowing a hand into his hair and turning his head, dragging his mouth back to hers whenever he paused to draw breath. Who needed air? If they stopped for even a second, she might start to think again. She might remember all the reasons she shouldn't be doing this, shouldn't be reveling in the feel of him, all that thick hair curling beneath her fingertips, the delicious friction of their jeans.

She wouldn't release his mouth, but his hands were free to roam. His fingers left hot trails everywhere they touched: the delicate skin of her throat, where his thumb traced light circles as he burned a path toward her collarbone, shoving at the edges of her sweater to push it off her shoulders, then sliding down the curve of her back and settling there.

He made a noise low in his throat. Something possessive, primal. Distantly, the thought intruded that maybe he hadn't planned to take it this far. Maybe his only aim had been to teach her a lesson, to show her how irresistible he really was. Just a quick, hot kiss to make her melt and leave her gasping. She was gasping, all right... but so was he. The rapid thud of his heart shot a thrill straight to her core.

He murmured her name. She willed him not to speak. She wasn't done with him yet, not even close. All that time she'd spent denying what she wanted, who she wanted, had left her starving, and now she intended to have her fill. She was playing with fire and she didn't care. She wanted to be burned.

Tonight there was no reality. No before, and definitely no after. Right now he was hers. If this was the only chance she ever got, then she wanted it all: the warmth of his mouth, the feel of his skin, the solid pressure of his body... even that faint prickle as his stubble scraped along her face. Her heart bucked against her ribcage as his hands skimmed further down her spine and curved around her ass, lifting her against him. Heat coiled in her belly. There was no mistaking the hard ridge in his jeans. When he caught her lower lip with his teeth, teasing it gently, she actually moaned.

A kiss shouldn't be like this, she thought hazily. Not so erotic, not so quickly. But this was so much more than a kiss.

This was surrender.

She had been waiting for this forever. Fighting it forever. Wanting it forever. An eternity of aching.

"We should slow down," Whit rasped, even as he shoved her back against the car again and his hands slipped under her blouse. The shock of his fingertips along the bare skin beneath should have sent her crashing back down to earth. Instead it set her on fire. His mouth dipped to her neck and when he unhooked her bra, his palms sliding up to cup her breasts, she felt herself arch toward him. He breathed hot words against her skin. "We need to slow down."

"No." Her response came out half protest, half plea. If they stopped, they could never start again—ever. Didn't he understand this was only a lapse? Unrepeatable. Temporary. "Don't you dare stop."

That chuckle again. "That sounds a lot like lust, Miss McLean."

She didn't care what it sounded like. She wasn't the only one lusting. Slowly, deliberately, she lifted her right leg, easing it up, up along his calf, his thigh, curling it halfway around his waist to pull him even closer.

"Jesus," Whit gasped. And then he went back to kissing.

Reason probably would have returned, eventually. There were only so many mistakes Nell could make in one night, and she was fast approaching her limit. The fog of hormones clouding her brain would have lifted, common sense would have come screaming back, her judgment would have reasserted itself, and Nell somehow—*somehow*—would have managed to put on the brakes. Probably. But in the end, she never actually made it that far, because the universe chose to do it for her.

Noise buzzed in her ears. Dimly she became aware of a sound that wasn't just the ragged churn of her breath or the wild kick of her heart. It tickled at the edge of her thoughts, a faint hum that became a deep mechanical rumble, low and gravelly and oddly familiar, sort of like... an automobile engine.

An engine that was rapidly getting closer.

Her eyes flew open. That dizzy spill of light in the distance wasn't just Nell seeing stars.

It was headlights.

Pure panic rushed through her. "Oh my god."

"Yeah. No kidding." Whit's voice was a gruff whisper as his stubble grazed her neck.

Nell's own voice came out thin and wheezing. "You have to stop now."

His only answer was a growl.

He had her pinned to the car, his hands under her shirt, his mouth still leaving hot trails along her collarbone. She did the only thing she could think of to stop him. She dropped a hand to the stab wound in his ass and squeezed.

Instantly, he released her. "What the fuck?"

"Someone's coming!"

"You could have just said that," he grumbled, rubbing at the sore spot while he glared at her.

"Oh my god," Nell groaned again. Her mind was shrieking *caught in the act! caught in the act!* like she'd just been discovered robbing a bank while burning down a house and burying a couple of bodies. Frantically, she yanked up the fallen fleece blanket, cocooning herself inside it like it would somehow hide her from view. Her bra was still unhooked, her lips were swollen, her hair a mess. She rounded on Whit. "What were you thinking?"

"*Me?*"

"We're in a high school parking lot! There are probably cameras all over this place. This time we'll probably end up on *TMZ*!"

"For making out? Hardly." His gaze skimmed past her to study the approaching vehicle, which Nell quickly recognized as the powder blue pickup that belonged to his grandfather. Whit lifted his hand in a short wave before turning back to Nell. "It's just Grandpa. It's dark and his night vision is crap. I doubt he saw anything."

A hope that was swiftly dispelled when Bucky pulled up alongside them, rolled down the passenger window, and said genially, "Figured I should interrupt before the two of you did something to get yourselves arrested."

Nell wanted to melt into the pavement. She thought she'd be perfectly happy if a giant meteor came hurtling out of the sky and smashed her to cinders.

Whit just looked irritated. "You couldn't have done a few laps around the lot?" he asked his grandfather.

Bucky's voice crackled with amusement. "Who says I didn't?"

Nell was reasonably certain Bucky was joking, but that did nothing to lessen her mortification. A giant meteor would not be nearly quick enough. Her only prayer was spontaneous human combustion.

Whit was apparently impervious to embarrassment—and not all that concerned about Bucky's supposedly terrible night vision—because he tugged open the truck's passenger door and started maneuvering Nell inside. The truck didn't have a backseat, which meant she was going to have to spend the ride wedged between Whit and his grandfather. Lucky her.

This was her just desserts, she thought glumly, keeping her gaze aimed firmly downward as she climbed into the seat next to Bucky. Her punishment for giving in to her baser desires and letting her libido override her better judgment. As she sometimes had to remind her students, actions had consequences, and this was hers.

She'd have preferred the meteor.

"What are you even doing here?" Whit asked, sounding a lot more grumpy than grateful. He slid into the truck beside her, his arm brushing her shoulder and his thigh right up next to hers. Even through the thick blanket and two layers of denim, she could feel the heat of his body—a body she'd been doing her best to plaster herself to less than a minute ago. And since any attempt to move away would end up with her sitting in Bucky's lap, she was basically trapped.

Bucky shrugged. "It was getting late. I thought if I showed up, it might hurry things along."

"I was going to text you when we were done."

"Uh-huh," said Bucky. "Done with what, exactly?"

Nell slunk as low in the seat as she could.

Whit aimed a stern look at his grandfather. "Knock it off. You're making Nell uncomfortable."

She didn't want to tell him that *he* was making her a lot more uncomfortable through his sheer proximity, so she kept her mouth shut.

"I'm way too old for tact," Bucky answered, unabashed. He tossed a glance back at the mangled Audi as he steered his pickup toward the exit. "You're leaving your car here?"

"Sawyer said the tow company will pick it up in the morning." Whit's tone was casual, but Nell didn't miss the slight hitch to it, or the way his shoulders immediately tensed. "Thanks for letting me know he was in town."

"Hey, Whitney! Sawyer's back in town!" Bucky called, earning himself another glare from his grandson. "You hear his dad kicked it a year ago?"

"Yeah. So what the hell made him come back?"

"You'd have to ask him."

Whit just muttered something that sounded like, "I'll get right on that."

By the time they made it out of town and reached the long dirt driveway that led to Bucky's farmhouse, Nell realized there was something worse than an unbearably awkward drive sandwiched between a cranky jock and an octogenarian with questionable eyesight—and that was the conversation waiting for her at the end of it. There was zero chance Whit was going to agree to pretend the past half hour or so had never happened. The second they were alone again, he would corner her, and Nell was in no way prepared for the reckoning she had in store. For her part, she intended to develop a sudden fascination with jigsaw puzzles and spend the rest of the night helping Bucky assemble them. Maybe not the most inspired plan, but she was desperate.

In hindsight, it probably would have gone a lot better if Bucky hadn't straight up thrown her to the wolves. They'd barely started work on a thousand-piece painting of sailboats when he stood up yawning and declared his need for beauty sleep. Whit, the wolf in question, had been biding his time by playing with one of the cats and throwing the occasional comment their way—but as soon as his grandfather disappeared down the hall, he turned to Nell with the sort of focused intent that would have made her squirm even if she hadn't just spent the better part of twenty minutes playing tongue hockey with him.

Nell shot to her feet. "I'm tired, I'm crabby, I'm concussed, and I need a shower," she told him in the best no-nonsense teacher voice she could muster. "So don't even think about following me. I'll see you in the morning, O'Rourke." Then she rocketed toward the door.

Okay, so she was a coward.

She could live with that.

***

Escaping into the shower got her away from Whit. Unfortunately, it left her alone with herself.

And herself was someone she really didn't want to deal with.

Nell grimaced. The steady, soothing pulse of the water might have cleared her head and calmed her nerves, but it did nothing for her guilty conscience. And she *was* guilty, there was no denying that. It was time for her to face some ugly truths—the ugliest of which was that she'd known exactly what she was doing in that parking lot. And she had known exactly what it meant. All it had taken from Whit was a sexy grin and a couple of bone-melting kisses, and she'd tossed away all of her carefully constructed disinterest. She'd basically hurled herself at him.

The worst part was, their make-out session had done nothing to get Whit out of her system. So much for her cure-with-a-kiss plan. He had completely invaded her senses. She swore she could still smell him—his warm skin, that tang of sweat. Just the thought of his hands sliding down her body made her hot all over again. Instead of being properly ashamed of herself, she was more than half hoping he'd ignore her command not to follow her. A soft knock... a heated look... in the cramped space and thick steam there would be no time for words, just the anonymous rhythm of flesh, two strangers responding to mutual need.

Except that he wasn't a stranger. That was the whole point. She didn't want some faceless, forgettable hookup. She wanted him. Just like she'd wanted him four years ago—only more, because now there was something real between them. Maybe not something she could define or label, but *something*. A connection. As foolish as it was, she didn't want to lose that.

The look on his face when he'd told her he wasn't worth defending… she'd wanted so badly to comfort him in that moment, to just pull him into her arms again and keep him there. He'd let her see that raw and vulnerable part of himself, and her own defenses had come crashing down.

One thing was certain: she needed to limit the amount of time she and Whit spent in private. Despite her earlier threat, she had no intention of leaving. Nell had given him her word, he'd held up his end of the deal, and she owed him. And recent evidence to the contrary, it wasn't as though they were a couple of horny teenagers who couldn't keep their hands to themselves. Any sort of physical relationship between the two of them would only complicate an already complicated situation. Even Whit would be able to see that.

Steeling herself with that knowledge, she toweled herself dry, pulled on her pajamas, and slipped back out into the hall, tiptoeing past the wedge of lamplight that spilled out from the living room.

She pushed open the door to the guest room and found her reckoning waiting for her.

He was—predictably—lounging on the bed, idly tossing a baseball back and forth between his hands. That long, athletic body looked ridiculously large on the narrow mattress, even with his ankles crossed and his back tucked up against the headboard. He'd changed his T-shirt and swapped his jeans for a pair of baggy sweatpants, but he still looked just as gorgeous, if a little grumpy. He hadn't bothered to drag a comb through his rumpled hair—though Nell supposed she couldn't criticize, seeing as she was the one who had rumpled it.

"Took you long enough," he said. "I thought I was gonna have to break in there and perform mouth-to-mouth."

Nell shot him a glare to let him know just how hilarious he wasn't.

He gave the mattress a little bounce. "You know, with Grandpa's objection to sleepovers, I never actually got to nail anyone in this bed."

"Well, you're definitely not doing it now, so up and out." She crossed the room and perched on the edge of the window seat, folding her hands in her lap. She'd already decided that the only way she was going to get through this was to be as brisk and professional as possible. Not the easiest task, considering she was dressed in corgi print pajama bottoms, her hair was wet, and her thin cotton top was clinging to her still-damp body. She'd scripted it all out in her head: a new set of rules they needed to establish, boundaries that had to be set. She was posing as his girlfriend, so she couldn't simply order him to keep a permanent ten-foot distance between them, but anything more intimate than holding hands had to be strictly off-limits. Simple and logical, in theory. But when she finally forced herself to meet his gaze, all that came out of her mouth was: "I'm not sleeping with you."

"Bummer."

Bummer? She'd spent the past half hour agonizing over this, and all he had to say was *bummer?*

But Whit wasn't through yet. He maneuvered himself to the end of the bed and sat facing her, holding up a hand. "Before you launch into whatever speech I know you've been preparing, let's get one thing straight. You have nothing to feel guilty about."

"Who says I feel guilty?"

"Me. I can just see you've been tying yourself into knots because you've managed to convince yourself you somehow betrayed big sis. You haven't."

"You aren't exactly an unbiased source on the subject."

"That's right. I'm one of the people involved, which means I know what I'm talking about. Paige and I dated for about five minutes *four years ago*. Are you gonna try to tell me she's never moved on?"

Paige had met an attractive Tai chi instructor three days after Nell's disastrous PEDs revelation, plus there was that whole *desperately-in-love-with-Gabi* thing, but Whit didn't need to know that. "You're going to be dating her again in a couple of weeks."

That annoyed him. He dragged a hand through his already rumpled hair. "A completely bullshit relationship I doubt Paige has even fully thought through. I'm not her territory, her property, or any other part of whatever sacred girl code you think you've infringed on. You and I are two unattached, consenting adults. Whatever happens between us is our business and no one else's."

"Happened," she corrected quickly. "*Happened* between us."

Whit's eyebrow shot up. "You're not going to start denying we're attracted to each other again, are you?"

"I'm not denying anything. I'm—"

"Because it's like I said, we've got chemistry. We always have. We tried to deny it four years ago, and look where that got us."

"You were dating my sister!"

"Only because I saw her first."

Just like that, he defused her outrage. Something hot and painful twisted inside her. Nell dropped her gaze. She needed to say this now, immediately, or she was going to end up throwing herself at him again, begging him to peel off all her clothes and toss her onto the bed so he could start carving notches. "It's not just about Paige. Casual may be your thing, but it isn't mine. I'm not built that way. I can't do the physical without the emotional, and neither of us wants that."

"So you won't sleep with me because you have a crush on me."

"Pretty much."

His expression turned serious. "I don't want to make you uncomfortable, Nell," he said softly. "And I won't hold you to anything. If you want to go home, I'll bring you to the airport tomorrow."

She hopped up from the window seat. "You're kicking me out because I won't sleep with you?"

"What? No!"

"We made a deal, and I don't go back on my word. I just think we need to have some rules."

"That's not what you said earlier."

"Earlier I was pissed off." She was being an idiot, but she couldn't seem to stop herself. Here he was, letting her off the hook, and instead of taking the excuse and running, she was digging her heels in. "I'm your week-long plus one. In name only. Unless you're worried that *I'm* so irresistible you won't be able to keep your hands off *me*."

Which was a completely laughable idea, but the calculating look that came into Whit's eyes made her uneasy.

"So, wait, what are these rules of yours?" he asked. "Besides not sleeping with me."

"That's the main one."

"I assume that kissing is also off the table."

"Everything is off the table. Except hand-holding. You can hold my hand—in public—*if* you aren't weird about it." She thought about it a moment. "And I guess you can put your arm around my shoulders."

"Kinky." He rolled to his feet, stretching languidly. "What do I get if I win?"

She blinked. "Win what?"

"No worries. We'll figure that part out later." A wicked smile pushed at the corners of his lips. He moved toward the door in full swagger—impressive for a guy with sweatpants and bare feet. When he reached the doorway, he swung back, hitting her full on with another of those hot, lingering looks that she felt from the top of her head to the tips of her toes, and everywhere else in between. He tugged ever so slightly at the waistband of his sweatpants. Then he was gone, his voice drifting back to her as his footsteps faded down the hall. "Sweet dreams, Nellie."

Seventeen

It didn't take Nell long to figure out that Whit was trying to get her to break the rules.

He wasn't even subtle about it. He'd turned the Whitney O'Rourke seduction machine up to full blast, complete with sexy smiles, flirty comments, and suggestive looks that convinced her he could scorch the clothing right off her body if he really put his mind to it. In public, he more or less behaved himself, but when they were alone... he was temptation personified. A fallen angel daring her to sin. His dark, smoky eyes promised her the fulfillment of every fantasy, every suppressed desire, every naughty urge. That silky voice whispered that he was the bad boy of her wildest dreams; all she needed to do was say the word, and he'd haul her off to the nearest horizontal—or vertical—surface they could find. And until she did, he'd be keeping his hands to himself.

It was another game, of course. She'd set him a challenge, the one thing he couldn't resist. He wasn't going to touch her, not without an explicit invitation. But that wasn't going to stop him from trying to get her to touch him.

She could have put an end to it. If he'd seemed remotely serious, she probably would have. Whit might be pathologically competitive and obnoxiously aware of his own good looks, but all Nell would need to do is tell him to stop, and she knew he'd do it. He was clearly enjoying himself, however, and she didn't want to spoil his fun. At least not when she had every intention of winning.

And she *was* going to win. For every sly innuendo, she countered with confusion. For every lazy stretch that teased those hard muscles lurking beneath his shirt, she faked a yawn.

"You realize what an easy target for reverse psychology you are, don't you?" she asked, mostly to hide how effective that testosterone overload actually was.

Whit leered in response. "Implying I only want you because you said I can't have you. Try again, Nellie. That just makes it more interesting."

She considered telling him that not everything in life was a competition, but she'd already heard enough about the infamous O'Rourke family rules to last her a couple of lifetimes. There were four of them, she'd discovered, each one loonier than the last. Her own edict of *don't tell Grandmother* was starting to seem downright normal next to: constant competition, a bloodthirsty need for revenge, the declaration that mercy was for suckers—nine-year-old Whit had apparently come up with that one—and a general reminder that rules were merely suggestions. Nell thought that last one a contradiction in terms, but when she'd mentioned it to Whit, he'd clarified they meant *other* people's rules. Their own were ironclad. Then he'd given her his sideways grin, licked his lips, and dropped his gaze to her breasts.

The next two days kept them busy, so there wasn't much opportunity for Whit to get her alone—to both her relief and disappointment. Monday included a charity brunch at the local senior center, which was followed by a silent auction at a nearby country club. Nell did her part as doting girlfriend to provide a buffer between Whit and the more inquisitive town elements, including another former classmate who made a couple of snide remarks before Nell stepped in and shut him down, since, once again, Whit wasn't doing anything to defend himself. But aside from the guys who had gone to school with him, no one seemed to have much of a problem with Whit. A few rude comments aside, most of the town was waiting with open arms to welcome their prodigal son. Literally, in some cases. There was a whole queue of women ready to swoop in and reminisce about the good old days—and probably to do a lot more than reminisce, if Whit hadn't kept Nell plastered to his side. Nell wondered how many of them he'd slept with, then felt disgusted with herself for wondering.

When Whit got pulled into a debate about pitching mechanics with one of the players from the old-timers game, Nell found herself in conversation with Maggie. A conversation that confirmed Nell's initial impression of her: Maggie was sweet but shy, and seemed completely in over her head when it came to Skip's world of baseball jargon and business decisions. Probably because she *was* in over her head. Apparently Maggie's late father had been a friend of Skip's, and the job she'd taken with him was a temporary position Skip had offered to help her get back on her feet after her father passed. A lot less illicit than Whit had been imagining, though he wouldn't abandon his belief that the two were sleeping together. According to him, Skip wasn't nearly that altruistic. If he'd really wanted to help Maggie, he could've just written a check.

Skip himself was too busy with stadium details to do more than toss a couple of comments in their direction—though he'd gone nuclear when he heard about Whit's car. He didn't think the tiny Fallen Oaks Police Department was up to the task of finding the culprit and wanted to bring in an outside investigator. That had led to another blistering father-son argument, but since Nell was actually on Skip's side on this one, she let Whit handle it himself.

On Tuesday, their morning was spent at the elementary, where Skip, Whit, and a few members of the Fallen Oaks Fishers gave one-on-one baseball lessons to dozens of starry-eyed children in the tiny field that adjoined the school. Nell sat on the makeshift bleachers with Allie and Freddie, trying not to melt every time some remark of Whit's earned him another mile-wide, gap-toothed grin, or when he bent to accept hugs from a few of the more affectionate students. She didn't need any reminders of how good he was with kids. He was going to make a great dad someday, a piece of knowledge that made her heart squeeze painfully.

The lessons were followed up by photo-ops, some with the children, some with local media—the exact sort of publicity Whit had been hoping for, though Nell knew him well enough by now to realize he'd have been just as kind and patient with those kids without the flash of cameras. It was clear he genuinely liked children, and understood them better than some of the teachers she'd worked with. He'd even roped her into helping him with a particularly anxious seven-year-old who couldn't get past being awe-struck long enough to speak.

I know how you feel, kid, she thought. She'd been annoyingly awe-struck herself lately. Among other things.

Although maybe awe-struck wasn't quite the way to put it. She wasn't tongue-tied or stammering, she was... having fun. More fun than she wanted to admit. Spending so much time in Whit's company should have been exhausting, or at least uncomfortable, but instead of feeling awkward and out of place, Nell was more relaxed than she could remember being since she'd been a kid. Relaxed, and at the same time, wholly and acutely alive. When Whit wasn't trying to seduce her, he was laughing with her, arguing with her, discussing books and TV, pop culture and politics—and, god, even *sports*—and getting into more silly competitions than she could count.

All of which led to Allie cornering her on Wednesday while Nell was helping set up Bucky's booth at the fairgrounds for the town's annual Harvest Fest. Whit and Bucky had gone to unload some extra shelving and a couple of hay bales from the pickup, which was all the opportunity Allie needed to pounce.

"You know, Whit doesn't bring his girlfriends to meet the family," she said, pushing aside a couple of baskets of sweet corn to perch on the booth's countertop. "Ever."

Nell darted a quick look around, but the only people in earshot were a couple of middle-aged women setting up a pie stand. She lowered her voice. "He still hasn't. Remember?"

Allie cocked her head. "Yeah, what's that about? You get along really well and you *seem* normal—which would definitely be an upgrade, from what I know of the last one."

That didn't feel like a compliment. Nell gave her a bland smile. "All part of my diabolical plan."

"So I misjudged you. I can admit when I'm wrong." Allie leaned forward, casting a furtive glance at the pie sellers before turning back to Nell. "Anyway, I need your help."

Nell groaned. Over the past several days, she'd learned enough about Whit's youngest sister to know those words couldn't possibly lead anywhere good. "If this is another weird O'Rourke contest, leave me out of it."

"As Whit's girlfriend, you're O'Rourke adjacent. That means you're obligated."

"Thankfully, I am *not* actually his girlfriend."

"Keep telling yourself that." Allie apparently took Nell's irritated grumble as assent, because she hopped off the countertop and took a step toward her. "It'll be quick, I promise. I just need you to call my sister."

Nell blinked. "Rory? Why? She doesn't even know who I am."

"That's the point. You call, tell her you're with *ESPN* or something, say you're doing a story on her marriage to Satan, and ask for a comment."

"You want me to actually say Satan?"

Allie ignored that. "She might recognize Freddie's voice, so he can't do it. And Maggie already turned me down."

And so it was up to Eleanor Lacey, sports journalist, to rise from the ashes. "Won't she just send me to voicemail?"

"Leave a message."

It didn't take Nell long to realize it would be easier just to give in. And she had to admit, she was dying of curiosity about Whit's other sister. Rory had been dodging Whit's calls—which, according to him, was a sure sign she was lying about the whole thing, because he would see through her bullshit—and when Whit had finally managed to get his mother on FaceTime, she hadn't shed any light on the situation. Instead of giving him an answer, she'd pokered up. The bubbly, bright-eyed Allie lookalike that Nell had glimpsed on Whit's phone had told him to ask his father.

"All right," Nell said, wondering if it was a bad sign that she didn't even feel guilty. Though really, what was one more lie added to her list? "But I take no responsibility for this."

She wasn't expecting Rory to answer the phone and had a moment of panic when the line connected and a breathless voice offered a thin hello.

"Oh, hello!" Nell winced as her own voice came out in a high, singsongy chirp, and made an effort to smooth it into something approaching professional. "This is Eleanor Lacey with *ESPN*. I'm doing a story on your marriage, and—"

"*No hablo inglés*," Rory said and hung up.

Well, Nell had tried, anyway. She slipped her phone back into her pocket and shrugged at Allie. "The Bride of Satan says no comment."

"What do you mean, no comment? She has to comment!" Allie set her hands on her hips and scowled, but since Whit and Bucky were on their way back from the truck, she let the matter drop.

Once the booth had been set up, Bucky shooed Nell and Whit off to amuse themselves until it was time to pack up. That was fine by her. She hadn't been to a festival, or any sort of fair—not counting book fairs—since before her mother got sick. The scents of caramel corn and pumpkin pie shot her straight back to childhood, but it wasn't nostalgia she felt walking beside Whit, her hand tucked neatly into his. It was something both deeper and more fragile than that, something more peaceful, something a lot like... contentment. The day was perfect: the sky a bright, dizzying blue; the fairgrounds rich with fallen leaves and blazing autumn colors; the air crisp but not biting—though it had proved chillier than expected, and she was wearing another of Whit's too-large sweatshirts under her jacket. It should have made her panic, how easy it was to pretend she really was his girlfriend, how good it felt. But panic would be for later. She was in the now, in the *right now*, and she intended to hold onto it as long as she could.

The Harvest Fest was traditionally held at the end of October, but Bucky had explained that the city council had delayed it a couple of weeks to coincide with Skip's groundbreaking plans. That meant a few of the usual activities had been altered, but Nell couldn't see much was missing. In addition to food stands and farm goods, the festival boasted an assortment of arts and crafts, live folk music, a hayride, a petting zoo, and several games that had been borrowed from the local county fair. Including a dunk tank. Which someone—Nell suspected Allie—had thoughtfully signed Whit up for.

"Hasn't anyone ever told you lunatics it's too cold to have a dunk tank?" Nell asked, eyeing the rickety-looking collapsible bench and giant plastic tub while Whit ducked into a tent and swapped his jeans for a pair of hideous green and orange striped shorts he'd procured from god knew where. *Take A Dive For Charity!* was painted in glittery letters on the side of the tub, along with the pricing guide. A dollar for kids, a few more for adults for the chance to send the Blizzards' ace for a frigid dip—along with the already drenched high school linebacker and burly volunteer fireman who had preceded him. "You're going to get hypothermia."

"Feel free to help warm me."

She could hear the smirk in his tone and did her best to sound scolding. "I changed my mind. You could use a good dousing."

Whit gave her his sideways grin as he emerged from the tent and handed her his neatly folded jeans, but before he could reach the tank, someone stepped in front of the ladder.

He didn't tense up quite as completely this time, but Nell still knew exactly who she would see when she turned. Sawyer Brewster, leaning back against the ladder with one arm draped across the top step, barring the way. He was off-duty at the moment, casually dressed in a pair of dark jeans and a rumpled gray sweatshirt—but Nell suspected that was the only thing casual about him. From what she knew of the guy, he could give Whit a run for his money in intense. He was the very definition of broody.

"What are you doing?" Whit asked him, voice tight.

"It says dunk tank, not *drunk* tank," Sawyer tossed out. "I'm a last minute substitution." Then, in one swift, sleek motion, he climbed up to the tank and seated himself on the bench, fully clothed. Nell could only assume it was some sort of demented, macho attempt to show

Whit up. But if Sawyer wanted to be the one to freeze into a Popsicle, well—let him.

Whit must have agreed with the sentiment, because he turned to leave.

Sawyer's next words stopped him. "Running away again, O'Rourke? Come on, let's see the fabled arm in action. A hundred bucks says you can't dunk me."

A completely ridiculous wager, since Whit could probably hit the target a block away and blindfolded. But then, that was what Sawyer was counting on, Nell supposed. Whit O'Rourke never backed down from a challenge. It was that same competitive drive that had propelled him all the way to the majors... and pushed him to betray his friends. Now he could either lose face, or betray Sawyer again—at least symbolically. Miss on purpose, or send him diving. No matter how he played it, Whit couldn't win.

Whit turned, and the small group of onlookers that had gathered instantly parted for him. The starstruck teenager behind the sales counter took the money he'd dug out of his wallet and handed him a faded yellow tennis ball. A total hush fell over them as Whit tested the weight of it a moment, bouncing it gently in his right hand, and did a quick warm-up with his shoulder and arm. Playing it up for the audience—or, more likely, delaying the inevitable. Nell wasn't sure what he intended; she wasn't even certain *he* knew what his plan was. His face was totally unreadable, his eyes focused solely on the target. She said his name and he ignored it.

She had to do something.

The second Whit lifted his arm to throw, Nell let out a sudden gasp, stumbled, and careened sideways into him. Reflexively, he turned and caught her, even as his fingers released their grip. The audience groaned as the ball went spiking into the ground.

Crisis averted. Temporarily.

Allie clearly had no scruples about dunking her brother's former friend. She peeled herself out of the crowd, slapped a five dollar bill onto the sales counter, plucked the ball from where it had rolled in the dirt, and whipped it directly at the target—proving that she might not have the O'Rourke family interest in athletics, but she definitely had the talent. Bullseye. The target slammed inward. The bench collapsed. Water splashed out of the tub as the crowd lurched back.

Sawyer came up sputtering.

"You owe me a hundred bucks, *officer*," Allie said. She smirked, tossed her hair, and then maneuvered the grinning Freddie toward the barn that housed the petting zoo.

Nell didn't waste any time in steering Whit away from the dunk tank. "Concussion relapse," she said, rubbing at her forehead. "I should probably sit down."

Whit's look told her he wasn't buying a word of it, but since she'd shackled herself to his arm, he had little choice but to guide her over to one of the nearby benches. "I could've handled that."

"Cannon fodder," she said.

"That felt more like the cannon. I guess I should count myself lucky you didn't stab me again."

She thrust his folded up jeans at him. "Here. Put these back on. Those shorts are an atrocity."

"You sure you don't want to come with me? I might need protection."

What she wanted to do was kiss him. He was doing his best to cover it, but she could see he'd been shaken. She wanted to push herself up on her tiptoes, curl her arms around the back of his neck, drag his head down to hers, and kiss away all the sadness that lurked in his eyes.

Instead she gave him a wobbly smile. "I don't think the big bad wolf will be knocking down any houses for a while yet."

But *yet* turned out to be a lot shorter than she thought. When they returned to the farmhouse later that evening, the wolf was waiting for them.

Eighteen

Whit had spent the last three days thinking about sex.

This wasn't unusual. He spent a lot of time thinking about sex anyway. Maybe not as much as he had when he'd first hit puberty and all those slowly simmering hormones had finally reached full boil, but the blast of testosterone that had rampaged through his body as a fumbling teenager was still doing its part to keep his mind on the goal. Hell, he'd probably be three days dead before he *stopped* thinking about sex. But for the better part of a week, the section of his brain that should have been keeping his sex drive at least partially under control had seriously malfunctioned. Nell couldn't walk into a room without him feeling that familiar tightening of his groin, and as a result he was in a constant state of semi-arousal. He was driving himself crazy with it. *She* was driving him crazy. It was a miracle he could still somewhat pass as a normal human being, since whenever they were alone together, all he could think about was stripping off her clothes and sinking into her, hilt deep, then watching her face as he coaxed out little moans.

It was his own fault. He should never have kissed her. Yeah, he'd been imagining a dozen ways to undress her even before then, but that was nothing in comparison to the explosiveness unleashed by that kiss. Chemistry didn't cover it. Neither did simple attraction. It had been like fusion, like a drug—irresistible and utterly intoxicating. That hot, sweet burn of desire; that frantic, all-consuming need to feel her skin against his. The second it happened, he'd gone into total sensory overload. He'd needed to touch her, to taste her. The more he'd tasted the more he'd wanted, until he'd been ready to throw her down on the trunk of the car and take her right then and there.

Ever since then, he'd been acting completely demented. There was no excuse for it. He hadn't let his libido make decisions for him since he was nineteen years old, but here he was, his entire being awake to the sight of her, his heart giving a swift, obnoxious kick every time she so much as smiled in his direction. Like a kid with a crush, except with a grown man's body and a grown man's lust. *She* was the one with the crush, dammit! And since she'd asked for hands-off, he'd told himself he would *be* hands-off. But that didn't mean he couldn't torment her a little. Make her sweat. Make her squirm. He told himself it was another game, that teasing her was just too delicious to pass up.

Except that it could never be a game, not for her; she'd told him that straight up. Her feelings for him, past tense or not, made things complicated. Whit had his own rules, and right now he was breaking them. Worse, tempting her did nothing but leave him frustrated and aroused. He wasn't sure which one of them he was torturing any longer, but he knew it had to stop.

It would be so much simpler if they weren't attracted to each other. Then they could just relax and have fun. And they *had* been having fun, in spite of the drama with Sawyer and the occasional argument flaring up. Nell was easy to talk to, even if she was pretty clueless about baseball, and she had a quick, infectious laugh that made her whole face light up. Now, instead of getting into silly fights over who had the best deep dish pizza in Chicago or discussing their unexpected mutual love for cheesy horror films, he was going to spend the rest of the week playing board games with his grandfather—because if there was anything less sexy than an eighty-year-old fussing over checkers in his long underwear, Whit had yet to find it.

He had just turned his dad's new Maserati down the road to the farm—Bucky following behind in his pickup—and was trying not to dwell on how depressing the prospect of game-night-with-Grandpa was when Nell's sudden, sharp inhale made him glance toward the house.

"Are you fucking kidding me?" His knuckles tightened on the steering wheel. Deep shadows blanketed the yard and the small path that led to the porch, but in the glow of the headlights, he could make out the sleek white and blue frame of a Fallen Oaks squad car. And where there was a Fallen Oaks squad car...

He didn't even feel surprised this time. He just felt pissed off.

Three nights ago he'd been caught off guard, a decade of guilt and regret crashing into him with all the force of a freight train. The relentless pull of memory had dragged him into its undertow, and for a moment he'd been seventeen again, back on that dark road, watching helplessly as his friend's life fell to ruins. And he'd let it happen, because deep down he'd known he deserved it. All the bitterness in Sawyer's eyes, all the contempt—Whit had that coming. But neither of them were seventeen now, and there were limits even to penance. He'd tried to reach out to Sawyer again and again in the years since the accident; each time he'd been rebuffed. Eventually he'd stopped trying.

Now he couldn't seem to get rid of him.

The cold knot of fury that had been lodged somewhere inside him for the past twelve years slowly began to unfurl.

"Twice in one day. Lucky us." He threw the Maserati into park.

"Whit—"

"I'll handle it," he said, not waiting for a response as he jerked the seat belt free and thrust himself out of the vehicle. Four long strides brought him to Sawyer, who stood leaning against the squad car, the picture of nonchalance. Whit curled a lip. "I hope you're here to tell me you arrested whoever trashed my car. Otherwise I think this qualifies as stalking."

"We're still looking into that," Sawyer replied smoothly, his voice cool and carefully neutral. He was back in uniform, all business now, afternoon swims and quips about drunk tanks forgotten. Officer Brewster was on what passed for his best behavior; he straightened up and gave brief nods to Nell and Bucky as they approached, without even a hint of his usual sneer. They had Bucky's presence to thank for that, Whit figured. The one O'Rourke whose opinion still mattered to Sawyer.

Still, Whit sincerely doubted the Fallen Oaks boys in blue had done anything about the vandalism except have a good laugh. "Yeah, I'll bet."

"We'll keep you updated if we come up with any leads. Right now, I'm here to speak with Ms. McLean."

"Funny."

"What's this about, Sawyer?" Bucky asked, stepping between them, a too-wide grin plastered on his face.

Nell moved up alongside Whit. "You're here to speak to *me*?"

"You're not in any trouble, ma'am," Sawyer answered. "The chief sent me out here as a courtesy."

Whit snorted. "The chief sounds like an idiot."

"Whitney," Bucky warned.

"We've had some complaints over the past couple of days—"

"Complaints? About *Nell*?"

"—and we need to follow up."

"Bullshit," said Whit.

"What sort of complaints?" Bucky asked.

"Disorderly conduct, threats of violence, inappropriate behavior on school premises."

The rage that had been building inside Whit expanded. "Since when is making out in a parking lot against the law? And the only person she's ever threatened with violence is me."

"I don't think you're helping," Nell said, laying a hand on his sleeve.

Whit was too angry to listen. He shook her away. "This is between you and me, Sawyer," he snarled. "You want to use me for target practice, that's one thing. But Nell is off-limits."

"You know him better than that," Bucky said quietly.

The edge was back in Sawyer's voice, though he kept his gaze on Nell. "It's our belief the accusations aren't credible. The calls were anonymous and can't be independently verified. The more likely scenario is that someone is trying to cause trouble for you, Ms. McLean. Do you know of anyone who might have a grudge against you?"

"Uh, I did sort of piss off someone named Petey."

Whit snorted again.

"Pete Henderson? Anyone else?"

"Maybe a couple of other guys Whit went to school with. I didn't get names. But... no one here even knows me. My only connection to this place is Whit."

A smirk slid onto Sawyer's face. "No shortage of grudges there."

Bucky's expression turned grim. "You play nice, Sawyer Brewster, or you can see yourself off my property."

But Whit didn't need anyone defending him—not Bucky, not Nell. Not this time. He took a step toward Sawyer. "You have something to say to me, say it. I've never known a Brewster to pull punches." It was a low blow and he knew it, but he was too angry to care.

Sawyer looked at him with all the disdain in the world. "Sorry, O'Rourke. You're just not worth it."

Walk away, Whit told himself. *Just walk away. Let it roll off.* But all the rage that had been festering inside him kept him rooted. "What the fuck more do you want from me? Another apology? I'm fucking sorry. I've been fucking sorry for the past twelve years."

"I'm sure you were real broken up about it," Sawyer scoffed. "But hey, whatever it takes to give you an edge, right? Doesn't matter who you screw over in the process. Who needs integrity when you've got a multi-million dollar contract?"

"I won't apologize for my success."

"Yeah, I heard all about your *success*. How long was that suspension of yours again? Eighty games?"

"Sixty," he shot back. A year ago—a week ago—that taunt might have had teeth. Now it just annoyed him. "That's all you've got? Everyone in the world knows I cheated. I've paid for my fuck-ups. I'm done trying to pay for yours. You're the one who crashed that car, Sawyer. Not me."

"And you shouldn't have been behind the wheel at all with how wasted you were the last time. I'd ask how you kept your license, but I think we both know the answer to that one."

"You think Dad only cleaned up *my* messes? Who the hell do you think took care of your medical bills? Or did you really believe the state covered it?" He'd finally rattled him, Whit saw. But he was on a roll now. "I said I was sorry, and I meant it. I'm not doing it anymore. You want to be bitter, you want to blame me, go right ahead. But I'm not your excuse, Sawyer. You really think you'd have made it to the majors? I can tell you right now exactly how it would go. You'd get drafted—ninth round, maybe tenth. High enough to dream you might be a prospect, plus get a nice chunk of money as a signing bonus. Nothing life changing, but enough to hope. Then you'd spend a couple of years in the minors. A season in rookie ball, another two in Low-A. Maybe with a little luck you'd get up to double. Brutal hours, bullshit pay, and eventually you'd burn out. You'd still end up back here, another Brewster with a badge in a town you hate, only this time you wouldn't have me to blame. You think I stole all that from you? I did you a fucking favor."

Whit saw the punch before it came and didn't bother to move out of the way. He braced himself and let the blow land, a clean jab to the left side of his jaw that made his head rock back and a sudden, slight tang of blood well in his mouth—but Sawyer was too angry to stop, and with a low growl he aimed a second punch straight at Whit's gut. Ducking sideways, Whit hooked a foot behind Sawyer's knee and sent him sprawling into the dirt, then stood sneering down at him. Before Sawyer had a chance to recover, he went in for the kill. "There's that daddy's boy I knew was in there," he jeered. "I guess some things *do* run in the family."

It was the one knife he knew exactly how to twist. But the shame he saw bloom in Sawyer's eyes didn't bring the satisfaction he'd thought it would.

Bucky stepped between them again, jabbing a sharp finger into Whit's chest. "One more word out of you, and *you* can see yourself off my property."

He didn't need to see the reproach on his grandfather's face or hear the disgust in his voice to tell him he'd fucked up. Again. He couldn't look at Nell. Couldn't look at any of them. "You can both go to hell," he whispered and stalked off toward the barn.

***

The rickety wooden ladder that led to the hayloft had seen better days, and Nell grimaced at the array of cobwebs that had collected between the rungs. Since Whit hadn't bothered to turn on the lights, she had to fumble along the wall, her hip bumping an old snow shovel that had been propped nearby before her fingers landed on a switch. Bingo. A few scattered wall lamps flickered on, giving the barn a warm, dusty glow as she hauled herself noisily up the ladder. She paused when she reached the top, taking it in. With a little work, she thought, the hayloft might be charming and picturesque. It had a homey feel to it, cozy without being cramped, bales neatly stacked on one end while two or three cats lay curled on a pile of flannel blankets at the other, and a single window had been thrown open to let in the stars. But from there it swerved past charming and straight into run-down: holes poked through the walls, at least one of the beams looked to be splintering, and the grimy floor gave it a general air of neglect. Still, it was the perfect hideout. A quiet place to lick your wounds and brood.

Whit was definitely brooding. He was seated on one of the bales of hay, leaning forward with his elbows on his knees and his hands loosely clasped between them. His head was bowed, his shoulders hunched. All he needed was a little rain cloud.

"Brought you an ice pack," she said, lifting the bag of frozen peas she'd filched out of Bucky's freezer. "Doubles as dinner, since you've been banished for the night." Not that she thought Bucky had been serious, but he *had* ordered her to cart out a couple of blankets, so that—in his words—*the idiot doesn't freeze to death*. She'd left the blankets on the sofa, gambling that Bucky would change his mind and grant parole.

Whit glanced up long enough to aim a blistering glare in her direction. "Keep it. I'm fine."

She wasn't scared off that easily, and she stepped over a couple of cats to make her way across the loft toward him. "Want to try that again without the macho, tough-guy attitude?"

Now he just looked sulky. "I'll live."

Since he showed no indications of moving, she sank down on the bale beside him and dropped the bag of peas in his lap, along with a thin dishcloth to wrap it in. "You made me get into a freaking ambulance for a bump on the head. You can deal with an ice pack."

"Frozen peas?"

"I thought they'd work better than carrots."

"Grandpa doesn't have an *actual* ice pack?"

"He sent it home with Sawyer."

"Of course he did. His favorite grandkid." He folded the dishcloth around the bag and touched it gingerly to his jaw. A frustrated sigh huffed out of him. "Go ahead. Tell me I acted like an asshole."

"Twelve years of torturing yourself about something you had no control over? I think you've earned a little pissed off." She wanted to pull him into her arms and had to tuck her hands beneath her legs to keep them from betraying her. "You never told your friends why you really got kicked off the team, did you? You never told them you were covering for someone."

He turned his head away. "I never told *you* I was covering for someone."

He didn't have to. Her own high school experience might have been the definition of tame, but she'd heard enough sordid tales of out of control jocks and subsequent cover-ups to know drunk driving wasn't considered much of a crime to athletics departments. She also knew that wasn't Whit.

"It wasn't all that hard to figure out. Not once I started thinking about it. I just had to narrow it down a bit. Who would Whitney O'Rourke protect with such devotion even after all this time?"

"And I suppose you think you have an answer."

"Your mother," she said quietly.

She hadn't been entirely certain she was right, not until the sharp look he turned at her. Then she saw it in his eyes, in the slight parting of his lips. She felt a surge of anger for the boy he'd been, losing the thing he cared about most because the adults in his life had failed him.

Apparently she wasn't very good at keeping her thoughts from showing on her face, because Whit's gaze hardened. "That reaction is exactly why I don't tell anyone."

"What reaction?"

"You're judging her."

Judging a woman who hung her own kid out to dry when she was the one who screwed up? Absolutely she was. But clearly Whit was sensitive about it, so she hedged a little. "I don't know her," she said carefully.

"If you want to blame someone for it, blame my dad. It wasn't as simple as whatever you're thinking."

What she was thinking wasn't anything charitable, and she bit her lip to keep herself from answering.

He set the makeshift ice pack down on the hay beside him. "I'm sure it'll shock you to hear my dad screwed around on my mom pretty much constantly. You remember that woman at the bar?"

The sudden change in subject left her a little bewildered. "The one in your lap?"

"She wasn't in my lap, but thank you for making my point for me," he drawled. "When you're a pro athlete, that's what happens—whether you invite it or not. Women are everywhere. Whatever you want, whoever you want, whenever you want. Yours for the asking. Some guys are better at resisting than others. My dad basically scored a negative on that particular test."

Do you resist? she wanted to ask. But since she wasn't sure she wanted to know the answer, she kept her mouth shut.

"Mom wasn't stupid," he continued. He leaned backward on his palms, gazing upward to where glimpses of moonlight spilled in through the holes in the roof. "She knew it was happening, even if she tried to ignore it. But she loved him, and she was naive enough to think she could change him. And when she couldn't... eventually she started drinking."

"How old were you?"

"Twelve, maybe? Thirteen? We didn't notice at first, because she did a decent job of hiding it. It got worse after my dad retired. The worst night"—he sucked in a breath—"the worst night was when she found him in bed with one of her friends. Normally she did her drinking at home, but that night she stopped by a couple of liquor stores, then drove out to the country club and sat in her car waiting for my dad to show up." He paused, glancing toward Nell. "You don't need to hear all of this."

"That was the night you covered for her?"

"It wasn't really intentional," he said. "It just happened. When Dad never showed, Mom gave in and called the house. Rory answered, figured out what was going on, and told her to stay put while we came to get her—which she didn't. It was pure luck we found her before anyone else did. She'd gone off the road and ended up in a ditch about a mile from the club. The whole thing was mostly brush, or it could've been a lot worse. Rory took her home while I stayed to try to get Mom's car back onto the road... pretty stupid, looking back, especially since Mom had spilled beer on me climbing out of it. You can probably figure out the rest. The cops made an untimely appearance, and since I was stuck in a ditch with about a dozen open bottles and reeked of alcohol, they hauled me in. They never actually bothered to test me, so Dad was able to get the charges dropped. Didn't matter to Principal Engel. Remember the friend of Mom's my dad was screwing? Yeah, that was Engel's wife. Good going, Dad. So I got kicked out of sports for the year and Engel got his payback. And before you go all avenging angel—no, it wasn't fair, but it's ancient history."

Not so ancient, given the scene with Sawyer. Tough-guy attitude or not, she'd be surprised if Whit didn't end up with a nice bit of bruising on his jaw.

Whit shrugged. "So that's what happened. I wish I'd left the damn car in the ditch, but I don't regret taking the fall for it. It was the wake-up call my mom needed. She's been sober ever since. She got herself into rehab, found her spine and left my dad, and got her life together."

"At the expense of yours," Nell said softly.

"Weren't you the one pointing out all the billboards with my face plastered on them? I think I'm doing just fine."

"Except for the part where you didn't want to face your hometown so you bribed a woman you hate to play bodyguard."

"Are we back on this again? I don't hate you. Or do you need another demonstration?"

Yes! the completely traitorous part of her answered. The less traitorous part tried to look snotty. "You still hated me when you made the bribe, so it counts."

"You're too hot to hate. By then it was already down to mild irritation." Her heart did an annoyingly predictable flip, but Whit thankfully wasn't paying attention. "Anyway, bribing you was one of the best ideas I've ever had. You've got Dad on his best behavior and I haven't heard a single crack about *Meltdown*."

"Your car was still vandalized," she pointed out. "And now your stalker has decided to multitask and come after *me*."

"I don't have a stalker. That complaint bullshit is all Sawyer, and I'm going to take care of it."

He was sounding cranky again, but Nell had never yet learned to leave well enough alone. "I think you should tell him about your mother. Both him and James. If you want to mend fences, you need to start there."

"Who says I want to mend fences?"

Your face. Your voice. "I'm not always going to be available to bodyguard. Our contract's up in three days." A fact that depressed her a lot more than she cared to acknowledge.

"Three and a half. Your flight's Sunday morning. And after that, it's *adiós, Fallen Oaks*."

"Then do it for yourself. So that you can finally start to forgive yourself."

"I don't need to forgive myself."

"Yes, you do," she murmured. "For a lot of things."

She expected an argument. Or maybe to be told to mind her own business—she certainly deserved that. But Whit didn't speak. He just closed his eyes and tipped himself backward until he lay flat against the hay, like he was too tired to hold himself up any longer. Nell lay down beside him, drawing her knees up and shifting to her side so she could watch the light play across his face. She wanted to trace her fingertips along his skin, to smooth out the wrinkle in his forehead, skim down the slope of his cheek, follow the curve of his lips. He was all angles and edges, like something out of a painting, something sculpted, too perfect to be real. Except that he was real, and he was anything but perfect.

He was so beautiful, she thought. So utterly, achingly beautiful.

Not just his body. His heart. His soul.

She bolted upright again.

The disaster had happened after all. All the warnings she'd given herself... all the ways she'd tried to convince herself there was nothing beneath that dazzling surface of his... all the admonitions and recriminations and guilt—all for nothing. She'd walked right up to the edge of the cliff and, without a backward glance, had thrown herself right over it.

She didn't have a crush on Whit. She was in love with him.

In love with this beautiful, flawed, stubborn man who had a much bigger heart than he'd ever admit. She'd probably been in love with him all along.

And this was all the time she'd ever have.

The question was whether she'd be too much of a coward to do anything about it.

She had no illusions. There was no future ahead of them, even without the complication of Paige. There was no fairy tale waiting for her at the end. Not with Whit. But that didn't mean she was going to be another revolving-door romance to fizzle out and fade away after a couple of months. This was going to be her choice, and she was going to do it on her terms.

Three and a half days. She would allow herself that. Three and a half days to love without guilt. And when it was done, it was done.

Beads of sweat started to prickle between her breasts. Her heart hammered against her ribs.

She licked her lips. "About that demonstration..."

His eyes flicked open. "Yeah?"

Panic took over. Instant heat climbed up her face as she did a quick scan of their surroundings. God, what was she thinking? How was she going to do this, smuggle him back into the house and hope they didn't get caught? They were in a hayloft! She might be in love, but she hadn't completely lost her senses. That meant safety first.

On the other hand...

"Let me see your wallet."

Whit sat up again. "Excuse me?"

"You heard me."

"What do you want with my wallet?"

"I'll tell you in a second." *If I find what I'm after.* If she didn't... well, she hadn't quite worked out what she'd do then. This was a make-it-up-as-you-go seduction, and she had no idea what she was doing.

Whit's lips twitched. "Are you mugging me?"

"Yes. Now hand it over."

He shifted his hips, reached into his back pocket, and handed her the worn leather wallet she'd already known he carried. Biting her lip, she flipped it open and began to search through it. Driver's license, with a criminally good photo; credit cards; a crumpled receipt from a gas station, a few hundred dollar bills—which made her frown, since he really shouldn't carry that much cash around, what if she *had* been mugging him?—and a note about an upcoming bowling tournament. Nothing else.

Frustrated, she tossed the wallet aside.

"Hey!"

"You're a professional athlete! How can you not have a condom in your wallet?"

"Why are you searching my wallet for condoms?"

She really should have left the seducing to him. She'd been going for cool and casual and instead landed smack in the middle of mortified. "Why do you think?"

The grin that spread across his face stole all the breath from her lungs. "Give me two minutes and hold that thought."

He vaulted off the hay bale and disappeared down the ladder almost before she could blink. There was a short scuffling noise. Then—

"Just in case," his voice called from below. Nell moved to the edge of the hayloft and peered down just in time to see him vanishing out of the barn. It took her half a second longer to realize he'd removed the ladder.

She fell back onto a pile of hay and laughed.

NINETEEN

WHIT WAS BREATHING HARD by the time he made it back to the hayloft. He'd been breathing hard before he *left* the hayloft, but after sprinting into the farmhouse, rummaging hastily through his suitcase for the box of condoms he'd bought a few days ago, just in case—because even if he didn't carry them around in his wallet like some people seemed to think he should, he did like to be prepared—and then dashing all the way back to the barn, he was huffing along like an out of shape DH trying for an inside the park home run.

And with the exact same objective, come to think of it. Metaphorically, anyway.

Nell stood peeping down at him from the loft when he shifted the ladder back into position. She'd pulled her hair free from its ponytail, letting the long, loose mass of waves tumble to her shoulders so that it framed her face in shades of chestnut and bronze. With the mischief in her eyes and that cloud of hair catching the light, she looked like a naughty angel ready to tempt some poor mortal into sin. Namely him.

He couldn't wait.

A naughty, *impatient* angel, from the way she was tapping her fingers along her arms. "What if you'd fallen and hit your head and never come back? I could've died up here."

"It's like a nine foot drop." He gave the ladder a quick test to make sure it was sturdy, then climbed upward into the loft. "You could just toss down a couple of hay bales. Anyway, I come bearing gifts. Sorry they don't come in a bouquet."

Her lips curved. "That was at least three minutes. Did you sneak in or just murder your grandfather?"

"He's asleep in his recliner. And I wasn't going to murder him. Just find a piece of plywood and knock him out."

"You're all heart." She eyed the box he was carrying and gave him a saucy look. "Someone's feeling optimistic."

Someone was feeling horny as hell, a circumstance he was going to have to set aside until they talked a few things out. As desperately as he wanted to spend the next several hours making love with her until they collapsed from exhaustion and their bodies were fused together with sweat, he wouldn't—he *couldn't*—so much as touch her unless he knew it was what she really wanted. He set the box aside and dragged in a breath. "Before this goes any further—"

"Save the speech, Whitney."

"—what happened to hands off?"

"I changed my mind. We're going to be hands on. Very hands on. Starting now." To prove her point, she placed her hand against the front of his shirt and began to trace a slow path downward.

He caught her wrist. "What about that whole '*I can't do casual*' thing?"

"I'm making an exception."

"And you decided this when?"

"Not nearly as soon as I should have. The way I figure it, I've only got about three and a half days left to do what I want with you. So if you plan to keep talking, you should start losing clothes."

It took every ounce of willpower he possessed not to yank her off her feet and toss her onto a hay bale so he could have his wicked way with her, but somehow he managed it. "I don't want to take advantage of you, Nell."

"Good thing I'm the one taking advantage of you." She gave him a silky smile and raked her gaze down him like the sexy seductress he knew she wasn't—well, seductress anyway; take off a layer or two of clothing, and she'd have sexy down to a science—but then the smoke in her eyes turned abruptly to panic. "Oh, god. That's what I'm doing, isn't it? Throwing myself at you like every other woman on the planet."

"No! Christ. Do you have any idea how crazy I've been going the past few days trying not to touch you? I just don't want you to do anything you'll regret."

"The only thing I'd regret is not doing this." Her words were quiet, but the look she gave him was fierce and determined and so full of heat he wanted to drop to his knees and beg her to have him.

His throat went dry. "Nell..."

"In a few days, I'm getting on a plane back to Chicago and never seeing you again. I'm not expecting anything from you, Whit. I'm not asking for some lifelong commitment. All I'm asking for is here and now." She closed the distance between them, lifting herself onto her toes to loop an arm around his neck, and tugged him downward to brush a soft kiss over his lips. Just the barest hint of contact, but he felt his already rapid pulse skyrocket. He wanted more and angled himself toward her, but she drew back. A frown flitted across her brow. "Unless your jaw hurts too much. I didn't think of that."

"To hell with that," said Whit. He'd put up with a little pain. He dragged her back to him, and there was nothing soft about his kiss. It was hot and hungry, and by the time he let her go again, they were both gasping. He leaned his forehead against hers. "Damn, you're good at that."

"Really?"

The delight in her voice made him chuckle, and he caught her hips to lift her, pressing her firmly against his erection. "Any questions?"

Her breath hitched out of her. She shook her head. Then her knees slid apart and she raised herself upward, wrapping one long, slender leg around his waist.

He backed her against the wall to keep them both upright, one hand hooked behind her knee, his hips rocking against her of their own accord as his mouth found hers again. Her hands clutched at his jeans, trying frantically to tug him even closer. "We're wearing too much clothing," she panted when they came up for air.

She was filling his senses, the taste of her mouth, the scent of her skin, the heat of her body through the layers of fabric that separated them. He wanted her, as simple as that. Wanted her so badly he could scarcely breathe, much less think. Every inch of him was burning, every molecule screaming to take what she was offering, to surrender whatever was left of his self control and lose himself in that sweet warmth, but when he felt her fingers move between them and fumble at his jeans, he caught her wrists.

"Not yet." Reluctantly, he eased away from her, settling her back on her feet, pressing her hands to her sides before releasing his grip. He reached to tuck a lock of hair behind her ear, tracing his thumb down her jawline. "I need to know this is really what you want."

Because at that precise moment, he couldn't think of a single thing he'd ever wanted more—which proved just how insane this was. Because it didn't *feel* casual, no matter what she said. It felt complicated as hell. And, god help him, he wanted it anyway.

If she told him no—if she changed her mind, or hesitated—somehow he would find the strength to walk away. It might actually kill him, but he'd do it.

She didn't.

"This is really what I want," she told him. "*You* are what I want. So would you please stop talking and start stripping?" She moved away from the wall to kick off her shoes, then stuck her hands on her hips and waited.

He took it back, he decided. She could make any number of layers look sexy. She could probably turn a paper bag into the peak of eroticism. But she was right, she was wearing way too much clothing.

Something he was about to change.

Now that her choice was made, he had no intention of letting her be the one in charge, so he removed his boots and socks, but left the rest of his clothing exactly where it was. "You sure are bossy, Miss McLean. Are you gonna give me detention if I misbehave?"

She aimed another of her seductress gazes his way. This time she licked her lips. "Definitely."

"Good." He had every intention of misbehaving. He stalked toward her, lowering his head for a kiss, and when he saw her eyes close, he let his fingers drop to the hem of her sweatshirt, tugging it upward.

She tugged it back down again. "What are you doing?"

He grinned. "You said to start stripping."

"I meant *you.*"

"Didn't we already talk about the importance of specifics?" This time he kissed her before he started tugging at her shirt again. He teased her mouth a little, tasting her leisurely, then drew her lower lip between his teeth and gave it a playful nip. She made a soft noise low in her throat, but when he started to inch the sweatshirt toward her ribs, she shoved his hands away.

"Wait," she said breathlessly. "Sweatshirt stays on."

"What? Why?"

"Because I'm not going to be naked in a hayloft in the middle of November."

Quickly, he ran through his options. He couldn't take her anywhere else, unless he wanted to end up in the backseat of his dad's car or the great outdoors—neither of which was an improvement—and even if he'd been willing to drag her off to some cheap roadside motel, he didn't think he could wait that long. He could barely stand upright as it was. "It's the beginning of November. And it's *my* sweatshirt."

"I'm wearing it, so right now that makes it mine."

"You have a T-shirt on under it."

"I'll get cold."

"That's what you think," he smirked. But who was he to argue with neurosis? "How about this: sweatshirt comes off, T-shirt stays on. And I want your bra. Deal?"

"We're negotiating now?"

"Damn right."

A calculating look came into her eyes. "What'll you give me?"

"For your bra?"

"I'm assuming *you* don't have a problem with being naked in a hayloft." She smirked right back at him.

He knew a lot more about negotiating than she did, and he had a pretty good idea just who would be winning this round. But give a little to get a little, so he pulled his shirt over his head and cast it aside.

The hungry look she fastened on him was gratifying, but she'd apparently decided to play tough. After she'd removed the sweatshirt and dropped it to the ground, she crossed her arms. "If I'm giving you my bra, I want your baseball."

He unhooked the chain and handed it to her. "Fair warning. If you lose that, I'll have to punish you."

"Punish me how?" She slipped the chain around her own neck and fumbled a moment with the clasp. He had a sudden vision of her wearing nothing but his good luck charm and decided that first thing tomorrow, he was finding a hotel room *somewhere*.

"I'm sure I'll think of something." He held out his hand. "Pay up. You got your trophy. I want mine."

A fresh blush scorched up her cheeks and she suddenly couldn't meet his eyes, but she obeyed him. After a bit of wriggling, she tugged her pale floral bra out through her sleeve and placed it in his open palm. He rubbed the warm, silky fabric between his fingers a moment, then tucked it neatly into his back pocket and turned his attention to the woman who was driving him crazy.

She stood barefoot in the hay, shoulders straight, the look in her eyes an irresistible blend of shy uncertainty and bold challenge. Her faded maroon University of Chicago T-shirt was the same one she'd been wearing last Thursday, the thin cloth stretching across her breasts and doing nothing to disguise the hard points of her nipples. Her lips were parted, her hair mussed. She didn't look anything like an angel now, naughty or otherwise. She seemed earthier somehow, that softly swollen mouth of hers meant for dirty words and steamy kisses. She made him think of sex and sweat, and the glint of that silver chain along her neck marked her as his, whether she knew it or not.

He had to touch her.

"Hands on, right?" he murmured huskily as he gripped her by the shoulders and drew her toward him. He slid his fingers down her bare arms and then up under her shirt, exploring, caressing, flirting along her stomach and rib cage until he found what he was seeking. He cupped her breasts, testing the weight of them, learning her body by feel. He wanted her in his mouth, but since they were playing by her rules—for now—he teased her slowly, circling her nipples with his thumbs until her eyes grew smoky again.

Screw it, he thought. "Up isn't off," he grunted. Then he yanked her T-shirt up over her breasts and bent downward, dipping his head and silencing her protests by taking first one rosy crest into his mouth and then the other. She leaned into him as he tasted her, his mouth hot on her salty-sweet skin, her breath coming fast, her fingers tangled in his hair.

"Wait... wait," she panted. "Jeans next." She moved his head away, then skimmed her hands down his spine to grip his belt loops. "*Your* jeans next. Specifically."

When her fingers trailed to the front of his jeans and unbuckled his belt, he pulled away and shackled her wrists. Holding her arms over her head, he backed her against a hay bale. "We're making a trade." He kept her pinned with one hand while he let the other drift, drawing his fingertips lightly across the tiny scar on her upper lip. "I want this. This is mine."

Her breath tickled against his hand. "My mouth?"

"That, too. But this scar right here." He ran his thumb along it, then leaned down and traced the path with his tongue. *Time to get serious*, he thought, releasing her wrists. When she tipped her faced toward him, he took her mouth, all of it, doing his damnedest to kiss her senseless while his hands found their way to her waist, undid her jeans, and slid the snug denim down off her hips, down her thighs, her knees, until her jeans were all the way at her ankles and she pulled back to stare at him.

"Hey, that's—"

Whit raised an eyebrow. "Cheating?" he asked, shrugging. He was going to have to get over that word eventually; it might as well be now. He gave her his wickedest grin. "Absolutely. And don't think I won't do it again."

He let his gaze wander up and down her legs, taking in those smooth, firm thighs, the soft curves of her calves, the bend of her knees, and...

There they were. Red panties.

God he loved being right.

They even had lace. He sighed happily.

"What?"

"You're perfect," he said. And she was, even with her shirt bunched over her breasts and her jeans around her ankles, her face flushed, her lips parted and deliciously moist, her tangled hair clinging to her face. She looked bewildered and aroused and rumpled. But not nearly rumpled enough.

He hauled her against him again, lifting her off her feet and kicking her jeans away, but she wasn't done ordering him around just yet. "Grab one of those blankets," she commanded. She squirmed out of his arms, but the breathy quality to her voice revealed she wasn't quite as in control as she wanted to pretend. "I'm not having sex on a dirty floor, and I don't want hay ending up in weird places."

"Maybe you should describe those places." He slid his fingers under the band of her panties and parted the soft curls beneath. "Is this one?"

"Um..."

Her breathing turned ragged as he began to massage gently. "Here?"

"That's... that's one," she rasped. "Maybe you should get that blanket."

"In a minute." He wasn't going anywhere without teaching her a little thing about submission first. He wanted her limp and moaning his name—or at least moaning—and he intended to torture her until she was. His free hand curved into the small of her back, keeping her in place while he carried out his assault. "I need to make sure you're ready," he told her. He moved gradually at first, easing her into it, drawing hot, languid circles against her flesh. When he slipped his forefinger inside her and began a slow, stroking rhythm, her eyes glazed over and her head tilted back. She arched toward him, her hands clutching his shoulders. Oh, yeah, she was going to moan, all right. Maybe even beg. He increased his rhythm, bringing her closer, closer—and then stopped abruptly.

Nell whimpered.

"You want to know what you've been doing to me?" he murmured in her ear as she mewled and pushed herself against him. He felt her shiver, her pulse throbbing under his hand, but he wouldn't give her what her body so desperately craved—not yet. "You want to know what I did the night after we kissed? I stood naked in the shower and thought about you. About touching you. Throwing you down and coming inside you. I used my hand and thought about all the things I wanted to do to you. All the ways I wanted to have you. Did you think about me?"

She gasped a yes.

He began to stroke again. "Did you use your hand? Like this?"

"Oh my god."

"That's not an answer, Nell."

She leaned her head forward, burying her face in his chest. "I am so"—another gasp—"not answering that."

"I think you just did."

Her grip on him tightened. "I... I think maybe we should slow down."

No chance in hell. He had her exactly where he wanted her, and he wasn't going to be satisfied with anything short of utter capitulation. "Look at me. I want to see your face when you come."

He thought maybe he'd pushed her a little too far, but she drew her head back and locked her gaze with his.

He nearly lost it right then.

"Say my name," he whispered. "I want to hear you say it."

"Please."

"That's not what I asked."

"Please, Whit."

There we go. Fuck, she felt good. She really was perfect—so warm and wet and responsive, so starkly beautiful in her arousal. He reveled in the feel of her, watching her face, gasping right along with her. When those soft gasps started to quicken, he slipped another finger inside, teasing and tormenting until she writhed and bucked against his hand. The sounds she made when she came were almost too much for him, and he had to peel himself away from her to keep from following her over the edge.

Christ. If he wanted to last long enough to make it inside her, he really was going to have to slow things down. So much for teaching her a lesson. Breath heaving, body trembling, he snatched one of the flannel blankets from the pile near the far end of the loft and tossed it over a hay bale.

Nell was standing where he'd left her, looking at him in a daze. "Why are your pants still on?"

He had no idea.

As he jerked his belt free and flung it to the ground, he jabbed a finger toward the hay bale. "There's the blanket. Get on it."

She must have realized he meant business, because instead of making any demands, she scrambled to obey.

Finally.

Since he had Nell properly compliant—and he needed to cool off a bit—he took his time removing his jeans, folding them carefully and setting them next to hers. He was slick with sweat, so hard it was almost painful, his hands shaking as he hooked his thumbs in the waistband of his boxers and eased the garment down over his hips.

The *holy shit* Nell uttered might have boosted his ego if she hadn't immediately followed it up with, "Wow. You really are bare ass naked in a hayloft."

Well, *properly compliant* had lasted all of a minute.

He grabbed the box of condoms and tossed it onto the bale, then stood peering down at her—absolutely, one hundred percent naked, cock at full-mast—and gave her his best bad-boy jock sneer. "That sounds like a challenge, sweetheart."

She scooted backward, tugging her T-shirt back into place and folding her arms across her chest. "I told you the shirt stays on."

"I'm more interested in the bare ass part right now." He caught her by the shoulders and pushed her onto the blanket, lowering himself over her. "In case you were wondering..." he said, reaching down and giving the front of her panties a little pat. "These are now your lucky underwear." He pulled them off. Then, to prove his point, he flipped onto his back, taking her with him, and cupped her ass.

She opened her legs to straddle him, his erection straining against her upper thighs, then she bent and captured his mouth in a swift, demanding kiss. His hands moved again, trailing along her curves, over her breasts, but hands were no longer enough. He wanted to see all of her, touch all of her, taste all of her. "You're killing me with this shirt," he murmured against her lips.

She drew herself upward, pressing the heel of her hand into his chest to keep him down. "You already broke the rules once. It's my turn. I want to touch you," she told him.

Then she did.

When her hand closed around his cock and began a smooth, steady stroke he groaned her name.

"Payback's a bitch, isn't it?" The satisfaction in her voice should've made his competitive instincts kick in, but he couldn't seem to move.

"Isn't that word on your naughty list?" he panted instead. For a moment he just lay there and gave in to sensation, but it was too much, too soon, and he couldn't stand it. "You'd better stop that unless you want this to be over a lot faster than planned."

"Really? In that case, I probably shouldn't do this." Her lips were on him again, only this time she started on his chest and moved lower, down, down, along his ribs, his stomach, his navel, and—

"Fuck," he rasped.

A low, guttural noise tore out of his throat as her tongue circled the head of his cock and she took him into her mouth.

It was bliss. It was agony. That warm, silky mouth sliding over him. Her hand wrapping around him as she took him deeper. His fingers curled in her hair, clenched.

"No," he managed, gritting his teeth. "I want... I want to be inside you when I come." He was on fire, pulsing with need, his self-control hanging by a thread, but somewhere he found the strength to lift her away. Trembling, he fumbled in the box of condoms, tore open a wrapper and sheathed himself, then rolled her onto her back, spread her thighs wide, and sank into her in one long, slow thrust.

"Don't move yet," he whispered hoarsely.

So of course she moved.

Her hips tilted upward, drawing him further in, the look in her eyes hot and wicked as she locked her legs around him and began to rock gently.

"Jesus, Nell."

"I thought you pro athletes had endurance."

Oh god. Now he had no choice.

He was on the edge, so close he thought he might explode any second, but he wasn't going anywhere without taking her with him. Pressing her down into the blanket, he began to move in a careful, gradual rhythm, straining for control with each steady thrust. His hand moved between them, finding the space where their bodies met, caressing even as he quickened their movements. He teased and tantalized until she started writhing once more, driving them both closer and closer to the brink with each thrust, and then—only then, when her head fell back and he felt her body tightening, shuddering around him and she called out his name again—*then* he let himself go, his climax so intense he nearly rolled them both to the ground with the force of it.

As soon as the aftershocks subsided, he heaved himself away to avoid crushing her, then let himself collapse. He lay beside her, both of them spent and panting, their thighs brushing as he idly twined his fingers in hers.

A second or two of silence ticked past. Then—

"It's a good thing you brought the whole box."

At least he still had the energy to laugh.

TWENTY

In Nell's opinion, there were some things that were worth a bit of a broken heart.

Waking at the crack of dawn to the sound of a rooster crowing, snuggled up in a narrow bed that really wasn't wide enough for two people when one of those two people happened to be six-foot-three and two hundred pounds—strangely enough, that was one of them.

What that *wasn't* worth was forgoing her morning coffee, so she pried herself free from Whit and slipped out of bed, then rummaged around in her carry-on to locate a few necessary items, like pants. And underwear. The rest of her clothing from the night before, along with Whit's, lay discarded in a haphazard pile near the bed.

It was a good thing his grandfather was such a heavy sleeper.

She heard Whit stir and glanced toward him, trying to ignore the way her heart constricted as she watched him blink his eyes open and stretch his long, muscular body, still half covered by the bed quilt. It wasn't fair that he could look so gorgeous with his hair mussed and sweaty and sticking up on one side and his eyes bleary from sleep. He should at least have some defect. A puffy face. Maybe a little drool. But even the faint bruise beginning to show on the right side of his jaw just added a bit of rugged allure.

"Hey," he murmured drowsily.

And *she* should be feeling awkward, she thought. Or guilty. Not this giddy, foolish happiness that rushed into her chest when he smiled at her. "Sorry. I didn't mean to wake you."

"The rooster pretty much took care of that." He yawned. "What time is it?"

"Caffeine o'clock. Want me to smuggle you some?"

"I've got a better idea." He leaned out of bed far enough to capture her wrist and yanked her back toward him.

Okay, given the choice between sex and coffee, coffee could probably wait.

Nell was running on borrowed time, and she knew it. Whit would be driving her back to Minneapolis Saturday evening after the groundbreaking festivities concluded, then bright and early Sunday morning she'd be headed to the airport, back to the real life she was so desperately keeping at bay. No lingering. No looking back. A clean break.

She'd spelled it out to him plainly the night before. They weren't going to have a relationship, not even the three-month blip that passed for a relationship in his distorted pro athlete worldview. This wasn't an affair, it was a *fling*, and it was ending the moment she got on that plane back to Chicago. He was still expected to follow through with his end of the bargain and carry out Paige's silly PR romance scheme—and if he ever breathed a word of what had gone on between them, she would make him regret being born.

"That's the most romantic speech I've ever heard," he'd told her, pretending to wipe away tears.

"I mean it, pal," she'd replied, poking him in the ribs. "You think you O'Rourkes are a vicious lot, wait till you meet a pissed off McLean."

"I've met one. She's hot." Then he'd dragged her on top of him, effectively putting an end to the conversation.

Since Skip needed to make a trip to Minneapolis to meet with investors, they had the next two days free—or they did once Whit finished helping with a sudden venue crisis. A ruptured pipe at a hotel ballroom necessitated a change of location for the Saturday night charity gala, which led Nell to discovering there was a Saturday night charity gala. And since she didn't have anything remotely approaching a dress among her recent clothing purchases, Whit whisked her off to Duluth for a bit of shopping... and booked a hotel where he proved to her just how much endurance pro athletes actually had.

Her plan to ignore reality as long as possible hit a snag Thursday evening when she received a series of texts from Gabi, who had taken Nell's recent evasiveness to mean something was going on with Paige. Nell didn't have time to worry about her sister's messed up love life when she was busy pretending the outside world didn't exist, but she *had* been lying to everyone for the past week, so she figured she was at least partially responsible for Gabi's current fears. It took a good twenty minutes of damage control to convince her that Paige hadn't already rebounded and was only in Cabo for work, and then another twenty minutes to think up an excuse for why she couldn't go out to brunch on Saturday. Then she made the mistake of mentioning the matter to Whit when they returned to their hotel after an early dinner.

His eyes flashed with instant outrage. "Wait a second. Paige was already in a relationship when she came up with her stupid scheme?"

"A stupid scheme you copied," Nell reminded him. "And they're currently broken up. Paige has commitment issues. And Grandmother issues."

"Why does that not surprise me?"

"This coming from Mr. Casual."

"I don't have commitment issues. I have a realistic outlook when it comes to ballplayers and long-term relationships—and don't even start to give me shit about that. You're the one who decided on this three-days-and-done crap. Or are you looking to reopen negotiations?"

Not a chance. That was the problem with being in love: she wanted more than he could give, and she wasn't going to waste her energy on might-have-beens. She crossed her arms. "Take off your pants. I like you better when you're not talking."

"Don't think we're done with this," he said ominously. And then somehow she ended up being the one with her jeans around her ankles, gasping and incoherent while Whit's mouth wreaked havoc between her thighs.

The hotel suite Whit had booked for them was nearly the size of her apartment back home—and came equipped with a much nicer bathtub—and after indulging herself in a bubble bath (alone, since nice or not, there was no way that thing was going to fit both of them), she started quizzing Whit on a subject that had been bothering her most of the week.

"What do you do with all that money?" she asked, climbing onto the bed beside him after he'd finished up a few phone calls. "Aside from splurge on fancy hotel rooms."

"This really isn't all that fancy. And I'm not buying you a private jet." He turned an amused glance at her, his gaze traveling down her terrycloth robe to where her bare feet poked out at the end. "Have I mentioned I like your toenails?"

"Yes." She'd had to resist the urge to run out and buy a bottle of nail polish to apply a fresh coat. "I'm serious, though. Your house just seems so... normal. I was expecting, I don't know, koi ponds and fountains and multiple swimming pools."

"Or the High Church of Baseball, like Dad's?"

"Or that."

"Just a whim. It felt homey. It felt like what I needed at the time." He shrugged. "I'm not saying I'll live there forever. I'll be on the lookout for a couple of fountains next time."

She toyed with the baseball charm that was hanging around her neck. "So where does the rest of it go? You don't seem to be hiding a coke habit. That I've noticed."

Whit poked her in the stomach, making her squirm away from him. "I have some investments. I like to travel in the off-season. And a lot of it actually goes to charity."

Nell sighed. "I was afraid you were going to say that."

"Charity's bad?"

"You're ruining my image of the spoiled, self-centered jock."

That made him grin. "I also partner with a couple of local animal shelters."

She rolled to her side and buried her face in a pillow. "Stop."

"I did buy a ridiculously overpriced penthouse in Chicago that I only used for about six months, if that makes you feel any better."

Images of her cramped apartment with its closet-sized kitchen and leaky sink popped into her head. "No, that just makes me hate you."

"I really should sell the place, I just haven't been able to make myself do it."

"You still have it?" That surprised her, since he hadn't lived in Chicago for over a year. "How overpriced?"

"There's no way I'm telling you that. You have enough dirt on me as is. I need something on you."

"You already know how I got fired. And"—she smacked him in the head with her pillow—"you laughed about it!"

"Because it was hilarious. If you ever tell another parent to go fuck himself, please record it. Now, come on—what's the worst thing you've ever done? You already know mine. It's only fair."

But when she told him about leaving her ex-boyfriend at a campground with nothing but his boxers and a cell phone, Whit just started laughing again.

"So what happened to him?" he wanted to know.

"I have no idea. I blocked his number. If he didn't get eaten by bears, I assume he made it back home."

"I guess I really should beware of pissed off McLeans," he said, and kissed her.

Nell thought she'd be perfectly happy to never get out of bed again, but Friday morning, Whit informed her they couldn't just spend the entire day having sex—total waste, in her opinion—and made her get dressed so he could show her the sights around Minnesota's north shore.

"You do know I grew up next door to Lake Michigan, right?" she asked sulkily.

"And this lake is called..."

"Seen one, seen 'em all," she retorted, though she loved the quick lighthouse tour he took her on, loved the old buildings smelling of dust and history, the low hum of the water as waves lapped the shore. They had to be back in town by six for dinner at Skip's, but that left them with most of the afternoon, and after a quick debate, Whit drove them to nearby Gooseberry Falls, where they hiked along the stream beds and picked their way up long wooden staircases that seemed to rise straight from the earth. When they stopped to eat lunch on a picturesque outcropping of rocks, Nell tilted her face to the sun and closed her eyes, trying to breathe everything in. She wanted to freeze this moment, keep it suspended in time. Whatever came after, she told herself, she had this one beautiful day where everything was perfect and none of it was pretend.

At least until Whit brought her back to reality. "I've been thinking about that prickly temper of yours," he said, nudging her foot with his. He was leaning back on his arms, his legs stretched before him, his aviators hiding his eyes.

Nell was enjoying herself too much to take that bait, but she tried to look huffy. "I don't have a prickly temper."

"Trust me on this one, sweetheart. You're the soul of kindness and patience until someone flips the outrage switch. Then it's time to run for cover. You're like... the Hulk."

"Very flattering."

"She-Hulk, then. Totally sexy. The point is—I think we should rehearse what you're going to say to Frank Grantham."

"We?"

"I'll be his stand-in." His roguish grin made an appearance. "Go ahead. Hit me."

She wasn't going to spend even a second of her precious borrowed time on Frank Grantham. "I rehearsed what I was going to say to you. Look how that turned out."

"Pretty damn well, from where I'm sitting."

"You don't believe he'll listen to me, anyway," she reminded him.

"Maybe you just need the right argument."

"This had better not be leading to another bet."

"It relates to our last bet. I have a vested interest in the outcome."

"You won't even *know* the outcome."

"Why, are you planning to block my number as soon as you get on the plane?"

What did he think three-days-and-done meant? That she'd want to stay friends? Watch him move from one lover to the next? Proof positive that whatever feelings he had for her didn't run very deep, otherwise he would realize what a painful prospect that was. But she didn't want him to think he'd struck a nerve, so she tossed him a teasing smile. "Maybe."

"Harsh. But just so you know, I have my ways."

Nell didn't even want to guess what that was supposed to mean, and she changed the subject. "Have you thought about what you're going to say to James and Sawyer?"

"Yeah. Nothing." Behind his sunglasses, his brow furrowed. "Like I said—all of that is ancient history."

Not if it still hurts you. "That doesn't mean you can't make peace."

"Why, so we can be pals? Reminisce about the good old days? Who cares? We used to be friends. Now we're not. End of story."

Not if you still miss them. "They should know why you were kicked off the team."

"It wouldn't change anything. I still set that fire."

He hauled himself to his feet and held out his hand, but Nell stayed where she was. "How will you know if you don't try?" she asked.

"I do know, so let's drop it."

"I just think—"

Whit's patience snapped. "Nell, stop. I don't need you to fix me, or rescue me, or whatever it is you're trying to do. I've gotten by just fine for twenty-nine years without your help. I think I can manage a little longer. We've had a great time the past few days, but you're not actually my girlfriend, and you're definitely not my therapist."

Nell thought a punch in the gut might actually have hurt less. Fitting that a cloud chose that exact moment to move across the sun. She stood, rubbing her arms. Her throat tightened. "I'm sorry."

"Shit. Nell—"

"You're right. It's none of my business." She forced another smile. "I guess the champion of the underdog just can't help herself." He started to speak again, and she lifted her hand, pressing two fingers lightly over his mouth. "Don't worry about it, okay? I was out of line. I won't mention it again."

***

It started to snow on the drive back to Fallen Oaks. And not big, fluffy, hang-in-the-air-like-a-holiday-movie flakes, either—the sort of wet, heavy snowfall that meant they were in for a couple of inches by morning, and within an hour or so the streets would be thoroughly covered. The trees along the highway already looked like they'd been sprinkled with powdered sugar, and the sudden drop in temperature had left a thin glaze of ice over everything. Probably not the best conditions for a groundbreaking, Whit thought, but if his dad wanted to build a stadium right when winter was set to make an appearance, well, that was on him.

He had his own problems to worry about. Specifically, the woman sitting next to him in the passenger seat.

He didn't have a damn clue what he was going to do about Nell. He knew what he *didn't* want to do, and that was drive her to the airport on Sunday morning and never see her again. He also knew she wouldn't want anything to do with him once she realized he had no intention of going along with Paige's rekindled romance idea. His best chance of smoothing that one over was to have a viable alternate plan for fixing—or at least reducing—the epic scandal Paige was about to find herself immersed in, but so far, the phone calls he'd had with his publicist hadn't been especially productive.

He hadn't dared mention that to Nell, since he already hurt her feelings once that day and he didn't feel like wasting what remained of their time arguing.

Which brought him back to... what the hell was he supposed to do about her? He wanted to yell at her for being such a stubborn idiot about the time limit thing, except that he knew she was doing it to protect herself. And with good reason. It was the exact same reason he'd set up his own rules about dating: keep it casual and no one gets hurt. They ended it here, and it became nothing but a fun week and a fond memory. They could enjoy their last two nights as lovers and then part as friends. That was a hell of a lot more than they'd had beforehand. It just... wasn't enough.

And it wasn't only the sex—though, god, the sex was incredible. Beyond incredible. Nell was everything he hadn't known he wanted in a lover: equal parts tender and bossy; shy at times and playful at others; all sass and sweetness and enthusiasm, with a little chaos thrown into the mix. He'd never laughed so much with a woman, or even wanted to. The night before, she'd made him laugh so hard he'd rolled right off of her. And then before he could fully recover, she'd climbed on top of him, riding him into oblivion while he was still trying to figure out what had happened. Afterward she'd lain nestled against him, her head on his chest, and he'd been shocked by how good it felt having her there. How the hell was he supposed to put her on a plane and give all of that up?

He stole a glance at her through the rearview mirror. The stupid thing was, he could just picture her sitting in the stands, leaping out of her seat to cheer when he struck out the side, her face flushed and her eyes laughing. Or coming to meet him after a game, driving home together, the two of them lying curled up in bed after a long night at the ballpark, warm and sleepy and serene. Absolute fantasy; that wasn't how his world worked. That first rush of excitement, that heady feeling of utter contentment? It faded fast. He knew the reality of it. He'd *lived* the reality of it. He'd seen the toll his father's career had taken on his mother, the way the separation had eaten at her nearly as much as the infidelity, the parts of herself she'd given up even before she'd started drinking. Theirs was an extreme example, Whit understood that—not every guy he played with kept his wife tucked away in another state, and not every guy he played with cheated. But none of them were ever free from temptation. Far too many of them eventually gave in.

Whit had never cheated on a woman and he never would, but that didn't erase all the other complications in his life. It didn't erase the hectic schedule or the media scrutiny. He had a full no-trade clause now, so that at least took care of the uncertainty factor a lot of players' girlfriends had to contend with, but how could he promise *any* woman that it would all be worth it in the end? The expectations and demands that came along with Major League Baseball could easily overwhelm someone unaccustomed to the rigors of professional sports, especially someone as sensitive and caring as Nell. Sure, some of his friends seemed blissfully happy with their wives and girlfriends and were cheerfully producing new additions to families they didn't see half the year, but how long could that last? There was too much at stake, too much risk involved, and Whit wasn't going to be responsible for anyone's broken heart.

But that didn't mean they had to end things quite so soon. He had three months yet before spring training started, and there was no reason he couldn't spend at least part of that time in Chicago. At a minimum, they could have a few more days of fun.

The trick would be somehow convincing Nell to agree to an extension.

He was busy trying to formulate a plan to persuade her—the first step of which would obviously involve getting her naked—when his phone rang. A quick glance at the screen told him it was Allie.

"Hey, what's up?" He assumed she was calling to complain that he was late, since the sudden snow and an unexpected stretch of road construction had delayed them. Ironic, considering Allie had never been on time for anything in her life. "We're about five minutes out."

Her words came out in a rush. "You're not at Dad's yet?"

"I thought *you* were at Dad's."

A pause. "Call me when you're done talking to him." Then she hung up.

That was odd.

What was even more odd was that his father wasn't in the house when they arrived. He was out in the backyard, hitting baseballs.

"Dad?" Whit called, following the telltale sound of a bat meeting a ball to where his father stood, faintly illuminated by the spill of light from the deck and the haze of cloud cover overhead. The snow was falling more softly now, thick flakes dusting his hair and melting into the fabric of the battered old O'Rourke 15 jersey he wore—his second-to-last game jersey, one of the few parts of his career he hadn't locked behind a glass case. That he was wearing it now signaled… something, though Whit was at a loss as to what.

He hesitated a moment, gazing out at his dad. From this distance, it was nearly impossible to tell how the passage of years had changed him. He could have been thirty again: tall, strong, indestructible, that same familiar silhouette Whit had seen countless times as a child—Skip standing alert and ready, the bat in his hands an extension of the body he'd honed through years of hard work and the relentless drive to win. Except that now he wasn't facing a rowdy stadium and a steely-eyed pitcher, and the baseballs he was launching into the ozone didn't come whipping over the plate, but from a large wire basket nestled at his feet. As Whit watched, his dad tossed one of the baseballs into the air, gripped the bat, and swung hard, sending the ball hurtling through the darkness. In a blink, it sailed out of the yard and disappeared somewhere in the woods beyond.

Whit's lips curved in a thin smile. Leave it to Skip to decide the first snowfall was the perfect time to head outside and take a few swings. Still, it wasn't exactly normal behavior—and Allie had been upset about *something*—so he asked Nell to wait for him in the house and then took a few steps toward his father.

"Nice one," he said, whistling as his dad hit another bomb that vanished into the line of trees. "But I seem to remember being grounded for a month when I tried that."

Skip turned, tucking the bat under one arm as he adjusted his batting gloves. He glanced at Whit, then bent down and reached into the basket to reload. "It was only a week, and you smacked a baseball straight into my windshield."

"A windshield you replaced the next day."

"Never did it again, though, did you?" Skip lobbed the next ball into the air, gripped, swung. "Goddamn, I love that sound," he murmured, watching the ball soar into the distance.

"What happened to dinner?" Whit asked, moving to his father's side. He wondered how long Skip had been out there. His jersey wasn't quite soaked through with snow, but it was getting there, and the basket at his feet was already half empty.

"I take it you haven't spoken to your sister."

"Assuming you mean Allie, she told me to talk to you."

"Well, I guess that's something." Skip's mouth twisted. "You came alone?"

"Nell's in the house."

"Good. Gerda can fuss over her for a bit." He paused, laying the bat over the top of the basket, then pulled off his gloves and tucked them into his back pockets. "Jerry Garwood flew in this morning. I'm giving him an interview tomorrow afternoon. I wanted you to hear this from me first."

The first prickle of unease crept up the back of Whit's neck. "We're having a talk out *here*?"

"I like the ambiance." Skip shifted slightly, nudging the basket with his foot so that the bat rolled from one side to the other. Then he looked back at Whit, his expression unreadable. "Did you know I was almost a two-way player?"

"Yeah, Dad, you've mentioned it a few times." More like a few thousand, but who was counting?

"We decided against it after I threw a couple of innings in Low-A. My bat was stronger, and I didn't want to risk an injury that could put me out of the game altogether, so I chose to play it safe. Biggest regret of my entire career. Except how it ended, of course."

"I sense this leading to Rory."

"I was a damn good ballplayer, Whitney. Almost as good as you."

"Dad—"

"Off the field, that's where I fucked things up. I never apologized to you kids for that."

"Are you dying? Are we having a cancer talk right now? Because Grandpa is gonna be seriously pissed you made him quit smoking if he ends up outliving you."

Skip's eyebrows snapped together. "Would you shut up and let me talk? I'm not dying. I have something to tell you, and I need you to let me have my say before you jump down my throat." He snatched up the bat and pushed it at Whit. "Here. Take a swing, kid. You're too old to ground."

"You could ask me to throw for you," Whit pointed out, his fingers automatically sliding around the grip.

"Could, but won't. We both know you can smoke me. Now take a swing."

Whit bent, plucked one of the remaining baseballs from the basket, and bounced it lightly in his hand. "You're never going to find these things again."

"I'll pay a couple of neighborhood kids to collect them. Come on, let's see what you've got."

Whit hadn't done this in years and his timing was off, but he still hit the ball with enough force to launch it quickly out of sight, the hard crack of the impact reverberating in his ears. It *was* a good sound, he decided. As long as it didn't come directly after he'd tossed a meatball dead center over the plate, anyway.

"Not bad," Skip conceded. His lips twitched. "For a pitcher."

Whit flipped the bat to the ground. "You want to tell me what we're doing out here?"

"I'm getting there."

His dad's gaze met his, then flicked away. Those hard lines around his mouth, Whit thought—those were new. And the faint webbing that fanned out from his eyes had deepened in the past few years. But underneath it all he was still Skip O'Rourke, a man who never showed weakness or allowed it, and the fact that he was hesitating now worried Whit more than he wanted to admit.

"July 2002," Skip said finally, lifting his shoulders in a faint shrug.

The date meant nothing to Whit, but he tensed anyway. "What about it?"

"I told you the biggest regret of my career. This is another one." He raked a hand through his snow-dampened hair and exhaled softly. "You remember I had a shoulder injury that spring that landed me on the DL for two months? Bitch of a thing. I was going stir crazy watching the season slide by without me, so when I had a setback in July, I went to see a new trainer. A specialized trainer."

Whit went utterly still.

He stared at his father, unable to form words. Unable even to fathom them. *A specialized trainer.* Whit knew what that meant without either of them speaking it. You didn't seek out that sort of specialist for a minor change in your workout routine or a couple of quick rehab tips, and you didn't lie about it for over twenty years if you did. There was only one reason to keep this particular secret, and Whit knew it better than anyone.

The problem was, he didn't believe it. Didn't want to believe it. It was impossible. Unthinkable. Not his father—not the great Skip O'Rourke, who preached about legacy, about respect for the game, who had once told him that winning meant nothing if you had to sacrifice your integrity in the process.

"No fucking way," he breathed. "You *doped?*"

Skip flinched at the word. "Twice. That's it. Then I realized my recovery wasn't worth it if I couldn't do it clean, and I put a stop to it." He shoved his hands into his jeans pockets. "I didn't tell anyone, and I got lucky. I never tested positive, and Mitchell didn't name me."

The Mitchell Report, an independent investigation into steroids usage in baseball, had sent shockwaves through the community and destroyed the reputations of nearly a hundred players, and if Skip *had* been named on it, it might well have kept him out of Cooperstown. But at that particular moment, Whit didn't care about the Hall of Fame or his father's place in it. His entire universe had tilted, and he had no idea how the hell he was supposed to react. He was reeling. His dad had doped. *His dad* had doped.

Their conversation in the aftermath of his own scandal came roaring back to him. *What the fuck were you thinking, kid? You had everything going for you, and you just threw it all away.*

This is your legacy now. They won't remember you threw two no-hitters before you were twenty-five or care how many strikeouts you had. They'll only remember you cheated.

And that had been the polite part of it.

Something like a laugh caught in his throat. "Jesus, Dad."

"I'm not proud of it," Skip said gruffly. "But I'm not ashamed, either. It was a mistake, but it didn't change who I was as a player."

Words Whit had been waiting four years to hear his father say—except with a different pronoun. How was that for irony?

And Whit *had* been ashamed. He still was. His breath skidded out of him. "You couldn't have told me that four years ago?"

That had always been the worst part of it, knowing how badly he'd let his father down. Forget the fans; forget the media backlash and the judgment from men and women who didn't know him and never would. It was the disappointment in his father's voice that had been the real knife twist. As much as he'd tried to deny it, tried to pretend that Skip's opinion of him no longer mattered—of course it had mattered. It had always mattered. It probably always would.

Skip's jaw tightened. "If you'd told me what you were planning, I'd have talked you out of it."

"*After*," Whit answered, struggling to keep his voice steady. "You could have told me after. You could have told me I wasn't the only who had made a mistake, instead of letting me spend all this time believing that I'd failed you. Failed your *legacy*. That I was the lesser O'Rourke."

"I never said that."

"You never said I wasn't. I needed my dad, and all I got was another lecture from good ol' Number Fifteen." This time Whit did laugh. "All that bullshit about dragging the family name through the mud... but I guess it's all right to cheat as long as no one finds out."

"I didn't cheat," Skip growled. "I wasn't juicing to give myself an edge. I wasn't trying to leave the yard every time I made contact. I just wanted to get back in the game."

The same argument Whit had made to himself dozens of times, first to convince himself that it was all right to bend the rules, and then to absolve himself afterwards. He'd told himself it wasn't about breaking records or needing to be the best, it was about wanting to play. But that was only an excuse, and Whit was long past trying to justify it. "No, Dad, you cheated. You cheated and so did I, and if you think Jerry Garwood or anyone else is going to see it differently, you are seriously deluding yourself."

Instead of firing back, his father seemed to deflate. His shoulders sagged. "I know. You're right, and I'm sorry I didn't tell you sooner. But I can't change the past, Whit. I can only try to do better in the future."

"And this is your idea of doing better? Blowing up your reputation?"

The enormity of just what his dad was planning finally hit him. Once Skip revealed his PEDs usage, the fallout would make Whit's scandal seem trivial in comparison. Everything Skip had ever done would be called into question. His two MVP awards, his thirteen All-Star berths... every stolen base, every jaw-dropping play, every home run... all of it, reduced to a single fact: Skip O'Rourke had doped. Those were the words that would define his legacy from now on. Two times or two dozen, no one would care; he had doped, and he'd lied about it for over twenty years. And unlike Whit, he wouldn't have the opportunity to move past it and prove his detractors wrong.

So why was he doing this? It was completely unprecedented. Almost no one admitted to using PEDs unless they had to, and Whit couldn't quite believe that his dad was suddenly eaten up with guilt, not after two decades of keeping silent. Not without reason. He was missing something here.

"You may as well tell me the rest of it," he said grimly. Though at this point, he couldn't imagine what else his father could possibly be hiding, since terminal illness was out. Tax fraud? Millions of dollars in gambling debt? An impending arrest on felony drug charges?

Skip's gaze sharpened. "What makes you think there's a rest of it?"

"Allie wouldn't care that you doped," Whit replied. And Rory... Rory would have stood by him, not faked an elopement with the man who ended his career. "So what other deep, dark secret are you waiting to confess?"

Skip turned, facing the backdrop of old pines that tangled together at the edge of the woods, veiled now with evening shadows and the frail dusting of snow. He shook his head slowly, his breath fogging the air as he exhaled. His voice went thick. "You know, I thought this would be easier. After Rory found out, and then Allie... I figured it couldn't get much worse than that. But you judge me harder than they ever did. Always have."

Whit held up a hand. "Hold on a second. *I* judge *you?*"

"I'm not saying I blame you. God knows I deserve it." Skip sighed, kicking at a clump of snow that had begun to collect in the grass. "I've thought of a thousand different ways to tell you, and none of them felt right. So I'm just gonna say it. Straight up, no excuses. Then you can tell me to go to hell, or cut me out of your life, or do whatever it is you're gonna do."

"Come on, Dad—"

"It's Maggie."

"Maggie?" Whit echoed. Another laugh sputtered out of him. "You think I care who you date?"

The moment it was spoken, Whit realized he was wrong. No, he didn't care who his father was dating, and neither would his sisters. At least not who their dad was dating *now*.

But there had been a time when it had mattered a lot.

Skip twisted around again, gaze blank. "What are you talking about?"

"You and Maggie."

He stared at his father, sudden certainty warring with disbelief. He'd been so convinced Maggie was Skip's latest feminine diversion, he hadn't even considered that there were other possibilities.

That she might have some other connection to him.

To them.

No fucking way, Whit thought again.

The outrage that exploded on his father's face confirmed it before his words did.

"For Christ's sake, Whit," Skip choked out. "Maggie's not my girl-friend. She's my daughter."

TWENTY-ONE

IT WAS STRANGE, WHIT thought as he gazed across the snowy darkness at his father, but he wasn't even angry.

He knew he *should* be angry. After everything Skip had just said, everything he'd failed to say during the past four years, Whit should be on anger overload by now. Maybe not *run off to Vegas with his father's worst enemy* levels of enraged, but at least enough to make a pointed exit like Allie had.

Instead he just felt numb.

Of course his dad had another kid. Hell, he might have twenty. Screw enough women and there was bound to be an accident sooner or later, no matter how careful you were. And Skip O'Rourke wasn't exactly famed for being careful. He probably had a slew of paternity suits discreetly hidden by his legion of lawyers. The only real shock was that it had taken this long for any of them to realize it.

Maybe they just hadn't wanted to.

He listened wordlessly as his dad filled in the details. Three months ago, Skip had received a letter from Maggie's father—the man who raised her—informing him of Maggie's existence. A deathbed confession, apparently, or close enough; he'd died of cancer not long after. Skip had been skeptical, but had been spooked enough to employ a firm to independently verify the man's claims. The report they'd given him mid-September had confirmed his paternity. Maggie was Skip's biological daughter, the result of a one night stand with a woman he couldn't even remember.

The least surprising thing he'd said all night, Whit thought wryly.

Maggie's mother had passed away when she was a child, and her dad hadn't told her the truth before his death. He'd left that particular task to Skip. His first job as her father: letting her know she'd been lied to her entire life.

Skip had hired her as his assistant instead.

"I was getting around to telling her," Skip said now. "I wanted us—all of us—to have a chance to get to know each other first. Then Allie found out, and Maggie overheard, and..." He sighed, lifting a hand to rub his forehead. "It went about as well as I expected. Maggie drove off and told me not to contact her again. She's heading home tomorrow, if she hasn't already left."

"Hence your little pity party."

"It's not a damn pity party."

"You're outside, in the snow, whacking baseballs after dark. What else do you want to call it?" Not to mention planning to torpedo the reputation he'd spent decades building. Whit had a feeling Skip's decision to do the Garwood interview was less about coming clean and more about some twisted form of penance.

Skip's eyes narrowed. "That's all you're gonna say?"

"No. Your plan sucked. Come on, Dad. *Hiring* her?"

He rubbed his forehead again. "I know."

"And I guess I know why Rory's pissed." He didn't know Maggie's birthday, but she was close enough in age to Rory for him to draw his own conclusions: Skip hadn't just spent the entirety of his marriage cheating on his wife with every groupie that crossed his path, he'd knocked up two women at the same time. And after having recently been cheated on herself, Whit didn't blame Rory for going nuclear. He just wished she'd told him about it. "Does Mom know?"

"Your mom doesn't have anything to do with this."

The mantra of cheating spouses everywhere. "Maybe not now. Back then she sure as hell did."

"Back then I was young and stupid. It's not like I planned this."

"Of course not. Women just fell into your lap and you were powerless to resist."

"Close enough," Skip muttered. "You know what it's like."

Exactly what he had told Nell: *Whatever you want, whoever you want, whenever you want.* Except you still had to be the one to say yes. "Why settle for leftovers at home when you're being treated to the all-you-can-eat buffet, right?"

Skip's voice was grim. "I wouldn't put it like that."

"Not in those words, at least," Whit retorted. He'd been in enough locker rooms to know that that was the *sanitized* version. It was a philosophy shared by more than one of the guys he'd played with over the years, and somehow they were always surprised when the "leftovers" served them with divorce papers. "And I do know what it's like, Dad—but I've still managed to go through life thinking with something other than my dick."

"You didn't wind up married with a kid on the way by the time you were twenty-one," Skip snapped.

"So it's my fault you screwed around."

"Stop putting words in my mouth. That's not what I said."

"Close enough," Whit echoed. He was finding his anger now and, as it turned out, he had rage to spare. "Did you know one of your girlfriends tried to come on to me? I was sixteen. You'd gotten tired of her, so I guess she decided to move in on the younger model. I said I wasn't interested in my dad's sloppy seconds and told her to get lost."

"You should've told me. I'd have taken care of it."

"And said what? Hey, Dad, one of your side pieces just offered to blow me?"

"You want me to say I was an asshole? I was an asshole. I was a shit husband and a shit father, and now I'm trying to make up for it."

"Mark it on the calendar. Skip O'Rourke admits he fucked up."

"You done yet?"

"Not even close." But when he opened his mouth to fire off another sharp retort, the words seemed to evaporate. His throat felt thick.

He glanced at the wire basket near his feet where the half dozen or so remaining baseballs had collected a light dusting of snow. Crouching, he reached a hand inside, letting his fingertips graze the leathery surfaces. Then he stood again and faced his father, ball in hand. "Pick up your bat."

Skip's eyebrows lifted. "What, so you can bean me? I don't think so."

"I'm not gonna be tossing fastballs at your head," Whit shot back. He moved away, rolling his shoulders to loosen up. He wasn't about to do any serious throwing, especially since he wouldn't have much of a warm-up, but he could still strike out his dad without risking high and inside.

At least he was pretty sure he could.

"How's this," he offered, "I'll show off my knuckleball."

Even in the low light he could see his dad's grimace. "So you're definitely gonna bean me."

"I thought you enjoyed life on the edge."

"I also like my nose where it is."

"If I see any blood, I'll call you an ambulance."

He went through an abbreviated warm-up while his dad put his batting gloves back on, took a couple of quick practice swings, and tapped the bat twice against his feet. The old, familiar routine. Whit closed his eyes and drew in air, searching for that calming focus he used to center himself before games. He hoped his dad was right and the housekeeper was busy fussing over Nell, because if she happened to be watching out the window, she'd probably think they'd both gone nuts.

Which, well, maybe they had.

His first pitch broke to the left, whizzing just past the reach of Skip's bat before vanishing somewhere near the treeline.

Skip adjusted his gloves again and glared. "The fuck was that? That was like a mile outside."

"You swung at it." He plucked another ball from the basket and tossed it back and forth in his hands. "So how did Rory find out?"

"Hell if I know. She said she won't reveal her sources, whatever that means." Skip paused, lowering his bat. "Look, what I said before—it wasn't how it sounded. I don't want you to think you weren't wanted.

Your mom and I got married because we were in love, not because we had to."

"Yeah. And look where that got you."

"Because I was a dumb fuck who didn't know how good he had it."

"You mean you *are* a dumb fuck."

His dad scowled. "Just throw the damn ball."

The second pitch was even further outside, but Skip managed to catch a piece of it, just enough to send the ball spiking into the grass at his feet. He glanced at it in disgust, then back at Whit. "You wanna try something in the same hemisphere as the plate next time?"

"I found my spot. Not my fault you forgot how to hit." He pulled another ball from the basket. "Did you tell Grandpa?"

"You think I wanted him lecturing me every day for the past three months?" Skip tapped his bat to the ground again and took a moment to brush the snow from his jersey before moving back into his stance. His eyebrows drew together. "Dad's on his way over. Figured there's no sense keeping it quiet any longer. A lot's going to change after tomorrow."

More than he knew, Whit thought. And Maggie was the least of it. As soon as Garwood published his interview, Skip's reputation would be shattered. No more legend. No more legacy. Instead of being known as one of the all-time greats, he would become exactly what his son was: just another doper. Another lying, cheating O'Rourke.

"You planning to toss that thing, or are we just gonna stand here all night?" Skip hollered toward him.

Whit's stomach twisted. He glanced down at the ball in his hand, tracing the seams with his thumb. "You know, for the first ten years of my life, I wanted to be just like you," he murmured. He felt the sudden catch in his throat, fought it down. "Every day since, I've done whatever I could to be anything but."

Skip grunted. "You should've picked a different career, then."

"I've never cheated on a woman."

"Congratu-fuckin-lations."

"Back when I hit free agency—any team you'd played for made me an offer? I turned it down flat."

"Now that's just stupid."

"Maybe," Whit agreed. "Since it turns out we're not so different after all." He swallowed hard, tightening his grip on the ball. "Giving that interview isn't going to fix anything, Dad."

Skip's gaze flicked away. "It's not about fixing things. It's about doing what's right."

"Bullshit. You could've done what was right twenty years ago. Or *four* years ago."

"Me coming clean four years ago would've only made things worse for you."

"And what do you think it's going to do now? You think the media will pass up the opportunity to gloat about the father and son dopers?"

"So it's not my reputation you're worried about, it's yours."

"It's all of it," Whit retorted. He could imagine the headlines already. The scathing rebukes and phony laments about scandals ruining baseball. There was nothing the sports world loved more than a fall from grace, and Skip had a long way down. "Have you actually thought this through? Like, even a little? You know what's going to happen, right?"

"I'm prepared for the fallout."

"I seriously doubt that." He flipped the baseball back and forth between his hands and shot a look toward his dad. "Here's how this is gonna go. I strike you out, you don't do the Garwood interview. There's no winning that one, Dad. For anyone. Besides—there's only one fuck-up allowed in this family, and I'm it."

Across the distance, he saw Skip's jaw clench. "The interview is already scheduled."

"So cancel it. Or talk to him about the stadium you've been trying to build for a decade. Isn't that the reason you flew him out here in the first place?"

Skip shook his head. "I'll keep you out of it as much as I can, but it's time for the truth to come out."

"All that does is punish the thousands of kids who grew up worshiping you." He didn't even know why it was so important to him, he just knew that it was. He'd been one of those kids, and the child he'd been couldn't bear the thought of what he was about to lose.

"I've been out of the game a long time. If they worshiped me, they aren't kids anymore."

"Do it for me, then," Whit said. "Because I'm asking you."

"I've made up my mind, Whitney."

"Then you'd better hit the ball."

Whit knew the moment the ball left his grip that his command was off. Half a second late on his release; not enough spin. The baseball hurtled through the falling snow toward Skip, dead center over the imaginary plate.

Skip swung.

The crack of the bat against the ball was all the answer Whit needed. He didn't turn to watch it fly. "I guess that's that."

Skip let his arms drop to his sides. The bat slid into the grass beside him. "Come on, kid, you weren't even trying with that pitch. *I* can throw better than that."

Whit closed his eyes, shoving his hands into his pockets. What had he expected? That for once in his life, his dad would actually listen to him? That he'd put someone else's wants above his own? Skip O'Rourke wasn't built like that. He never had been.

"You might want to stock up on baseballs," Whit said, nudging the basket with the tip of his boot. "Something tells me you're gonna be throwing a lot more pity parties."

Shaking the snow from his hair, he turned and headed for the house.

***

Whit had booked a room at a lakeside bed and breakfast for the night, a cozy, rustic lodge nestled by pines and situated a couple of miles out of town. He'd never stayed there before, but the proprietor was an old friend of Bucky's, the reviews were glowing, and Whit thought Nell might enjoy the prospect of a secluded hideaway before all the mayhem of the upcoming festivities. According to the website, their room came with its own wood fireplace and private balcony that looked out over the water, and in the cooler months, the kitchen served round-the-clock hot chocolate. The place even had a cutesy address, Snowsugar Road, currently earning its name with the soft, silvery glaze that glittered along the pavement.

Whit drove right past it.

They could spend the night at the farm, he thought as he pulled onto the highway. Bucky had arrived at Skip's with a six-pack and a promise to crash on the couch if he broke into the liquor cabinet—pretty much guaranteed—which meant Whit and Nell would have his place to themselves. The turnoff was only a couple of exits ahead, a long, winding gravel road whose twists and bumps Whit still knew by heart.

He drove past that, too.

"You want to talk about it?" Nell asked. She must have sensed how close he'd been to unraveling earlier, because she hadn't asked any questions when he'd stalked into his father's house, tight-jawed and tense. She'd just taken one look at his face and followed him back out to the car. Now she sat quietly beside him, fidgeting with her seat belt and sending him concerned looks whenever he glanced in her direction.

Whit kept his eyes on the road. "Nope."

"Okay. Do you want to tell me where we're going?"

"What would you do if I said Chicago?"

Her sharp inhale told him she'd misunderstood. "You're taking me to the airport?"

"Us. I'm taking *us* to the airport."

"You want to come with me to Chicago?" She stopped fidgeting and twisted around to face him. "*Now?*"

"I need to get out of here for a while."

"But... you can't come with me. That wasn't our deal."

"The deal is stupid. I have an empty apartment and three months of freedom ahead of me, and I say we spend that time as naked as possible, as soon as possible."

"I'm not going anywhere with you until you tell me what's going on."

"If your plan is to jump out of a moving car, I have to say, I wouldn't recommend it."

"You know what I meant," she gritted out. "What is the *matter* with you?"

A question he'd been asking himself for a good twenty minutes, and unfortunately, he couldn't just stay on the highway until he sorted it out. They weren't even headed in the right direction if he planned to make for the airport. At this rate, they'd probably end up in Canada.

With a sigh, Whit slowed the Maserati and guided it onto the turnoff for a county park that butted up against one of the region's smaller lakes—a wide, grassy area with an arrangement of barbecue grills and picnic tables, flanked by a couple of wooden gazebos. If he wanted secluded, this fit the bill. In the summer months, the place would have been packed from sunup to sundown, filled with kids hauling inflatable rafts and harried parents slathering their impatient offspring with sunscreen. Now the lot adjoining the park was open but empty, the asphalt littered with discarded beer cans and forgotten toys rapidly disappearing beneath the snow. The glare of the headlights skimmed off a battered sign that declared no lifeguard was on duty. After a quick glance confirmed the park was deserted, Whit pulled the Maserati into a space near one of the picnic tables and killed the engine.

Childhood memory flickered: late August heat beating down across his bare shoulders, the giddy shrieks of his sisters splashing at the nearby beach. The crackle of his mother's ancient radio spitting out game scores.

"I think I'd better take these," Nell murmured, reaching across him to pull the keys from the ignition. Before he could protest, they vanished into one of her jacket pockets. "Now... want to tell me why you're running away?"

"I'm not running away."

"This is the third time this week you've kidnapped me. I'm not getting in another car with you unless I'm the one driving."

"I'm not running away," he repeated stubbornly. "I just don't want to deal with my dad for a while."

"Well, you'd better not have brought us out here for a swim," she joked, tugging her jacket tighter.

Whit reached into the backseat for his own jacket and tossed it to her. "Bundle up. We're going for a walk." He shoved the driver door open and climbed out, heading toward the park with long, slow strides.

He hadn't thought about this place in years. Longer, probably. Over a decade had passed since he'd even set foot there, but every inch of it was familiar—proof, he supposed, that some things didn't change. Maybe someone had slapped a fresh coat of paint on the gazebos, but the tables were still scattered in the same haphazard layout, the same creaky water pump still jutted up near the hiking trail, and the ancient metal grills still smelled of old charcoal and burned food. Strange how comforting that was. He paused, glancing back at Nell. He'd intended to make for the beach, maybe stand on the shore for a while, watch the snowfall vanish along the water's surface, clear his head a little. Instead, he came to a halt near one of the picnic tables and perched on the edge, his legs stretched out, his palms flat against the cool wooden surface. Wordless, Nell slid up beside him and tucked her hand over his.

Frightening how comforting *that* was.

"We used to come here when I was a kid," he said, resisting the urge to turn his hand and twine his fingers with hers. "End of summer, right when school started. Mom would round us up on the weekends, drive us out here, listen to Dad's games on the radio while we ran around like maniacs and threw ourselves into the lake. Then we'd go for ice cream. That was supposed to be our consolation prize—swimming and ice cream."

Nell's voice was soft. "That must have been hard on you."

He hitched a shoulder. "At least he was around part of the time. I figure that's better than what you got."

"Maybe." Her thumb stroked the back of his hand idly. "Maybe not. I never really knew my father well enough to miss him. He'd show up and disappear again so quickly, I was never sure what to expect from him. I looked forward to his birthday cards mostly. At least until I was old enough to realize it was my mom who was actually sending them."

"Sounds like she was a good mom."

"The best."

The smile in her tone made him turn toward her. *She* would make a good mother, he thought. The idea had popped into his head out of nowhere, but now that it was there, he couldn't shake it. He could just picture her, the wind in her hair, eyes brimming with laughter as she waited at the bottom of a slide, a couple of adoring, adorable mini-Nells tugging at her, complete with sticky fingers and apple cheeks. He imagined she was like that in her classroom: patient, playful, as capable of holding her own with a passel of second graders as she was with a bunch of rowdy, aging ballplayers. Kind but firm—and ready to do battle with anyone or anything that threatened her kids.

She was watching him now with that same quiet patience, her eyes dark pools, her lashes tipped with snow. Her freckles weren't visible in the low light, but he knew they were there. He wanted to trace them with his fingertips, one by one.

How had he ever thought she wasn't beautiful? The look of tenderness on her face made him feel like he'd been punched in the gut.

"What?" she asked.

He wanted to tell her that—that she was beautiful in a way that made his heart stop and his throat close up, in a way that made him want to wake up beside her every morning and just lie there, watching her sleep. He wanted to tell her he'd been an idiot to think anything between them could ever be casual, and that he would be seven kinds of stupid to let her walk out of his life two days from now.

But she deserved more than that, she deserved a man who could *give* her more than that, and it would be better for both of them to leave some things unsaid.

He pulled his hand from hers, raking his fingers through his snow-damp hair. With a ragged exhale, he turned his gaze toward the lake. He supposed he should at least explain to her why he'd been acting completely unhinged.

"Maggie is my sister," he said softly. The words came out easier than expected, but his voice stuttered on the last syllable, and he paused a moment, took in a breath. "My half-sister. Dad got another woman pregnant while he was married to my mom. That's what we were arguing about. Part of it, anyway." As for the rest of it... Nell would find that mess out in a couple of days, along with everyone else on the planet. "Dad didn't even know until a couple of months ago, if you can believe that."

The way she was biting down on her lip told him she could.

"You don't seem surprised," he said.

"It fits better than her being your dad's girlfriend." She laid her fingertips on his arm, the lightest of touches. "Are you all right? Sorry—stupid question."

Whit shrugged. "I'll adjust."

"Does Maggie know?"

"She does now. Apparently it didn't go well."

"I guess that explains what's going on with your sisters. Your other sisters."

"Yeah. Remind me to thank Rory for keeping *that* little secret."

"I imagine it's a lot to process."

Especially for Allie, he thought. She was the baby of the family, and he and Rory had done their best to shield her from the chaos of their parents' marriage. As a result, she'd never realized the extent of Skip's infidelity. Pranks aside, she'd always been a daddy's girl. Rory, however... "She could've found a better way than running off to Vegas."

"I was talking about you," Nell said.

Of course she was. That big heart of hers couldn't bear to see anyone hurt. And right now, all her worry was focused on him—he could see it in the way her eyebrows had drawn together, that delicate wrinkle forming between them. He reached toward her, smoothing the wrinkle away with his thumb. "I'm sorry for freaking out on you."

"I'd say that's a normal reaction to finding out you have another sibling." One corner of her mouth tilted up teasingly. "Maybe not the kidnapping part."

He was too raw to rehash his entire conversation with his father, but he gave Nell the basics—how his dad had first learned about Maggie, Skip's asinine decision to hire her rather than simply tell the truth. "Obviously, that backfired," Whit said, working to keep the bitter edge from his tone. Overhead, the snow had drifted into flurries, and a spill of moonlight broke through the cloud cover to gleam on the lake. Whit let his hands drop to his sides, fingers tightening. "Dad says he's trying. That's the really screwed up part about this whole thing—I actually believe him." His mouth gave a wry twist.

Nell's voice was gentle. "What are you going to do?"

"Me? I'm not going to do anything. Maggie's leaving town. She wants nothing to do with us, and good for her. The last thing anyone needs is Skip for a dad."

"I don't know about that." She touched his sleeve again. "You turned out pretty well."

"Yeah, fuckin' fantastic."

"Except for being way too hard on yourself," she added.

He grinned.

"What?"

"You said hard-on."

Nell rolled her eyes. "Plus having the approximate maturity of an eight-year-old. Too bad for you, I deal with *actual* eight-year-olds. I'm familiar with diversionary tactics." She turned toward him, and he could tell by the stubborn set to her jaw he wasn't going to wiggle out of this one easily. The wrinkle he'd smoothed away was back with a vengeance. "All right, Whitney O'Rourke, sit yourself down. We need to have a little chat."

"I am sitting down."

"Then stay that way, and listen up. I have some news for you, Whit. You're not perfect. But guess what? Nobody is. You're a good man. You don't have to punish yourself forever just because you've made mistakes." She took his hand. "Repeat after me: *I'm a good man.*"

He leered at her instead. "You don't have to sweet talk me, baby. Just say the word, and I'll drop my pants."

"I'm being serious. I'm not trying to fix you. Or rescue you. I just want..." She let his hand fall, shook her head. "What I said to you in the bar that night—you know I didn't mean it, right?"

His skeptical look said it all. He assumed it did, anyway, because Nell flushed.

"Okay, maybe I meant it at that exact moment," she amended, "but I didn't *really* mean it. And I'm sorry I said it."

"You didn't say anything I didn't deserve." When she started to protest, he held up a hand. "At least at that exact moment."

Hell, he'd probably deserved worse.

He wasn't proud of it. The instant he'd seen her at Gills, he'd completely short-circuited. His mind had shut off, sheer instinct taking over; like a cornered animal, that instinct had been to lash out. He'd spent four long years trying to put the past behind him, and suddenly there she'd been, a specter from the darkest days of his career. A vivid reminder of his myriad sins.

And now here she was, absolving him.

He didn't know if that was irony or fate, but either way, it was high time he absolved her, too.

"You're wrong," he told her. "I'm not punishing myself for my mistakes, I'm owning them. *All* of them." He tucked a stray lock of hair behind her ear, his thumb following the curve of the helix and tracing a slow path downward. "It's your turn to listen. Not a word until I'm done, okay?"

She nodded against his hand.

"I've been trying to figure out what was going through my head when Paige called me last week. I was joking, yeah, but I guess some part of me wanted a little petty revenge." He let out a rueful laugh. "I definitely never thought she'd actually send you—or that you'd agree to it."

"Sister pact. I was bound by sacred oath."

Whit smirked. "Or maybe you just wanted to see me again."

Another eye roll. "That was absolutely *not* it."

"Remember what I said about not talking?" He pressed his fingers over her lips, keeping his gaze steady on hers, and drew in a slow breath. This was the hardest part, but he had to get through it. He owed her that. "For a while, I hated you. Seriously hated you. That video of yours haunted me. *You* haunted me. Everything went out of control so quickly—my injury... the scandal... It felt like my entire life was unraveling, and it was a hell of a lot easier to blame you than to admit I'd fucked up. And I did fuck up. Massively. I knew exactly what I was doing. That was my mistake, Nell. Not yours. You have nothing to apologize for. You never did."

And as for himself... he was through with apologizing. Whatever happened with his father's interview, Whit had done his penance and paid his dues. If the media wanted to paint him as the Bad Boy of Baseball, that was their problem, not his.

Nell's lips curved. "Hated, huh?"

"Past tense," he said hastily. To emphasize his point, he slanted another leer toward her. "*Very* past tense."

She laughed. "You can get to work on convincing me of that part in a moment, but first..." She reached up and unclasped his lucky silver chain from where it lay around her neck, eased it out from her jacket, and placed it gently in his hand, closing his fingers around it. "Here. This thing is making me nervous. I don't want to suffer the wrath of the baseball gods if I lose it."

Whit blinked down at it. "Why do I feel like I just got dumped?"

"I can't dump you. We're not dating."

"I sense a *but*."

She glanced away. Too quickly. "I didn't mean what I said in the bar..."

"Yeah, you said that already."

"...But I meant it when I said you can't come to Chicago with me."

"Right. Because of our deal."

"No. Not because of our deal." She lifted her gaze to his, held it. Something hot and unspoken passed between them. "Whit..."

Panic seized him. He didn't know what she was going to say, but he knew he couldn't let her say it. He curled his hand around the back of her neck and pulled her to him, crushing his mouth against hers.

It was a hungry, hurried kiss. Nothing tender or gentle about it. Pure physical need, desperate almost, like this would be the last kiss, the only kiss, and they had to make it count. She gave him everything and he took it, greedily, even when she bit down on his lip hard enough to make him wince. He held her there until they were both gasping, and when they finally came up for air, he kept his hand in her hair, breathed against her cheek. "Two nights left, huh?"

"Give or take."

"Then I guess we'd better stop wasting them."

***

They spent the night at the farm. The B&B would be a waste, they agreed—too little time, too much hassle. The farm was closer, and sitting empty anyway.

Neither of them wanted to say it, but something between them had altered. They'd tumbled into bed with wordless urgency, tearing at each other's clothes before they'd made it halfway across the room. Afterward, instead of lying curled against his chest, Nell had slipped out of bed and into the shower, and Whit hadn't offered to join her. He'd drifted off to sleep before she returned, and when he woke the next morning, she was already in the kitchen, brewing coffee. But the urgency hadn't left them, and this time they only made it as far as the living room wall. With her legs locked around him, both of them panting, he moved against her hard enough to make the wall shake. His mouth found the delicate flesh along her collarbone. His fingers dug into her hips. He wanted to leave his mark on her, imprint his body upon hers, so that weeks from now, years from now, she'd remember that hot, sweet ache that only he had been able to satisfy. It was irrational, it was unreasonable, and he didn't care. Dimly he heard the sound of a crash, but he was too lost in Nell's moans to do anything but keep going, keep pushing them both closer and closer to the brink, and then over it, until they just stood there, bodies quivering and spent, glistening with sweat.

When he came back to himself, it was to the guilty realization that they'd wreaked havoc on more than just each other. Not only were there a couple of knickknacks on the floor—along with his shirt and the panties he had literally ripped off her—but one of his grandfather's puzzles had slipped from the wall. It lay on the carpet, frame askew, a long, damning crack running the length of the glass.

Whit stared down at it, rubbing his nose sheepishly. "My grandpa is going to kill me."

Nell looked a little unsteady as she bent to retrieve her underwear. "Maybe he won't notice?"

Whit snorted and padded back into the kitchen to search Bucky's tool drawer for glue.

Bucky had texted to say he wouldn't make it back to the farm before noon, which gave them plenty of time to put the house back in order—provided they could keep their hands off each other—but barely twenty minutes had passed before the faint chime of the door-bell sounded. Nell poked her head out from the bedroom, where she'd been packing the rest of her clothing into the small canvas carry-on she'd brought from Chicago.

"Are you expecting someone?" she asked.

"It's probably Allie." Whit hadn't returned his sister's call the night before, and her patience at the best of times was thin bordering on nonexistent. No doubt she'd decided to take matters into her own hands, which meant he had another thrilling conversation about his father's infidelity ahead of him. With a sigh, Whit hopped up from the table where he'd been engaged in a futile attempt at puzzle repair and headed for the entrance. He reached the door with a couple of loping strides and yanked it open.

But the woman who stood scowling on the porch, arms folded, mouth a red slash of disapproval, wasn't his sister.

Her words came out in a teeth-clenched hiss. "Hello, Whitney."

Whit swallowed a curse and plastered a smile on his face. "Paige."

TWENTY-TWO

OF ALL THE WAYS Nell had imagined Paige finding out about her and Whit—and over the past few days, she'd spent a lot of time imagining—this had to be the worst. They had *recent lovers* written all over them. Whit was wearing nothing but a pair of shorts and his sweaty T-shirt, and though Nell had put on clean clothing, her disaster zone hair and the swollen red splotch that had formed on her collarbone could leave little doubt as to what they'd been doing. The only thing that prevented this from being the absolute pinnacle of nightmare scenarios was the fact that Paige hadn't arrived half an hour earlier. Just the thought of that possibility made Nell want to hyperventilate.

Not that she had ever envisioned this precise situation. Mostly because it hadn't occurred to her that Paige would somehow find her way to a nameless farm in the middle of nowhere. She was supposed to be in Cabo! She should be two thousand miles from here, relaxing in the hot sun and drunk-dialing Gabi, not skewering Whit with a death glare icy enough to make their grandmother proud. Paige shouldn't even be in the same country as them, let alone the same room.

But since she *was* here...

Nell straightened her shoulders and lifted her head, trying to steel her nerves. Paige was always going to find out, and Nell had been deluding herself to pretend otherwise. She'd made her decision that first afternoon, when she'd agreed to stay in Fallen Oaks instead of doing the responsible thing and getting on a flight back to Chicago. And the hard truth was, she wasn't even sorry for it. Whatever happened now—and she had a strong suspicion the next several minutes would count among the most painful of her life—she was long past regrets.

Her borrowed time was up, and now she had to face the consequences. This was the bargain she'd made. Her deal with the devil. A few days of reckless happiness with the man she loved.

And all she'd had to give up was her heart.

Whit hadn't moved aside to let Paige into the house, but she didn't wait for an invitation. She pushed past him, still glowering, and darted a quick glance around the room. "I'm tired, I'm jet-lagged, and I'm crabby as hell, so let's cut to the chase. Where's my sister?"

"I'm here." Nell stepped out from the bedroom doorway, surprised at how steady her voice sounded. She managed a weak smile. "Hi, Paige."

Paige swung toward her. She didn't look tired or jet-lagged, Nell thought. She looked as beautiful as ever, her shiny blonde hair falling around her shoulders with careful artistry, her makeup dramatic and flawless. Her black silk halter top and wrap skirt had been meant for warmer weather, which told Nell she'd been in too much of a rush to bother with a change of wardrobe. Her strappy six-inch heels put her nearly at a height with Whit. Intentional, Nell knew, since Paige only wore heels when she had to.

"Well, now, isn't this cozy," Paige drawled. She tapped her fingers along her arms as her gaze swept over Nell, taking everything in—bare feet, mussed hair, puffy lips, the faint bruise at her collar. Her eyebrows lifted. "Forget to mention a couple of things in your last text?"

What was there to even say? "I was going to tell you." Eventually. Probably. But only because she'd never been very good at keeping secrets from Paige. Nell wiped her sweaty palms on her jeans and turned to Whit. "Can I have a moment with my sister?"

He crossed the room at a jog and tucked her hand into his. "I'm not going anywhere."

The concern she saw in his eyes made her heart constrict, but this was her mess, and she had to be the one to deal with it. "I'll be okay."

Paige made a gesture of impatience. "That's sweet, but unnecessary," she told Whit. "We're not staying." Her gaze flicked back to Nell. "Consider this an intervention. Playtime's over, Nellie. Time to go home."

Nell opened her mouth to respond, but Whit was quicker. "How are you even here?" he demanded, keeping Nell's hand firmly in his grip. "I don't remember giving you this address."

"*That's* your main concern right now?" Paige huffed. Her shoulders lifted in a faint shrug. "Some groupie put it together. Imagine my surprise when a Whitney O'Rourke superfan messaged me, telling me all about how my ex-boyfriend was hooking up with my scheming little sister—complete with photographic evidence. They sent me the address, I guess to convince me to come fetch her. Which, well, mission accomplished, so bravo to them. You might want to get that checked into, though, because it looks like you have a stalker with a serious voyeurism fetish."

Nell felt sick. "Someone's been taking pictures of us?"

"Don't worry, they're flattering," Paige said, flashing her teeth. Nell couldn't tell if she was being sincere or sarcastic. Knowing Paige, it could be either.

Whit had skipped right past the *stalker* part and was busy skewering Paige with a glare of his own. "Your ex-boyfriend?" he retorted in a tone that was half disbelief, half disgust. "We broke up *four years ago*. Nell and I are two consenting adults, and what we choose to do with our time is our business, not yours."

Paige tossed her hair. "You think I hopped on a plane from Mexico and drove for three hours at the crack of dawn because I care about *you*? Please. I'm here to save my sister from herself. I know how quickly you go through women, and I don't want to see her get hurt." A thin wrinkle worked its way onto her brow. "Though from the looks of it, I arrived too late."

Oh, god, Nell thought. Panic surged as understanding dawned. Paige wasn't here because she was angry. She was here because she was overprotective.

That was so much worse.

Nell heard the roar of a freight train in her ears. Breakneck speed, collision course, bearing down on her. Desperately, she tried to derail it before it could come crashing into them. She pulled her hand free from Whit's and took a step toward Paige. "I know I messed up," she began, "and I'm sorry for not telling you. But this isn't going to interfere with your plans. My flight home leaves tomorrow morning, and Whit already agreed to go along with your PR"—she couldn't make herself say *romance*—"idea."

"Really. He told you that." Paige's skepticism was palpable.

"I made him agree to it before we left Minneapolis. The second I'm gone, he's all yours." She heard the faint catch in her voice and winced.

Paige's stormy expression smoothed. "I would never do that to you, Nellie," she murmured. Louder, she said, "Anyway, your boy toy lied to you. He never had any intention of going along with my plan."

Nell frowned. "That's not true. He—"

"Then why do I have his publicist calling me to discuss the best way of handling my quote-unquote situation?"

Whit swore under his breath. Nell's gaze flew to his, searching for a denial.

Instead she found guilt.

A muscle in his jaw twitched. Those deep brown eyes that had become so familiar to her were full of remorse. His mouth formed a word he didn't speak.

He reached for her hand again and she jerked away. "I told you I would help Paige with her problem," he said finally, softly. "And I fully intend to."

"How magnanimous," Paige sneered. "Thanks, but I no longer want your help."

Whit rounded on her. "Tell me something, Paige. Did you ever actually contact Frank Grantham?"

"Who?" Paige asked, too quickly. She moistened her lips and toyed with one of her chunky dangle earrings.

"Nell asked you to help her get her job back. You were supposed to call him. Did you?"

Paige drew herself up to her full, six-inches-extra height and aimed another death glare at Whit. "Don't try to turn this around on me."

"You didn't call him?" Nell could only stare at her sister. For the second time in less than a minute, she felt like her legs had been kicked out from under her. She backed toward the wall, pressing her fingers flat against the cool, hard surface.

"I was going to. I had a lot going on, and it slipped my mind."

"You told me you'd called him."

"You told *me* you were back in Chicago." Paige stopped toying with her earring and let her arms fall to her sides. "I'm sorry. I didn't come here to argue."

Whit wasn't having it. "Then what the hell *did* you come here for?" he bit out. "To punish her? Why? Is it jealousy? Or are you just pissed she did something without your permission?"

There was a dangerous glint in Paige's eyes. "I shouldn't have sent her. That's on me. I knew she had a thing for you back when we were dating—I'd just hoped she'd gotten over it by now."

"Like I told you," Whit said through his teeth, "what happens between Nell and me is our business."

"And who do you think gets to pick up the pieces after you break her heart?"

Nell's voice was a strangled hiss. "Paige, stop talking."

Paige didn't listen to her. Her gaze was locked on Whit. "God, I knew you were selfish, but I didn't think you were enough of a bastard to take advantage of her like this."

"I'm not taking advantage of her," Whit snapped.

But Paige smelled blood. She went in for the kill. "What would you call it?" she asked him. She jabbed a finger toward Nell's stricken face. "Look at her. She's completely in love with you, and you're using her for sex."

Whit's words came out in a growl. "Get out."

Every line of his body was rigid with fury, but Nell saw the doubt in his eyes. Her stomach plummeted. There it was. The truth that they'd been able to ignore only as long as it remained unspoken. She was in love with him. Helplessly. Painfully. And he would never believe that he *hadn't* been using her, that she'd given her love to him freely because that was the way love worked. Instead of leaving him with the fond memory of a torrid fling, she'd just become one more transgression to add to his list of sins.

Screw that.

She pushed herself away from the wall, struggling against the panic that threatened to overwhelm her. The freight train had slammed into her and now she had to do what she could to salvage the wreckage. "Paige, *stop*. The only person hurting me right now is you."

Paige started to speak, but Nell held up a hand.

"Setting aside the fact that *this is my private business*"—a futile effort, Nell knew, since Paige didn't consider much of anything private—"you're completely wrong about what's going on between us. Whit and I are just having fun. Fun, frivolous, meaningless sex, and flying across two countries to rescue me from the evil clutches of the hottest guy I'm ever going to see naked isn't just *way* overstepping the bonds of sisterhood, it's honestly kind of mean."

The frown Whit aimed at her told her he was about to make some sort of protest, and Nell hurried to cut him off. "I'm as angry at you as I am at her, so don't even think about opening your mouth right now," she warned him. His eyes narrowed, but he knew better than to test her, and she turned back to Paige. "Hot or not, I need to yell at him for lying to me. And since I don't want an audience, you have to go away. I'll call you in a couple of hours."

Paige must have recognized how close Nell was to coming unglued, because she didn't try to argue. She just smoothed her hands down the front of her skirt and gave her hair another toss. "Sure. I'll go play tourist for a bit." With one last withering glance at Whit, she headed for the door.

Nell waited until she heard the low rumble of tires on gravel that signaled Paige's departure, then turned and stalked into the bedroom. Her pulse hammered in her ears. She needed to finish packing. She needed to do *something* before she started to come apart at the seams. Her self-control was in tatters, and if she didn't find a distraction, some way of calming herself down, she was going to do something really humiliating. Like curl up in a ball and weep.

Not an option, she told herself. There was no way she was going to cry in front of Whit. She was going to remain dry-eyed and clear-headed, and the only way she was going to do that was to focus on something other than how close her heart was to shattering.

Incandescent rage seemed like a good place to start. The one person in her life she'd thought she could always count on and the man she'd fallen so stupidly in love with had both let her down. That should give her enough anger to fuel the sun.

Except that the person she was angriest at was herself.

Her small carry-on sat open on the bed, next to the laundry basket that held the last remaining articles of clothing she'd been attempting to cram into it. Too small, she decided; she'd have to leave a few things behind. She picked up the cardigan she'd worn to last Sunday's baseball game and shoved it in, wedging it between a long-sleeved button-down and her new corgi print pajama bottoms. The lacy red panties Whit had called her lucky underwear went in the garbage.

"Meaningless, huh?" Whit said from behind her.

Nell didn't turn. "Don't forget fun." She stuffed her University of Chicago tee into the bag and set aside a couple of pairs of socks. Those could stay. And the dress for the gala that she would never wear was still hanging in the closet. Whit had paid for it; he could return it.

"Are you going to look at me?"

"Are you going to feed me some pathetic excuse about how you never actually said you'd go along with Paige's plan?"

"No," he said quickly. "But I wasn't lying when I said I intend to help Paige. I asked my publicist to look into it. She wasn't supposed to make contact for a couple of days yet."

"So the problem isn't that you lied to me, it's that I found out."

"You know that's not what I meant."

Nell swung around to face him. It annoyed her that even now he looked sexy. He was rumpled and sweaty and somehow had dirt in his hair, but every pore of him exuded that subtle masculine confidence that made her weak in the knees. If he had any sort of human decency, he would at least try to take it down a notch. As it was, he needed about ten more layers of clothing. And a bag over his head. "I think the words you're looking for are *I'm sorry.*"

"Would you believe me if I said them?"

"Probably not."

"I'm sorry for hurting you. I hope you'll believe that." He took a step toward her, then seemed to think better of it and made his way to the window seat instead. "Can we talk about what happened back there?"

"I thought that was what we were doing." She'd known he wouldn't be distracted for long, but she couldn't face him, and she turned toward the bed again, tugging at the zipper of her carry-on. "If you mean that BS about you using me, you know that isn't true."

"Do I?" His voice was soft.

"We already had this discussion before getting naked in the hayloft. And since you've apparently forgotten, I was the one who did the seducing."

"Then why aren't you looking at me?"

"Because, believe it or not, having my sister show up and embarrass me in front of the guy I'm sleeping with isn't the most enjoyable experience I've ever had. In fact, it was actually sort of traumatic, so I'd appreciate it if you'd drop the subject."

"I can't do that," he said with quiet steel. "Something tells me we need to have this conversation."

"Oh, would you get over yourself?" she snapped. "It's not that deep. You're pretty, but you're replaceable. I already have my next lover lined up." A total lie, since she'd decided a few days ago that she wasn't going to call Evan. It wouldn't be fair to him, not when he wouldn't even be a rebound. You couldn't rebound until you hit rock bottom, and Nell had the feeling she had a long way left to fall. She yanked at the zipper again, tried to keep her tone light. "How did you know Paige never called Frank Grantham?"

"A hunch."

"Good hunch."

"Cut the crap, Nell."

She heard the scowl in his tone and groaned in frustration. "Paige was just trying to push your buttons. She's good at that."

"So she was lying?"

"What, you think she took one look at my face and decided I was in love with you?" She was going to have to give him something, she realized. After last night, Whit would never believe she didn't feel anything for him. She may as well have been holding a flashing neon sign when she told him he couldn't come to Chicago. "I have a mild case of infatuation. It's nothing I won't get over once I've got a good four hundred miles between me and your pheromones."

She heard his breath hiss out. "Jesus. You *are* in love with me."

"Are you even listening to me?"

"I'm listening to you. And the fact that you won't give me a straight answer is starting to scare the shit out of me."

"Just what every woman wants to hear."

"Nell."

The slender thread keeping her temper in check finally snapped. She shoved her bag aside and whirled to face him. "Fine. I'm in love with you. Happy?"

Shut up shut up shut up! she screamed at herself. Her throat tightened. Her hands balled into fists. But she had been pushed to her limit, the floodgates had been opened, and any hope she'd had of holding back vanished when she saw the panic that bloomed in his eyes. White hot fury took hold. What the hell had he expected? He was the one who had forced a confession!

Well, if he wanted a confession, he was damn well going to get one.

"I'm in love with you, Whit," she repeated, her voice breaking. All the air seemed to have been sucked from the room. Tears burned a path down her cheeks and she ignored them. "I am passionately, deliriously, desperately in love with you. I was in love with you four years ago. I love you even though you lied to me. I want us to get married and have babies and sit in matching rockers when we're old and wrinkly. I want to go to your stupid baseball games and wear your stupid jersey. I want it so much I can't breathe, and the fact that it's not what *you* want is killing me. Is that good enough for you? Is that what you wanted to hear?"

She hugged her arms and backed toward the bed, struggling against the sobs that threatened to break loose. She wanted to be anywhere else in that moment. In a cavern. On the moon. Why couldn't he have just let it be? She'd had this vision of herself at the airport, saying goodbye to him with a wave and a smile, no bitter tears, no hint of the gaping hole he was leaving in her heart. She'd wanted to set off into the sunset, holding the memory to her like a happy dream.

Instead it was becoming a nightmare.

Whit hadn't moved. All the color had drained from his face. He didn't look panicked now. He looked horrified. And this time, he was the one who wouldn't meet her gaze.

"Nell, I..."

If her heart hadn't already been in pieces, the quiet pain in his voice would have done the trick. As quickly as it had come, her anger deflated. It left her feeling limp, boneless. She sank onto the bed, heaved in breaths. Her hand fluttered toward her throat. "It's crazy, right? Believe me, I know it's crazy. I barely know you." Except she felt like she did. Maybe not every part of him, but enough to matter. Enough to know he would spend the next few months riddled with guilt and torturing himself unless she did something to stop it.

And her love didn't feel crazy. It felt right.

She let out a shaky laugh. "I didn't mean for this to happen, and I know you didn't, either. I'm not blaming you. Whatever Paige says, you didn't take advantage of me. I'm a big girl. I knew exactly what I was getting into."

She just hadn't known that it would hurt this much. That she would want so much.

Whit still wouldn't look at her. He perched on the edge of the window seat, his elbows on his knees, his head bowed. The early sun slanting in through the glass painted his skin in shades of bronze and gold. "I get that this week has been really intense—"

"Stop. You're not responsible for my feelings, but you don't get to erase them, either." Strange how calm she suddenly felt. Like the aftermath of a storm. It was cleansing almost. Freeing. "I make my own choices. I stayed because I wanted to. I slept with you because I wanted to, and the only thing that will piss me off right now is if you try to twist this into something it isn't. I'm not going to be one more reason for you to feel unworthy. I want what I can't have, so I took what I could get. If there's a guilty party here, it's me, not you."

Whit cleared his throat. "Nell... you're a beautiful, kind, incredible person."

She scrubbed at her face with both hands. This was even worse than she'd imagined. "Oh, god, please don't. You don't need to let me down gently. I know you don't feel the same way, and if you say any guy would be lucky to have me, I might actually scream."

It was like talking to a brick wall. A brick wall that also happened to have a serious guilt complex. "This week has meant a lot to me. *You* mean a lot to me. I just..."

"Whit, I get it. I really do. I don't need you to explain."

That finally got through to him, but instead of sounding relieved, he turned surly. His head jerked up. "Then what the hell do you expect me to say here?"

"You don't have to say anything. You don't have to *do* anything."

"I *told* you what my life is like," he said hoarsely. He sliced a hand through the air. "I *told* you why I don't do long-term relationships."

"I know. I'm not blaming you."

"Bullshit. You just said you wanted to marry me."

"It wasn't a proposal!" Why was he so angry? She was letting him off the hook! He should be thanking his lucky baseball she wasn't trying to prolong this. Something he would probably realize the second she was out the door. She took a steadying breath, somehow forced a smile. "No regrets, okay? We had a great time this week. It was fun while it lasted, but it's over now."

He stared blankly at her. "Over?"

"Paige can take me to the airport. I'll call her once I finish packing."

"So... that's it, then." His voice was gruff.

"That's it."

"All or nothing. Because I didn't fall in love in a fucking *week*, you're running away."

The words stung, but his hostility confused her. "I'm not running away. I'm going back to the real world." Whit gave her a stony look, and she fought another flare of temper. "I was leaving today anyway!"

"Tonight. *After* the groundbreaking ceremony. That was our deal. What happened to not going back on your word?"

She shot to her feet. "That's really the argument you want to go with? After you lied to my face?"

"You're glad I lied," he retorted hotly. "Admit it, Nell—you never wanted me to go along with Paige's plan." The crook of his eyebrow dared her to deny it. The faint sneer on his lips said he wouldn't believe her if she did.

"That isn't the point."

"No. The point is we had a deal, and now you're trying to back out."

Nell gaped at him. "You can't seriously expect me to go to the ceremony with you."

"Why not?"

Because I just told you I'm in love with you and you told me you're not.

Because every minute I spend with you will be agony.

Because I'd like to get out of here while I still have some pride left, and if I don't go now, I'll be falling on my knees, begging you to love me.

She couldn't say any of that. *Wouldn't* say any of that. Instead, she just stood there sputtering. "Because... because..."

"I don't want you to leave yet," Whit said, which might have had more of an impact if he hadn't growled it. He leaned back in the window seat, arms folded. "And *you* didn't want to leave, either, until big sis showed up and gave you a scolding."

"I'm pretty sure it was you she was scolding. Paige isn't the problem."

"Then stay, so we can figure this thing out."

"What *thing?*"

He gestured vaguely. "This. You and me. Us."

"I told you I'm in love with you. You told me I'm a nice person. What could there possibly be to figure out?"

"Kind. I said you were a *kind* person." He made a frustrated noise and ran his fingers through his hair. "Look. You're upset, I get that, but leaving now isn't the answer. You have to"—another gesture—"I don't know, give it a chance to run its course."

"Run its course. Right." Like she had the flu; another day or two, and she'd be cured. But she supposed in Whit's world, that's what love was—something you caught if you weren't careful. She swallowed down a laugh. "Thanks, but I think I'd rather just rip the Band-Aid off."

"That sounds to me like you're scared."

"Of what? Having my heart broken? Because I'm right in the middle of been there, done that, and I'd like to get it over with as quickly as possible."

"Of taking a chance."

God, she wanted to. The wild hope that stirred in her heart urged her to say yes, to let her deal with the devil go on just a little longer. But what if she did? Whit wasn't going to fall in love with her. Not in two weeks, not in two months. He would never allow it. She wasn't deluded enough to believe that she could change him, that maybe, just maybe, she'd be the one to make him finally decide to commit. If she didn't end things now, she'd only be setting herself up for more heartache, and she'd already had as much as she could stand.

"There wouldn't be any point," she told him.

"You said it yourself—we had a great time this week. There's no reason that can't continue. And once things are less intense—"

"I'll magically fall back out of love with you?" She shook her head slowly. "I can't stay here, Whit. I have to go back to Chicago. My *life* is in Chicago."

"I already offered to come with you. Let me know when you come up with an excuse that isn't total bullshit."

Her eyes narrowed. "You want to talk bullshit? All right. Let's talk bullshit."

"Nice language, Miss McLean."

She didn't bother to respond to that. "Bullshit is cycling through girlfriends every couple of months so you don't have to worry you might get attached. Bullshit is thinking a relationship can just *run its course* without anyone getting hurt in the process. You didn't mean to hurt me, but you did, and I'm not going to be your next female distraction just so you can try to figure out some way of fixing it. I may be in love with you, Whit, but I still have *some* self-respect, so if you're looking for someone to keep you entertained over the winter, you'll have to find somebody else."

He was on his feet now, too. "You think that's all this was for me? Entertainment?"

"I didn't mean it like that."

"I like my relationships uncomplicated. I'm not going to apologize for that. That doesn't mean I'll screw any woman who crosses my path."

"I never said it did!"

Whit wasn't just surly anymore; he was fuming. He stalked toward her, his gaze burning into hers. "This isn't casual for me, either. Just because I'm not ready to declare eternal love doesn't mean I don't fucking feel anything. Jesus, Nell, it's been a *week!* I'm sorry if I'm not on your schedule, but it takes normal people a hell of a lot longer than that."

"I don't want you to declare anything!" she cried. "I don't need you to love me right now, Whit! I..." Her voice broke again. "I just need to know you someday can."

"How the hell am I supposed to know something like that?"

"You're not. You can't. But that's what I need, and since I can't have it, I'm going home."

The words hung in the air between them, a fraught, tense silence. Nell wanted to sob in frustration. It wasn't supposed to happen this way. It wasn't supposed to *end* this way. All her beautiful memories were turning to ash.

Whit's shoulders sagged. He turned away. "If that's what you want, go ahead and go," he said bitterly. "But don't expect me to come chasing after you. If you leave now, it's done."

It's done. The finality of his statement rang in her ears. Her throat closed up. Her legs turned to rubber. She ordered herself to go—to grab her bag, walk out the door, race, skip, run, climb out the window, do *anything*, just go—but she no longer seemed to have any control over her body. She stood rooted, staring at Whit's back, at the taut outline of muscles that showed beneath his shirt and the hint of warm skin that was no longer hers to touch. She couldn't just leave. Not yet. Not like this. If this was over, if this was it, she needed something else to burn away the hurt and the guilt. Both of them did. Instead of taking the escape he offered, she whipped her shirt over her head.

Then she hurled it at him.

It him square in the shoulder. He spun around again. "What are you doing?" His gaze went straight to her breasts.

She had absolutely no idea what she was doing. "I don't want us to end angry." Her bra landed on the floor.

"This isn't angry?"

Maybe it was. But it also felt necessary. "This is getting you out of my system. For good. Now hurry up."

He scowled at her, but he was already breathing hard. "You just dumped me. I'm not going to have sex with you."

"Who's the terrible liar now?" She slid her jeans down her thighs, past her knees, let them pool at her ankles. Stepped out. "And I didn't dump you, because—"

"We aren't dating. Whatever." His shirt disappeared, and she could see his erection straining against his shorts.

She removed her panties before he could rip them off her a second time in one morning. "It's up to you," she whispered. "I'm leaving either way."

The faint twinge of fear that he would leave her standing there, naked and embarrassed, vanished along with his shorts. He reached her in two long strides. His hands clamped down on her shoulders. A breath stuttered out of him as her own hand moved between them. "Goddammit, Nell." His voice was hoarse.

He pushed her onto the mattress, grabbed one of the condoms they'd left in the nightstand, and shoved her thighs apart. She gasped when he entered her, but she didn't want gentle. This wasn't about love or tenderness. This was an act of pure lust, stripped of emotion, two bodies seeking one final, frantic release. His hands were rough as he jerked her hips upward. She started to come after a few hard thrusts and bit down on her lip to keep from crying out. She held tight when his own climax rocked through them both, and as soon as it was finished, slid out from underneath him.

"You can have the shower first," she said as she scavenged around the floor, retrieving her clothing. She pushed his shirt at him. "And cover up, before I get the urge to jump you again."

He was slower to recover, dragging himself from the bed with graceful lethargy. After he pulled his shirt back on, he gave her a narrow look. "You'd better be here when I get out. Don't just slink off without saying anything."

"I won't," she lied.

The moment he was out of the room, she texted Paige. *Come get me.*

TWENTY-THREE

THE CHAMPION OF THE underdog had one last stop to make.

"I don't get why we can't just leave a message," Paige said, leaning back in the passenger seat of the sleek Lexus rental car with her bare feet up on the dashboard, legs crossed, a silver bangle winking from one ankle. She'd traded her wrap skirt for a pair of jeans and bundled herself up in one of Nell's new sweaters, but she hadn't thought to bring a jacket, and she reached sideways to crank up the heat.

Nell shifted the car into the left lane as her GPS alerted her of an upcoming turn. "Because I want it done right, and since I still haven't decided if I'm speaking to you, you have to do what I say."

"You're speaking to me right now."

"You're on probation pending final judgment."

"I said I was sorry."

"And now you get to prove it."

Nell flicked a glance in her rearview. The snow that had fallen overnight had turned to a layer of grimy slush on the streets, spattering tires and making the Chevy behind her fishtail briefly as it pulled into a nearby gas station. Behind that, the road was clear. She wasn't exactly on the lookout for a silver Maserati—even if Whit had decided to drive into town, he wouldn't know what Paige's rental car looked like—but after she'd run off without so much as a goodbye, the fact that she hadn't made a quick exit from Fallen Oaks left her uneasy. What if she ran into Skip? Or Bucky? She had no idea if Allie and Freddie were still in town, but Nell's status as Whit's (supposed) girlfriend meant there were plenty of other people she'd prefer to avoid. And *that* meant she needed to get this done, and fast.

No matter how angry Whit would be when he found out.

With a quick check to make certain the intersection was clear, she made her turn, then slowed the Lexus as the GPS informed her the destination would be on her right. She could see it already, a squat brick building with an arched entranceway flanked by flagpoles. The Fallen Oaks Police Department shared the space with city hall, but thanks to the early hour—and the government offices being closed for the weekend—the small lot was mostly empty. Nell parked, then sat for a moment clutching the steering wheel, staring at the building ahead of her.

This was a terrible idea. Worse than terrible. Phenomenally, fantastically bad. Not to mention poorly thought out. What if he wasn't even there? He could be off duty. Or out on patrol. How many officers could a town the size of Fallen Oaks have, anyway? A dozen? Half a dozen? Odds were good this whole escapade would turn out to be pointless, and Nell's foolhardy, half-baked plan—concocted while waiting for Paige at the end of Bucky's driveway—would be nothing more than a big waste of time. But her luck held. When Nell finally summoned the courage to head into the station, the fresh-faced twenty-year-old behind the reception desk was so dazzled by Paige's bright smile, he ushered them straight to the small, cluttered alcove where Sawyer Brewster sat brooding behind a desk.

No turning back now, Nell thought.

Paige's gaze had already zeroed in on him. "Please tell me we're here to talk to Officer Hottie."

"Can you at least *attempt* to not be totally embarrassing for the next twenty minutes or so?" Nell groaned.

The answer to that question was apparently no. As soon as they approached Sawyer, Paige went into full-on flirt mode. She fluffed her hair, moistened her lips, and when they reached his desk, she held out her arms, wrists together, hands hanging limp. "Arrest me, Officer. I've been bad."

"Do you want to go wait in the car?" Nell hissed.

Sawyer ignored Paige entirely. His eyes were fixed on Nell, his expression wary. "Can I help you, Ms. McLean? If this is about the complaints..."

"It isn't. I'm here to talk about Whit's stalker."

"Supposed stalker," Sawyer replied, not even attempting to keep the derision from his voice.

"Someone has been taking pictures of us."

Sawyer leaned back in his chair, his hands tucked behind his head. "He's a professional athlete. People take pictures of him all the time."

"On private property? Through a window?" Nell had skimmed through the photos Paige had been sent, and while none of them were particularly intimate, the thought of someone spying on her and Whit made her skin crawl. That wasn't the behavior of an overly-invested fan, and neither was the vandalism to Whit's car. It was behavior rooted in obsession, and Nell wasn't leaving town until she knew someone was treating it seriously. She grabbed Paige's phone and thrust it at Sawyer.

His expression turned sober as he looked at the photos, but when he asked Nell if she had any suspects, she was forced to admit she didn't. That meant the best he could do was take a statement, log the photos into evidence, and advise her to be on the alert for any further incidents—unnecessary, since she would be gone within the hour, a piece of information she kept to herself. Anyway, that was only part of the reason she'd come.

The other reason was a bit of none-of-her-business meddling that Whit would probably never forgive.

Good thing she'd already dumped him.

She pressed her fingertips to the edge of the desk, using the cool, polished surface to steady herself. She didn't know much about Sawyer Brewster, and what she did know wasn't particularly favorable. He seemed to her a spiteful, angry man with too much resentment and too little compassion. But he'd once been the closest thing Whit had to a brother, and that had to count for something.

Please let it count for something. "You need to talk to Whit," she said softly.

Irritation pinched at Sawyer's lips. "Someone will head out to take his statement in a couple of days."

Whit would be back in Minneapolis in a couple of days. Nell shook her head. "No. *You* need to talk to him."

Ice-blue eyes burned back at her. "Look, lady—"

"I won't pretend to know everything that went on between the two of you," she began, letting the words rush out before her common sense could kick in and stop her. "But I know that what happened twelve years ago wasn't Whit's fault. And I think you know that, too."

Sawyer's irritation turned to full-blown hostility. His palm came down hard on his desk, making the stack of papers in front of him bounce. "You don't know a damn thing."

Paige touched her arm. "Maybe we should go."

Nell shrugged her off. "He wasn't driving drunk that night. His mom was behind the wheel, and he took the fall for her. That's why he was kicked off the team. He got punished for something he never did, and he was too stubborn to tell you and James. He's guilty of being an idiot, but that's all."

"That and a slight bit of arson," Sawyer said with a sneer. "Or didn't he tell you that part?"

"He already hates himself for that more than you ever could."

There was nothing more she could say. Sawyer would either believe her or he wouldn't; he would make peace with Whit or he wouldn't. But twelve years was a long time to carry around so much animosity, especially for someone you used to love. Maybe he was looking for a little forgiveness, too.

She felt lighter as she left the station. Not happy—it would be a long time before she found her way back to that—but lighter. The cool, pine-scented air that brushed against her brought to mind the thick winds rolling off Lake Michigan. She closed her eyes and breathed.

"You might have given me some warning," Paige said as they headed to the car. "For a minute there, I thought he really was going to arrest us."

"I bet Grandmother would've just *loved* that. Though I suppose you could've always said you did it for her, so she wouldn't be the first Forrester to land behind bars."

Paige made a face. "That isn't funny."

"And speaking of Grandmother..." Nell let out a shaky exhale. "You need to work with Whit's publicist."

This time she scowled. "When hell freezes over."

"You screwed up, Paige. You were supposed to have my back, and you didn't. You want to make it up to me? This is how you do it."

There was a bit of muttering, followed by a sigh of resignation. "All right, fine. If she contacts me again, I'll listen."

She would, Nell knew. Whit would make sure of it.

A moment of silence ticked past, then Paige reached over and gave Nell's shoulder a squeeze. "You're going to be okay, sweetie."

"Yeah."

She slid into the car, turned the ignition, put it in drive. A few minutes later they were on the highway, Fallen Oaks vanishing behind them.

***

Whit didn't leave Fallen Oaks on Saturday. He didn't leave Sunday, either. Or Monday. By the time the following Saturday rolled around, Bucky had given up asking him how long he was planning to stay.

Which was good, because Whit didn't have a clue how to answer that question. If he had been following any sort of plan, he'd have left for Minneapolis directly after the charity gala. Instead, he was still sleeping in his grandfather's guest room, still driving his dad's Maserati, still dutifully mucking out the barn every morning and confiscating any cigarettes he found lying around the house. He'd also added a workout routine into the schedule and bullied Bucky into letting him paint the porch. Since that wasn't enough to occupy him, he'd considered starting a new throwing program—but Bucky would've tossed him out on his ass the second he saw a baseball, so Whit decided any adjustments to his arsenal could wait.

"Don't know why you want to hang out with me anyway," Bucky told him, after threatening to make Whit detail his pickup failed to dislodge him.

"You're pushing ninety," Whit said. "I figure I should spend as much time with you as I can before you keel over."

"I just turned eighty, smartass. And my mother lived to be a hundred."

"Which is about a hundred years younger than that pickup. It doesn't need detailing. It needs a metal compactor."

"Go do your moping in the barn," Bucky huffed. "It depresses me to look at you."

Whit wasn't moping. He was taking a breather. A perfectly normal response to the recent upheaval in his life, only part of which was due to the infuriating woman he couldn't seem to purge from his thoughts. He wasn't dejected, despairing, or whatever other adjective Allie wanted to fling at him. Which was exactly what he told her when she called to demand what the hell he was still doing there.

"You hate Fallen Oaks even more than I do," she hissed over the phone line. She and Freddie had left town the night she'd learned about Maggie, and since Allie's preferred method of demonstrating displeasure involved spending as much of Skip's money as possible, as *quickly* as possible, she was currently enjoying the nightlife in Singapore—which she intended to follow up with two weeks in Hong Kong and a month in Australia.

"I'm just taking a little time to clear my head."

"You're not the first guy to ever get dumped, you know," she said.

"Nell didn't dump me. We were never actually dating."

"Mm-hmm. Just taking a guess here, but... when was the last time you shaved? Or showered?"

"I don't know. What does that have to do anything?"

"You're holed up in a farmhouse at the ass end of nowhere and have abandoned personal hygiene. You got dumped."

"At least I haven't peed on any statues."

Allie hung up on him.

Okay, so maybe he was moping a little. But after discovering he had another sister, learning his father had doped, and being not-exactly-dumped by the woman who had begun to occupy his every waking moment, he figured he deserved a good mope.

On the other hand, he was sort of starting to resemble a caveman—or at least some kind of paranoid off-the-grid survivalist who lived in the woods and slept with a gun—so he shaved off the beard he'd been haphazardly growing and made a point of washing his hair.

He finally got Rory on the phone, and it felt good to have someone to yell at, but after he went into a tirade about the stupidity of keeping important family secrets from siblings, she hung up on him, too.

Rebecca called to let him know Paige had agreed to work with her, which surprised him. He ended *that* call before he could humiliate himself by grilling her for information she couldn't possibly know.

He heard nothing from Nell.

Not that he wanted to. Every time he thought about her, he felt like someone had taken a sledgehammer to his chest. What had she expected him to do? Beg? Get down on one knee and propose? They'd been together a fucking week! Less than that, if you took into account they'd spent the first couple of days arguing. She knew he didn't do long-term relationships. She knew why. He'd told her about his parents' train wreck of a marriage and the endless misery that had come as a result. And even after all of that, he'd offered to come with her so they could take time to figure things out. Instead, she'd chosen to run out on him, sneaking away while he was in the shower like she was fleeing a hotel after a cheap one-night stand. All that talk about how she couldn't do casual, about how desperately in love with him she was, and she'd walked away without a second glance.

It pissed him off that he missed her. The way she tilted her head back when she laughed... that sly smile she sometimes got. He missed talking with her. He missed how perfectly she fit in his arms. He fell asleep remembering the scent of her skin and woke with his body aching for her. She flitted through his dreams, tempting, teasing. Even her voice seemed to haunt him.

He would get over it eventually. He'd have to. It had taken Nell a week to turn his world upside down, it couldn't take much longer than that to get himself back to normal. By the time spring training rolled around, she'd be a distant memory, an object lesson in becoming involved with someone who made him feel too much.

He just wished the getting over it part would hurry the fuck up.

"Now who's having a pity party?" his dad asked when he stopped by the farm and found Whit attempting to keep himself busy by painting the barn.

Whit tossed a roller toward him. "You can get to work or you can get lost. Those are your options."

Skip grabbed the roller. "From what your grandfather says, you're gonna run out of things to paint."

The cool weather that had brought with it the season's first snowfall hadn't lasted, and the late autumn sun beat down on them, thick and hot. "The house needs to be reshingled," Whit grunted, wiping the sheen of sweat from his forehead with the back of his hand.

"Since when do you know how to shingle a roof?"

"Since the invention of YouTube."

"And what happens when you break that million-dollar arm of yours?"

"It's worth a hell of a lot more than that," Whit retorted. "And I'm not going to break it."

Skip rubbed the back of his neck, sending Whit a sidelong glance. "I didn't do the interview," he said gruffly. "If that's what this whole thing is about."

Whit had figured that much out by now. Instead of a shocking tell-all that exposed the darkest secrets of one of baseball's most respected figures, Jerry Garwood had published an in-depth feature on the struggles of Bellamy Swan.

It should have relieved him. His father's legacy was safe. There would be no blistering condemnations or sordid scandals, no intrusive articles dredging up the past. No one would use a youthful mistake to call into question whether Skip O'Rourke really belonged in the Hall. Skip's penance would be his silence, and even if neither of them said it, Whit knew his father had done it for him.

But somehow he just felt... numb. "I suppose you want a thank you."

Skip sighed. "And if that's *not* what this is about..." He shifted uncomfortably. Cleared his throat. "Have you considered just giving her a call?"

Every minute since she'd left. Whit turned away. "If there's one person I won't ever be taking relationship advice from, Dad, it's you."

"Fair enough."

It wasn't until the following day that Whit realized his dad had moved in with them. He went to bed early and woke to find Skip had installed himself on the sofa, deposited a duffel bag of workout clothes in the hall closet, and set up a makeshift office in the laundry room. A couple of Bucky's cats were already making themselves comfortable in his lap. Whit just stared in disbelief.

"Quit lurking, kid," Skip called from the couch. "I can hear your teeth grinding from all the way over here."

Whit stalked into the living room scowling. "You're kidding me, right? You live like ten minutes away."

"Misery loves company." Skip flopped back against the cushions, dislodging one of the cats as he propped his feet on the rickety coffee table in front of him. "You're stuck with me." Apparently Maggie was still refusing all contact, and both Rory and Allie were dodging Skip's calls, so he had decided to—in his words—strengthen his bond with the one kid who didn't totally hate him.

Whit told him to stop reading self-help books.

Three generations of O'Rourke men living under one roof. It was a recipe for disaster. Or at least a lot of yelling.

"The two of you are pathetic," Bucky said in disgust after Skip announced plans to redo the kitchen cabinets. "If either one of you tries to fix one more thing on this farm, I'm giving you both the boot."

"You won't let us play baseball," Skip protested. "What else are we supposed to do?"

"You're both richer than god. Buy yourselves an island if you need somewhere to brood."

But he didn't kick them out. One week slid into two. A cold front brought with it a fresh fall of snow, and this time the sun didn't burn it away. The temperature dropped, the wind picked up, and in every direction, the ground vanished beneath layers of silver and white, signaling the end of autumn and the beginning of the long, frigid winter ahead of them. Whit finished one coat of paint on the barn and started a second. Gerda materialized, insisting on cooking Thanksgiving dinner, and took over Bucky's kitchen. Bucky muttered to himself and tried to oust them by flooding the house with Christmas music.

Then, thirteen days after Nell had returned to Chicago, Whit got a call from the police.

He knew even before he answered whose voice would be on the other end of the line. "What do you want, Brewster?"

Sawyer was all business. "I need you to come down to the station."

"Funny. I didn't think legalizing weed meant you got to smoke on the job."

"Your choice, of course," Sawyer drawled. "But there's someone here you might want to have a chat with. Your stalker just turned herself in."

TWENTY-FOUR

The last time Whit had been to the Fallen Oaks Police Department, he'd been in handcuffs.

Twelve years hadn't done much to change it. Same ugly brick building perched like a gargoyle in the center of town. Same pervasive smell of Lysol and musty carpet. He breathed it in, his chest tightening at the memory as he strode past the city's government offices and into the section of the building that housed their meager police force. Same beige walls lined with pictures and plaques. He even recognized a few of the faces, old friends of Sawyer's dad who had to be at least approaching retirement. Bit of a different reception this time, he thought, as the rookie at the front desk asked for an autograph.

Sawyer hadn't been particularly forthcoming with details, and Whit wasn't certain what to expect. Fans, even overly-invested fans, came with the territory. So did groupies. A lot of guys didn't mind it—a few even welcomed it—but every now and then, someone crossed a line. Spread rumors, faked photos, tracked down phone numbers, contacted relatives. Harmless fantasy twisted into obsessive delusion, and then it needed to be shut down, fast.

He'd dismissed the possibility of a stalker when Nell first suggested it, partly because he hadn't felt like dealing with it. These situations had a tendency to get messy, and Whit hadn't wanted more of his personal life dissected by the press. But this was so far over the line, it wasn't even in the same galaxy. Forget the vandalism to his car. Whoever had done this had targeted Nell, and that made his blood run cold.

He stopped in his tracks when he recognized the slender, tear-streaked woman seated in front of Sawyer's desk.

"*Lilah?*" The word croaked out of him.

He blinked, but she didn't vanish. That was Lilah, all right, her lower lip wobbling and her misery coming off her in waves. Still beautiful, in spite of the puffy eyes and smeared makeup. She'd cut a few inches off her hair, lost a little weight. She flinched when he said her name, then sat wringing her hands, a box of tissues in her lap, her shoulders trembling with the soft, hiccuping sobs that kept escaping.

Whit's thoughts churned. He hadn't seen Lilah in... what was it, two months now? Longer? Not since they'd decided to end things. He didn't like to break up during dates—it seemed disrespectful—so they'd taken an afternoon walk in the park, and when he'd seen she was upset, they'd gone back to her place. There had been a few tears then, but nothing on this level. She'd been a hell of a lot more reasonable than Nell, when it came to it.

Lilah dabbed at her eyes with a tissue. "Hi, Whit," she said when he reached her. Her voice came out small and creaky.

He stared at her, trying to process. *Lilah* was the one who had trashed his car? She was the one who had messaged Paige? He couldn't believe it. Lilah was the very opposite of aggressive. She was warm, bubbly, affectionate—the sort of woman every guy wanted, which was exactly what he'd told her the day they'd broken up. He remembered the faint smile she'd given him at that. *Not every guy.*

He also remembered telling her on their first date that he wasn't looking for anything serious, and that he never dated anyone more than a couple of months. She'd given him a smile then, too. *Perfect. I'll try not to break your heart.*

Apparently *perfect* had been a bit of an exaggeration.

Whit had no idea what to even say to her, so he just snarled out the first thing that popped into his head. "What the fuck, Lilah?"

Her already anguished face crumpled. "It was a mistake."

"You think?"

"I didn't mean for this to happen. Any of it."

"So you *accidentally* spied on me? You accidentally took a baseball bat to my car?" His raised voice was drawing looks, and he made an effort to lower it. "You don't accidentally stalk someone, Lilah. You don't accidentally harass them."

She must have sent the video to *Meltdown*, he realized. He hadn't seen her at Gills that night, but after his run-in with Nell, Babe Ruth could've walked into the bar without him noticing. And the video edit, sloppy as it was, wouldn't have required much effort for a woman who made a living recording modeling shoots and makeup tutorials.

He was too disgusted to look at her, and he turned his snarl on Sawyer. "She just showed up and turned herself in to you? Just like that?"

"Actually, she turned herself in to Keane. He's letting me handle it." A thin smirk slanted across Sawyer's face. "As a favor."

"Yeah, I bet you're just loving this."

"Hey, don't kill the messenger." Sawyer leaned back in his chair, swiveling it slowly from side to side. "And just so you're aware... she's not technically under arrest yet. She said she doesn't want a lawyer, she just wants to explain things to you."

Whit glowered. "That's standard operating procedure?"

"I assumed you'd prefer to keep it out of the press."

He wasn't wrong, though Whit had no idea why Sawyer would give a shit. He forced his hands to unclench and turned back to Lilah. "You couldn't have tried calling me first?"

"This was the only way I could think to prove how sorry I am." Her voice caught. "I loved you, Whit. I... I couldn't say that before."

He recoiled, which only made her cry harder. "And *this* was your way of showing it?" He was close to shouting again, and took a deep breath before continuing. "I don't understand. We agreed to end things months ago."

Lilah's watery gaze flicked toward Sawyer, then back to Whit. "Maybe we could do this privately."

"Like hell." He might not enjoy Sawyer having a front row seat to this disaster, but he didn't trust Lilah not to twist things around on him, and he wanted witnesses. "If you're going to say something, say it here."

"But..."

"Say it here, or I walk out and you can say it to a judge."

It was an empty threat and Lilah knew it. He wouldn't allow her to go to jail, no matter how furious he was. But she nodded anyway. She gave her eyes another dab. "It didn't start out as stalking. At least... in my head it didn't. I just wanted to see you. Someone mentioned they'd spotted you out at Gills, so I went there every night for a week, hoping you would show up." She grimaced. "And then when you did, there were women all over you. I couldn't stand it. I was so jealous I couldn't think."

"You were thinking clearly enough to edit that video," Whit retorted.

She stared at the floor. "I regretted that right away. I knew you were going to Fallen Oaks that week, so I followed you here to apologize. I thought maybe I could make it up to you. But you were already with someone else, and when I saw you with her... I guess something inside of me snapped. I'm sorry. I'm really sorry, Whit. I didn't mean for it to get so out of hand."

"Out of hand? Lilah, you totally wrecked my car." He let out a soft curse as sudden realization hit. "You had my spare set of keys."

"That really was accidental," she said quickly. "I didn't know I had them until after we'd broken up."

Whit snorted.

Lilah had managed to stop crying, and she set the box of tissues on Sawyer's desk, folded her hands in her lap. "I know it doesn't make any sense, but it's like—like I wanted to punish you for not loving me back. Stupid, right? None of it made me feel any better. And after a while I realized the person who did all those things wasn't who I wanted to be." She heaved in a breath. "So I went home. I decided to put it all behind me. But after this morning..."

Whit was on instant alert. "What happened this morning?"

"I take it you haven't seen *Meltdown* today," Sawyer said mildly.

Dread pooled in Whit's stomach. Rebecca had texted him a few hours earlier, before he'd even dragged himself out of bed. A single, short statement: *Don't worry, I'm handling it.* He'd disregarded the message at the time, assuming it was referring to Paige. Now he fished his phone out of his pocket and felt bile rise in his throat as he stared at the photo of him and Nell that was once again splashed across the tabloid's main page. *Meltdown* had updated its article to include the identity of the woman with him in the bar. *Eleanor McLean, a schoolteacher from the Chicago area, sister of O'Rourke's former flame...*

He felt like he'd been sucker punched. Beneath the picture of Nell on her knees was a blown up and cropped version of a press photo that had been taken a couple of weeks ago. That Tuesday, he thought. The day before they'd first slept together. It had been at the elementary, where Whit and some of the guys had been giving baseball lessons to the kids. When the media had set up their photos, Whit had dragged Nell into one of the group shots without even thinking. Her bright smile beamed out at him. She looked radiant and happy, so lovely it made him ache. He'd drawn her close to him, nestling her hip against his thigh, and his hand was curled possessively at her waist. She was dressed in those tight-fitting jeans that drove him crazy... and the exact same sky blue jacket she'd worn that night at Gills.

It may as well have been a giant guilty sign. A scarlet letter. For the past two weeks, Whit had been trying not to wonder how Nell's meeting with Frank Grantham had gone; now he didn't have to. If she'd had a job when she woke up that morning, she wouldn't for much longer, thanks to him. He'd given her the chance to save her career, and then stolen it right back from her.

Lilah must have read the fury in his eyes, because she scooted her chair backward a couple of inches and lifted both her hands. "It wasn't me, I swear."

"Bullshit."

"As soon as I saw the article, I drove straight here," Lilah was saying. "I didn't *have* to come here, Whit. I didn't have to tell you anything. I'm trying to make amends."

Whit was barely listening to her. "Release it," he breathed.

Lilah stared up at him. "What?"

"The unedited video. The entire thing. I assume you caught more than just those few seconds." His publicist would have some choice words for him about that, but it was the only way to absolve Nell. "You want me to believe you're sorry? You want to make amends? Prove it."

He could issue a statement. He *would* issue a statement, of his own, on his own, whatever Rebecca had to say about it. But if he wanted anyone to believe the video had been taken out of context, he'd need to provide that context.

Lilah was still gaping at him, and he struggled to rein in his temper. "Or send it to me, and *I'll* release it," he ground out. "I'll keep your name out of it, if that's what you're worried about."

"I—I'll release it."

Whit wasn't taking any chances. "Why don't you send it to me, just in case?" he told her, and tried to ignore the rapid drumming of his pulse when the video popped up on his phone.

It was worse than he remembered. Lilah's focus had been on him, not Nell, and even from a distance, he could see the hard, angry sneer on his face, hear the cold mockery in his tone. Every word dripped with venom. And Nell... she looked so small in comparison, but she faced him down without flinching, without fear, the same way she'd faced down his father less than twenty-four hours later. His gut churned. He closed the video, slid his phone back into his pocket. Swallowed hard.

Lilah lifted a hand toward him, then thought better of it. "Whit—"

"We're done here," he said flatly. "Release the video in a couple of hours, or I'll do it."

"You're not going to have them arrest me?"

"You knew that before you walked in the door." His rage had burned itself out. It left him feeling numb, empty. He turned away. "I'm sorry I couldn't be what you needed."

He didn't watch her leave. He needed to think. He'd have to come up with a statement, warn his publicist. Lilah had enough of a social media following that the second she dropped the video, some news outlet or another would pick it up. It would be all over the internet within minutes. That probably wouldn't be enough to undo whatever damage had already been done to Nell's reputation, but it might help mitigate it.

His own reputation was another matter.

Sawyer was smirking at him again. "Did you really just apologize to the woman who vandalized your car?"

"She needs therapy, not a jail cell." Whit was too tired to care what Sawyer thought. He was bone-weary, wrung out. But since Sawyer had done him a favor, even if he didn't know why, he managed to grumble out, "Thanks."

"I heard your girlfriend left town."

Great. Did everyone know he'd been dumped? He should just walk out, but he couldn't seem to make his feet move. They just sat there like cement blocks. Really big cement blocks. He tried to work up another snarl. "Haven't you gotten your fill of gloating today?"

"She came to see me."

That surprised him enough that he straightened up. "*Nell?*"

"Didn't you date her sister, too? The hot blonde? She was with her. That makes three in the past couple of weeks. I'm a pretty popular guy with your exes."

Whit could feel his teeth wanting to grind and tried to think of something calming. When that failed, he folded his arms and glared at Sawyer. "What did she want?"

"Would you believe my number?" Whit just went right on glaring at him, and after a moment Sawyer relented. His voice lowered. "She told me about the night you were arrested."

He should've known Nosy Nellie wouldn't be able to mind her own business. "She shouldn't have done that."

"Is it true?"

"Does it matter?"

"Yeah, Whit, it matters."

"Then think whatever the hell you want. You always did."

"What the fuck else were we supposed to think? You shut us out. You wouldn't talk to us."

"And then I switched schools, started a fire, and nearly got you and James killed. Yeah, I'm familiar with the history. If we're making a list of my sins, let's not forget the time I wrecked a motorcycle or when I got suspended for doping."

Sawyer let out a soft whistle. "Damn, you *are* a mess."

"I'm not the one wearing a uniform I swore I'd never be caught dead in."

"You want to say that a little louder?" Sawyer hissed. He leaned back in his chair again. "I never said I *wasn't* a mess."

"What are you looking for here?"

"I'm not sure."

"If it's another apology—" He broke off, frowning. After Sawyer's accident, he'd tried so hard to reach out. Again and again, more times than he could count or remember. If this was an olive branch, shouldn't he take it? If somehow, beneath all the anger and bitterness, there was something left to be salvaged, shouldn't he at least try? Nell's voice was in his head, gently urging.

Then do it for yourself. So that you can finally start to forgive yourself.

Whit shifted his feet, feeling awkward. "What I said the other night... I didn't mean it. You were good, Sawyer. One of the best I've ever seen. You would've made it. All the way."

"Maybe. Maybe not. I guess we'll never know."

Whit shifted again, rubbing the back of his neck with his hand. "Anyway... thanks for helping with Lilah."

He was nearly at the door when Sawyer called after him.

"Hey, O'Rourke."

Whit turned.

Sawyer sat at his desk, flipping him the middle finger. "Go fuck yourself, man."

Sheer surprise made him bark out a laugh. It had been twelve years since he'd last seen the designated farewell of the Fallen Oaks boys' baseball team, but he still knew there was only one accepted response to it. He cupped his hands around his mouth and hollered back. "Every time I see your mom!"

***

True to her word, Lilah posted the unedited video, along with a less-than-detailed confession about her brief "lapse" into harmful behavior. From what Whit could tell, it didn't do much to damage her image. She recorded a couple of videos discussing the importance of mental health and inviting her followers to *accompany her on her journey of self-discovery*, which Whit thought sounded ridiculous—but at least she confirmed that she'd signed herself up for counseling. He noticed she'd left out the part about trashing his car.

He thought about calling Nell.

For three days, he could hardly think about anything else. He even clicked on her name in his contacts and stared at the screen long enough that he started to sweat. But what could he possibly say to her? That he was sorry? His statement to the press had been his apology. Entirely personal. Nauseatingly heartfelt. Clearly she didn't want to hear from him. If she had, she would have called him herself. Instead, radio silence. He'd set his reputation on fire to save hers, and she didn't so much as text.

Not that the fallout from the video had been as bad as he'd feared. The inevitable rehashing of his PEDs usage was quickly overshadowed by the fresh scandal of a prominent hitting coach with a gambling problem. Whit's years-old doping incident was barely Little League drama in comparison to one of the cardinal sins of baseball, and his latest transgression was out of the news cycle before he could even have his lawyers demand a retraction. But instead of being relieved, Whit was filled with a vague sense of panic. There was an air of finality to it all. The last thing, the only thing connecting him to Nell had come to an end.

Unless—what if she'd gotten pregnant? They'd used protection, but a couple of times they hadn't been quite as careful as they could've been, and nothing was a hundred percent. She would have to contact him then, wouldn't she? It was probably still too early to tell, but it would be the right thing, the responsible thing for him to check in.

Only the worry that she might have blocked his number stopped him from calling her that time.

And even if he did reach out to her, what would it matter? Nothing had changed. Anything lasting between them was still out of the question. Dating was impossible; the logistics alone would be a nightmare once he had to report for spring training. They lived four hundred miles apart, and managing a relationship during the season was difficult enough without adding long distance into the equation. He couldn't ask her to hop on a plane every weekend just so they could steal a few hours together in between games. If he gave in now and asked her for a second chance, it would only lead to more heartbreak. She'd understood that when she ended things. She was *right* to have ended things.

If only he could convince his own heart of that.

I don't need you to love me right now, Whit... I just need to know you someday can.

So maybe he *was* in love with her. He knew damn well that wasn't a guarantee. And that talk about marriage and babies, about getting old and wrinkly... people fell in love all the time. They fell right back out of it just as quickly. In the real world, there was no such thing as always. Ever after only lasted until the ink was dry on the divorce papers. People grew apart. Chemistry faded. And who knew? Maybe Nell would be the one to wake up one morning and decide she was bored with him.

Maybe she already had. She'd claimed to have her next lover lined up. What if she hadn't been lying?

That thought depressed him so much, he almost wished he hadn't outgrown reckless behavior. Pushing a motorcycle to its limits on a lonely stretch of highway, feeling the bite of the wind on his face, the rush of adrenaline as the asphalt blurred away beneath him—that might be enough to distract him from the woman who had turned his life inside out and then left him restless and wanting. Instead, he added a two-mile run to his daily workout routine.

"Don't you think this has gone on long enough?" Skip asked him, two weeks and five days—he was keeping track of the days—since Nell had returned to Chicago. Whit had just finished showering after his run and found Skip waiting outside his bedroom, an old gym bag slung over his shoulder.

Whit brushed past him. Skip was one to talk. His hair was getting shaggy at the ends and he'd been wearing the same pair of sweatpants for a week straight. "If you want to go home, go home. We won't miss you."

Skip grunted. "Come on, kid. Let's go destroy some baseballs." He lifted the gym bag slightly, slapped a hand against it. "Dad went into town for a couple of hours, so I smuggled in contraband."

"I hope you didn't go out in public like that."

"If you want to shit talk, do it outside. We're on a schedule here."

Whit wasn't in the mood to whack more baseballs into the snow, but he was in even less of a mood to argue with his dad, who had apparently been serious about that fatherly bonding crap. He would've told him it was too little, too late, but the truth was, he sort of felt sorry for him, so he pulled a cap over his damp hair, shrugged into a jacket, and followed Skip out of the house and around the barn, where the farmland turned from rolling pasture to snow-covered cornfields. The sky was a clear, crystalline blue, the sun just reaching its zenith. A beautiful day for baseball. If it hadn't been about twenty degrees out.

A faint breeze whistled against them as Skip dropped the bag to the ground, digging out a bat and a couple of baseballs. "This is for you. You'll find out why in a minute." He shoved the bat toward Whit.

It didn't surprise Whit that his dad immediately brought up Nell.

"I won't pretend to understand what actually went on between the two of you, but you've been miserable since she left," Skip said. "And I know you don't want my advice as your father, so let me just say this as an outside observer. You're being an idiot."

It didn't surprise him, but it *did* annoy him. "You're right. I don't want your advice."

"Well, I'd ask your grandpa to do it, but he thinks you're smart enough to figure it out on your own, so I'm what you get."

"Don't you have three estranged daughters to worry about?"

"Allie and Rory aren't estranged. They're on vacation. And as for Maggie... I'm working on it." Skip grimaced, rubbing at the bridge of his nose. The sunlight sparked off the glints of silver in his hair. "Okay. This is gonna be as awkward for me as it is for you, so let's just get it over with. Do you love her?"

Whit had never in his life discussed relationships with his father, and he wasn't about to start now. *His dad,* of all people. His dad, who had once kept a different mistress for each day of the week. It would be laughable, if his chest hadn't squeezed painfully at the question. How could he explain what he felt for Nell when he barely understood it himself? He tried to tell Skip to mind his own business, but what came out was a hoarse whisper. "It feels like I do."

"Then what the fuck are you still doing here?"

A dozen sarcastic retorts came to mind, but it was as though someone else had control of his body. "I don't know if I can be what she wants," Whit heard himself answer.

"Don't know or won't try? Because if you don't love her, that's one thing. If you do love her, you fight like hell."

His voice cracked the way it hadn't since he was fourteen years old. "Maybe love isn't enough."

"Or maybe you're just scared."

Almost exactly what he'd said to Nell. Having it flipped around on him only made the knot in his chest tighten further. "Thanks for the chat, Dad." He tossed the bat into the snow and would have stalked off, but Skip stepped in front of him.

"I'm not saying I blame you. You've got plenty of reason to be scared," Skip told him. He nodded at the bat. "Pick that up—we're not done here." Whit just stared stonily at him, and Skip sighed. "Christ, you're difficult. Always have been. Your mom and I used to have to sit in the car with the engine running for hours at a time just to get you to stop crying. And that was when I was on a minor league salary, so believe me, we didn't want to waste the gas money. Now would you pick up the goddamn bat, Whitney?"

He did, mostly because he figured it was the quickest way to end the conversation, and he needed to get out of there before he completely broke down. "Is there a point to all this?"

"I'm getting to it." Skip crouched, pulling a few more baseballs from the bag and arranging them in a small pile in the snow, then glanced up at Whit. "You know, with your mom, it was like a lightning bolt. I knew immediately, that first day we spent together. No other woman ever came close."

It hadn't been a lightning bolt for Whit. More like a grenade. One he hadn't even known he'd been holding until it had detonated.

He aimed a half-hearted sneer at his dad. "And it took you how long to start cheating on her? One week? Two?"

"I won't try to excuse it. I ruined one of the best things that ever happened to me because of my selfishness, and I didn't figure it out until it was too late. But the point is—just because I screwed up doesn't mean you're going to. You're not me, Whit. And thank god for that."

"It's not that simple."

"Why the fuck would it be? Playing ball isn't simple. I don't hear you bitching about that. You want something badly enough, you find a way to make it work." Skip flipped one of the baseballs into the air, caught it again. "Here's how we're gonna do this. I strike you out, you go after her."

It wasn't until his father said the words that Whit realized how much he wanted to.

Desperately. More than desperately. With every fiber of his being. He wanted to go right now, not waste another second—just throw the bat to the ground and take off running, climb into the Maserati and whip down the highway until he reached the airport. And if there weren't any available flights, he'd just keep on driving. He'd be in Chicago by morning, and then—

And then... what? Everything would magically fall into place? Whit knew better than that. Going after her wouldn't be fair to either of them. He'd been through all of the arguments. He'd spent the past two and a half weeks torturing himself with them.

You want something badly enough, you find a way to make it work.

He had never wanted anything more.

His hands felt clammy. A line of sweat popped up on his brow. "You're not a pitcher," he told his dad.

"Almost a two-way player, remember? And I wouldn't get cocky if I were you. I've seen you try to lay down a bunt, kid."

Whit's heart was slamming against his ribs, but he did his best to sound casual. "I've been called on to pinch hit before."

Skip retreated a few paces, stamping the snow to form a makeshift mound, and did a couple of warm-up motions with his right arm. "Yeah, in the sixteenth inning, after you'd lost the DH and everyone else left on the roster had the shits."

"It was the fifteenth. And we won that game."

"No thanks to you. Now are we just gonna stand here, or are we gonna do this thing?"

Whit wrapped his fingers around the grip of the bat. For all his bluster, there was no way Skip could strike him out, and both of them knew it.

Skip gazed down at the ball in his hand, turning it slowly. "The way I see it, you're at a crossroads. Thirty years ago, I stood at one, too. I can't tell you which way is right for you—I only know I regret the one I took. It's your choice, Whit. It's your future. You just have to decide if you want her in it."

A future with Nell. Whit froze.

He could imagine it so easily. That picture he'd had of her, smiling at him from the stands—he wanted it so much it was like a physical ache. He thought of her curled up on a sofa, a blanket draped across her knees and a book in her lap. Or standing in the kitchen with the early sun on her face, a mug of coffee in her hands, her hair a mess, her eyes misty with sleep. He wanted to wake up with her body nestled against his. He wanted to argue with her until her temper sparked, and then seduce it away again.

He'd told her no one fell in love in a week, but what the hell did he know? He'd never been in love before. He'd felt more for Nell after a few days than he had for any other woman after a few months.

I want us to get married and have babies and sit in matching rockers when we're old and wrinkly.

Why had that seemed so frightening? The only thing that frightened him now was the thought of a lifetime without her.

"You get one shot at this," Skip called to him from across the snow. "Try not to mess it up, will you?"

He peeled back his arm and threw.

TWENTY-FIVE

NELL HAD THOUGHT A room full of two dozen second graders was a handful. That was before she'd met Mrs. Nielsen's kindergarten class from hell. She'd only spent four days with the legion of adorable demon spawn and she was already tempted to take up day drinking. She was pretty sure that was what Mrs. Nielsen had done. No way she had shingles. She was on a beach somewhere, sipping margaritas and enjoying a much needed mental health break. And who could blame her? The few students who weren't possessed by creatures from the netherworld were possessed by feral cats. They didn't need a teacher, they needed an exorcist, but since Nell hadn't yet been able to find a permanent faculty position and was relying on subbing to pay the bills, she'd take what she could get. There was no way she was going to let a bunch of cute, conniving little monsters get the best of her. She was determined to find the inner sweetness that had to be lurking in there somewhere and drag it out of them before Mrs. Nielsen got back.

At least the daily battle provided Nell with a distraction from her crumbling life and shattered heart.

The subbing part of it was her own fault. If she'd simply swallowed her pride, it was possible—not probable, but *possible*—that she'd be back teaching at Bellwater. Her own classroom, her own kids. But instead, five minutes after her meeting with Frank Grantham had started, she'd walked right back out again. It had taken her less than half that time to realize Whit had been correct. Grantham was every inch the bully his nephew was, and he wouldn't be satisfied with an apology, no matter how sincerely meant. After the tumult of the past couple of weeks, Nell had developed a newfound sense of clarity, and as much as she had loved her job, it wasn't worth sacrificing her self-respect. If she hadn't been willing to give that up in order to be with Whit, there was no way she'd do it for the minor perk of a steady paycheck. There would be other jobs. Just as, she told herself, there would be other men.

Until then, she was taking it day by day. It wasn't a fresh start, but it was a fresh *something*. A new perspective. She needed a change, but doing anything dramatic to her hair felt too obvious, so she stripped all the polish from her toenails and dumped her favorite bottle of Cherry Apple red in the trash. Then she cut her hair anyway. No job meant no apartment, so she gave notice at her building; beginning in January, she would be staying with Paige—at least temporarily.

"Just like when you finished college!" Paige had said, like that was a good thing. Though it wouldn't be *just* like then, since the space was a bit more crowded these days. Paige had made up with Gabi, and this time, it seemed like it might actually stick, since they had decided to move in together.

Nell was genuinely happy for them, but the biggest surprise was that Paige had stood up to their grandmother about it. The news about the company's deceptive advertising had finally hit, and the imminent downfall (or at least stumble) of Forrester Cosmetics had given Paige the freedom to be herself. Rather than cut ties, she had taken control; instead of a fake relationship, she was going public with her real one. She was still working with Whit's publicist while riding out the scandal, but for the moment, it appeared that Paige Forrester had successfully reinvented herself.

Nell only wished she could do the same.

Nearly three weeks had passed since she'd last seen Whit, and she was no closer to moving on than she'd been when she'd left. Aside from her work, distractions hadn't helped. Paige had dragged her out of her apartment a couple of times, and she'd been out to dinner with friends, but somehow, everywhere she went, something reminded her of Whit. She wanted to turn back the clock, go back to when her life made sense and she didn't spend every moment feeling like some part of her was missing. Maybe she'd had a vague sense of dissatisfaction back then, a certain restlessness, but nothing she could describe or name. Now she could name it. Name him. Now the whole world felt empty without him. Colors didn't seem as vibrant. Winter in Chicago grew dreary, especially after the first snowfall turned to slush in the streets. And as awful as it was having herself named in a national tabloid, Whit's statement to the press only made the emptiness worse. How was she supposed to move on from a man who had bared his soul to save her career? She'd read his words so many times she had them memorized.

Ms. McLean was on her knees because I had unfairly demanded an apology for exposing the greatest shame of my career. The truth is, I should have been thanking her...

Thanking her for forcing him to confront his actions and accept his mistakes. Because it had made him a better man.

Nell had used up every tissue box in her apartment crying when she'd read that.

She'd wanted to reach out to him, but how could she after the way she'd left? It should be enough to know that he didn't totally despise her. Even if his words had been motivated by guilt, at least she had that knowledge to cling to. But she hadn't slept well since her return to Chicago, and the deep shadows that had taken up permanent residence under her eyes had Paige asking a constant stream of well-meaning questions that Nell didn't have the energy to answer.

She assumed that was what had prompted Paige's latest text. *Gabi and I are going out of town for the weekend, but I left a surprise for you in the condo. Could you stop by after work?*

Nell fought a sinking feeling in her stomach. Paige's most recent attempt at a distraction had involved a blind date ambush with an attractive med student who had taken Nell's awkward explanation that she wasn't looking for a relationship as an invitation to suggest a one-night stand. This time, Paige had probably hired a stripper.

She was tempted to ignore the text. A week of wrangling hell beasts hadn't left her in the mood to deal with anything more strenuous than a glass of wine and a bubble bath. But Paige would only keep pestering her about it, Gabi would back her up, and Nell didn't see any point in delaying the inevitable—especially since she needed to start moving her things over, anyway. The bubble bath would have to wait. After finishing up at school, she swung by her apartment to load up her car, made a quick pit stop to fuel up on coffee, and was at Paige's building by the time night fell. Gloom settled over her as she trudged down the lushly-carpeted hallway. The condo was on the eighth floor, and even with access to an elevator, she wasn't looking forward to an evening spent hauling in boxes. She sort of hoped there *was* a stripper in there. At least she could put his muscles to good use.

She was amusing herself with that thought when she stepped inside, balancing a box on one hip, and flicked on the overhead light.

Then she screamed.

Or rather squeaked. Most of the scream was swallowed the moment she recognized the large masculine form draped across the living room sofa. She had just enough time to register the fact that it was Whit before the box she'd been carrying tumbled from her grip and went crashing to the floor. The impact made a couple of light fixtures rattle, but Nell's pulse was thudding so loudly she never even heard it hit the ground.

Whit jolted into instant awareness. And then promptly fell face-first off the couch.

Nell squeaked again and rushed toward him, heart in her throat, box forgotten. He rolled to his side, lying sprawled on Paige's three thousand dollar rug, one hand on his chest, the other arm flung haphazardly across the glass coffee table he'd narrowly missed cracking his skull on. He blinked at her, looking dazed. "Jesus, Nell, you scared the shit out of me."

"*I* scared *you?* I'm not the one lurking in the dark in someone else's apartment!"

"I wasn't lurking. I fell asleep. And it wasn't dark when I got here." He touched the bridge of his nose and winced. A thin flow of red oozed from one nostril toward his upper lip.

"Oh, god, you're bleeding." She gripped his arm and tugged at him. It was like trying to lift a concrete slab. "Tilt your head back or something. Paige will kill me if you bleed on her rug."

"Your sympathy is touching." He pushed himself upward with a grimace and stalked toward the nearest bathroom, where he grabbed a handful of tissues from the sink and crumpled them against his face. "Happy?"

Incredible how he could manage to sound sarcastic with a wad of tissues pressed under his nose. Nell might have laughed, if her emotions hadn't been thrown into turmoil the second she'd seen him. The best she could manage was a weak nod.

He glared at her from behind the tissues. "Yeah, this is exactly how I pictured this going."

She slipped past him, avoiding eye contact. "I think there's a first-aid kit in here somewhere." But after rummaging through the cupboards and medicine cabinet, all she came up with was a half-empty bag of cotton swabs and a box of tampons.

Whit took one look at them and actually growled. "No way. I'm not having this conversation with a tampon stuck up my nose. If I bleed on anything belonging to Paige, I'll replace it."

Nell hesitated, hugging her arms. "Maybe you should go to the hospital."

"It's probably not broken. Just ugly." He peered at himself in the mirror, withdrew the tissues, and winced again. "Good thing it's the off-season. I'd have a hell of a time explaining this one. Not the worst injury I've had, but definitely the stupidest. Except for the time you stabbed me in the ass."

"That was an accident," she said dully.

"And this wasn't?"

Nell retreated a step. She was starting to put the pieces together, and the picture they formed made it hard to draw breath. Paige. Paige had done this. Nell didn't know how, she didn't know why, but she did know that the only way Whit would have gotten into the condo was if Paige had invited him.

Surprise.

All he needed was a bow around his neck.

Her legs didn't seem to want to hold her up, so she sank onto the fuzzy pink toilet cover, wedging her hands between her knees. Ever since she'd seen Whit lying on the sofa, she'd been trying not to think. She'd resisted looking at him, really looking at him. Now she caught him in glances—the dark hair he'd clearly been running his fingers through, the slope of his jaw showing the faintest hint of a beard. Instead of his normal jeans and T-shirt ensemble, he was wearing charcoal trousers and a blue dress shirt rolled up at the elbows, where the pale crescent of his scar was just visible. She remembered trailing a path of kisses along that scar. Remembered the warm tang of his skin beneath her lips.

He was so achingly familiar, every part of him. She wanted to touch him, to curl her body into his and feel the rhythm of his heart against her, but she couldn't until she understood what was happening.

"What are you doing here, Whit?" she asked softly. Had Paige called him? Told him what a pathetic mess Nell had become? That would be the ultimate humiliation. Nell hadn't wanted Whit's guilt, and she wanted his pity even less. She felt a thread of anger and seized it. "And make it quick, because I have a date."

She was more than a little horrified by her own rudeness, but Whit saw right through it. He tossed the crumpled tissues into the wastebasket and turned toward her, folding his arms across his chest. "Nice try, McLean, but you're still a terrible liar."

Instead of apologizing, she doubled down. "Make it quick anyway."

"Can we do this somewhere else?"

"Not until you answer my question."

"Well, I'm not telling you I love you in a flippin' *bathroom* unless we're both in the shower and naked, so either take off your clothes or come with me."

He walked away without giving her time to answer.

Not that she could have answered. She couldn't even move. Her heart screamed at her to run after him, but her body wouldn't obey her. He didn't mean it. Couldn't mean it. The words they'd thrown at each other that morning at the farm were seared into her memory, as bitter and painful as they had been three weeks ago. And the statement he'd released to the press—he'd done that because it was the right thing, and whether he believed it or not, he was the kind of man who did what was right. Maybe not always, but when it counted.

But she wanted him to mean it. She wanted it so badly she couldn't breathe.

Whit must have realized she wasn't going to follow him. A moment later he reappeared, giving her a grumpy look as he set a slim gray duffel bag on top of the vanity. "Are we seriously doing this here?" he demanded. "Is this really the story you want us to tell our grandchildren?"

Grandchildren. Nell somehow forced her mouth to work. "Did you just say you loved me?"

"This whole thing was way more romantic in my head."

"Whit—"

"I have a lot I want to say to you, and I'd like you to hear me out before you make any decisions. I figure you owe me that much after the way you ran out on me. But first—this is for you." He unzipped the duffel bag and reached inside, withdrawing what appeared to be an old Little League trophy with the tiny, faded gold figure of a baseball player swinging a tiny, faded gold bat. He held it toward her.

She took it automatically, gazing up at him questioningly.

"It's the O'Rourke Family Trophy. Congratulations. You won."

"Uh, what did I win?"

"The Piss Off Dad Contest. He was really upset when you dumped me." Nell immediately started to argue, but Whit cut her off. "You were sleeping with me and now you're not. That counts as dumping."

A bubble of laughter rose in her chest. "So your dad is pissed off I'm no longer sleeping with you."

"I have to say I'm not really happy about it either." He reached into the bag again, this time pulling out a carefully folded jersey of gray and blue fabric that he laid in her lap. "That's for you, too. For around the house. We'll get you other game day gear."

Nell pressed her fingertips against the cloth. She didn't need to hold it up to know the gold lettering on the back would spell out O'Rourke.

"We can start there, if you're willing," Whit said quietly. "I don't think we're ready for marriage and babies just yet."

"That wasn't—"

"A proposal, I know. That's why I'm making one." He grabbed the chair from the vanity and seated himself across from her. "I want to be with you, Nell. Girlfriend, boyfriend, lovers, partners, whatever you want to call it. No deals. No expiration date."

This was exactly what she'd hoped for, everything she'd hoped for, but instead of throwing herself into his arms, she stuck her hands between her knees again to keep herself from touching him. "What about your realistic outlook about long-term relationships?"

"That was before I fell in love with you."

Her heart did an erratic little skip. "I thought normal people didn't fall in love in a week."

"Neither of us is exactly normal."

"That's not what you said at the farm."

"I'm not as in tune with my emotions as you are. It took me some time to catch up. And technically, we met more than four years ago. That's plenty of time to fall in love."

"You hated me four years ago!"

"Only because I was an idiot. And only for a little while. If I'd spent a week getting to know you, I'd have loved you back then. It's a good thing I didn't, since you'd have turned me down flat."

"Probably," she conceded. She could feel tears beginning to form and blinked them away.

Whit's smile was rueful. "I think I knew that night at the lake, and it scared the hell out of me, so I told myself it was better to just let you leave. But it wasn't better. I missed you so much I couldn't think. Couldn't sleep. I couldn't go back to who I'd been before I found you, and I don't want to." He rose to his feet, sliding the chair away, and reached into his pocket. Then he hesitated. "I have something else for you. It's not a ring, but... do you want me to get down on one knee? It's kinda cramped in here, but I'll do it."

She shook her head mutely.

"Here." Gently, he drew her to her feet, sliding his fingers along her arm until he found her hand. He brushed his thumb along her skin, making her shiver, then set the slim silver chain of his charm necklace into her open palm. "I love you, Eleanor Lacey McLean. I don't know the future, and I can't promise you forever any more than you can promise it to me. But I can promise you that you're the one I want to be with. I'm hoping you still want to be with me."

His hand was trembling, his beautiful dark eyes suspiciously damp. Nell would have wrapped her arms around him, but his troubled expression told her he wasn't finished yet.

His voice caught when he spoke again. "It won't be easy. You need to know that. As soon as spring training starts, you'll have to get on an airplane any time you want to actually see me. That's just the beginning. My life revolves around baseball, which means yours will, too. If we decide to move in together or get married, you'll have to leave Chicago—it will have to be you, not me. I'm locked into a contract for the next five years, and I have an obligation to my team. After that, we may end up moving, and god only knows where we'll end up. You might have to pack up and start over in a new city. More than once. If we have kids, you'll be spending a lot of time on your own with them. And there will be expectations placed on you. You'll have to participate in baseball activities, and it's more than just going to games."

"You don't think I'm up to that?" she asked softly.

"I know you are. You just need to decide if I'm worth it."

This time she couldn't blink back the tears. "Haven't you gotten that through your head yet? Of course you're worth it. I love you, too, Whit O'Rourke, and you're going to have to work a lot harder than that if you want to scare me away."

"Thank god." He dragged her into his arms. His strong, solid body pressed against hers, his warmth steadying her.

Nell smiled up at him. She was crying and she didn't care. "Grand-children, huh?"

"I'm choosing to be optimistic." He bent to kiss her, then swore and drew back sharply when his nose bumped against hers.

"I still think you should go to the hospital," she said, pulling away reluctantly. "Or at least get an ice pack."

"I thought you hated hospitals."

"You'll note I said *you*."

"What, you're going to send me off all by myself after I traveled four hundred miles to confess my love to you?"

"I'm willing to drive you there," Nell teased.

A wicked glint came into his eyes. "I've got a better idea."

That bubble of laughter rose again. God, she'd missed him. Even more than she'd wanted to admit. "Let me guess. It involves sex."

"Obviously. But not here. I've mentioned my penthouse, right?"

"Once or twice."

"It has these windows. Floor to ceiling. One-way glass. Overlooks the whole city."

"It must have a great view," she murmured.

The wicked glint turned straight up sinful. "Incredible. But that's not why I'm mentioning them."

"Should I be worried?"

"I've been having this fantasy of you. Pressed up against those windows. Bare ass naked."

"That sounds a little uncomfortable," she said, even as a delicious shiver shot up her spine.

"I'd settle for the naked part."

She laughed, looping her arms around his neck. "I'll indulge your fantasy, as long as you indulge mine of unloading my car."

"Deal."

With Whit's help, moving the boxes from her car to the spare bedroom Paige had set up for her use took less than half an hour. It wouldn't have even taken that long, except that Nell spent the first ten minutes of it arguing with Whit that she couldn't just move into his apartment. They had all the time in the world, and she had no intention of rushing things.

In between box loads, Whit told her how he'd devised his plan to—as he put it—win her over. Paige *had* been in on it, but only because Whit had called her first, just in case Nell had blocked his number. And then Paige had made him swear on his pitching arm, his Cy Young Award, and his immortal soul that he wouldn't break Nell's heart.

"Seems like she meant business," Nell said. She supposed she'd have to let Paige off the hook for barging in on them at the farm.

"So do I."

"You fell asleep waiting for me!"

"I was exhausted. I've been up for two days straight, and I haven't slept well for weeks."

"I know how that feels." She sucked in a breath. Since they were beginning a real relationship now, it would be best if they did it with a clean slate. "I have something to confess."

"If this is about Sawyer, I already know. We had a talk before I left town."

"And...?"

"And what? We're not miraculously best pals again. But... it went better than I expected."

"That's a start," she said gently.

"It's something, anyway."

Whit's apartment was only a ten minute drive, which would be convenient once Nell was officially living with Paige. But the moment she stepped inside, she felt a twinge of regret that she'd insisted on keeping her own place. She'd expected decadence, but realized quickly she should have known better—even sparsely furnished, the spacious condo with its warm tones and understated, wood-accent architecture felt more graceful than luxurious. And Whit hadn't been kidding about the view. To the east, Lake Michigan spread dark and endless, and everywhere else the Chicago skyline glittered with a thousand points of light, dappling the river in sparks so that the entire city seemed to glow. Incredible had been an understatement; *breath-taking* was more the word for it.

She turned to Whit, who stood watching her with a hungry, heavy-lidded look that made her heart flip over. She fought down a flutter of nerves. "I see why you haven't wanted to sell this place."

"At least now I have a reason to use it."

A trickle of sweat started to form between her breasts. "Maybe you should tell me more about this fantasy of yours."

He was across the room in three strides. "Why don't I show you instead?"

The faint worry that had been building inside her—*what if it wasn't the same between them?*—melted away the moment he reached her. They moved together hurriedly and then languidly, first against the windows and then in front of them, with the desperation of two bodies that had been starved for each other and the fierce joy of reunited lovers. When they finally made it to the bed, sated and spent, sheets tangled around them, Nell propped herself up on one elbow and traced a finger along his ribs, over his heart.

Whit watched her with a drowsy smile. "The angry sex was hot, but tonight was so much better."

"Any other fantasies I should know about?"

"This one is pretty good." He stroked her hair idly, then shifted his arm, drawing her against him. "You know, I keep wondering what would've happened if you hadn't run into me at the bar that night."

She'd wondered the same thing. If she'd arrived a minute earlier or a minute later... if her tire hadn't gone flat... "I still would've shown up at your house the next morning. I had an apology to make, remember?"

"You might have missed me. Or I'd have slammed the door in your face."

"I don't believe in fate, if that's where this is going."

"What would you call it then?"

"Good timing. Four years ago, we had bad timing. Maybe this is just... balancing the scales."

A low chuckle stirred in his chest. "So—fate."

She wasn't willing to concede that just yet, even if she was thinking she might have to reconsider her opinions on destiny. "Coincidence. A very *lucky* coincidence."

"Best luck I ever had," Whit murmured.

She snuggled against him and closed her eyes. "Me too."

Epilogue

Eleven Months Later

"Someone told them we're getting married!"

Whit glanced up from his cereal as Nell flounced into the kitchen, her hair still damp from the shower and her phone in her hand. He took that to mean she'd seen *Meltdown*. "We *are* getting married."

"But we haven't announced anything!"

"You were wearing your ring in Paige's wedding photos." He leaned back in his chair and looked at her, enjoying the way the early sunlight played along her skin and caught her freckles. Ever since she'd officially made the move to Minneapolis at the beginning of June, mornings with Nell had become his favorite time of day.

Except for evenings with Nell.

And every other hour in between.

She waved a hand in dismissal. "That was over a month ago." Scowling, she stalked toward the coffee pot, poured herself a mug, and turned back toward him. "I bet it was my grandmother. She's desperate for good publicity."

"If there's one person in the universe I can't imagine ever speaking to a tabloid, it's your grandmother."

"Then she had her minions do it."

"Are you allowed to have minions in prison?"

"You've met her. She's been there for weeks now. She's probably got the makeup mafia running the place." Nell took a sip of her coffee, then set the mug on the counter and folded her arms. Her scowl deepened. "This is her revenge. She still thinks we scheduled the wedding specifically so she'll miss it."

"I hope you told her that was just a delightful bonus."

After her indictment on fraud charges that summer, Nell's grandmother had chosen to accept a plea bargain rather than go through the ordeal of an embarrassing and highly publicized trial. Her four-month prison term would conveniently prevent her from attending the wedding, which had been scheduled for early January to coincide with MLB's off-season. But convincing Josephine Forrester—who was trying to reform her image from conniving CEO to benevolent matriarch—that their chosen date wasn't an intentional slight was an ongoing battle.

One that Nell was determined to win. "If we were having the wedding at the farm, she'd never have come anyway. She wouldn't be caught dead within fifty feet of a barn."

"If we were having it at the farm, your wedding dress would be a snowmobile suit." Whit thought it was sweet that Nell had wanted to get married in Bucky's backyard, but a winter wedding in the frozen north would've meant guests turning into icicles, so they'd decided on an indoor venue off Lake Minnetonka—with a second reception in Fallen Oaks after they returned from their honeymoon. That was at Nell's insistence. *So you can see how much the town doesn't hate you,* she'd said. *And we're inviting Sawyer and James.* Since Whit had already made peace with his former friends, he didn't think that was strictly necessary, but it was important to Nell, and that was good enough for him. No harm in doing what he could to please his wife.

His wife. A year ago the very thought of marriage would have been unfathomable. Now he couldn't imagine his life without Nell in it.

It hadn't all been smooth sailing, of course. Those early months of separation had been hell. If he'd had his way, he'd have moved Nell into his house right at the start of the season, but since she'd wanted to finish out the school year in Chicago, they'd had to survive on late night phone calls and weekend rendezvous. Each time they said goodbye, doubts had begun to creep in. Some part of him hadn't been able to let go of the fear that she'd wake up one morning and decide none of the chaos and complications were worth it. But that little voice had grown softer and softer, and it had been silenced forever the day she told him she was ready to move in with him for good.

The addition of four hundred miles between her and her grandmother hadn't made that relationship any less contentious, however. Nell was still stewing. "The farm probably would've ended up backfiring, anyway," she grumbled, "since arctic wastelands are Grandmother's natural habitat."

"You could always stop speaking to her."

Nell's indignant look told him he was an idiot for even suggesting it. Whit held up his hands. If there was one thing he'd learned over the past year, it was that trying to understand the tangled dynamics of the Forrester-McLean women was beyond the capabilities of mortal men. "Quit worrying about some stupid tabloid and come here," he told her. "I want to celebrate our anniversary."

"This is *not* our anniversary." An argument they'd been having for the past several weeks. Whit thought they should count the day she'd run into him at Gills as their anniversary. Nell thought it should be the day he'd come to find her in Chicago.

"It's our almost-versary."

"That isn't a thing."

He crooked a finger at her. "Come here anyway."

Mischief danced in her eyes. "What'll you give me?"

"My love and devotion aren't enough?"

"Save it for the altar, O'Rourke. What'll you give me right *now*?"

That was just asking for the sort of lewd remark guaranteed to turn her cheeks pink—god, he loved that he could still make her blush—but since he did actually have something he wanted to give her, he reached into his pocket to withdraw a small, slightly creased piece of notebook paper, and then set it on the table.

Her brows went up. "Paper?"

"It's a list. Reasons why you should date me."

"As opposed to marrying you?"

"I wrote it last year. I was going to give it to you that day in Chicago, but the timing didn't seem right, so I decided to save it for our"—he broke off at her glower—"for a more appropriate moment."

She crossed to the table, took one glance at the list, and snorted. "Really? You started with sex?"

He grinned, scooting his chair closer to her. "Yeah, I thought you'd appreciate that."

"Reason number two: handy around the house." She sent him an amused look. "I think you're missing an *S* in there somewhere, pal."

"Hey, I'm not *just* handsy. I did paint my grandpa's barn."

"According to your dad, you did it wrong."

"That just shows you can never trust his opinion."

"Reason number three—" Another snort. "You didn't seriously think I was pregnant."

"You could've been. I wouldn't have complained, but it's probably better we've had some time to ourselves."

"Reason four, a rich boyfriend. Okay, I have to admit, that one does have its perks. But I'd love you anyway."

"I know."

"Five. Good hygiene?"

"You're always saying you like how I smell. Though the whole showering thing fell off for a bit after you left."

Reason six earned him an eye roll. "*I promise to let you win at least half of our arguments,*" she recited. Her skeptical look said it all.

"I was trying to be realistic," he explained. "I didn't think you'd believe it if I said *all* of our arguments."

"I wouldn't have believed it anyway. But if we're keeping score—"

"Which we are. Obviously."

She lifted a hand to shush him. "*If* we're keeping score, we're at O'Rourke 2, McLean 15."

Numbers she had definitely made up on the spot, but since it was their anniversary—whether she believed it or not—Whit decided to let her have that one. "This is going to get a lot more confusing once it's O'Rourke versus O'Rourke."

"You could always stop arguing with me," she suggested.

This time he snorted.

"Reason seven... you look good naked?" A laugh gurgled out of her. "You made *two* of these about sex?"

"That one is about aesthetic appreciation," Whit replied. "Not my fault your mind went straight to the gutter."

"Uh-huh. Reason eight: we could get a dog." She glanced up again. "How exactly is that a reason for me to date you?"

"Well, it's kinda hard for me to take a dog on the road. But that reminds me—we should get a dog. Or a couple of cats. I'm not picky."

"I'm willing to negotiate," she answered, then shook her head as she turned back to the list. "Reason nine: see reasons one through eight. Now that's just lazy."

"I wanted an even number. Keep reading. You're almost to the best one."

She smiled when she got to the end, her eyes growing misty. *I love you.* "That was the only one you ever needed."

Whit's eyes turned a little misty, too. Nell might not believe in fate, but Whit knew deep down that some things were simply meant to be. Even if you had to wait a while to find them. "I don't know. I thought that first reason was pretty good," he said, giving her his very best leer.

Nell leered right back. "Oh, yeah? Care to provide a demonstration?"

He laughed and pulled her into his arms.

Looking for more?
Watch for the next book in the Making the Play series

Sort of Undeniable

C.J. AND RORY'S STORY

COMING EARLY 2025

9 798990 870703